CAGE THE WOLF

ALEX STEWARD: BOOK 2

STEFANIE GILMOUR

Library of Congress Control Number: 2023924023

Printed in the United States of America
First edition 2024

Hardcover ISBN 979-8-9883745-5-8
Paperback ISBN 979-8-9883745-6-5
E-book ISBN 979-8-9883745-7-2

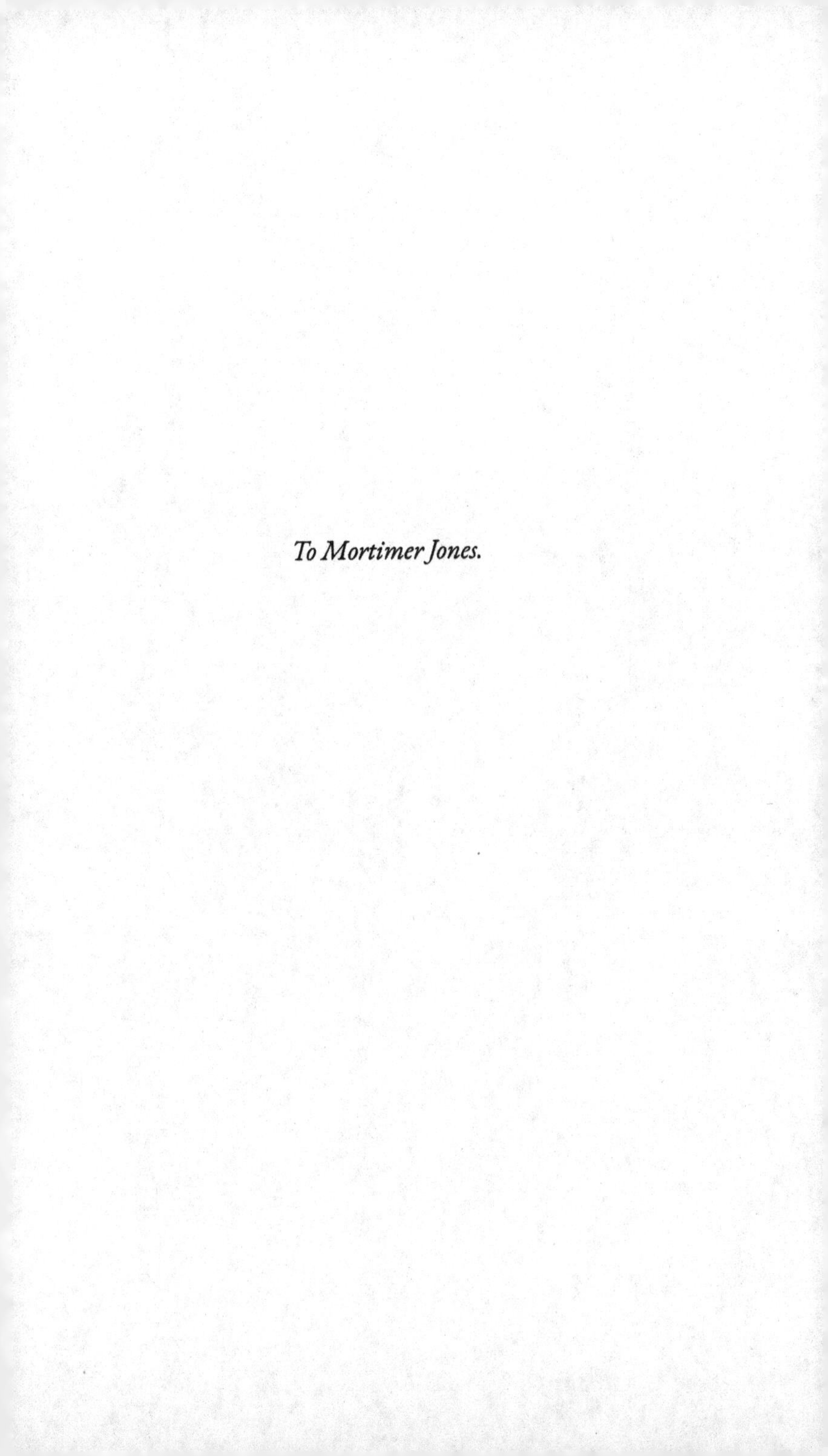

To Mortimer Jones.

1

I CROUCHED BY the entrance of the shabby building, the heat causing my shirt to stick to my back. The cracked pavement of the deserted parking lot emitted that baked-in-the-sun sort of smell. When I tried the doorknob, the door was unlocked. I pulled it open wide enough to slip silently inside. The aromas of cigarette ash, stale beer, and faded perfume surrounded me. There was another scent, too, something more primal and musky.

In another life, getting good marks on school exams or work evaluations meant something to me. I wasn't that person anymore. But tonight, I was taking a different kind of test that I wanted to ace. It would prove I could control the deadly creature living inside my body.

That I wasn't a mindless monster.

Within seconds, my eyes adjusted to the darkened interior. A buzzing neon sign, the only light source in the room, cast a halo onto the bar. Outlines of low tables, worn sofas, lounge chairs, and mismatched lamps solidified within my heightened field of vision. I let my breath out slowly and moved deeper into the room. I crept along the left wall, ensuring one side of my body was protected from attack.

I'd crossed the lot to the building undetected, and this room was the last stretch of the test. Compared to previous attempts, it all seemed too easy. My muscles tightened and twitched from the doubt and anxiety crowding my mind. What was the catch?

I paused, trembling, to inhale through my nose and slowly exhale again.

My goal, the glass bottle, was so close. It sat atop the bar just ten feet away, bathed in the neon-orange glow. Capturing the bottle meant my hard work had been worth the repeated failures, the injuries, the tears and frustration. I'd have to cross the room, leaving my body exposed on all sides. I scanned the area, scenting the air and straining to hear any disturbance. Still nothing.

I invited my inner wolf closer to the surface of my consciousness to share this space with me. Maintaining control of her was necessary and a skill I'd honed for months. That goddamn bottle would finally be ours tonight.

My upper body remained motionless as I gathered my feet underneath me like a coiled spring. Warm energy charged the muscles of my legs. The joints in my fingers ached and enlarged as my fingers lengthened. Mercilessly chewed fingernails thickened and grew pointed. My body lowered further, and my claws rested lightly in front of me on the worn floor. I was a runner at the blocks, making the last adjustments to my position before I made my move.

I saw it then, the source of that earthy scent, as an ever-so-slight shift in the deep shadow to my left. I was found.

It was now or never.

I feigned forward, and a figure leaped from the shadows. The man-sized silhouette landed, his combat boots striking the floor where my body would have been. I slashed at him with my claws, hoping to dispatch my opponent before he could engage me.

The man spun out of my reach and turned glowing copper-colored eyes on me. A low growl erupted from his throat as he bared pointed canines. He stood between me and my prize. I maintained eye contact with him so I didn't broadcast my next move. Now I had to decide what that move would be.

I threw one punch and another, which he effortlessly dodged. The man lunged at me, and his claws latched into the flesh at the back of my neck. My teeth clenched as he yanked my body toward his own. Clasping his wrists, I raised my knee and leveraged the forward momentum to strike the area right above his knee. He yelped in pain, released me, and pivoted out of my reach again.

I rushed toward the bar.

My claws grazed the bottle before I was seized from behind, lifted off my feet, and hauled away from the counter. The attack drove a wedge of terror through me, and the beast inside me responded. Self-control snapped, and I became a flurry of talons and teeth. The man lost his hold on me.

The prize at the bar was forgotten. The test was forgotten. Growling, I advanced on my attacker . . . the new goal being to rend him into bloody ribbons.

His sleeveless shirt made satisfying ripping sounds when my claws caught the fabric. My relentless attacks drove him deeper into the room until he was forced to leap over one of the sofas. I circled the furniture, my body buzzing with anticipation. How glorious it would feel when I broke him apart.

With a fierce snarl, I dove for him. The base of a large, very solid, lamp collided with the side of my skull. An explosion of black dots marred my vision. It jarred me from the haze of fury fueled by the creature inside me. I gasped and held my head. My knees weakened.

In that brief moment, he made short work of me. A heel was placed behind mine and a solid shove brought me crashing to the floor. With a knee on my chest and secure hold of my wrists, he held me down. His eyes narrowed to slits. "Say it."

"No." I didn't want to surrender the win to him. I didn't want to fail. Not again.

"Say it!"

"No!" I tried to twist loose of his grip.

There was an awful noise in the back of his throat. He leaned forward, and a wad of saliva and snot threatened to drip onto my forehead.

"Stop!" I squeezed my eyes shut and turned my head away. "Okay, stop! I'll say it! The Stooges are superior to the Ramones!"

The weapon of snotty spit was retracted with as awful of a sound as it was conjured. Convulsing with laughter, my friend Nate pushed himself back to sit on the floor against the sofa. His clawed hands smoothly shifted back to their normal state. "You should have seen your face."

I sat up and rubbed my aching temple. "You're disgusting, Nate."

He gave me a toothy grin and scratched behind his ear. "And you're getting better."

I shook my head. "Getting better isn't good enough. I should have had it tonight."

There was a whisper of footsteps in the hall, and the lights behind the bar flickered on. A woman wearing a simple red sundress, her dark hair shaped into a sleek bob, opened the prized bottle and brought it over. "How did it go, Alex?" She handed me the beer and settled onto the sofa behind Nate.

I took a sip of beer. "Awful. He caught me in the last stretch." My gaze turned on Nate. "Was the lamp necessary?"

The woman ran her fingers through Nate's soft mohawk, smiling at him. "I would prefer you don't destroy our lighting, love."

"Utilizing the environment given to me, Trish." His mood sobered. "Tell me what happened near the end, Alex. What were you feeling?"

I looked at the beer bottle to conceal my frustration and discomfort. "You grabbed me from behind." My inner wolf never responded well to a man seizing me.

"When you lose balance between you and her, you lose focus. A clever opponent will use that to take you down," he said. "You should've seen that lamp coming from a mile away."

I frowned. "I don't know how to maintain control if I'm taken by surprise. Suddenly, what she wants isn't unreasonable." That's what made her deadly. If I couldn't control her, I'd endanger the wolf community I wanted to be a part of and help protect.

"She broke free to protect you," Trish said, referring to the day I met my inner wolf. "Your safety will always be her concern."

"I understand, but I wish she'd check in with me first." Seven years ago, I was attending college on a running scholarship. It was the last semester of my senior year when the man assaulted me. Glimpses of that horrific day were only available to me in lingering nightmares.

"You're growing to know each other," Trish said. "Be patient."

Nate flashed another grin. "Like I said, you're getting better each time. We'll work through it with you."

"What if, in the meantime, I accidentally hurt someone?" I threw up my hand. "Not only would I be tethered, but I'd be used as an example that werewolves don't belong in Hopewell. It'd be awful for the rest of you." I wanted to be an asset, not a risk. "Mitch messed with my head at the Mind Center this past winter, and now my shifting is harder to control and accelerates faster."

"I understand you're frustrated, but there is no instant solution, Alex," Trish said. "You've been working hard, and the space between you and your wolf will continue to shrink."

"But it's taking forever!"

Trish smiled and nudged Nate's shoulder. "That sounds familiar, doesn't it?"

Nate chuckled, turned, and climbed up onto the couch with her. He wrapped his arms around Trish, growling and mock-attacking her throat. She dissolved into rich laughter, causing me to smile.

For the past six months, I'd grown to know these two and the community of werewolves they protected. They'd taken me into their pack, no questions asked. Almost daily, they gave their time to work with me and help me understand the creature with whom I shared a body.

I'd lived in Hopewell for three years, but it hadn't felt like a home until I met Trish and Nate. They were my family when I'd had to leave my parents and grandmother in New York.

I savored one of those sacred moments when my heart was full and content. At the far edges of my mind, self-doubt and anxiety lurked. If I couldn't master control of my inner wolf, it would only be a matter of time before I messed up. The Committee would brand me as a monster by slapping a tether on me, a punishment most werewolves don't survive.

2

EVEN AFTER THE sun went down, the summer heat didn't break. Unlike many other nightspots in Hopewell, Hell's Bells was situated on the west side of the river. The surrounding businesses didn't offer evening hours, so no one other than the club's patrons were in the neighborhood at night.

The front windows of the building were obscured by layers of show posters, new pasted over top of the old. Trish and Nate owned the intimate lounge and music venue and lived in a tiny single-bedroom apartment within it. In addition to overseeing the well-loved congregation space for local werewolves, Trish was a leader in the wolf community. Until a few months previous, she'd been our representative in Hopewell's supernatural political scene.

Hopewell being a Midwestern town, some club-goers socialized in the parking lot to enjoy the brief season of warm weather. Others, like my friend Emma and me, sought fresh air as a break from the intense music and damp heat of the basement venue.

"Any leads on a job with a steady paycheck?" asked Emma, perched beside me on the trunk of my car. She looked misplaced in the grungy parking lot, dressed in a designer mini, strappy sandals, and a wispy top that looked more like it was made from a cloud than fabric. Her hair was pinned up in intricate twists of blonde and pink strands. As usual, it made me feel a bit dumpy in my threadbare thrift store clothes.

"Nah," I turned the Solo cup in my hands. "I have some money saved, so I haven't looked for anything." What I didn't tell her was that after intercepting a sizable chunk of change from her evil ex, Mitch, this past winter, I'd made the executive decision that the money would live out the rest of its days in my bank account. If I watched my spending, it would last me a couple more months. "I've been running rides here and there through my rideshare gig. I'll get to another job eventually."

"What about a place to live?" she asked. "It's too bad the rent was raised on your old place."

"Yeah, imagine a landlord taking advantage of renovations to double the rent," I said. "If I hadn't experienced it myself, I'd suspect she'd paid to set the place on fire."

Emma frowned. "It was a great location for the price."

"Well, it's out of my reach now, and forget about getting a lease without that income you mentioned." I shrugged. "I was staying over at Ben's, so I'll keep covering the rent while he's away. As long as the money shows up every month, his landlord doesn't care."

Benjamin Sharpe was a wizard I'd been seeing since January when we'd met at the Sound Refuge. After opening as the local act for Derezzed, Ben was invited to join the Midwest leg of her Electric Arc tour. We'd shared his apartment for a brief three months, him offering me the bed while he slept on the couch, before he left for an additional three. I missed the guy.

"But he'll be home any day now," Emma said.

"Tomorrow." Saying it aloud made me smile. If he and my inner wolf were up for it, I hoped nobody would have to sleep on the couch when he got back.

"Are you going to look for an apartment, or do you think you'll stay?" Poorly concealed giddiness shone in Emma's eyes. She'd introduced Ben and me, so she took full credit for any happiness it brought us.

Ben was the antithesis of the toxic masculinity that so often tested my ability to not lose my shit. We complemented each other well, and with him I could relax. He was patient, gentle, and quick to smile. I felt safe, and my wolf was close to accepting him, too. Ben and I were cautiously figuring out the relationship thing, but yeah, I'd fallen pretty hard.

I took a swig from my cup to hide my smile. "I can move my stuff out of your garage if you need the space." The few material bits of my life were stowed in boxes there. I only kept some clothes and a couple items precious to me, like my grandfather's jacket, at Ben's.

"Alex!" She laughed and swatted my arm. "Stop it. Answer my question."

"I don't know. We didn't really plan that far ahead."

"He bought an extra motorcycle helmet for you before he left for the tour! *You're* part of his plans."

I shrugged. "I'm not sure what I'm going to do yet, Em. My energy and time are spent with Trish and Nate. It's important I get better control of my shifting." Learning to communicate with the creature inside me was not only crucial for my safety but also those around me. "I don't want to accidentally take off someone's head."

"I haven't had to patch you up for weeks. That's an improvement, right?" She knew how impatient I was with myself, so she always wanted me to acknowledge my progress.

"I guess so, yeah." It was handy to have a wizard as a best friend, especially since Emma's magic focus was healing. "Do you remember some of those wounds Nate gave me when we first started training?"

She mock-gagged. "They were awful. I almost passed out."

"And all the names you called him?" I chuckled. "What was that one? I think it was at least five different expletives strung together."

Emma giggled. "I don't think I can repeat it without blushing."

I spaced my forefinger a tiny distance from my thumb. "I was *this* close earlier tonight but lost my grip at the last minute."

"It sounds exhausting," she said. "I think you need a night off. Want to join me at an event my parents are hosting?"

I laughed. She might as well have asked me if I wanted to stab myself in the eye with one of her family's silver spoons. Then I realized she wasn't laughing. "Wait, are you being serious?"

"My mother organized a fundraiser for Joe Stone, one of the mayoral candidates. As director at Another Chance, it's important I be there. We need cooperation from the city for our new mental health programs to get off the ground. I'm putting a bug in both candidates' ears so when either of them are elected, we can get started."

Another Chance Ministries was a shelter and food pantry downtown offering support to the city's more vulnerable citizens. I had a hard time believing subjecting myself to an evening with Emma's parents would help the organization.

"I don't want to spend *all* evening pandering to a politician," Emma said. "It'd be nice to have friendly faces there. Bring Ben along. I'd love to hear how his tour went." She folded her hands together and held them up. "Please?"

I hesitated. "I'm not sure it's a good idea. Remember what I said about struggling with self-control?" Emma's mother, Susan, didn't care for me—and the feeling was mutual.

"There'll be delicious free food and drinks," she said.

The proposal suddenly sounded better, especially the part where the food was free. The dollars in my bank account would last even longer. "Nothing in my wardrobe is going to meet Susan's standards." I motioned down to my dark tank top and denim shorts. "You know this is as good as it gets."

This excited rather than deterred Emma. "We can go shopping!"

I disliked shopping. "Let me think about it."

There was a sharp whoop and an outburst of laughter nearby. A guy in his midteens, all elbows and knees, approached us. From his scent, I could tell he was another werewolf. He was obviously being urged on by his friends. The handful of kids stood in a huddle not twenty feet away. He eyed up Emma, close to fifteen years his senior.

I fixed him with a flat look. "What do you want?"

Emma drew a lot of attention when we hung out here, but the young ones especially fell over themselves to talk to her. The guy's confidence was bolstered by the smile Emma gifted him. The light from the club's sign caught the sparkling dust she'd used to powder her face. "Hi there."

He froze and then introduced himself in one go. "Hey, I'mRogerit'snicetomeetyou."

I rolled my eyes and took a drink from my cup.

Showing kindness to yet another love-stricken stray, Emma introduced herself. "Hello, Roger. I'm—"

"Emma Arztin," he said with a grin. His hands in his pockets, he rocked back on the heels of his Chucks. "Yeah, I know. We all know. You're the wizard who saved Nate."

It wasn't an exaggeration. Nate had been dealt a nasty wound with a silver weapon by one of the same people who'd torched my apartment. Silver was extremely bad news for us wolves, and wounds inflicted by it were something our accelerated healing couldn't fix.

Emma smiled. "It was a team effort."

Wolves and wizards rarely moved in the same social circles, so Emma being here—in a den of werewolves—was abnormal. Everyone knew Nate and Trish were okay with wizards visiting Hell's Bells, but there was tension. Wizards tended to think they were better than other supernatural beings, especially werewolves. However, since she'd healed Nate and was my closest friend, Emma didn't have to worry about much trouble.

Roger glanced over at his friends and looked back at Emma. "So, um, I was dared to come over here, and um, talk to you. I said I could do one better and . . ." His cheeks turned rosy. ". . . ask for a kiss?"

Emma's perfect brows lifted. "Really?"

He nodded. "They don't think I have a chance." His next grin was for me. "They said Alex would kick my ass first."

Emma laughed and I snorted. "How do you know it's me you have to worry about?" I asked. Beneath her bubbly exterior, Emma was ruthless when it came to men. Never short of choices, she'd toss one at a moment's notice. This behavior had become exacerbated by the aforementioned evil ex, Mitch. But Roger, still a pup, was safe from her.

Eyes sparkling, Emma gave an impish smile and wiggled a finger at Roger. He went for it, leaning in with closed eyes and a comical, puckered face. Emma caught his peach-fuzz-covered chin, turned it aside, and placed a light, chaste kiss on his cheek.

Roger's friends exploded with howls of laughter. His eyes flew open, and his face burned a bright red. He rubbed at the back of his neck, grinning. Roger mumbled a "thank you" before he ducked away and returned to his group. They greeted him with a mix of cheers and more laughter.

I smiled, warmth spreading in my chest. Where many people saw a dirty, loud nightclub crawling with delinquents, Trish and Nate had carefully crafted a community. Proof of it was in the carefree laughter and companionship of Roger and his friends.

Emma giggled. "Oh my goodness, he's adorable."

"Should we go back inside and catch the last set?" I stood and finished my drink.

She hopped down. "I'll try to. Why do you and Ben like this music?" She wrinkled her nose as we walked toward the entrance. "The singer sounds so angry, and it's hard to dance because everyone is flailing around and trying to kill each other."

I chuckled, imagining how much Ben would enjoy Emma's critique of punk music. Ben and my shared love of music was something that'd drawn us to each other. I was so busy daydreaming about welcoming him back, I walked headlong into a wall.

The wall growled.

"Alex, are you okay?" Emma asked from behind me.

My vision swam. Confused, I shook my head and looked up into a face I didn't recognize. A guy stood in front of me, blocking the doorway with his wide frame. Under the scent of cigarette smoke and sweat was the musky odor of a fellow werewolf.

"What are you doing?" I drew myself up to my full five feet, seven inches. Unfortunately, I still stared at his chin. "Move out of the way. We're going to miss the rest of the show."

He crossed his arms and shook his head. "Not until you get rid of her." He pointed over my shoulder at Emma. "They don't do shit for us. We don't want them here."

"Come on. Don't be a dick." I nudged the front of his shoulder. "Move."

"Alex, it's okay," Emma said. "It's late and I'm getting tired anyway." She often deterred me from giving obnoxious men black eyes. She'd done so the night we first met.

But tonight, her quick surrender stoked my simmering anger. "No." Growling, I narrowed my eyes at the guy. "It's not okay."

"If you're with her, you can't come in." The guy shrugged and smirked. "I can stand here all night. We're not letting some magic-using whore into our—"

My fist collided with his mouth, cutting his words short. His teeth sliced the skin of my knuckles, and his head snapped up and to the side. There were rules forbidding us to throw a punch with a Commoner, a non-supernatural being. In most instances, we weren't even allowed to use our gifts to defend ourselves against them. Those rules didn't apply here among each other.

He turned a shocked expression toward me. I landed another punch straight to his gut. He doubled over. Why were they always so surprised? Commoner, wolf, wizard—it didn't seem to matter.

Snarling, I hauled him by the back of his shirt from the doorway. I gave him a rough shove, and he stumbled into the parking lot. He slowly straightened, glaring at me with gold-colored eyes. My nose was tickled by the scent of blood before he spat out a dislodged tooth. He wiped his mouth clean on his forearm. With the dull popping of cartilage, his ears and fingers lengthened. Each fingernail turned talon-like.

His shifting form caused my own beast to tear her way to the surface of my skin. My body flared with dull pain as it distorted bits of itself. Eyes glowing, I watched the other werewolf pace. I ran my tongue over my enlarged canines and flexed my claws. My inner wolf strained against my control. It'd felt great to deck the guy, and she wanted to do more than take out a few of his teeth.

We held our transformation here. If we didn't, we could become the dangerous and unruly canid-like monsters similar to those found in Hollywood films. Even the most skilled werewolves avoided giving themselves completely over to their inner wolf.

The altercation drew the attention of others in the parking lot. "Alex," Emma's voice filtered through the growing noise. "Stop! It's okay! We can go watch the band now." The guy started toward me, and a growl rumbled in my chest. Emma's voice receded. "Alex!"

His punch hit my jaw like a sledgehammer. I reeled, completely taken off guard. How did he reach me so fast? He seized my shoulder and drove me down to the pavement. The stored heat in the cement warmed my cheek, and the odor of spilled oil and gasoline flooded my nostrils. I struggled, but he held me prone on my stomach.

No, no, no . . . A cold sweat broke out across my forehead.

The shouting around us blended together, but the guy's words were clear as he whispered close to my ear. "We're tired of this playing-nice-with-their-kind bullshit. You're going to have to pick a side. Are you with us or not?"

Being held down by the unknown man triggered panic throughout my body. The last threads of control slipped from my fingers. The edges of my vision blurred, and I snarled and thrashed like a trapped animal.

The guy's weight was suddenly lifted off me, freeing me to move. I rose to my hands and knees. He landed on his ass beside me with a yelp. Someone had stepped in to help me.

My opponent attempted to prop himself up, but I was already on him. Sitting astride his lap, I took the first wide swipe with my claws to open up a deep set of gashes from his ear, across his cheekbone, and over the bridge of his nose. I'd barely missed his eye.

I wouldn't make the same mistake again.

I readied my next strike, but my raised wrist was seized and I was hauled up onto my feet. Blind with rage, I swung and only succeeded in having my other wrist restrained. My body was given a rough shake. A voice called my name from somewhere. It sounded muffled, as if from underwater. I froze, listening.

"Alex!" The voice was clearer and familiar this time. Panting with effort, I tried to latch onto it to bring my mind back into focus. There was a person in front of me.

Nate held my wrists stationary between us. My hands and fingers had shifted further than usual. They were not only more distorted with deadly claws, but also covered in a thin layer of fur. Nate searched my eyes. "There you are."

A splitting pain shot through my core, and I whimpered. The beast within me ripped at my insides as if she were attempting to escape the cage of my body.

Only twice has my inner wolf taken complete control of my body. The first time was when she awoke. I still couldn't fully recall what happened that day. The second time was six months ago when I was strapped into a lab chair at the Mind Center. What frightened me most was how fast the creature inside my body had dominated my consciousness.

I threw a panicked look toward the werewolf I'd been fighting. He lay moaning in a puddle of blood . . . the same blood under my claws.

"Hey, stay here with me," Nate said. "Don't worry about him. He'll be okay."

I took a slow, trembling inhale and exhaled as purposefully. My shirt was soaked through with sweat.

"Alex, look at me so I know you're here with me."

My gaze fixed back on Nate. I heard my voice say, "Okay, yeah. I'm here." My vision blurred from the tears that welled in my eyes.

I bit hard on my lip to stop them. Would I ever learn to control her? Wasn't I more than a beast?

"I'm going to let go of you," he said. "Think that'll be okay?"

Sniffling, I nodded. Nate released me, and I covered my face with my hands to hide my humiliation from the other wolves. Staying in control was *Werewolfing 101* to them.

"Can I talk to her?" It was Emma's voice, wrung tight with anxiety. I turned toward the sound and was enfolded into her should-be-patented vanilla-scented hug. She held me, her hand rubbing my back. "Nate, I offered to help him, but he didn't want me to."

"Don't worry about it." Nate's voice turned rough. "On your feet." There was a scrambling noise of claws on pavement and another yelp. "Get your ass inside. Now."

I lowered my hands. Nate followed the injured werewolf back into the club. Thankfully the crowd had thinned. I didn't like to be the center of attention, especially during such a blatant display of my shortcomings. It had felt great to take the guy down, but since we were required to remain hidden, not having control of my inner wolf made me a liability.

Emma released me. "I thought you promised Ben no brawls while he's away." I gave a weak smile, and she giggled. "Are you hurt?" she asked.

My mind felt a bit foggy, and my jaw hurt like hell. I rubbed at my jawline and winced. "He didn't hold back with that punch."

"Can I check if he broke anything?" Emma regarded me with more concern than usual. The attention made me squirm. We'd been close for years, and she'd never seen me completely lose control. She referred to my shifting as *wolfing out*. The phrase made it sound comical, but I wondered if now she saw it differently.

Seven years into the werewolf gig and some would think I'd have a handle on it by now. Shame washed over me. Averting my gaze, I answered, "I'll be fine, thanks."

"Maybe you shouldn't be alone tonight. You could stay with me."

"Em," I said, "I'll be fine."

"Alex, are you okay?" someone asked.

I spun to face the person. "Back off!" My irritation dissolved into embarrassment. I'd met the young man but couldn't recall his name.

He wasn't bothered by my outburst, but the woman beside him frowned at me.

"I'm sorry." My jaw throbbed. "I didn't mean to snap at you."

"It's okay." He smiled. "That punch looked hard enough I felt it in my own teeth."

Emma, far more skilled than me in interactions with people, introduced herself. "Hello. I'm Emma. You are?"

"Isaac." He indicated the woman beside him. "This is Julia."

Julia embodied the typical Dutch heritage of this part of the Midwest: tall, blue-eyed, and blonde. Unlike Isaac, she didn't wear the earthy scent of a fellow wolf.

"Hello, Julia." Emma shook both of their hands.

When Isaac reached for Emma's hand, my memory was jogged by an intricately tattooed cross on the inside of his forearm. He and I had chatted because I'd admired the artwork. The same artist rendered my own Shield, a type of inked mark of protection against hostile magic. Shields were worn by most wolves and some wizards.

"Why'd he attack you, Alex?" Isaac asked.

Emma gave me a look. "She was defending my honor. Again."

"He didn't want her here because she's a wizard," I said.

Julia shot a glare toward the club. "As if that should make a difference. Maybe wizards would feel more welcome if people like him weren't here. What an ignorant ass."

Isaac's forehead creased. He looked toward the club as well. "Nate threw people out last week, both wolves and wizards, when the confrontations turned violent. These don't feel like the usual scuffles we have around here." Isaac looked back at me. "Everyone is on edge. The Committee should have been more willing to help you guys investigate those kidnappings this past winter."

The Committee was a local organization of representatives that was *supposed* to keep the peace among Commoner and supernatural citizens of Hopewell. What it *really* did for the wolves was a whole lotta nothing, except for enforcing the laws it outlined.

"Do you think the wolves are pissed because Trish left the Committee?" I asked. "She said the Committee wasn't working as it was meant to, and we'll get more done without them. The only other supernatural representative is Reginald, and he's a wizard."

"No, I don't think so, but a lot of wolves believe Reginald should have left when Trish did," Isaac said.

"But then who'd represent the wizards?" Emma asked.

"Yeah, everyone deserves a voice, but like Alex said, Reginald is the only other non-Commoner rep. Where is everyone else?" Isaac asked. "Can you see how one of the most prominent wizards choosing to stay with a Committee packed with Commoners instead of showing solidarity with the wolves looks bad?"

"The wolves don't seem to have a lot of love for the Committee," I said.

"Not in my lifetime," Isaac said. "Tethering is the largest problem. The Committee doles out the punishment to werewolves for even minor infractions of Commoner laws. They don't care that it's a death sentence for us." He frowned. "I've lost friends to it. One was tethered for shoplifting, the other for drug possession."

I shuddered. I couldn't imagine dealing with a tether as a werewolf. For wolves, the punishment blocked our ability to shift. All the raw emotion we harnessed for our gift remained trapped inside us, channeled directly into our minds.

"Isaac, I'd like to go now," Julia said. She was still frowning and gave an occasional glance over her shoulder at the club's entrance.

"I'm sorry, I didn't mean to make you uncomfortable." He took her hand into his. "I'm worried this pent-up anxiety is going to fly out of control, and people are going to get hurt."

"You should talk to Trish, Isaac," I said. "She'd be interested in hearing your concerns."

"Yeah. Maybe." He didn't look convinced.

Julia gave his hand a tug. "It's time to go." She looked at Emma and me. "It was nice to meet you."

"Nice to meet you two as well." Emma smiled and gave a little wave.

I exchanged a nod with Isaac, and the two started toward their car. I'd been so absorbed in my own goal of getting my shifting under control, I hadn't realized how bad tensions had become between the wolves, the wizards, and the Committee.

A few weeks ago at Hell's Bells, when Emma and I had gone to the bar to get another drink, Emma was catcalled. Like any other night, she turned her nose up, and I gave the guys the finger. In addition to calling me a "wolf bitch," they used words like "dirty" and "mangey." It'd drawn growls from other werewolves.

I was familiar with the insults a frail male ego slings at a woman, but that was different. The guys were wizards, and their verbal assault was targeting me as lupine. The situation with Emma tonight was of the same nature. A feeling of unease crept into my stomach as I remembered the words whispered to me.

You're going to have to pick a side.

3

THE CANOPY OF *dancing spring leaves overhead is stunning. A light breeze kisses my wet face and carries the fragrance of newly emerged greenery and thawing earth. I am drawn to another scent, one that is bright, sharp, and tastes like copper. My gaze lowers to the broken man at my feet.*

He is sprawled amongst the mud and clumps of disturbed leaves. His sobs for help waver in intensity. A human body is not meant to bend at those angles. There are fractured bones and so much blood.

An electronic beeping noise distracts me. I crouch to brush aside leaves, and the man gives a garbled scream. Saliva, blood, and bits of teeth drip from his chin. I pick up a watch face and a broken band. My hands feel awkward. They are the wrong shape.

I can't shut off the alarm.

The man's keening is constant now, hot needles in my sensitive ears and hazy mind. I realize I can stop his noise.

I know how to shut him off.

I raise a large hair-covered hand, fingers ending in dirty claws, above my head. His eyes widen and he gives one last distorted cry before my arm swings downward.

MY EYELIDS SNAPPED open to a dark, empty room. My pulse raced and my breath came in gasps. Then all the familiar scents of

Ben's apartment flooded my consciousness. They anchored me back into the present.

It's okay. You're safe.

Groaning, I sat up. It'd only been a few hours since I got home from Hell's Bells. The side of my face throbbed. A huge headache had bloomed in my sleep, making my skull feel like it was in a vise. Just because werewolves healed faster than Commoners didn't mean we couldn't feel pain.

There was an upside to waking up feeling so rotten. It brought me back more quickly from the nightmare—my companion ever since my inner wolf surfaced. At first it was constant, robbing me of hours of sleep. Eventually, several nights and then months would pass where I was granted a reprieve. But a situation like the attack at Hell's Bells happened and the nightmare returned.

This time, though, the nightmare had been different. My inner wolf was one step closer to eliminating the man who assaulted me. I worried about this new development, wondering what had caused it. Was I opening up too much of myself to my wolf?

I flipped the sheet aside and stood up from the mattress that lay on the floor. It didn't take me long to reach the bathroom. Situated on the second floor of an older building in downtown, the studio-sized apartment held only the bare essentials: a compact kitchenette, a washer and dryer that worked, and a functioning shower.

I opened the medicine cabinet to get something for my headache. Ben's medicine cabinet was woefully understocked on a good day. It usually held nothing but toothpaste and deodorant. After I started training with Trish and Nate, I picked up a bottle of painkillers. I wasn't going to bother Emma with every bump and bruise.

With pills in hand, I walked to the kitchenette and got a glass of water. When I'd returned after my night out, the apartment stank from the A/C window unit. Ben paid the huge electric bill to keep his extensive vinyl collection comfortable during summer.

Since I wasn't fond of the chemical smell from the A/C, at night I shut off the unit and ran a small window fan instead. It hummed in the window as I downed the pills.

Something clicked at the front door. I froze, nostrils flaring. The fan continued to spin, throwing off both my sense of smell and my hearing. Had the werewolf I'd fought followed me home? I crept toward the door of the apartment, straining to detect anything above the sound of the fan. Nothing.

I unlocked the door and turned the handle ever so slowly. The door, layered with years of paint and barely fitting the frame anymore, stuck a moment before it popped open. Smooth. I waited, every muscle tense. Still nothing. I stepped outside onto the landing.

A siren shrieked to life several blocks away. There were distant shouts of late-night revelers, but no sign of possible intruders outside the building. I took a slow inhale through my nose. There were only the aromas of food from restaurants, the odor of car exhaust, and the faint scent of the flowers in the container downstairs.

After a final glance around, I turned and walked back inside. The nightmare must have made me jumpy. According to Ben, there were wards on the apartment to prevent magic-based spying or forced entry via magical means. It was like a home security system built out of spells. But I knew from experience that wards didn't keep someone from kicking down the door.

I tried to close the door but it stuck again. Growling in irritation, I looked down. The toe of a tattered sneaker was wedged between the door and the frame. I jerked my gaze up in time to receive my second punch to the face for the night.

My vision exploded into spots. I stumbled backward and covered my nose. Blood rushed from it anyway. The door burst open and a thin silhouette of a woman charged into the apartment after me. It was fortunate for her that she'd got the jump on me because her next punch was slow and clumsy. I caught her by the arm and yanked her forward off her feet. She shouted in surprise and fell into the small table in the kitchenette. The table legs screeched on the linoleum as it tipped and she tumbled to the floor.

I reached down to flip her over and get a better look at her. She rolled onto her side and raised a hand, open palm lifted toward me. Her hood fell back from her face, revealing a woman with light eyes and a wild mane of dark hair. The telltale prickling of energy rapidly drawn through the room and past me was collected by her. The woman was a wizard. She yelled a command in a language I didn't understand, and the energy was released in the form of a spell.

I instinctively raised my arm in front of me and turned my face away. The tattoo across my breastbone, my Shield, flared to life with a stinging sensation. I was still acclimating to the protection it gave me. The woman made it to her feet as the spell's blast caused me to take a step back, but otherwise split harmlessly around me. The front door wasn't as lucky. It was wrenched from one of its hinges.

How had she cast a spell if Ben's apartment was warded against magic?

"Where is Benjamin?" the woman yelled. She trembled, her face flushed and her eyes blazing. If my nose wasn't so swollen already, I had a hunch I would smell fear.

Scared or not, there was no way in hell I was going to tell this crazy person where to find him. The same bad guys hired by Emma's evil ex also had an interest in Ben. One of the criminals was still MIA. I lowered my arm, my knuckles aching as my fingers lengthened and my claws appeared. "Who's asking?" Glaring at the intruder, I took a cautious step toward her.

She raised her palm again and another draw of energy brushed over my skin, giving me goosebumps. "Stay back," she said.

Hadn't she noticed my Shield? I took another step. "What do you want from Ben?"

My next step was too close for her. She yelled another command, pulling her hand down and to her side. I waited for the spell to deflect off my Shield again. Instead, I was blindsided by the kitchen table as it flipped up on end, flew at me, and knocked me off my feet. The table pinned me in place.

Being held on my back against my will would be an automatic loss to the beast roiling inside me. But a) it wasn't a man restraining me, and b) it was a table. I was more confused and annoyed than enraged.

The kitchenette light flickered on, and from my angle on the floor, a pair of sneakers approached. The pressure on the table increased as she drew near. She came into view, her brow furrowed. Her shaking had subsided in both her body and voice. "Tell me where he is or I swear I will flatten the breath right out of you."

I remained silent, growing more frustrated by the second as I struggled to free myself. Who the hell gets her ass kicked by a piece of furniture? It was humiliating. The woman stepped closer and I bared my teeth, letting loose a snarl of warning.

She frowned and raised her fist gradually toward her body. The pressure on the table increased, and the cheap surface cracked. She locked eyes with me. "Tell me what you did with my brother."

I saw the family resemblance. It was in the dark, thick hair and gray-blue eyes. I recognized the drawn brows as she concentrated on maintaining the spell. And that must be why she was able to cast. Ben had excluded her from the wards. She raised her fist higher and the table continued its merciless application of pressure. "Wait!" I gasped. "I know Ben. He's my . . . friend."

She hesitated, a small frown appearing. "How do I know you're not lying?"

"Would a criminal be lounging around at the scene of the crime in a nightshirt?"

"Most criminals aren't very smart." The pressure receded slightly. "He didn't mention a roommate." She took a second to glance around the dark apartment. "Where is he?"

"He's out of town," I said. "Let me up so we can have a civil conversation about this."

Her expression remained skeptical, but the table relented further. It allowed me a more comfortable inhale. "When will he be back?" she asked.

"Soon. Hopefully later this morning?" My whole face ached, and I could taste the metallic tang of blood running down the back of my throat from my nosebleed. "Please. Call off your table."

A small smile slipped past her lips, and the resemblance was unmistakable. Ben's eyes brightened when he smiled. So did his sister's. She threw her hand aside like she was tossing away a piece of trash. The table flipped effortlessly off me and clattered to a stop. Her features relaxed, and she offered me a hand.

I accepted it and pulled myself up to stand. My nose immediately discharged blood down the front of Ben's t-shirt. I cursed and dashed to the kitchenette for something to stop the bleeding.

"I suspected Benjamin was in trouble again." She turned the single kitchen chair upright and sat down. "I'd thought he was past the problems with those two tethered guys. When I saw you, I wasn't sure anymore. Benjamin keeps to himself at home, so it was odd someone else was here."

"Yeah, I get it." I tried to grab some ice cubes from the freezer while also staunching my bloody nose. Half of the ice slipped from my hand and shattered across the floor.

"Let me help." She took some ice cubes and folded a kitchen towel around them as I rested back against the counter.

"I didn't notice you at all," I said. Between my souped-up senses of smell, hearing, and sight, it was rare that someone snuck up on me. "How'd you do that?"

"I'd cloaked myself before coming to the door." She handed me the wrapped ice.

That was useful. Goddamn wizards. I gestured at the table. "And you weren't worried I was a Commoner?" A blatant display of magic in front of a Commoner was forbidden. All supernatural beings, even wizards, were expected to conceal our gifts.

"Your eyes gave you away," she said. "You should be careful."

It wasn't the first time it'd been suggested. "Was Ben expecting you?"

"No, I thought I'd surprise him with a visit." She winced as I placed the cold compress on my face. "I'm sorry about the nose."

"Thanks. It'll heal." I raised my free bloody hand briefly in greeting and smiled. "I'm Alex, by the way."

She nodded. "I'm Joan. I wish we could have met under different circumstances."

I shrugged. It seemed appropriate. How else would I meet the family of the guy I'm dating except through hand-to-hand combat, in the middle of the night, wearing only a t-shirt and my underwear?

Joan tipped the small table back into an upright position. It wobbled. "Leave it to my baby brother to keep a werewolf in the house and not bother telling any of us about it."

The comment didn't sit well with me. Was Ben embarrassed to have me living with him? I arched my brow. "Maybe he feels it's no one's business."

Her laugh was abrupt and sharp. "More than likely, yes." She took a moment to study me from my bare feet to my head full of curls, now a tangled mess streaked with blood. "What are you to Benjamin?"

The blunt nature of the question caught me by surprise. The fact I wasn't sure how to answer made me uncomfortable. *Girlfriend* felt juvenile. *Partner* felt stifling. Hopefully someone who made him feel as happy and cared for as he made me feel?

"That's really no one's business, either," I said. He and I were still figuring it out.

Joan's eyebrows lifted. "Fair enough. I'm sure if he hasn't told us about you, you don't know much about us."

I knew Ben was the youngest of three, and that everyone but his grandfather moved away from Hopewell. That was the extent of it.

She took my lack of response as confirmation. "Didn't think so. Once he's home and settled, can you have him message me?"

"Why don't you stay on the sofa?" I readjusted the ice. "I don't mind." But I did mind. It had been a shitty night, and I selfishly wanted Ben to myself when he walked through the door.

"Thanks, but I'll stay with Granddad." She gave me a final glance over, seemingly convinced I wasn't an immediate threat to Ben. "I guess I'll see you later?"

I nodded and held my hand aloft again. As she left, Joan made several attempts to shut the door before it latched into place. The door was broken and there wasn't a screwdriver in sight. Once it was closed, at least the deadbolt still slid into place.

I had too much adrenaline left in my system for sleep to be possible. Plus, Joan and I had made a mess out of the kitchenette area. Both the table and door were broken, and I hoped my nose wasn't as well. I cleaned the blood from the floor, started a load of laundry, and showered.

With a fresh batch of ice cubes wrapped and pressed to my nose, I curled up on the sofa with a copy of *Ms. Marvel* to wait for Ben. Since he didn't talk about his family, I wasn't sure how he'd receive the news that I met his sister. I wondered what she thought of me . . . if she would view a *last-in-her-class* werewolf as good enough for her brother . . . and how much that would matter to Ben.

4

I WAS POURING my third cup of coffee when I heard familiar footsteps on the apartment stairs. The sound sent a thrill of excitement through me. Grinning, I set my mug aside, rushed to the door, and opened it. Ben looked up at me from the stairs, a giant duffle bag over his shoulder, and returned my grin.

He was tall, lean to the point of skinny, and, like his sister, had beautiful gray-blue eyes. While her complexion was sun-kissed and freckled, Ben was fair-skinned. His skin and eyes stood in stark contrast to his dark hair and eyelashes. Elaborate tattoo art on his throat curved back along the side of his neck and wound down and around his left arm.

I rushed to meet him, threw my arms around his neck, and was surrounded by his deliciously warm and spicy scent. The creature inside me recognized it and uncurled from where she rested. Warmth spread through my body. I kissed him. A lot. His hand grasped the railing to maintain his balance on the narrow stairs.

We parted and I held out my hand. "Let me take that for you."

Ben surrendered the heavy bag. He touched his fingertips to his lips before lowering his flattened hand toward me, like blowing a kiss, in an ASL gesture meaning "Thank you."

I practically pulled him up the stairs. When we got inside, I tossed the bag onto the kitchen table and moved to embrace him again. Ben pushed the door mostly closed but was confused by the damaged hinges. He turned to me with his eyebrows raised in question. It was a frequent and common exchange between us.

"It can wait," I said with a crooked grin. I seized the front pockets of his jeans. He smiled as I pulled him toward me with a low, hungry growl. When it came to Ben, my inner wolf and I were so close to being in sync. I almost had her convinced . . . *He's safe.*

I attempted to kiss him again, but he stopped me. His forehead wrinkled, and he ran his thumb lightly along my bruised jaw. The bruise from the fight at Hell's Bells wouldn't last long, but my body had to work through the healing process.

"I'm okay." I took his hand from my jawline, smiled up at him, and slowly ran my tongue along the length of his index finger.

He inhaled sharply through his teeth.

There was a large crash behind me. We both jumped from the sudden noise. The hair at the nape of my neck stood on end. The table's leg, weakened by my scuffle with Joan, had collapsed beneath the weight of the duffle bag.

Ben's expression flipped back to concern. His quiet voice was only audible because of my sharpened hearing. "What happened?"

Dammit. My face flushed. Emma was only partially joking about my promise to stay out of fights while Ben was away. He realized I could take care of myself. I'd been very vocal about that. But it didn't prevent him from worrying about my safety.

Despite the signs that something indeed happened, I was annoyed that Ben had foregone the more polite "*Did* something happen?" I tucked my hands into my back pockets and shrugged, determined to downplay the incident. I mean, no one had been *permanently* injured. "Your sister stopped by."

He frowned. "What? Why was Joan here?"

I squirmed and shrugged again. Couldn't this wait until later? "She wanted to surprise you with a visit but surprised me instead. You're supposed to message her when you're unpacked and settled."

Ben glanced from the door, to the table, and then to me. "Is she okay?"

"She's fine, just a bit confused." I was thankful the swelling across the bridge of my nose had gone down and the bruising wouldn't appear until later. "She didn't know who I was, so she was afraid I'd done something horrible to you. And apparently she wasn't expecting a 'roommate'." I knew it wasn't fair, but I was miffed. The mood for my long-awaited and often imagined steamy reunion with him was being spoiled.

Ben's pale complexion turned pink. "Alex, please don't be offended. I don't share everything with my family. I'm not as close to them as you are to yours." He held his hand out.

I latched my fingers with his, and he drew me toward him to encircle me with his arms. But doubt lingered. "They wouldn't be disappointed in you for 'keeping a werewolf in the house?'"

"No." He leaned back from me and smiled. "Besides, I'm a tethered wizard. They have no disappointment left to give me."

Years before I'd met him, Ben had broken the Committee's laws and was branded with a tether. My fingertips settled on the cross-like mark, hidden within the inked artwork on his throat. Since he was a wizard, it suppressed his voice, therefore cutting off his access to magic.

I gave the mark a light kiss. Ben had puzzled out a way to partially cheat the tether, but no one knew that but me, and I'd found out by accident. Trying to break a tether was forbidden and could get him executed by the Committee. It was a secret I'd sworn to keep for him.

He brushed my curls back from my face and placed a kiss on my forehead. "So, the first time you meet my sister, she hits you in the face?"

I might as well have been talking to my friend Anne. Her inquisitive police officer's mind guaranteed at least one round of twenty questions in any given conversation. "Well, yes . . . but the jaw is from a disagreement at Hell's Bells. Some guy wouldn't let Em into the building because he doesn't like wizards."

The corners of Ben's mouth dipped downward. "So he hit *you*?"

My ears burned. "Well, *I* punched *him*. Then he hit me."

"Right." He nodded. "That seems like a natural progression."

"The bickering between the wolves and wizards grew worse while you've been gone." Shaking my head, I frowned. "The guy seemed pissed that Em is my best friend. He said I have to choose between the wolves and wizards."

"That's some narrow-minded bullshit," Ben said. "This disagreement with the guy you fought—is it settled?"

"Yes." I was too embarrassed to share my failure of control with him. "Nate helped take care of it."

"Good. Please be careful."

Ben preferred to avoid physical conflict if he could. It was one of the qualities that attracted me to him. He was tethered because of a mistake that resulted in someone's death. I didn't know the details, but my gut told me it was exactly that: a mistake.

I tightened my arms around him, having missed the sensation more than I'd like to admit. "I'm glad you're back," I said. "I mean, it's okay you were gone . . . but it's nice to have you here."

"I missed you, too."

I sighed. "We weren't supposed to have clothes on at this point."

"Yeah?" Ben smiled. "Should we attempt to fix that?"

"Later?" I released him, my cheeks warm. "I have to meet Anne."

"Take all the time you need," he said. "I'll be here when you're ready."

I CHANGED MY clothes and left to meet Anne at the gym. She was tough as nails, smart as a whip, and determined to make detective. She'd excelled at hand-to-hand combat when training at the police academy. When Anne offered to introduce me to boxing as an addition to my exercise routine, I took her up on it.

I'd never needed to learn the mechanics of fighting. When I was in college, how to throw a punch never crossed my mind.

After my inner wolf awoke, my increased strength could drop a guy with one hefty hit. But now that I was involved with beings at least as strong as me, a bit of technique could help.

Anne waited for me outside the gym's entrance, wearing a light tank over her sports bra and a loose pair of shorts. Her auburn hair was fastened back in a ponytail, and she held a bulky gym bag.

"Good morning." She smiled. "I was going to call. I didn't know if you'd chickened out."

"Sorry I'm a bit late." I looked down at my oversized t-shirt and ill-fitting sweats. "Am I dressed right for this?"

She laughed. "It's boxing, not a night out with Emma. Wear whatever you want."

I grinned. We often joked that Emma could wear a potato sack and still outshine us. I'd met Anne through Emma, and our friendship grew when Anne became my running buddy. Running was a love of mine that I could share with her. What I couldn't share, since she was a Commoner, was that I was a werewolf. She didn't know Emma's secret either.

I followed Anne into the gym and was bowled over by the rank scent of sweaty men. The place crawled with them. I wrinkled my nose, having second thoughts. Maybe this wasn't a good idea.

Anne noticed and encouraged me along with a smile and wave. "Let's head over to the heavy bags and I'll help you get started."

Sticking close, I followed her along the edge of the room. I kept my gaze averted from the occupied weights and machines so as not to make eye contact. My skin crawled as I imagined possible stares tracking us.

The gym wasn't owned by the police department, but many officers liked the setup. Anne seemed perfectly comfortable, but she was also a woman on the city's police force. Working within a majority male environment was just another day for her.

Anne set her bag on a bench. She sorted through and pulled out gloves and fabric bandaging. "These are my old gloves, but they should work while you decide if you enjoy this."

I sat down beside the bag and watched her wrap bandaging around my left hand. "How long have you been boxing?"

She grinned. "I haven't stopped since school." She picked up the next strip of cloth and glanced at my bruised jaw. "Getting a head start on our lesson?"

I knew the question would come up. Not much slipped by her. I shrugged. "Em and I were out and ran into some jackass."

She looked up at me. "You couldn't walk away?"

"Why should I? Maybe instead he could not be a jackass."

Anne shook her head. "Alex, he could've broken your jaw." She never lectured me, but she insisted on laying out the facts. She began wrapping my right hand. "And this?"

I looked down at my knuckles. The cuts already sealed but were still visible. "Jackasses have teeth."

"I think this is going to help with your pent-up frustration."

I scowled. "I'm not frustrated about anything."

"Will Ben be home soon?" She winked. "Three months is a long time."

Laughing, I gave her a mock punch in the shoulder.

She finished wrapping my hand, chuckling. "Boxing helps me vent a lot of stress. As a bonus, I'll teach you how to block the next punch thrown at you." She helped me put on the boxing gloves, and I waited as she suited up in another pair.

Anne showed me a basic stance, how to hold my gloves up to protect my face and head, and several basic punches. I appreciated her patient and precise teaching skills.

"I'm right here if you have any questions," she said. "I'll set the timer and we'll work through a few rounds. Sound okay?"

I nodded, focusing on the points she'd designated on the worn heavy bag. My first punches were unsure.

Gradually I relaxed as the world shrunk to only me and the leather bag hanging in front of me. A slow burn began in my arms, shoulders, and back. The sound of the gloves colliding with the bag was gratifying.

As my blood started to flow from the workout, my jaw began to throb. I thought of the guy I'd fought at the club. I recalled his smug expression as he used his larger body to exclude us. The heavy bag rocked on its chains as it absorbed my punch.

And what had he called my dearest friend, a woman he doesn't even know, because of a bit of flirting? A whore?

I pummeled the bag with a series of punches, the strength coming from deeper inside.

Was it because she was a wizard or a woman? Probably both. Would it have been overlooked if she were a man? Or maybe the guy was jealous because she'd accomplished more for the wolves in a span of weeks than he'd accomplished in his entire life.

A sharp snarl left me as I drove my fist against the bag. It bucked and jumped at the end of its chain, swinging forward and back to almost slam into me.

The erratic movement shook me from my tunnel vision, and I fumbled to slow the bag's chaotic swing. I'd put a crack in the worn leather. Breathless and covered in sweat, I gave Anne a panicked glance. She stood beside her heavy bag, watching me with raised eyebrows. Some younger guy, dressed in gym shorts and a t-shirt with the city police department's emblem, waited next to her.

He chuckled. "Don't worry about it. They're old bags. It looks like she's a natural, Anne."

"Mmm-hmm. Yeah, looks like it." Anne wasn't smiling. "Alex, this is my new partner, Jakob DeBoer. Jakob, Alex."

Focusing on the new guy allowed me to avoid Anne's analytical gaze. I gave him the rehearsed smile I kept on file for such occasions. "Hi, Jakob."

Anne patched the tear in the heavy bag with some duct tape as Jakob nodded in greeting. "I was on my way out and saw Anne. Thought I would stop by and say 'hello.'"

"As if I don't see enough of you already," she said with a smile.

Jakob seemed nice enough, with brown eyes, open features, and a friendly smile. He was tall like Anne, but more thickly built with broad shoulders. He had the clean-shaven features and neat haircut I'd seen on many other officers. More important, he wasn't setting off my "Bro Beam" (as Ben called it), my uncanny ability to sense ill intentions. Another werewolf perk, it gave me highly accurate first reads on people.

But there was something else there too, nagging at me.

I wiped the sweat from my brow with the back of my forearm and stepped toward the two. "Have you taken any of Anne's classes? She's a great teacher." I almost had it ... disguised beneath the strong scents of soap, deodorant, and aftershave.

Anne waved away the compliment, and Jakob took a step back, smiling. "No, unfortunately not." He held up a finger. "But I have been her sparring partner. Watch out for her left hook."

"Okay, enough!" Anne said. "Goodbye, Jakob."

He smiled. "It was nice to meet you, Alex."

"Yeah. Same." I watched him leave, curiosity piqued.

"Ready?" Anne asked. She was waiting to start the timer again. Part of me was nervous I'd more blatantly slip up, but I also didn't want to cut out early and alert her to something being wrong. I squared up to the bag, focused my control, and nodded. "All right. Go."

WHEN I RETURNED to the apartment, Ben had unpacked, showered, and was on the sofa reading. The washer ran in the small hall to the bathroom, and *The King Is Dead* spun on the record player. I was still flushed and my muscles had that nice ache of a good workout. With a bit of effort, I closed the broken door behind me.

Ben looked up from his book. "How'd you like it?"

"It was fun," I said. "Anne said boxing is a good stress outlet. It did feel great to pummel the bag, and the bag doesn't hit back." I paused, reconsidered the statement, then added, "Most of the time, anyway."

"A stress outlet that doesn't hit back sounds good for you." He watched me walk to the record player. "Do you think you'll go again?"

"Yeah." I turned up the music to give us some privacy with the open windows. I stared back over my shoulder and hit him with the most overblown *come-hither* look I could conjure, complete with fluttering eyelashes and pursed lips. I'm positive the alluring sweatpants, a tad big and stained with sweat, sealed the deal.

He laughed, set his book aside, and met me where I'd flopped down on the mattress. "I've waited months. I can wait a few more minutes if you want a shower."

"I'm tired of waiting." I pulled him down onto the mattress. The afterglow of the workout and Ben's scent immediately drew the beast inside me forward.

His lips were light on my skin as he kissed me . . . my earlobe, my jawline, my throat. My inner wolf pushed against my hold, wanting to be closer to the surface of my skin . . . wanting him. I clenched my teeth. The dull ache started in my hands and knuckles. "Wait!"

Ben flinched and drew back. "What's wrong? Too much?"

"Uh . . ." I sat up, pulled my shirt off, and wiggled out of my sweatpants. "Too hot."

"Are you sure this is okay? We don't have to—"

"Yes." I kicked my sweatpants aside. "Please, yes."

He chuckled and leaned toward me. I tackled him. His skin felt wonderfully warm under his shirt and tasted even better. My hands started to shift again. This time, I was the one to jerk back. "Dammit!"

Ben rubbed my arm. "Alex, it's okay."

"No." I pushed the heels of my hands into my eyes. "It's so. Goddamn. Frustrating. My body isn't listening to me." I dropped my hands into my lap. "I messed up the last time with you, but I thought I . . . she . . . we were ready now. I even practiced."

Ben arched an eyebrow. "Practiced?"

"Yeah," I shrugged. "I thought if I surrounded myself with your scent while I got hot and bothered—" I motioned vaguely to my body. "—she'd grow more used to you and listen to me when we're actually together."

A corner of his mouth twitched upward. "Would you feel comfortable showing me what you mean?"

Holy. Hell.

My entire body ignited with heat. "Absolutely."

We spent the remainder of our day relaxing at the apartment, in various states of dress, enjoying each other's company. With the pressure to perform removed, we explored different ways to please each other without my inner wolf turning our play dangerous.

In his whispered voice, Ben answered my litany of questions about his time away. While he was touring, our exchanged text messages hadn't allowed for in-depth conversations. His eyes lit up as he narrated to me the nights filled with various venues, crowds, and local musicians he'd met.

By evening, I lounged on my stomach, sweaty but satisfied, with my chin resting on my folded arms. "Ben?" My eyelids were half-lowered as I enjoyed the light back scratch he gave me. I turned my head toward him and settled my cheek on my arm.

"Hmm?" A small smile lingered on his lips. He was stretched out on his side next to me, his eyes closed, his eyelashes thick and dark against his skin.

"Have you ever heard a werewolf purr?"

He chuckled. "No. Why?" The areas of his breastbone and lower throat were still flushed, and strands of damp hair clung to his temples.

"It's possible you might." I smiled. "I can't remember the last time I felt this relaxed."

Ben was an accidental lover. Since I was a werewolf, I hadn't realized allowing someone so close was a possibility. Would my struggles to control my wolf drive him away? Would he eventually lose patience and see me as a monster?

But then Ben's hand halted its movement across my back, and he opened his eyes to look at me. My stomach did one of those giddy flips I found so embarrassing. Sure, he was an attractive guy, and I got a second-hand high seeing him happy, but it was the way he looked at me that really did it. He seemed to genuinely enjoy being with me—the entire me.

Ben pulled me close and tightened his arms around me. His scent was so strong, I tasted him on the back of my tongue. I exhaled a sigh against his skin and decided to fully enjoy this while it was available to us.

5

I SMELLED THE body before we saw it. Anne and I were out early the next morning for a run along my favorite stretch of the riverside. There was enough light without having to dodge the heavy pedestrian traffic of the afternoon. Our breathing and footfalls set a nice rhythm, and the already warm air brushed over my bare arms. After a winter cooped up indoors and a temperamental spring causing flooding, finally being able to run along the riverfront felt great.

We'd descended stairs to a wooden walkway, the water's edge running parallel on the left, when the sickly sweet smell of death hit me. My stride broke and I slowed. There was too much of it to be an animal like a racoon or some other urban critter.

Anne noticed I was no longer beside her. She reduced her speed until she came to a halt and looked back at me. "Everything okay?" She waited with her hands on her hips, her chest lifting and falling. Sweaty strands of her auburn hair had come loose from her ponytail, and a healthy blush brightened her cheeks.

I scanned along the boardwalk, seeking the source of the scent. We'd passed the area where the lawn met the river and tree branches draped over the water. In this stretch, a concrete retaining wall, designed to protect the sidewalk and streets above from flooding, rose up high beside us on our right.

"I'm getting a stitch in my side." I pressed a hand into an area of my waist and winced. "Mind if we walk for a bit?"

Anne nodded. "Sure, we can walk."

We continued down the boardwalk. My nostrils flared as I surveyed the water's edge. Yes, I knew if it was a corpse it shouldn't be hidden from the police. But under the smell of decaying tissue and extinguished life, there was another scent. It was intimately familiar . . . something that was part of my world but not Anne's.

I kept my secret from Anne, not only because I was expected to by Committee rules, but also because I didn't want her in danger as a result of my shenanigans. Activities in the supernatural community often flew under the radar of the city police. Whenever the police force got involved, everything got much more complicated.

"Alex?"

"What?" I looked at Anne. She'd caught my attention wandering. I was glad I was already flushed from the run. Otherwise my guilt would be literally painted on my face.

Anne studied me. I'd stumbled closer to setting off her bullshit detector. "I said, do you want to get in another run tomorrow before we go shopping with Emma?"

"Sure. What time were you thinking?" I asked.

The sinister smell strengthened as we approached Opal Street bridge. It ran perpendicular to the river and brought traffic in and out of downtown. A white-haired man stood near the railing tossing bits of bread to the ducks below. An equally white cat lounged on the railing in the sun beside him. The man and his pet shared the bridge with numerous fishermen whose lines were cast into the water.

The boardwalk stretched ahead of us and continued underneath the bridge. But my gaze snagged on a set of stairs leading up to street level and the bridge. The body floated between the boardwalk and the retaining wall to the right, caught beneath the stairs by the river's current. A moment later, Anne noticed it too.

"What the . . ." She frowned and her pace quickened.

I followed, the strength of the scent increasing sharply. I pulled the edge of my shirt over my nose to dampen the smell. Anne crouched on the boardwalk beside the corpse before retrieving her phone. Her features were grim as she stood, took a few steps away, and dialed a number.

My heart plummeted when I drew closer and got a better look at the body. It was Isaac. I thought of our conversation about growing tensions among the Committee, werewolves, and wizards. News of his death wouldn't land lightly in the wolf community.

Anne talked on the phone as I crouched at the edge of the boardwalk. Isaac floated face up, his hair fanned softly around his head. His eyes stared blankly at the bottom of the stairs, his lips parted. He was fully clothed, so he'd obviously not been in the middle of a recreational dip in the river.

The most evident trauma to his body was the large puckered gash across the front of his throat. The edges of the grisly wound were dark despite the water erasing most traces of blood. I reached out toward the body.

"Alex!" Anne stood beside me, eyes wide. "Don't touch him. This is a crime scene." She frowned and extended her hand.

I accepted it and stood. "Sorry. I wasn't thinking." I actually was. I'd caught the scent of singed tissue mingled with the heavy smell of the body. Since I wasn't completely sure what had happened, I didn't feel safe telling Anne I had known Isaac. "Did you call it in?"

"Yes. I have to wait here and make sure nothing is tampered with until they send an investigator and a medical examiner." She studied me. "You're remaining surprisingly calm for having seen a dead body."

I was still shielding my nose. Anne was not. I removed my hand, and the collar of my shirt fell back into place. I immediately regretted it. The strong odor of the corpse turned my stomach. Yes, that was definitely the stink of charred flesh. I suppressed a gag and took a few steps away.

Anne was at my side. Her sweat and deodorant was added to the soup of nausea-inducing aromas currently assailing my nose.

"I'm sorry. That was a stupid thing to say." She placed a hand on my shoulder. "You don't have to wait for me. You can go."

I dismissed her concern with a shake of my head. "Any idea about what happened to him?"

"It seems like he was attacked and more than likely dumped. There isn't too much of a smell yet, so it must have been recent." She frowned. "I shouldn't speculate too much. I'll find out more after he's out of the water and an ME sees him."

Nope, I wasn't going to make it. The stench became unbearable. My stomach clenched again and I gagged. I held the back of my hand up to my nose and stepped away. "I'm sorry. I thought I could keep you company, but I need to go."

"Of course. Go." She waved me away. "I'll see you tomorrow."

I turned, retreated up the stairs to the street, and didn't stop jogging until I was a few blocks into downtown. I took big gulps of air, preferring the scent of exhaust fumes to the awful odor that lingered in my nose.

The underlying reek of burnt skin had thrown my mind back several months. Nate hadn't been the only one attacked with a silver weapon. The first time I'd smelled the stench of a wound inflicted by the metal, it had been on my own body. The ME would only find a young man with his throat slashed, but I knew silver was most likely the cause of Isaac's death.

AFTER A QUICK shower and change of clothes at Ben's apartment, I went to Hell's Bells. I wasn't confident Trish and Nate would be awake but felt the news I brought was important enough to get them out of bed. The lot was empty except for Nate's rusted sedan, the size of a small watercraft, parked beside the building.

I knocked, and when no one answered, I pounded my fist on the door before placing my hand against the glass and peering in. A figure moved through the darkened room. I stepped back, locks clicked, and the front door opened. Standing in the doorway, rumpled and squinting out at me, was Nate.

He lifted a hand to shield his bloodshot eyes against the morning sun. "Christ, Alex, what time is it?"

I raised my hand to shield my eyes too. "Where the hell are your pants, Nate?"

He gave a groggy smile and scratched behind his ear. "You're lucky I put on underwear." He stifled a yawn and stepped aside. "Come on in."

I entered the building, and he shut the door behind us. My eyes adjusted to the dark room, and I followed him across the lounge. "Is Trish here too?"

"Nah. She's doing something downtown." He flipped on a tableside lamp and dropped into a chair. "What do you need that couldn't wait until a more humane hour?"

I hesitated before I sat down across from him. Telling them together would have been preferable. I chewed at my thumbnail. "Do you know when she's going to be back?"

He became more alert as the dregs of sleep fell away. "What's wrong, Alex?"

"Um, Anne and I were out this morning for a run." My chest tightened. I barely knew the kid, but I was having a difficult time breaking the news to Nate without becoming upset. "We were running along the boardwalk when we came across a body."

Nate's brows knit together as he frowned. "One of ours?"

"Yes," I said. "Anne suspects a homicide. I'd agree."

"Who was it?"

"Isaac. I don't know his last name, but he wore a cross on his forearm as his Shield," I said.

Nate cursed and lowered his head. "Isaac Laska." He ran his hands up over his hair. A rumbling growl sounded from his hunched frame. I leaned back as he abruptly stood, cursing again. Nate's eyes shifted from brown to a bright copper. He strode away to an open area by the bar.

I heard a car door close outside and looked to the front door before it opened. Trish entered the lounge. She pushed her sunglasses up onto her head. "Alex? You're here early." Her attention jumped to Nate's pacing, and she moved to him. "What is it? What happened?"

Nate stopped, closing his eyes when Trish touched the side of his face. She took a hold of his hands. Attempted restraint tightened his voice. "Someone killed Isaac and dumped him in the river. Alex and her cop friend found his body this morning."

"What?" Trish turned to me, eyes wide.

"The medical examiner hadn't even got there when I left. I wanted to let you know right away in case there's anything we can do to prevent . . ." I let my words trail off, not sure how to phrase it. To prevent more agitation in the werewolf community?

Trish nodded, switching to problem-solving mode. "Good thinking. Thank you."

"There's something else," I said. "He was attacked with silver. I could smell the burns."

Another low growl escaped Nate. "I'm going to kill that priest."

Trish scowled. "No. Aiden has always been impartial, even to a fault. We need him in place for our safety."

Nate snarled, "We don't need his protection!" His intensifying anger caused the hair on the back of my neck to rise.

"Yes, we do!" Trish didn't usually raise her voice. First, she didn't have to. The majority of the wolves respected her as a leader. Second, she had the uncanny, and admirable, ability to remain calm in high-stress situations.

Nate dropped his gaze, his hands clenched at his sides. Trish's tone softened. "I know you're hurting, love. I am too. We'll find who did this to him." She brushed Nate's damp cheek with the back of her hand and gave him a gentle kiss. He sniffed and wiped his nose on his arm before abruptly leaving down the hallway to their apartment.

"Um, I think I'll go." I stood. "Sorry to bring such bad news."

Trish turned to me, her eyes now a liquid gold hue. She joined me near the sofas. "I'd like to stay here with him. Can you visit Aiden and tell him what happened?"

I frowned. The quiet nature and hawk-like persona of the priest unsettled me. "Can I call him instead?"

"No. Isaac was a member of his church. It's not news to mention in a phone call," Trish said. "While you're there, ask Aiden to show you the silver daggers. If he resists, call me. I would do it myself, but Nate and I have to discuss how to share this awful news with everyone."

Trish was pulling me deeper into the complicated web of supernatural politics. Last year, agreeing to help her would have been the furthest thing from my mind. But the events we'd weathered together had created a bond between us. Because of Trish, Nate, and the other wolves, Hopewell became more than a hiding place for me. I wanted to help my community because they were my family and this was my home.

I nodded. "Yeah, I'll do it. I'll try, anyway. I can't promise I'll do it well."

"Do you have any pressing plans this afternoon?" she asked.

"Ben got home yesterday." I wanted to spend the day with him before he returned to work tomorrow. Trish waited as if I hadn't answered her question. My conscience wrestled with what I wanted to do versus what I felt I should do. "So no, nothing urgent."

"There's a Committee meeting this afternoon," Trish said. "Considering what happened to Isaac, and that you found him, I'd like you to attend the meeting with me."

"What? When did you decide to rejoin?" I'd hoped to never attend the Committee meetings again. Trish's frustration had caused her to leave her seat.

"A colleague convinced me to do so. If I'm at the meetings, it might help to mitigate this rising tension," Trish said. She placed a hand at my shoulder. "Thank you for agreeing to visit Aiden. I'll see you again this afternoon. We can get dinner afterward."

I nodded and glanced toward the hall leading back to Nate and her apartment. "Can you give him a hug for me?"

"Of course."

SAINT ANTHONY'S WAS one of two cathedrals downtown. In an area where real estate was at a premium and people struggled to find a place to live, the huge building and landscaped square unapologetically took up an entire city block. I'd only been here once before, but not much had changed. Then, I'd crossed a courtyard with snow and icy walkways; now, heat rose off the sun-baked stone. The only relief for a pedestrian was the occasional tree.

I liked the heat, but the humidity I could do without. I paused in front of the building's enormous portal-like door to wrangle the halo of flyaways back into my ponytail. The damp air had transformed my head of curls into a comical poof. Father Aiden had a way of both making me feel small *and* irritating the hell out of me. The ridiculous state of my hair didn't help my confidence. I took a deep breath, steeled myself, and passed through the doorway.

Goosebumps rose on my exposed arms and legs from the temperature change. Thick yellow limestone walls kept the summer heat at bay. The dusty aroma of ceremony reached me, containing incense, books, and candle wax. Since it was a weekday, the main hall was empty. My steps echoed loudly, an uncomfortable feeling considering I moved silently through most spaces.

I passed the sanctuary entrance on the left and continued to the administrative offices on the right. I gave a light knock on the door before I entered. A blonde wisp of a woman wearing large glasses looked up from her typing at a desk behind the main counter.

"Good morning." She took in the tattoo peeking above my tank top's low neckline and the ragged state of my blue nail polish. Her pale lips pressed into a thin line. "Can I help you?"

I gave her a pleasant smile anyway. "Is Aiden here?"

"*Father* Aiden," she emphasized the title, "is available by appointment. Would you like to make an appointment?"

The sound of movement came from the office behind her. The door opened, and a dark-haired man with graying temples stood in the doorway. He was dressed in black pants and a black short-sleeved button-up shirt with a white priest's collar. His brows rose in mild surprise. "Miss Steward. What can I do for you?"

"Trish sent me over to share some news." I glanced at the older woman and back at him. "Can we talk in private?"

"Of course." Aiden spoke to the seated woman. "I won't wander far, Mrs. Murphy."

"Remember your lunch appointment, Father," she said as he walked past her.

"Thank you." Aiden rounded the counter and I followed him out into the hall. "Patricia couldn't visit herself?"

"No. You got me instead." I jabbed my thumb over my shoulder, down the hall. "Mind if we have a chat downstairs?" It was where the cathedral's lesser relics were stored.

"There's no need," Aiden said. "We can sit in the sanctuary."

"Someone killed a young wolf, Isaac Laska. Silver was involved. Trish wants me to check the cutlery you keep in the basement."

Since I'd met him, the priest had been a challenge to figure out. He kept his emotions and intentions veiled. Every once in a while he slipped. I caught the slight widening of his eyes when I said Isaac's name.

"My condolences. Isaac was an exceptional young man," he said. "Patricia can rest assured the daggers are safe."

His refusal wasn't surprising. "She'll rest better if you show me," I said.

The priest studied me from down the length of his curved nose. I wondered if he was tallying all my faults into a lengthy list. I almost broke my stare when he nodded and turned. "Come along, then."

I followed him down the hall to a gated stairwell. He fetched a set of keys from his pocket and unfastened a shiny padlock. "Has Patricia decided if she will rejoin the Committee?"

"She said she would." We descended the stone staircase, and the air cooled even more. The large, low-ceilinged room smelled of damp stone and age. With its dim lighting, the space seemed more eerie than sacred.

"A mayoral election will be occurring soon. I feel it's important she is in place as the lupine representative when it does." He stopped beside a lit alcove. A decorative wooden container, about the size of a shoebox, sat atop a stone pedestal within it. "She has refused my calls and requests for meetings. Would you pass the information about the election to her?"

It irritated me that he thought of me as an errand girl. "She'll be at the meeting this afternoon. You could tell her yourself. Now . . ." I motioned to the gated alcove.

Aiden gave a cool smile as he unlocked the gate. "Patience doesn't seem to be your strongest virtue, Miss Steward." He pushed aside the collapsible gate, stepped into the alcove, and retrieved the box. Aiden turned toward me and lifted the wooden container's lid. Nestled into a purple velvet interior were three silver daggers. Each dagger's handle was engraved with a swirling design and symbols echoed on the pedestal and box.

All three blades had been stolen from the bowels of the church this past winter. One had given me the scars on my palms and side. Trish had returned the daggers to the cathedral with Aiden's promise it wouldn't happen again. Nate had wanted to hold onto the weapons for safekeeping, but Nate also didn't trust the priest.

"So now we know someone is running around with more silver." I looked up at Aiden as he lowered the lid. "Have you heard anything?"

He replaced the box. "No. I would have told Patricia." Aiden pulled the gate closed, resecured the lock, and started back toward the stairs. "The use of silver weapons within Hopewell has been outlawed by the Committee for several decades."

I studied the elaborate scene carved on the stone pedestal. The carving depicted a man in medieval clothing brandishing a spear. He stood among a flock of sheep, his spear driven down through the skull of an enormous wolf. "Who is this guy again?" I called after the priest.

"Saint Hubertus, the patron saint of hunters." Aiden ascended the stairs.

"Hunters?" The word stirred unease inside me, especially when paired with those awful daggers. I followed him back up into the hallway. "When the daggers went missing, and Mitch attacked me with one, Trish had said we're protected from Hunters and their weapons."

"Yes, she's correct. That is why the daggers are guarded here." He relocked the gate. "Hunting was a cruel method of managing supernatural citizens. It's an archaic practice no longer allowed in Hopewell by Committee law."

Managing citizens by hunting them? "Do you know if Hubert has a fan club around here? Any die-hard groupies?"

He spared me a glance before he started back toward the offices. "Despite what your personal experience suggests, not every malicious act in Hopewell leads back to a religious fanatic."

"Is that a no then?" I growled. The constant effort to extract bits and pieces of information from the priest wore on my patience, and the new information had me on edge.

At the animal-like sound, Aiden stopped. He turned and looked at me. Judgement weighted his stare. "Miss Steward, you are dangerously close to overstepping your boundaries. Patricia sees something in you worth cultivating. I do not. But I hold her opinion in high regard. For that reason alone do I currently extend to you my respect and cooperation."

Every word he spoke pushed my irritation further toward anger. The hair on the nape of my neck rose as he closed the distance between us. Another low rumble, one of warning this time, sounded in my chest.

He halted, but the severity of his tone didn't waver. "However, I expect you to at the very least honor the guidelines the Committee has put into place for everyone's safety. Do not think because Patricia favors you that you are above its laws." The volume of his voice lowered. "Actions have consequences. Control yourself."

I did so . . . with a great amount of effort. My face burning, I bit back my retort and retreated a step. I shouldn't escalate conflict with Aiden. As Committee Chair, he was a direct path to getting disciplined. I was allowed to live in Hopewell as long as what I was—the growling, the teeth, and the claws—was kept hidden and in check. And under no circumstances could I harm a Commoner. Like Isaac had said, the Committee didn't need much of an excuse to have werewolves tethered.

Aiden's tone turned conversational again. "If you'll excuse me Miss Steward, I have an appointment. Again, please send my condolences to Patricia on the loss of her young friend." He re-entered the office suite.

I slunk from the gloomy cavernous hallway and escaped into the bright day. The change in temperature caused condensation to gather on my fingernails. I texted Trish. *All accounted for at St. Anthony's. Aiden sends his condolences. See you this afternoon.*

Tucking away my phone, I started back to the apartment, my gut still simmering. *Control myself?* The beast inside me paced. His warning felt like a smack on the nose with a rolled newspaper. It was condescending, humiliating, and infuriating. I wasn't a mindless beast. Did he believe I wasn't trying?

Most wolves knew how to navigate a conversation without a snarl, but not me. Even now, I struggled to suppress her—our—frustrated growls. If I didn't learn control, I'd get slapped with a tether. And as a wolf community member, my failure would be held up as an example that werewolves were dangerous and shouldn't be allowed in Hopewell.

6

THE APARTMENT WAS empty when I returned from the cathedral. Ben messaged me that he was with Joan to run errands and go to lunch. My reply let him know I was joining Trish for a meeting and dinner. I sighed and tucked away my phone. So much for spending the day together. After a quick lunch, I walked farther downtown to meet Trish.

I waited for her outside Union Street Church, the Romanesque building where the Committee held their meetings. The summer heat cooked the city while I basked like a lizard on the edge of a cement-edged flower bed. The warmth on my skin felt wonderful, and I drifted close to falling asleep.

"Ah, Miss Alex!" A familiar voice greeted me. "Are you joining us at the meeting today?"

"Hey, Reginald." I sat up and smiled at the older man. "Yes. Trish asked me to be here."

Reginald Sharpe was Ben's grandfather, a close friend of Trish's, and served as the wizards' representative on the Committee. He was tall and slender like Ben and wore a light-gray suit and bowler. His short white beard and mustache were neatly kept, and his gray-blue eyes were alert despite the deep lines of age at their edges.

"I'm glad Ms. Drake has decided to rejoin us. We are in dire need of her insight." Reginald had invited Trish to join the organization in the first place, and I suspected he also convinced her to return. He rested his hands on the pommel of his walking cane. "I hear you've met my granddaughter, Joan?"

My eyes widened. "Oh . . . you heard about that?"

"Joan is more forthcoming than Benjamin. She told me the two of you met. I'm pleased Benjamin took the initiative to introduce you."

I picked my words carefully so as not to contradict whatever falsehood Joan had peddled. "It was an exciting evening of intimate conversation."

"The two of them have always been close." His chest inflated. "She's a remarkable young woman."

"She seems really . . . nice."

"Who's nice?" Trish asked.

"We were discussing my granddaughter, Joan. She is here visiting." Reginald tipped his hat to Trish. "I'm delighted to see you again, Ms. Drake." The same pride that'd shone in his eyes moments before remained as he regarded her.

"It's good to see you too, Reggie." She placed her hand on his sleeve, and gave his whiskered cheek a light kiss.

Reginald's smile waned. "Aiden notified the Committee members of what occurred earlier this morning. Please accept my condolences on the loss of your friend."

"Thank you." Trish, concealing any emotion, looked at the church's entrance. "Shall we?"

Reginald held open the door, and I followed Trish inside. My nose was assailed by the scent of a pungent cologne. A man dressed in a suit, darker gray and with a more contemporary cut than Reginald's, paced the tile floor. His voice echoed in the entry hall as he gestured and spoke to himself. He would've seemed like a raving madman if I hadn't noticed the small device lodged in his ear. The man halted, scowled at the floor, and then shouted, "I told you, the numbers are wrong! Run them again!"

Trish fixed the stranger with a cool stare. Reginald murmured, "Shouting seems a bit distasteful here."

The man jabbed at a phone secured to his belt. "Goddammit why can't anyone do their job anymore?" He stormed through one of the stone arches that led into the sanctuary.

I'd been so distracted by the spectacle, I hadn't seen the police officer in full uniform waiting for him. The officer turned, and our eyes met. It was Jakob. He didn't acknowledge me and followed the other man.

"I met that cop yesterday. He's Anne's new partner," I said to Trish. "I wonder why he's being allowed to attend the meeting."

"I do as well," she said.

We walked through the inner doorway closest to us, past rows of pews, to the front of the vast sanctuary. A balcony wrapped around three quarters of the room. Towering stained-glass windows led the eye upward to a vaulted ceiling. We joined about a dozen people who sat at a circular table on a raised platform. The loud-talking man from the hall sat across from us. Both men and women served on the Committee, but the majority of the representatives at the table were older white guys.

Aiden, seated to our right, looked up from documents he was reviewing. Seeing me, he spoke to Trish, "Ms. Drake, your name is on the agenda, but not Miss Steward's." He stared over the top of his glasses. As Committee Chair, Aiden was a strict enforcer of its rules and operations, a trait that either pleased or irritated the hell out of the members, depending on the situation.

"These meetings are open to any supernatural citizen in Hopewell. Has something changed that she now needs a special invitation?" Trish asked. The conversation around the table fell quiet. Reginald shifted in his seat.

Aiden looked back at the papers. "She does not, but she does need an invitation to sit at this table. I'll have to ask her to take a seat in one of the pews."

His apparent pettiness made my pulse quicken. Was this because of one little growl earlier? "Like it makes a difference," I said beneath my breath.

"Did you have a question about Committee procedures, Miss Steward?" Aiden asked without looking up.

Trish placed her hand on my arm and gave a slight nod. *Got it. Don't argue with Aiden before the meeting even begins.* I stood, descended the stairs, and sat in a front row pew next to Jakob. He sat upright and alert with his eyes fixed ahead of him.

"You people run a tight ship around here," Mr. Loud-talker said from his seat at the table. He briskly rubbed his hands together and grinned. "I like it."

Aiden turned his stare on the man. "Mr. Stone, I know you are a new member and still familiarizing yourself with how we operate. This is a kind reminder to turn off devices during meetings."

New member? So he wasn't a guest. Trish and I had uncovered information this past winter that cost a previous Commoner representative, Pastor William Jansen, his Committee seat. This Stone guy must be the replacement.

"Sorry about that, Father." Stone stowed the speaker from his ear in the pocket of his suit jacket.

As the meeting got underway, I slid closer to Jakob, intending to ask how he got his invite. The scent I couldn't place at the gym was stronger. It was also absolutely familiar. I whispered, "I didn't know there were wolves on the police force."

Jakob blushed and spared me a sideward glance.

"Officer DeBoer?" Aiden said.

Jakob stood. "Yes, sir."

"You've been nominated by City Commissioner Joseph Stone and Detective Samuel Grey to serve on this Committee as a representative for the lupine. Do you accept this responsibility?" Aiden asked.

"Yes, sir."

What? Wide-eyed, I looked at Trish. For years she'd asked to have another wolf at the Committee table. She was the sole representative for werewolves living in and around Hopewell. I was startled to find naked shock on her face.

The legs of her chair screeched as she stood. "What is this? Since when do Commoners hand select members to represent the lupine?"

A tense silence fell across the table again. "Ms. Drake," Aiden said, "we could not halt our activities in your absence. The lupine community is fraught with anxiety. It was already strained before you parted ways with us."

"It was." Trish's eye color turned golden. "And the Committee refused to make us a priority at that time."

"When Officer DeBoer returned to Hopewell, he was concerned by this tension and felt it important we be informed. For everyone's safety, including the lupine, we moved forward without your guidance." Aiden motioned to Jakob. "Officer DeBoer has an outstanding service record as a police officer from his previous city."

"Being a cop doesn't prepare him for navigating this Committee," Trish said.

Aiden frowned. "He is willing to provide additional insight into your community's needs."

Trish drove her fingertip down onto the tabletop. "Lupine representatives should be elected by the lupine," she snarled. Her glare swept around the table and settled on Reginald. "Even in my absence, this should have been defended."

Unlike the Commoner representatives, whose seats were refilled by Committee member nominations, Trish had been nominated and voted in by the werewolf community. She'd insisted upon it. Then the vote moved to the Committee.

Why had the Committee cut corners and picked Jakob? And with wolf and wizard tensions at an all-time high, wouldn't one wizard to two wolves on the Committee cause issues?

"Please, Ms. Drake, take your seat," Aiden said. "We are past the point in the process to voice objections."

Reginald touched Trish's elbow, his voice quiet, "Patricia ..."

Trish sat down, her eyes glowing, a portrait of composed fury. Jakob's nomination as a lupine representative was seconded and voted upon. Trish, Reginald, and a few others opposed it, but the motion carried. Jakob sat back down beside me.

"Officer DeBoer?" Aiden motioned to Jakob. "You may join us at the table now."

Jakob blushed again and stood. "Thank you, sir." He climbed the steps and took the seat beside Trish that I'd vacated.

"Now to the business of Isaac Laska's death," Aiden said. "Ms. Drake, on behalf of this Committee, I'd like to extend our condolences on your loss."

Trish's eyes blazed. "Thank you for your words, but they don't alleviate the 'anxiety' with which everyone here is concerned. The most effective action is to expedite an investigation into Isaac's death. Prove to the lupine that this Committee considers them a priority."

"You think the kid was murdered?" Stone asked. "I mean, I'm sorry for your loss, but are you sure he didn't OD? Kids are doing that all the time over there."

I was liking Stone less with every word leaving his mouth. Trish's low growl was audible to me from the pew. Jakob frowned and glanced at her. I struggled to keep my own brewing frustration locked in my chest.

Detective Grey, a middle-age man seated to Stone's left, spoke up. He wore a rumpled gray suit and a look of annoyance. "The body was discovered this morning, so the narcotics test is pending." He referenced a small notepad. "The body had multiple lacerations and severe trauma to the throat. The canine teeth were missing. Currently, the injury to the throat is believed to be the cause of death. We're looking at some sort of attack."

Someone had taken his teeth? I swallowed back a sudden feeling of nausea.

"Was this a gang thing?" Stone asked.

Serenity, a young woman wearing a priest's collar and glasses, answered. "Isaac collaborated with my church. They founded a mentor program to aid young adults in navigating gang politics."

Aiden nodded. "Isaac was a parishioner of mine. To be part of a gang or not isn't always the choice of the young adult. We often discussed his past involvement, but I do not believe he was an active member."

"The wound was caused by silver, Detective Grey," Trish said. "The killer is someone who knew Isaac was a werewolf."

I rubbed at the scars on my palm. All supernatural creatures were expected to keep our gifts hidden, so those who knew Isaac was a wolf would be others like us or those close to him.

Detective Grey frowned and flipped through his notes. "We don't have details on the murder weapon yet, Ms. Drake. Nothing was found at the scene. The medical examiner's best guess is a blade of some sort."

"Seems like we're wasting time on speculation since the investigation hasn't concluded, right?" Stone said.

"Mr. Stone." Trish conjured her polite smile. "Once they've smelled it, a werewolf doesn't forget the scent of flesh seared by silver. Thankfully, Alex was one of the people who discovered Isaac's body."

Trish's words prompted another rustling of pages from Detective Grey. Stone looked around the table. "I'm sorry, who is Alex? Is he here?"

My face warmed and I raised my hand.

"Here it is." Detective Grey looked up. "Alexandria Steward? Her name was given by Officer Reid." Realization lit in his eyes as he connected my first name to my last, which Aiden had mentioned. His gaze settled on me. "Is that you, miss?"

I lowered my hand and hesitated, glancing at Aiden. He nodded and I stood. "Um . . . yes, I'm Alex. Anne—Officer Reid and I found Isaac near the Opal Street bridge while we were running along the river. I smelled the silver burns. They were on Isaac's throat where it had been slashed."

Stone looked at Detective Grey. "I don't remember reading about burns on the throat."

"I don't see mention of burn marks, either," Grey said.

"Officer DeBoer," Stone said, "have Detective Grey take you to the morgue. Check for the burns the ladies are worried about."

"Yes, sir," Jakob said.

Why wouldn't Trish and I go as well? Were we being cut out of the investigation? At least one werewolf, Jakob, would see the evidence of silver used to attack Isaac.

"That okay with you, Sam?" Stone asked.

From Detective Grey's forced smile, he was less than okay with Stone making calls on next steps in his investigation. "We can do that," he said.

Stone held up his hands and grinned. "Done! What's next?"

AFTER THE MEETING concluded, Trish and I found Jakob waiting for us in the entrance hall, his uniform hat in hand.

He gave Trish a friendly, albeit hesitant, smile. "Hi, Trish."

"Hello Jakob." Trish lifted her chin. "You followed through with your planned career in law enforcement. Congratulations."

"Thank you." Jakob turned his smile to me. "I've known Trish ever since she started dating Nate. He was my brother's best friend."

I raised my eyebrows and looked at Trish. Her expression and body language wasn't communicating "friend" to me. She studied him from his polished shoes to his precise haircut. "Why didn't you tell us you were selected for the Committee, Jakob?"

"We haven't spoken in years, and frankly, I thought you would've stopped it," he said. "I wouldn't have stood a chance."

"No, you wouldn't have," she said.

I lowered my gaze. Maybe I should've stepped outside to save Jakob any embarrassment.

"Being an officer gives me an advantage," he said. "I'll be able to make sure the law is upheld equally. I want you to know that's my promise to everyone."

Trish listened, but his words didn't seem to reassure her. "I wish you the best of luck." She turned, speaking to me as she fished cigarettes out from her handbag. "I'll be waiting in the park, Alex." Then she was through the doors and into the sun and heat.

I looked at Jakob. "Anne doesn't know, does she?"

"Know what I am?" When I nodded, he shook his head. "Nobody on the force knows except Detective Grey."

"That must be tricky. Be careful around Anne. She's so perceptive it's been a challenge to keep my secret from her."

"That doesn't surprise me." He chuckled. "She's amazing. I'm going to learn a lot from her." We walked out of the church together, and he put on his hat. "Are you good friends with Trish and Nate, too?"

"Yeah, we've grown close. They introduced me to the other wolves in Hopewell."

"Trish is great. It makes sense the lupine look to her for guidance," Jakob said. "And where Trish is, you'll find Nate. I'd like to work with them, but I don't have their trust. I'll need that to make any real difference."

"You don't have their trust? But you're one of us," I said. Nate had hammered that fact home in my mind. I was a wolf in Hopewell, so I was an assumed member of the city's Pack. Trish was our leader, and we all looked out for each other.

"This uniform complicates my relationship with the Pack. I'm willing to figure it out and make it work." He smiled. "I guess you and I will be seeing more of each other?"

"More than likely," I said. "If Trish has her way, which she usually does, I'll be at most of these meetings."

"And at the gym, right?" he asked. I gave him a puzzled look, and he raised his fists into a classic boxer stance.

I chuckled and shook my head. "Right. I guess so."

Jakob smiled again. "I should go. I don't want to keep Detective Grey waiting. Enjoy the rest of your day." He walked away in the direction of the police station.

Trish sat on a park bench across from the church. Her eyes were hidden behind dark cat-eyed sunglasses, but the way she worked through her cigarette suggested she was still agitated.

"Jakob seems like a decent guy." I sat beside her. "Even if we didn't elect him, it's good we have another voice on the Committee, right?"

"They picked him because they can manipulate him." She took another drag and exhaled a stream of smoke. "He's inexperienced with Hopewell Committee politics. They'll confuse and mislead him, and that will endanger us."

"Why is Jakob's brother not friends with Nate anymore?"

"He's dead." Trish ground out the spent cigarette on the bench seat. "He killed himself several months after being tethered for carjacking. The feedback from the tether was too much for him."

"I'm sorry." Another werewolf dead because of a tether.

"It was a long time ago." She pushed past my apology. "Nate told me he broke up a fight between you and another wolf."

I'd wondered when word would reach her about my scuffle in their club's parking lot. "He was giving Em and me a hard time because she's a wizard. I lost my temper."

Trish nodded. "Take care that it doesn't appear you're favoring a wizard's safety over your Pack's."

"Em's my best friend." I frowned. "She means everything to me. I'm not letting some guy, wolf or not, bully her around."

"I know. I'm not asking you to abandon Emma," Trish said. "Instead, consider walking away. Eliminate the chance it escalates. We don't need the Committee watching Hell's Bells, waiting to punish us for unruly behavior or any other fabricated excuse."

My face flushed. I dropped my gaze and clenched my jaw.

"Everyone is on edge. We're arguing among ourselves. Now with Isaac—" Trish shook her head. "A lot of people loved Isaac. Those people will be processing their anger and grief. Both the violent nature of his death and the bungled medical examiner's report worry me."

"Do you think we should investigate his death ourselves?" I asked.

"Not quite yet, but I don't think that should stop us from aiding Detective Grey's investigation. I'm furious that Jakob was selected without our knowledge, but the Committee is correct in saying the situation among the lupine has grown dangerous," she said. "If the wolves aren't given the full story about Isaac, rumors will spread. They'll feel unsafe. Fear and anger never mix well. Hopefully the investigation will quickly identify Isaac's killer and diffuse both."

"What will the Committee do when Isaac's killer is found? Is the suspect turned over to the police?" The covert nature of the local ruling body complicated how our laws were reinforced. I was still trying to puzzle it out.

"That depends," Trish said. "The trial itself will be held in front of the Committee, with the members being judge and jury. If the suspect is a Commoner and found guilty, he will be turned over to their prison system for sentencing. If the killer is someone like us, he will either be tethered or executed."

The punishment seemed more severe for supernatural citizens. It didn't seem fair. "Nate told me Reginald creates tethers, but who is responsible for carrying out executions?"

"Reginald."

"Really?" Shaking my head, I frowned. "It's hard for me to imagine he'd do that." Reginald always came off as a friendly, at times clueless, old guy. But then again, he did tether his own grandson. Would he have executed Ben if ordered to do it?

"Rules and tradition are the foundation of his moral code," Trish said.

But rules should be flexible and change . . . like the banning of silver weapons in Hopewell. I thought of the grotesque carving in St. Anthony's of the spear-wielding man and the large wolf. An eerie prickle traveled down my spine. "Trish, what do you know about Hunters?"

"They are Commoners who believe we should not exist." She smirked. "Unlike most other Commoners with that belief, Hunters track, trap, and kill beings like us."

My voice was hoarse. "Kill us? For existing?"

She nodded. "But Hunting in Hopewell has been outlawed by the Committee."

"Aiden said the same thing."

"I've never met a Hunter here, or anywhere for that matter."

"I can't imagine their success rate was too high," I said, seeking comfort by reasoning aloud. "How could a Commoner overpower someone like us? They're all so frail, like . . ." I sought the word, and the beast inside me provided it. ". . . sheep."

Trish's reply was quick and sharp. "Never underestimate Commoners, Alex."

My face grew hot, and I looked away.

"A Hunter is stronger than the average Commoner," she said. "Faster. Tougher. They believe they're warriors, blessed with special abilities, in a crusade to eradicate us."

"Wonderful. How do we know who's a Hunter and who isn't?" I tried to lighten the mood. "Do they wear sashes like the Scouts?"

Trish didn't smile. "They're also able to agitate our inner wolves and wield that against us. It's the trait that often gives them away."

Holy. Hell.

I swallowed. "How would we handle a Hunter if we have zero experience with them?"

"In the slim chance it was a Hunter who killed Isaac, we would cross that bridge when we came to it." She dug in her purse in pursuit of more nicotine. "I believe it is a misguided Commoner who got lucky, possibly a member of the Noble Sons."

Not again. "I thought that group no longer exists."

"The Committee ordered it to be dissolved," Trish said. "But that wouldn't stop the former members from continuing to believe people like us don't belong here."

I frowned. "I'd like to help with Isaac, but the idea that some-one is targeting and killing wolves is terrifying. I'm not at my best when I'm scared. My self-control isn't at 100 percent yet."

She gave up on the cigarettes, put her purse aside, and leaned back. "None of us are 100 percent in control at all times. Did you notice my underwhelming performance not even twenty minutes ago? All those small encounters . . . constantly being prodded, provoked, told who we should be and how we should act." She shook her head. "It's impossible not to make mistakes."

"Trish, my mistakes could cost someone a limb." I was thankful for my sunglasses so she wouldn't see me get upset. "I'm not sure what would've happened if Nate hadn't pulled me off that guy in the parking lot."

Trish nodded. "I understand your concern. So does Nate."

"Wrestling with her is exhausting. When I restrain her, she turns on me instead and starts to rip me up inside. It happened at the Mind Center, and again when Nate helped to bring me back to myself."

Trish's hand settled on my shoulder. "It's different for each of us, but we all struggle making peace with the creatures inside us. Your Pack is here to help, whatever that may look like for you."

"Maybe I should sit the investigation out until I'm more expe-rienced with controlling my wolf," I said.

Trish pushed her sunglasses up onto her head and studied me with her warm brown eyes. "Alex, do you believe lack of experience kept Joe Stone from running for city commissioner and now for mayor of Hopewell?"

I shrugged. "Probably not."

"Of course not. Mediocre men like him advance through life with little to no self-doubt. You're a smart, strong-willed woman. Stop limiting yourself."

I was being prudent, but she was pushing me to grow. "You're suggesting I should have the confidence of a mediocre man?"

She laughed. "Yes. I suppose so."

"I don't feel it, but I'll try," I said. "How did your talk with Nate go after I left?"

"We decided Hell's Bells will host a memorial show for Isaac," Trish said. "There will be a mixed guest list because his friendships reached beyond the wolves. I've asked Ben to provide the music."

"Oh." Ben hadn't mentioned anything, but I hadn't seen him since before my run with Anne. It felt like ages ago. "Will the wolves be okay with a wizard providing the entertainment?"

"I believe so. Music has the power to unite people. There's a lot of excitement around Ben being there." Her expression turned smug. "And Hell's Bells will host his first Hopewell show since his return from the tour."

"But will it be safe for him?" If there were people at Hell's Bells who had a problem with Emma, who could befriend anyone, how would they react to Ben? I'd brought him along a few times this past winter, but tensions seemed less volatile then.

"Nate will watch over him," Trish said.

"Great." I snorted. "Nate doesn't like him. I might as well feed Ben to the first wolf we see."

"It was Nate's suggestion to have someone at Ben's side. Then he volunteered."

My eyebrows rose. "Really?" Nate disliked most wizards, believing them to be arrogant and selfish. Emma was an exception because she'd come to his rescue, and "she smells nice." Was he warming up to having Ben around?

Trish winked. "But I wasn't the one to tell you."

"Ben and I have to survive an event Emma invited us to first," I said. "Her mother is hosting a campaign fundraiser for Stone. Now that I've met him, I'm looking forward to it even less."

Trish looked off across the park. "It makes me uneasy to think of him as mayor. Perhaps it's a good thing you're attending the fundraiser. You can hear what vision of the city he's selling his donors. You'll gain more insight into what type of person he is. That's valuable since we'll be working with him on the Committee."

"I can't say I'm looking forward to that," I said.

"Let's not give him any more of our time today." Trish lowered her sunglasses and stood. "I believe I promised you dinner."

As we walked to the retail district for a bite to eat, my anxiety grew about the fundraising event. Susan Arztin didn't have a track record of supporting diversity in Hopewell, especially concerning supernatural beings. Despite her husband and daughter being wizards, she often backed political policies that would further restrict our lives.

I didn't have high hopes for Stone's vision for the city, and even less confidence we wolves would have a place in it. My new home and supportive family, where I could strive to be more than the animal inside me, would be gone.

7

TRISH OFFERED TO drop me off at the apartment after dinner, but I decided to walk. I'd eaten too much, so stretching my legs helped settle my food. The warm evening thrummed with life. A blend of aromas and patrons spilled out of the restaurants onto the sidewalks as people enjoyed food and drinks together.

I lingered to watch a busker before I dropped a few bills into her guitar case. The city's sports arena flashed the names of national music acts, and queues of excited people waited outside its multiple entryways.

When I arrived at the apartment, Ben was seated outside on the small landing. He wore a large set of headphones hooked into the beat-up laptop balanced on his thighs. My movement on the stairs drew his attention from his project. He smiled, closed the computer, and pulled the headphones off to rest on the back of his neck. I stopped beside him and glanced at the door. "How'd the home repair go?"

His hand brushed up my calf before it came to rest behind my knee. "The door closes now on the first try."

"This could've been solved with a message to the landlord. It's a benefit of renting," I said. "I can call next time."

"Nah. I'd rather not have random contractors showing up. Random family is enough excitement for me."

I smiled. "How was your visit with your sister?"

"It was good to catch up," he said. "She'll be in town for a while. Your meeting?"

"Dinner with Trish was great, but I could have passed on the meeting." I combed my fingers through the top of his hair. "Sorry today didn't work out like we planned."

He shrugged. "Shit happens." He rubbed the back of my leg. "I'm sorry to hear about the guy you and Anne found. Are you doing okay?"

The image of Isaac's body floating in the water came to mind, and I hugged my arms to myself. "I feel terrible for his family and friends. Finding him like that . . . it spooked me. I guess he was a member at St. Anthony's. Laska was his last name. Sound familiar at all?"

Ben shook his head. "I haven't been there for a service since I was a kid."

"If you know about Isaac, you must have talked to Trish?"

"She called me about my upcoming show at Hell's Bells," he said. "After you'd been to the club this morning, she wanted to switch up the show to be a benefit concert."

"I thought they should know as soon as possible about Isaac since everything feels so charged right now among the wolves." I offered my hand. "Should we go out for ice cream and people watching? I need a distraction from the awful morning."

He stood. "I thought we could go for a ride tonight."

I immediately liked his idea more. "Sure! Where do you want to go?"

"Nowhere in particular." Ben didn't own a car, but he'd been gifted his dad's '71 Suzuki motorcycle. He used the motorcycle to get around during every season except winter.

Ben stepped inside to exchange the laptop and headphones for two helmets. He handed them to me and locked up the apartment. The black one was well-loved, scuffed up, and peppered with faded stickers. The other helmet was a spotless powder blue. My favorite color. Happiness tingled through me.

I tried not to appear *too* excited as I bounded down the stairs after him. I put in earplugs, pulled my ponytail's band lower, and wrestled with the helmet. The act took extra time because of all my hair. I tilted my chin up, and Ben checked that the strap was fastened correctly. He smiled, gave the top of my helmet a rap, and motioned me over to the bike.

Ben turned a key, flipped a lever on the side, flipped another lever lower on the bike, checked a light at the top, and then got onto the bike. With one forceful, downward step on a foot pedal, the motor roared to life. The crackling pops and loud idle gave me goosebumps.

I'd never ridden a motorcycle before, so I couldn't help my stupid grin when I hopped on behind him. I clung tight around his waist as he eased the motorcycle back out of its parking space. He pressed a handlebar lever, shifted another pedal, and we coasted toward the street. Ben paused the bike at the edge of the sidewalk. I felt him chuckle and tap at my fingers laced together in front of his stomach. I loosened my hold on him, and we were on our way.

The first thing I noticed was the immediate assault on my sense of smell. Scents were hurled at me in rapid succession. My mind buzzed as it tried to isolate and identify each. The breeze brushed across my skin, a pleasant feeling after the day's stagnant heat.

Ben drove up the hill, away from the river and the city's center. We cut through the neighborhoods of the historic district. The majority of the houses were old lumber baron mansions either divided into apartments for rent or owned as a residence by wealthier individuals. People were outside savoring the day as it cooled. They sat on wide front porches or strolled along the sidewalks.

The large houses became interspersed with modern corporate buildings, and then we passed into a medical campus. There were two hospitals in the city. This one sat perched at the top of the hill. A highway curved through its north side, and the west edge overlooked downtown.

We left the motorcycle in a parking garage and walked across a strip of manicured grass to a retaining wall that kept the hillside intact. The sounds of the city floated up to us as we surveyed the carpet of twinkling and flashing lights. In the waning dusk, I could still see the river and even the western neighborhoods.

"It's beautiful up here." I glanced at Ben. "Have you known about this place for long?"

He stood beside me on the wall, his thumbs hooked in his back pockets. "For a while now." His shoulders lifted and fell. "I don't remember who told me about it or when. I may have found it while wandering around."

I sat on the wide lip of the wall and dangled my legs over its edge. The cement was still warm. Ben sat down beside me. He slid closer, and I smiled and leaned into him. One of his long legs hung over the edge while his other braced up behind me.

"Alex, I've been thinking something over and wanted to run it past you," he said.

"Oh?" After my conversation with Trish, I hoped it was something simple like replacing the table or changing the toothpaste.

"I've been digging through the Committee's past minutes. They're available to any supernatural citizen in Hopewell."

"They are?"

"Yeah. We can request them from the Committee Chair," he said. "There've been wizards who've had their tethering sentences reduced. I didn't know that was possible. I thought I would . . ." He paused, and his face screwed up as if the next words were physically uncomfortable to say. ". . . talk to Reginald about it."

Ben's relationship with his grandfather was complicated.

"He could help shave off some time?" I asked.

"I'm not sure if the Committee will go for that, but Joan thinks they'd agree to be even more flexible about my travel. I only have two years left, and I've kept my head down for fifteen." The backs of his fingers brushed my bare arm. "I could pick up some more gigs, farther from here than before. What do you think?"

"It's worth a try, right?" I asked. Since his tethering, Ben had never been allowed to leave the city. The tour he'd returned from, restricted to the Midwest, was a first for him and only possible through special permission from the Committee. Now that he had a taste of travel, I wondered if wanderlust was setting in. "You and Joan would know more about how that works than I do."

He tilted his head and smiled. "I guess what I'm asking is, would you want to come along? The only thing I missed about this place was you." He looked out at the city lights again. "We could get a change of scenery. Maybe we won't come back for a while."

I laughed. "Benjamin Sharpe, are you asking me to run away with you?"

His eyebrows scrunched together, and he looked back at me. He wasn't laughing.

I blinked. "Oh. You're being serious."

Before landing in Hopewell, I'd spent almost five years fleeing across the country, wondering if the next stop would be somewhere safe to rest. Traveling wasn't the first item on my *stuff-to-do-in-my-free-time* list. But I'd be with Ben.

"Why would I joke about wanting to spend time with you?"

Shit. A stab of panic. "I'm sorry." My next words were rushed. "I mean, I've traveled a lot, and now Trish indirectly asked me to help with the investigation into Isaac's death."

He dropped his gaze, rolling the frayed hem of my shorts between his fingertips. "*Asked* you or *told* you?"

I put my hand over his. "Trish, Nate, and the rest of the wolves are part of my family here. You're one of my favorite people, but it's also important to me that I help them." Even if I wasn't sure I'd have enough control of my inner wolf to be good at it. "I *want* to help them."

"Yeah, I get it. It was kind of a stupid idea anyway."

"No, it wasn't." I squeezed his hand. "Hopefully we'll have some closure with Isaac before you're ready to leave again. Do you know when that'll be?"

Ben shook his head. "I didn't have a set date. I haven't even asked Reginald for a meeting." He looked up at me. "Maybe give it some thought? I don't need an answer right now."

I nodded. "I will. Even if I can't go, you should."

He searched over my features.

"I'd of course miss you, but you had such a great time on the tour," I said. "I like seeing you happy."

Ben gave a small smile. "It was exhausting but incredible."

"Trish sounds pretty thrilled about your gig," I said. "She's pleased that your first show back home is at Hell's Bells."

"She'd booked me months ago before I left." Chuckling, he shook his head again. "It pissed off the Sound Refuge, so I hope they'll still lend me the audio equipment." He turned his hand to interlace his fingers with mine. "We spent yesterday talking about what I'd been doing. Tell me more about what you've been up to. You mentioned Trish and Nate were working with you to finesse your shifting?"

I snorted. "I'd love to be able to use the word 'finesse.'"

"Why do you say that?"

"I feel like I'm stuck at the *Not Killing Everyone* stage when my opponent gets the better of me. I mean, I've made progress while you were gone, but that guy I fought at Hell's Bells—" I shook my head. "I'm not sure I could've stopped her alone. Nate saved the guy by coaching me back into control."

Ben's hold on my hand briefly tightened, and the edges of his mouth twitched downward. "You really believe she would've killed him?"

Hearing it said aloud made my stomach convulse. I pulled my hand away. "I don't want to leave that up to chance." I drew my knees up and folded my arms around them.

"I don't think she would've." He leaned back, his hands braced behind him. "Shred? Maim? Dismember? Yeah, but not kill."

"There's no way for you to know that," I said. "You're saying it to make me feel better."

"The more I know you, the more strongly I feel it." He gave my back a nudge with his knee and smiled. "You wouldn't let anger push you that far."

Wouldn't I? "What about us? You're not a little freaked out sharing a place with a werewolf who hasn't figured herself out? What if you and I get into a really intense argument and she hurts you? Or we're fooling around and she takes over again?"

"Whoa, Alex—"

I gestured at him. "Ravaging you would take on a completely new meaning!"

"Alex—"

"I don't want you to doubt being with me because you're scared." I hid my face in my hands. "I never want you to look at me like I'm some monster."

We were both silent. The sounds of the city buzzed below our feet. Ben's hand settled on my shoulder. "Hey."

My voice was muffled behind my hands. "What."

"Can you please look at me?"

I briskly wiped my eyes and faced him.

Ben was looking at me in that way that made my heart hum. "I'm sorry you're frustrated about your shifting. But I want you to know I feel really good when I'm around you. Things feel right, you know?" He smiled. "I'm not afraid of you, Alex."

Warmth bloomed throughout my chest. I wiped away a stray tear, leaned toward Ben, and kissed him. "I feel good around you, too."

Investing in a long-term romantic relationship was still new to us. Ben had buried himself in music and books for years to keep his nose clean. Until moving to Hopewell, my life on the go and need to keep a low profile had prevented it. If I went with him, would everything get messed up? The possibility scared me. What if I didn't get control of my inner wolf, and Joan convinced him he'd gotten too cozy with a dangerous beast? But Ben hadn't even approached Reginald yet. I was fretting over a choice I might not have to make. There were more pressing matters to focus my energy on, like uncovering who killed Isaac. Most urgent of all was how in the world I would make it through Susan Arztin's party.

8

"THAT MAKES YOUR ass look amazing," Emma said. She admired my reflection in the changing room mirror.

"Think so?" I looked back over my shoulder and studied how the skirt she'd picked out hugged my figure. It did look good. The snug fit accentuated my curves and ended in a flirty hemline above my knees.

"I want to see." Anne's head peeked through the curtains. She raised her eyebrows. "Wow, yeah, that'll be on the floor as soon as you get him back home."

"No need to waste time taking it off." I turned to get another angle in the mirror.

Emma cued us. "Why's that?"

All three of us quoted my dear grandmother in unison. "Because a lady has needs."

"Hell yes," Anne said.

My friends and I laughed. Then I checked the price tag. I stopped laughing. "Holy shit, Em. Did you even bother looking at the price?"

"What?" She glanced at the tag. "Don't worry about it. It's a gift."

I wondered what that would be like, to never have to worry about money. Shaking my head, I unzipped the skirt to change. "No. This is like a week's worth of food." I wouldn't have even been in the boutique without Emma. After one look at my second-hand clothes, the clerks would have profiled me as a shoplifter.

Emma placed her small hand on my wrist. "Please, Alex! It looks so nice. I don't want you worrying about my mother or her judgey friends."

Yeah, Emma was considering my comfort for the upcoming fundraiser. However, one of the ways Emma reconciled accepting money from her parents, even though the three disagreed on most issues, was to spend it on things that would irritate them. In this case, that would be me.

I hesitated and looked at Anne in the mirror. She gave me a smile and helpless shrug before she disappeared from view. The curtain swung back into place.

I lowered my voice. "Em, I can't get gifts like this for you. You know that. It doesn't feel fair that you're buying me something so expensive."

"Our friendship is not transactional. I wouldn't expect a gift like this from you in return." She paused and then added, "And I wouldn't want you picking out clothes for me anyway."

I chuckled.

She sensed my defenses weakening and went in for the kill. "This is my love language. Let me love you!" Emma pleaded.

A roll of my eyes signaled my surrender, and she squealed with delight. Emma ducked out of the changing room. Anne's laughter from the store made me smile.

I turned again and ran a critical gaze over the woman in the changing room mirror. Compared to the *Ideal Woman* image peddled to me throughout my life, her stomach could be flatter, and she'd look more symmetrical with a larger bust to balance out the swell of her hips. Maybe heels would help with her height.

I lifted my chin and tilted my head. But her neck was long and graceful. Her body was shaped by beautiful dips and curves. Her legs were strong, finely muscled, and *damn* I bet they'd look good wrapped around Ben. The mental image caused the creature inside me to stir, and a tingling warmth filled my limbs. My face flushed, and I quickly changed back into my clothes.

Emma bounded up to me as soon as I left the changing room. Her excited smile wavered. "Is something wrong? You're all red."

"Em, this is okay to wear to a fundraiser, right? It's not too short?" I thought the skirt looked good, but I wasn't as fashion literate as Emma. Plus, the social circles she was born into, located up in the stratosphere compared to my own, were completely alien to me.

"It's perfectly appropriate." She smiled. "If someone doesn't know women's knees connect to thighs, I think the problem is with them, not your clothing."

"Okay. Now that we've found something acceptable for me to wear, can we grab some lunch?"

"Yes, please," Anne said. She and I weren't as fond of shopping as Emma. Neither of us could afford to be. But, we joined Emma anyway because the three of us enjoyed being together.

"Okay, okay! Let me pay for this and we'll be on our way." Emma snatched the skirt from my hands and beelined to the store's register.

Anne grinned at me. "Did you even make an attempt?"

"A half-hearted one," I said. "She wasn't playing around. It was a pretty swift takedown."

Anne shook her head, chuckling. "I don't even try anymore."

Outside, I took a deep inhale of fresh air, savoring the escape from the heavily perfumed retail space. The designer scent clung to us, but it wasn't as overpowering as in the shop.

Emma linked her arms with ours. "Anne, Alex said she met your new partner. Are you going to invite him out some evening?"

"I'm not ready for him to know me that well. Plus, I don't feel like dancing around him if I meet any interesting women." Anne gave her a suspicious look. "You aren't jonesing for a man in uniform, are you? I have to work with him, and this isn't one of Alex's cheesy romance films."

Emma laughed, and I went on the defense. "Rom-coms are not romance films!" I said. "They're comedies that happen to have a relationship as a key plot point."

"You do know rom-com is short for *romantic* comedy, don't you?" Anne asked.

"Of course I do!" I said. "But I'm not in charge of naming film genres, am I?"

"Just admit you're a romantic at heart," Emma said. "There's nothing wrong with that."

I answered with a derisive snort, which caused both of them to laugh again. I'd thought romance was for other people, not a werewolf who was required to hide her insides. But I befriended Trish and Nate and witnessed what a relationship could look like for me. Then I met Ben and everything got turned further on its head.

After lunch, Anne left for her shift and Emma gave me a ride back to Ben's apartment. We passed by Saint Anthony's on the way. My thoughts turned to the daggers locked away in their alcove below ground.

"Hey Em, do you know anything about Hunters?" I asked, watching the front doors of the cathedral as we passed.

"That's a random question." She glanced over at me. "It's the Midwest. You can't step outside without bumping into someone who kills wild animals for food or sport."

"No, I mean, people who hunt us." Saying it caused goosebumps to rise along my arms.

"Oh." Emma frowned. "Why are you asking about Hunters?"

"Trish had me stop by St. Anthony's and check on the silver daggers they keep there."

"Why? Are they missing again?"

"No, they're still in their box," I said. "But apparently weapons like those were used by Hunters."

"I don't know too much about Hunters," she said. "When the lupine joined the Committee, my parents petitioned to have a Hunter installed. I guess they thought since werewolves had a voice in city politics, the werewolves would also begin to eat everyone? The petition failed."

"Weren't your parents worried the Hunter would come after you and your dad?" I asked. Emma and her father were gifted magic-users, but her mother was a Commoner. Susan Arztin was okay with her husband wielding healing magic as a surgeon. But when her daughter studied spellcasting, she was giving in to the sins of witchcraft.

"No, Hunters don't go after wizards unless they practice dark magic," she said. "My father assured me of that. I was terrified of Hunters when I was little. They were the bogeyman."

"*Dark* magic?" Wizards specialized in specific types of magic, like healing or protection, but I was still learning exactly what those were.

"Yes. It's a dated term for riskier magic . . . like necromancy."

"Which is?"

The edges of Emma's mouth turned down. "Magic that involves the manipulation of deconstruction, decay, or death. Think of it as the opposite of what Reginald Sharpe practices."

I shook my head. So, wizards harnessed energy and used it to manipulate matter, but heaven forbid my nails grew too long? It was oversimplified, but the differences in what was expected from the wizards and wolves were starting to add up.

And how was I supposed to keep track of this all? Was there a manual? "So, these Hunters go after werewolves, death wizards, and who else?"

"Supposedly, everyone else. I don't remember anyone mentioning a Hunter living here though, not even during my father's childhood." Emma was more tuned into the types of supernatural beings trying to covertly coexist with Commoners.

I, on the other hand, hadn't made the effort to even seek out another werewolf. Having Emma as my token supernatural buddy had been enough for me. But now I realized how much I'd needed the community Trish, Nate, and the other wolves gave me. "Every-one else? Like sprites, gremlins, vampires, and such?"

"Yes." She smiled. "Have you finally met someone who isn't a wizard or a wolf?"

"No. Nate mentioned them to me before." I drummed my fingers on my knee, frowning. "If we're hiding who we are, I don't see how a Hunter can find us."

"I don't know. That's part of what made them so scary when I was a kid."

Emma parked her car near the stairs at Ben's apartment. She reached into the back seat for a garment bag. She'd found a blazer in her collection of men's jackets to lend Ben for the party. Emma kept the clothing on hand to give her dates a fighting chance when she subjected them to being her plus one at her parents' events.

I hadn't told Emma the main reason I agreed to attend the fundraiser with her. I know she wouldn't expect me to, but it'd been bothering me since speaking with Trish. Endorsing Stone was important to her parents, but I wasn't sure how Emma felt. My gut told me she wouldn't care why as long as I was there. Emma handed me the bag. "Go grab your shirt and shoes. We have an appointment at the salon."

I took the bag from her. "I have a confession to make."

Emma glanced at the clock on the car's console. "Will it be a long confession?"

"I agreed to go to this event because I was asked to talk to Stone," I said. "He landed a seat on the Committee, and Trish suspects he'll be a headache for the wolves. She wants to know what promises he's running on for mayor."

A small crease appeared on Emma's forehead. "Nothing will get broken, will it? My mother has been planning this for months. I'll never be allowed to bring you to another party. Ever."

Dammit. Now I wanted to smash an expensive vase so I'd never have to go to a Susan Arztin event ever again. But that behavior, especially in a wizard's home, would do nothing but reinforce the idea that the wolves were people to be feared. Hell, Susan would amplify it and make sure everyone knew.

Emma frowned. I knew why she was asking. She'd witnessed me lose my shit at Hell's Bells. It frustrated me that her confidence in me had been affected. "I don't usually walk into a place with plans of wrecking it," I said.

She nodded. "I know. I'm sorry, Alex. Do what you need to do tonight." She motioned me out of the car. "Now go drop off the jacket and get your stuff so we're not late."

GETTING READY WITH Emma meant Ben and I would arrive separately. She dragged me through the gauntlet of primping and preening most women endure before presenting themselves to strangers. Because of her family's wealth, Emma's life had been spent in what seemed like a parallel dimension. Every step of the arduous process of preparation was amplified. I envied how Ben would probably wait until the last minute and then be ready in about fifteen.

"I feel like this is a waste, Em." A waste of time. A waste of money. At least this was another bill covered by the Charles and Susan Arztin fund.

"Hold still, please," requested the salon employee seated in front of me.

"When is the last time you've done something like this for yourself?" Emma watched the manicurist apply another coat of polish.

"For me, or for you?" The end of the marathon was in sight, but I'd already sat still for hours. My stomach growled and my head throbbed from the odors of hair and nail products. I was hungry and cranky.

"Alex, you know what I mean." She looked at me. "The last time you've spent time, effort, or money on something you feel is silly and a tad decadent but is solely for you."

"Is this solely for me?" It seemed to be for Susan's benefit, which didn't make me happy.

"Miss, please." The employee paused again.

I sighed and looked in the mirror behind the woman working on the gnawed disaster that was my nails. Hours previous a stylist conjured something out of my mess of curls that I didn't think was possible. She was probably a wizard.

Then her coworker had painted on my makeup. The eyeliner was lighter than I preferred, but she'd preserved my *I-don't-give-a-damn* look and elevated it. Now it might be acceptable among the type of reserved guest at a Susan Arztin party. All in all, the person in the mirror was me, but me if many more dollar signs were a norm in my bank account.

My reflection frowned. "It's not too much?"

Emma caught me studying myself and smiled. "You look lovely. We're almost done. Relax and think of the food."

"How do you think I've lasted this long?"

I WAS CONFIDENT Susan Arztin considered me her nemesis. She'd placed the blame for her daughter's resistance to Susan's life coaching squarely on my shoulders. True, I disagreed with the woman's approach to most things. However, Emma's independent nature had nothing to do with me. But Susan seemed incapable of believing her only child to be at fault for anything, let alone disagreeing with her mother.

Emma preferred not to witness Susan's last-minute, frantic verbal flogging of the staff, so we arrived twenty minutes into the event's start. We drove up a paved drive past immaculate landscaping to a large, decorative entrance of a colonial-style house. The size of the home verged on obscene. Most would describe it as an estate. We left the car with the valet at the front door, and I followed Emma through the entryway.

Scents of wood polish and old tapestries filled the air. The home's interior was as grandiose as the exterior. A wide, ornate set of stairs led upward to split at its summit toward the two wings of the home. Stately chandeliers were suspended from the high ceilings.

Stepping out onto the back veranda felt like passing through a portal into another world. The floral aroma of the magnificent garden wrapped around me first, followed shortly by fine food and the party guests' perfumes and colognes. The back facade of the home dripped with climbing roses of all colors.

A string quartet played near the base of a large, stone fountain serving as the garden's focal point. Set deeper onto the lawn was a banquet of food. Staff in matching uniforms bustled around, unnoticed by the party's guests. A young woman in a white shirt and black pants appeared beside Emma and me to present a tray filled with long-stemmed glasses.

Emma took two glasses and handed me one. She'd noticed my apprehension. "It seems overwhelming, but these events are very formulaic."

With a sweep of her hand, she said, "Everyone will arrive and spend time telling each other how amazing they are while simultaneously gossiping about the other guests." Emma flipped a curled strand of hair back over her shoulder and adopted a nasal tone. "Why thank you, darling. Yes, I've lost over twenty pounds! Can you believe it? My trainer and I returned from Greece last weekend. It must be that gorgeous Mediterranean air."

Her antics caused me to laugh and eased the tension between my shoulders. I lilted my voice to a sing-song tone. "But what will your husband, Stewart the Third, think?"

Emma leaned toward me and lowered her voice. "What Stewart doesn't know doesn't hurt him. Plus, ever since his affair with that intern, he's been positively dreadful in bed. Which reminds me, did you hear about Evelynn's husband?"

"Dante?" My fingers fluttered near my lips. "No! Do tell."

"He lost a bundle in that risky trade. They'll have to sell their summer home in Brazil!"

I managed a mock gasp before we laughed again.

"See? You'll do fine," Emma said. "But let's focus on your target. Joe will say a few words over there." She pointed to a low stage with a mic stand. "And then he'll move around the party promising favors in exchange for campaign money." She smiled. "With your sensitive hearing, you could pick up details without even having to talk to anyone."

"What will you be doing?"

Emma cocked her head, flashing a dazzling smile. "Playing the game."

I felt more confident knowing the layout of the evening. My phone chimed from the small purse Emma had lent me. The shirt I wore didn't allow me to tuck my phone into it without ruining the illusion I knew what the hell passed as fashionable. This meant I was stuck carrying around a stupid handbag that did nothing for me but hold my phone and make me worry I'd lose them both.

"Ben?" Emma asked as I checked my phone.

"Yeah," I said. "He'd like me to meet him out front."

Emma smiled. "I'm going to start mingling."

"Good luck." I set my untouched drink on a passing tray and retraced our steps back to the front entrance. Ben leaned against one of the two-story pillars, watching the dance of the valet staff. "Hey there."

At the sound of my voice, he turned toward me. He started to sign a greeting but stopped. A touch of color appeared high in his cheeks.

I smiled, pleased by his reaction, and treated him to a twirl as Emma had instructed. "What do you think? Does *Living-Beyond-Her-Means Alex* look good, or what?"

He walked over to me, open admiration and affection in his eyes. His hands settled lightly at my hips, and he drew me closer to whisper by my ear. "You look amazing, Alex."

Both the compliment and his breath tickling my ear caused my face to warm. "Thanks. Don't expect this often, though. There are no pockets on this outfit."

He smiled and removed his hands to gesture at the pocket of his blazer.

"No thanks. I don't have anywhere to put this thing." I held up the purse. "You look really good, too." Ben had shaved, found a fitted pair of black denim that wasn't threadbare, and chose shoes without holes.

I smiled at the album artwork, a black and white photo of a burning monk, on the shirt he wore beneath the designer blazer. Emma and Ben were both wizards and had grown up in wealthy families. Where Emma accepted and skillfully navigated that world, Ben refused to participate and verged on resenting it.

"Thank you for doing this with me," I said. "I'm thinking we hit the food first. Em had people poking and prodding me all afternoon without feeding me."

Ben chuckled and followed me through the large home to the back garden. I eyed the long table of food and my stomach growled. It took some juggling and an extra trip because of the handbag I was saddled with, but I was able to get a plate of food and settle at a bistro table. I leaned toward Ben and lowered my voice. "Did you notice how tiny everything is? The food portions, the plates, and what are these supposed to be?" I held up a miniature bamboo fork.

He smiled and withdrew a small notepad. Not everyone knew sign language, so he used it to bridge the communication gap. I'd attempted to learn the language between running rides for my gig job, but it was slow going, so our communication in public was hindered. He scribbled on the page. *Size being conserved for campaign donations instead?*

"Probably. At least they have good beer." I watched the people drift around the area as we ate and began to recognize a few faces. "There are Committee members here," I said. "Trish wasn't invited, so I know the whole Committee won't be here. I wonder if Stone knows these guys through some other organizations."

I scanned over the guests for Stone but located him by the volume of his voice. He flashed a bleached white smile, which appeared even more unnatural due to his new tan, at a semi-circle of people. The whole group erupted with laughter as Stone slapped the man next to him on the back.

I looked at Ben. "I'm going to see what I can pick up on this guy. Do you want to come along?" Ben raised an eyebrow as if to say, "Are you serious?" I grinned and stood. "Okay, I'll be back in a bit."

I left the table, beer in hand, to walk down onto the lawn. It took some extra concentration since the heels of my shoes insisted on sinking into the turf. I drifted around the garden's edge and feigned interest in the landscaping while I switched between nearby conversations. Like Emma predicted, most of the guests' chatter was self-flattery. I began to doubt I'd find anything useful to pass on to Trish.

A strong whiff of Joe Stone's cologne filled my nose. "Alexis!" he shouted from a new group of party guests. "Excuse me, folks. I'd like to say hello to this young lady I know."

I stopped and waited while he walked over. When he attempted to hug me in greeting, I backed out of his reach. I barely contained my instant scowl. "It's Alex."

"Relax, kid. I'm not going to bite. Alex is what I said." He looked me over and flashed that smile again. It was filled with so many teeth, he reminded me of a shark. "You clean up nice. Wow!"

I frowned, immediately feeling gross. I opened my mouth, ready with a reply when he continued talking. It was probably for the best. I wasn't going to get any info if I got kicked out for berating the guest of honor.

"I didn't think any of you people would show up to this little gathering. Susan was really selective when she made up the guest list. Will Patricia or that older guy be here?" he asked.

"Which older guy? There are a lot of those on the Committee," I said.

"You have a point." He guffawed. "The guy who's so friendly with your boss."

My tolerance for people like Stone was never high on a good day. I tried to keep my growing irritation from my voice. "Reginald Sharpe? He and Trish weren't invited."

"So how did you find your way onto the guest list?" He gave me a sly smile. "Do I have a secret admirer?"

I smirked. Of course, he would think that. Nailing Stone between the eyes seemed a more viable option by the second. What was Trish thinking when she assigned me this task? "I know Susan's daughter, Emma." I squeezed in a question before he could talk over me again. "So what made you want to run for mayor, Joe?"

The transformation was seamless. The bravado melted away, and he launched into his pitch. "Well, Alex, thank you for that question. I've lived here my entire life, and nothing would make me happier than to see Hopewell flourish again. Over the past decade, I've noticed a steady decline that doesn't reflect the intrinsic values of its citizens. Hopewell isn't as prosperous or as clean as before, and it's definitely not as safe."

"You think it's unsafe?" For the size of the city, Hopewell was considered fairly safe. Anne had shared the stats. I didn't feel any more threatened walking around Hopewell than I did in any other city.

"Yes. Look at the case of that kid killed on your side of town."

"My 'side?' What side would—" I began.

"Kids are in gangs, the homeless are blighted with drugs, and violence is off the charts."

The challenges he listed were accurate . . . to a point. "Do you think social inequities might be contributing—"

"We've lost our moral compass," he continued. "And when citizens try to speak up to voice their concerns and suggest improvements, they are reprimanded and silenced."

He was confusing me. I'd often wondered if the supernatural community wasn't more vocal because they feared being tethered, their gifts silenced. Eyeing him suspiciously, I lowered my voice. "Are you talking about how tethering is handled in Hopewell?"

"No. I'm talking about our citizens who attend houses of worship. When they attempt to spread the good word and mobilize for change, they are cast as villains! This past winter, an outstanding group called the Noble Sons was nearly dismantled because they were accused of harassing and attacking people."

"Nearly?" I frowned. William Jansen, the local group's organizer, was ordered by the Committee to dissolve it. Had that not been done?

"This, of course, was completely false," Stone said.

What the hell? "No," I said. "That's exactly what was happening. The Noble Sons are a hate group. Emma and I—"

"That's what some, like those in the media, would like you to believe." He winked as if divulging a little-known truth. "Someone needs to represent these good people and be a voice for restoring Hopewell back to what it once was. What it should be."

I actually laughed. "You can't be serious! Over three-quarters of the Committee already represents 'those good people.' It's not much different outside the Committee. No one like me is on the city council. Do they really need a champion in you?"

This was not the response the speechwriter had prepared Stone for. His mouth opened and closed a few times, searching for the next line in the script. A familiar perfume drifted to my nose, the odor of which instantly raised the hair on the nape of my neck.

"There you are, Joe!" Susan's voice was musical in its greeting as she arrived next to Stone. One well-manicured hand landed lightly on his arm while the other fluttered near her sparkling necklace. "I've been searching all over for you. I wanted to introduce you to some university colleagues."

Susan maintained her dazzling smile as she looked at me. Unlike her daughter's, there was no warmth in it. "Alexandria, what a surprise! Emma didn't mention you would be tagging along. Don't you look nice when you make an effort."

My jaw clenched, and I tried for a smile. It probably looked like indigestion. "Thank you, Susan. I thought you'd know I would be here. Em said the full spa day we enjoyed was on your dime."

Susan's smile flickered.

Oblivious, Stone chuckled. "That's Susan. The woman is brimming with generosity."

"Joe, why don't you go on ahead to the covered table by the stage," Susan said. "I'll be along shortly to introduce you."

Stone gave me one last look over and a wink. "Great talking with you, Alex."

I gave him another forced smile.

Susan watched him leave before she turned on me. All pretense was dropped. "What did you say to him?"

I blinked, taken aback by the sudden ferocity of the question. "I asked him why he was running for mayor."

"What are you even doing here? You can't possibly make a worthwhile donation to this campaign. Where is Emma?" Susan scanned the crowd for her daughter. I was yet another problem for her to deal with during an already busy evening.

She turned back to me. "And what are you trying to accomplish with 'this'?" She motioned to my outfit and sneered. Her previous passive-aggressive compliment had been for Stone's sake. "Are you trying to ruin this campaign to spite me? He's a married man, Alexandria. Try being a decent human being for once."

My mouth went dry, my chest tightened, and my face heated up. Susan shot me a parting glare and hurried after Stone. I exhaled a shaky breath and blinked back angry tears. The outfit Emma had helped me piece together was suddenly ill-fitting, and my hair probably looked ridiculous. Maybe the skirt was too short after all. I briskly wiped at my eyes and started back toward the veranda.

Burning anger caused the creature inside me to pace. Why was it so easy for some women to shame other women? Every since she met me, Susan made me feel less-than, like I was taking up space I didn't deserve. I was done playing proper and polite. If all Susan saw was an animal, she'd get an animal.

What I planned to do was stupid. It wouldn't help Trish or the wolves, but with extreme dislike for Susan flaring in my gut, I didn't care.

Ben noticed me walking toward him and stood. He must have also seen the determination in my eyes, because he looked uneasy.

I wrapped my arms around his neck and gave him a deep kiss, pressing as much of my body as I could along the length of his. I breathed near his ear, "Come inside with me." His face was flushed and he seemed confused, but he allowed me to lead him into the house.

9

WHEN I TOOK the first step onto the large staircase, Ben stopped. He urged me back with a light pull of his hand. His gaze darted around the empty front hall before he asked in his whispered voice, "What are you doing?"

I ran my hands under his blazer and smiled up at him through my lashes. "I've been informed the only reason I would ever look like this is to inappropriately ensnare a man."

"Did Emma's mom find you?" Ben was familiar with my Susan struggles.

"Maybe." I was reluctant to credit her with shattering my confidence.

"She's a sad and petty person. Don't let her get inside your head." He lifted one of my hands from his chest and pressed his lips to the inside of my wrist. "Let's leave. Emma will understand."

"But Susan expects me to behave a certain way. I wouldn't want to disappoint her." I moved up the first stair again. "And now, all I can think about is you and me on one of her expensive antique couches."

He grinned and shook his head.

"And this skirt's hem," I pulled it a bit higher, "up around my waist."

Ben looked from the raised hemline to me. "Are you sure about this?"

"Very sure."

He glanced down to the front hall a final time before he jogged up the stairs after me. We moved down the left hallway past a dark study smelling of cigars and more wood polish. My pulse thrummed in my ears at the thought of our impending mischief. I randomly selected a room a few more paces down and across the hall, pulled Ben inside with me, and closed the door.

We were in another study, this one filled with the perfume of roses from the fresh bouquet on the desk. All of the furniture was blonde wood. The large desk was in front of a window dressed with sheer curtains, and a leather sofa sat along the wall. The opposite wall held shelving for books and bits of sculpture.

Ben sat on the front edge of the desk. "I realize I'm arguing against my own interests, but you're sure you want to be here instead of out there working your spy gig?"

I set the purse aside on the desk so I could part his knees and slip my body between them. The primal being deep inside me responded and warmth unfurled inside my belly. Yes, I should be out collecting information on Stone. No, it wasn't what I wanted to be doing right now. "Desk or couch?"

Having finally exhausted any objections, Ben leaned forward and kissed me. His hands slipped beneath the skirt, up the sides of my thighs, and pulled me tight against him. The creature inside me delighted at his touch. She pushed forward and waited just underneath my skin.

He's safe.

Was my inner wolf finally on Team Ben? I placed a hand on Ben's chest to push him back onto the desk. Suddenly, a loud voice came up the stairs.

I froze, both the need for revenge and physical desire flushed away by a single surge of adrenaline. Ben began to ask a question, but I placed my fingertips lightly on his lips and shook my head. When the voice echoed down the hall, it reached his ears as well.

I stepped away from Ben toward the closed door. Several voices joined what I could identify as Stone's. A group of muffled footfalls advanced down the carpeted hallway toward us. My whole body tensed.

"Right in here, gentlemen." Stone said. Door hinges creaked across the hall. They were gathering in the study we'd passed.

I returned to the desk and grabbed my phone from the purse. "Stay here," I whispered to Ben.

"What are you planning to do?"

"I want to see who's in there and why they came up here instead of talking outside with everyone else." I listened at our door a moment before turning the knob and cracking the door open. The door across the hall was ajar, making it easier to hear Stone's conversation.

"I can assure you, gentleman," Stone said, "actions have already been taken to roll back the hunting ban within our city limits. By the time the election takes place, we can rest assured our citizens will be protected again."

I had to know who was in the room. When I snuck into the hall, a new sharp scent lingered in the air. Only a handful of steps brought me to the study door. The odor grew stronger. It was almost painful, stinging my nostrils. Bleach. I brought up the voice feature on my phone, crept as close as I could to the door, and hit the record button.

"How do you plan on convincing the others?" an unfamiliar male voice asked.

"Convincing won't be necessary when the other members witness the damage the werewolves are capable of," Stone answered. "Those monsters will dig their own graves. We'll just happen to have laid out the shovels for them."

My fist tightened at my side, and a growl brewed in my chest. I slowly inhaled through my nose to remain calm. The stink of the bleach burned and caused my eyes to water.

"And the other creatures? If they follow the laws by remaining hidden and unintrusive, the Hunter has no legal reason to exterminate them."

"Once the Committee members understand how dangerous the werewolves are, it won't be difficult to persuade them that all the others should be monitored," Stone said. "Our Hunter can take it from there. The beasts allowed to live here will either leave or will be dealt with."

Our Hunter? Stone had access to a Hunter? My hackles raised, and I clenched my teeth against the renewed urge to growl.

"What about Reginald?" asked another voice. "That bitch, Drake, is like a daughter to him. He'll help oppose the vote to lift the hunting ban."

"If he's in the minority, we don't have to worry," Stone said.

"Joe's right," another voice said. "Reginald is as bad as Aiden when it comes to following the rules to the letter. If the vote passes, he'd accept it. He won't be a problem."

The floor inside the doorway creaked, and the conversation halted. I stepped back and placed the phone to my ear. The door abruptly opened, and a towering, wide-shouldered man filled the threshold. His head was clean shaven, and he had a thick beard and eyebrows.

It took effort not to visibly recoil. Maybe it was his size that set off my "danger" sense. Who was this guy? Why was he in on a conversation about supernatural matters in Hopewell? I lowered the phone, covered the speaker, and gave him an apologetic smile. "Sorry. I hope I wasn't too loud. Do you know where the bathroom is?" My pulse pounded so hard, I worried he could hear it.

The man pinned me in place with his stony gaze. It didn't move over sections of my body—he looked directly into me.

And he saw her.

I doubled down on my effort to not retreat, but the beast inside my body betrayed me. A growl was pulled up into my throat. The guy didn't react as if it was anything unusual.

"Alexandria Steward." His voice was a low rumble. "Daughter of Scott and Kimberly Steward. Granddaughter of Alexander and Lunella Steward."

His words drove spikes of dread through me. Was someone digging through my past? Emma, Trish, and Nate were the only people who knew why I fled my home. Now, with Stone's new laws, those details could get me retroactively tethered. All the hair along my arms and the nape of my neck stood on end. "Who are you? How do you know me?"

He stepped into the hall. The floor creaked. "I've been searching for you, lupa."

I slunk back, baring my teeth.

"Shh. Be still, now." His gaze never left my eyes. "Our time will come, but not today."

My heel bumped into the hallway wall. I thought of what Trish had said about a Hunter's ability to draw out our inner wolves. My heartbeat stuttered, and I looked for the nearest exit. I was *not* going to die in Susan Arztin's upstairs hallway.

The door opened farther, and Stone stood beside the stranger. I caught a glimpse of the room beyond the two men and recognized several other Committee members.

"Alexis." Stone smiled. "Are you lost?"

"Yes." I swallowed, but my voice trembled anyway. "I was telling your friend he caught me looking for a bathroom."

Stone stepped into the dimly lit hall and glanced up and down its length. "Are you alone?"

"Well, sort of." I held up the phone, the receiver still covered. "I was chatting with a friend."

"On your way to the bathroom?"

I finally looked away from the stranger to Stone. "We ladies can't stand going to the bathroom by ourselves."

He held out his hand. "Give me the phone."

It'd been worth a try. I narrowed my eyes. "No."

Stone raised an eyebrow and gestured toward me with a jerk of his head. My shoulder blades struck the wall before I realized the larger man had moved. He held me stationary, his hand pressed against my sternum. Odors of dust and rotting wood, barely discernible beneath the bleach, clung to him. Dark eyes stared down at me, unblinking.

"Give me the phone," Stone said again.

My nails shifted and warped. The carefully applied polish cracked and peeled. I clasped at the stranger's wrist to free myself, but his arm was unmovable. "Let me go, asshole!" I snarled. The claws of my free hand sank into the stranger's forearm. The shirt's fabric was easily punctured, but my claws were inhibited by a layer of thick material beneath it.

"Last warning. If you don't give it to me, I'll simply take it," Stone said. "Give me the phone."

I growled, pissed they were getting the better of me. The larger man was an unknown variable. I didn't know who he was or what to expect from him. With bile in the back of my throat, I surrendered the phone to Stone. He gave a nod. I was released.

Immediately, I backed away and rubbed at my aching chest. "Taking my phone isn't going to stop me from telling Aiden about your private meeting." The agitated creature inside me fought against my efforts to calm her. My hands slid back into their human form, but my body continued to shake.

"That's true," Stone said. He passed my phone to the stranger. The guy snapped the phone in half.

The dull cracking noise made me flinch, as if he'd injured me instead of the phone. The blood drained from my face. No Commoner could do that. Who the *hell* was this guy?

The broken device was returned to Stone, and Stone handed the pieces back to me with a smug smile. "But now it will be your word against mine."

The door across the hall opened, and all three of us looked in that direction. Ben emerged from the room, hair mussed and blazer over his arm, zipping up his jeans. He stopped short and gave us a surprised expression. I bit my lip and dropped my gaze as if I were humiliated. As a woman, I was expected to act ashamed of seeking out and enjoying sex, so it wasn't hard to pull off.

Stone looked from him to me and back, thrown off by the unexpected interruption. Ben managed a sheepish expression as he stepped up beside me. He signed a question before he put his arm around me and settled his hand possessively at my hip.

"No, everything is okay. I found the bathroom. We can go." I looked at Stone. "Right?"

"Of course." Stone chuckled. His whole demeanor had returned to the friendly neighborhood politician. "You're not being held here."

I walked with Ben toward the stairs, my palms sweating and my heartbeat still racing. We maintained a casual pace, but the prickle of the larger man's gaze on my back made me want to run like hell. We reached the top of the staircase. Susan and two police officers stood in the entrance hall below. My stomach cratered. It was Anne and Jakob.

Out of all the cops in Hopewell, it had to be those two.

Jakob waited, his face expressionless. Anne, on the other hand, had spots of color high in her cheeks and a look of disappointment to rival any parent's. It confirmed my suspicion they were called here for Ben and me. How had Susan realized so fast we were missing from the party?

We reached the bottom of the stairs. Ben put the blazer back on as I asked the group, "Did something happen?"

Susan gave me a frigid smile. "I'd like you to leave. Immediately. Otherwise, these officers will see you out."

I glanced at Anne and Jakob standing behind her. "Isn't it a bit extra to call the police to get someone to leave your party?"

"Not when that someone is breaking the law," Susan said.

What reality was this woman living in? "It's not a crime to use the bathroom," I said.

"Of course not, but it is a crime to trespass and attempt to steal sensitive campaign information," Susan said.

I scowled. "I wasn't stealing anything."

"Then what were you doing in my private office?" she asked.

My cheeks warmed, but I lifted my chin.

"You don't think we would have cameras in case a guest abused our generosity?"

Cameras? The red spread across the bridge of my nose. "If you have cameras, you *know* I didn't steal anything."

"Or didn't have the chance to before you were interrupted." Susan's smile was smug—a replica of Stone's. "Goodnight, Alexandria."

I clenched my jaw and moved to walk to the garden. "Let me tell Em—" I stopped when Jakob stepped into my way.

"You can leave through the front door, Miss Steward," he said. "Thank you."

I narrowed my eyes at Jakob before glancing to Anne for some help. She crossed her arms and frowned. So . . . no help coming from her.

Ben's fingers brushed my elbow. He gave a nod toward the front door. I shot Susan a parting glare and walked out with him.

"Thank you for your help, officers." Susan's voice was sickly sweet behind us.

"Have a nice evening, ma'am," Jakob said.

Ben and I were down the steps before Anne called out to me. "Alex, wait a minute."

I stopped, my stomach in knots. Anne would want an explanation, and I'd have to choose how much to share. Ben looked at me and jerked his thumb back over his shoulder. I nodded. He leaned forward, kissed my cheek, and walked toward where he'd parked the motorcycle.

Jakob touched his index finger to the brim of his hat as he passed. "Goodnight, Miss Steward." He continued toward the police cruiser in the driveway.

I turned to come face to face with a very disgruntled Anne.

"Why would you purposefully poke a bear like Susan Arztin?" she asked. "You *know* she doesn't like you."

"I didn't do anything wrong!"

Anne pointed back at the large home. "You were trespassing in her house!"

This time the lie made my chest ache. Anne wasn't Stone or Susan—she was my friend. "I was trying to find the bathroom."

"With Ben? I know you're a woman who can take a piss by herself, so do you want to try another one on me?" She held up a finger to stop me from answering. "No, on second thought, I'll save time and let you know Susan shared the camera footage with Jakob and me."

A new wave of heat surged from my neckline to my scalp. Anne knew getting close to Ben was one of my favorite things to do, but I wasn't an exhibitionist. I wanted to melt into the driveway and disappear.

"Yeah." Anne nodded. "Pretty damn stupid. What the *hell* were you thinking, Alex?"

I got a whiff of vanilla. The sound of heels clicking down stone steps caused us to look back toward the house. Emma's eyes widened upon seeing Anne in uniform. "Oh no. Did she really request you?" She looked between us. "I'm sorry, Anne. I hope her call didn't take you away from anything important."

Susan was able to *request* which police officer be sent? Who does that?

"Requested me?" Anne asked.

Emma nodded, causing the pile of curls on her head to bounce. "Yes . . . because you're Alex's friend." She acted as if this should all be obvious. "The stress of this upcoming election is causing my mother to be even more spiteful than usual."

Anne and I looked at each other. I was more confident than ever that a full suite awaited Susan Arztin in hell.

Anne shook her head. "Emma, your mother is . . ."

"An awful person?" I said.

"I was going to say a force of nature," Anne said.

"I'm sorry you got called out here," I said to Anne. "It was childish of me to play *Who Can Be the Bigger Bitch* with Susan.

Ben tried to stop me, but I didn't listen." Anne was already less-than-thrilled about my friendships with Trish and Nate. The two of them were slippery when it came to Hopewell's police department, and Anne had noticed. I didn't need her suspecting Ben of bending the law, too.

"Let's make this a one-time event, okay?" she said.

"Okay." I hoped. I was running out of excuses and half-truths to keep Anne at arm's length from the supernatural goings-on of my life.

"I'll still see you tomorrow morning for boxing?"

I nodded. "I'll be there."

Emma waved at Anne and Jakob as they pulled away in the police cruiser. She turned to me with a frown. "What happened? Mother said you were 'defiling' her office and 'stealing' from her?"

I blushed. Again. "Em, I didn't steal anything."

Her hands rested on her hips as she searched my features. "I know you didn't want to come here, and I appreciate you coming despite that, but I asked you to please not upset her."

My chest tightened. "You asked me not to 'break anything.'" Despite Emma not agreeing with her parents' behavior, she expected me to make concessions so as not to upset them.

"Then I hear guests gossiping about my mother calling the police on someone, and I find you missing." Emma said. "I've been told I can never bring you back here because you're no longer welcome."

"You know what? I don't care." I crossed my arms. "She accused me of trying to seduce Stone. It's because I wore this goddamn skirt, that I didn't even want, to look nice for her goddamn friends, that I don't even know, at her goddamn party, that I didn't even want to come to in the first place!" I mirrored Emma's frown. "I'm tired of her treating me like trash. You're on your own with her from now on."

We glowered at each other a few moments before Emma bit her bottom lip. Her features twitched, and she started to giggle.

Raising my eyebrows, I asked, "Something funny?"

"I grew up in this *goddamn* house. I know all the camera-safe places. You should have asked me where to go if you wanted to hook up with Ben."

My shoulders sagged, and I shook my head. "I was hurt and angry. I wasn't thinking straight. I'm sorry, Em."

"Did you at least get any information for Trish?"

I glanced back toward the house, half expecting the large stranger to be watching us. The front doorway was empty. I motioned Emma to walk with me toward where Ben waited.

"Stone brought a group of men upstairs for a private meeting," I said. "He's championing rolling back bans on hunting."

Emma's eyes widened. "Wait, what? He can't do that! Can he?"

"I don't know. He said there would be a vote." We stopped beside the motorcycle, and Ben handed me a pair of jeans. He'd stowed them in the bike's saddlebag for the ride home. I pulled the jeans on under the skirt and lost the skirt. "Stone also had some huge guy standing in as muscle." I shuddered. "The guy tapped straight into my wolf. I think he's a Hunter. He knew my name, as well as my parents' and grandparents' names. Then he broke my phone in half like it was nothing."

"Did he threaten you?" Emma's features turned stormy, which was about as intimidating as gray clouds around a rainbow. "We should report Stone to the Committee."

I considered her offer, wondering if her supernatural class status of wizard would carry any weight. "There were Committee members there, so I don't know if that will do anything," I said. "Let me tell Trish and see what she suggests."

Emma nodded. "Call me if I can help." She gave Ben and me a hug and waved goodbye as we left on the motorcycle. I watched her figure shrink in the motorcycle's side view mirror. A pang of guilt tinged my conscience. I hadn't even considered fallout for Emma when I'd formulated my half-ass plan to spite Susan. Now I'd probably lost even more of Emma's confidence in me.

Then there was Anne, who would, no doubt, have more questions for me tomorrow. I'd have to predict what those may be and how to answer. Helping to solve Isaac's murder was going to be tricky without Anne taking notice. I didn't want to choose between helping the werewolves or keeping my friendship with Anne.

And what would my actions tonight—misbehaving in a prominent wizard's home—mean for the reputation of the wolves? Would Susan complain to her husband, Charles, and Charles to the Committee? The Commoner reps gathered in that study would love for that to happen.

Irritation with my short-sightedness agitated the beast within me. She forced a growl from behind my ribcage. I closed my eyes, rested the front of my helmet between Ben's shoulder blades, and focused on the hum of the motorcycle as he drove us home.

THE FIRST THING I tackled back at the apartment was getting a new phone. The phone's warranty didn't cover *Destruction by Freakishly Strong and Scary Unknown Men*, so that was an expense I hadn't planned for. Ben rode along with me, and I updated him on everything concerning Isaac's death. He was about as thrilled as I was with the possibility of a Hunter in the city. Not only was he concerned for me, but his tether would put him on the Hunter's radar as a possible repeat offender.

As soon as the new phone was working, a message came in from Trish. She asked for fundraiser highlights and told me I was expected at Hell's Bells tomorrow morning. She'd arranged for Nate and me to retrieve information on Isaac's murder. Instead of messaging back, I called. No one answered. I called Nate's number and was sent to voicemail. A message popped up from him a moment later.

We're sorting an emergency at the club right now. See you in the morning.

I chewed on my thumbnail, wondering if I should go to Hell's Bells. Nate would have said if they needed help, though. Should I alert them right away about what I'd overheard and seen at the fundraiser? But they were dealing with an "emergency mess." A low rumble sounded in my chest. I confirmed Trish's previous message and requested a joint chat asap with her and Aiden.

"What's going on?" Ben asked.

I looked up from my phone. "Huh?"

"You're growling," he said. "It's your frustrated growl."

"Trish wants Nate and me to pick up some info tomorrow morning, but I have boxing with Anne."

"Reschedule with Anne," he said. "It gives her time to cool off."

"I can't," I said. "Things are tense with Anne right now. I think she knows I'm hiding something from her. If I reschedule, she'll be even more suspicious of me. I'll fit in both."

He followed me to the bathroom. "You told Emma that guy knew your last name and the names of your family members."

"Yeah." I squeezed toothpaste onto my toothbrush. "I wonder if Stone looked up info on me. I'll talk to Trish tomorrow morning."

Up to this point, Emma, Trish, and Nate were the only people in Hopewell who knew my inner wolf nearly killed the Commoner who assaulted me. But if Stone knew, why hadn't he reported me to the Committee? Would he do it now that I'd interrupted his secret meeting? And if the Committee found out, I could be tethered. A cold lump of dread turned in my stomach.

Ben leaned against the bathroom door frame, watching me as I brushed my teeth. I stopped and spoke around the toothbrush to his reflection. "You're being a creep right now. One man ominously staring into my soul tonight is enough for me."

He didn't find it as funny as I did. "What precautions can we take in case this guy is a Hunter?"

"I don't know yet." I spit the toothpaste out into the sink.

Ben frowned. "You said he was in the room when Stone was talking about driving out werewolves. Temporary hires, especially

Commoners, wouldn't be sitting in on those conversations. And overpowering you? Destroying your phone? He *must* be the Hunter Stone was talking about."

"Ben! Stop." I rinsed off my toothbrush.

"You could ask Trish for a pass on this Isaac thing," he said. "She has an entire pack at her disposal. There have to be other people willing to help her sort it out."

"Isaac *thing*?" I faced him, leaned back against the sink, and crossed my arms. "I want to be one of the people to help her with the Isaac *thing*." Even though the maybe-probably-Hunter terrified me, I wanted to prove Trish correct. I could control my inner wolf and help. I was more than an animal.

Ben ran his hands through his hair and blew out an exhale. "Okay. If you insist on doing this, what can I do to help keep you safe?"

"Stop fretting over me like a mother hen?" It was mean, and I regretted the words as soon as I said them.

He shook his head and vacated the doorway.

"Wait, I'm sorry." I padded after him out to the couch. He didn't acknowledge me when I settled beside him. I shimmied as close as possible without sitting in his lap.

No luck.

I nudged him. "Hey, I'd rather you not help. You're tethered."

He awarded me a full-on scowl and opened his mouth.

Raising my palms, I said, "Let me finish." I lowered my hands. "And because you're tethered, your bar for good behavior is higher than mine. You're a prisoner on parole. Trish may decide we need to go independent with the investigation. If we do, and the Committee finds you're connected, an extended sentence would be your best outcome."

Ben dropped his gaze. He struggled daily with not having full access to his magic. It scared me to think what a lengthening of his sentence would do to his mental health. I didn't want him to face that because of me.

"It's hard to sit by and do nothing when you're endangering yourself," he said. "I care for you. A lot."

"I know, and I'm sorry I made fun of your concern," I said. "But I want to keep you safe as well. You mean a lot to me, too."

His wrinkled brow smoothed, and he looked up at me. "Yeah?"

My pulse skipped, and my cheeks warmed. "Yes." It made him smile, which only caused me to blush more and roll my eyes. I rested my head on his shoulder. "Having you at the party tonight was nice. That helped."

"Did it? We were tossed out."

"I wanted to spite Emma's mom so badly," I said, "I didn't think of what getting caught could mean for Emma or you. I'm sorry."

He put his arm around me and kissed the top of my head. Ben's phone buzzed atop the folding tray kept beside the couch. I sat up and he reached over and checked the message. "Joan wants to meet us tomorrow." He looked back at me. "Think you'll even have time for that?"

The question's tone caused a twinge in my chest. "Um, sure. Why does she want to see us?"

He shrugged. "I think this is her attempt at getting to know you. Maybe we could get that ice cream you mentioned yesterday."

The ice cream sounded great. Being interrogated by Ben's sister did not.

He sensed my hesitation. "I thought a public setting would be better, but we could hang out here. If you can't make it, we'll meet her some other time."

Ben had already considered my discomfort with meeting new people. I smiled again. "No, it's okay. Earlier in the evening would be better since I'm meeting Trish and Nate after dark."

"Thanks," he said. "I'll let her know." He turned his attention to the text exchange.

My nerves were still tweaked after my confrontation with Susan, Anne, Emma, and finally Stone and his large friend. I snuggled beside Ben and closed my eyes. The creature inside me curled in on herself to rest. Ben's familiar scent and the rhythm of his breathing relaxed us.

Tomorrow was a *scheduled* confrontation with Joan. I wasn't sure I'd made the best first impression. Then there were those comments she'd let slip about me being a werewolf. It was possible she didn't want a dangerous beast hooking up with her little brother. From what Reginald said, the siblings were close. I couldn't disappoint Joan because I didn't want to lose Ben.

10

"THAT SEEMED LIKE *some* party." Though it was early, the rhythmic clanging of weights and whirring of cardio machines filled the gym. So did the musky scent of all the sweaty bodies. Anne glanced up at me from wrapping my hand. "The skirt seemed to have worked."

Despite her small smile, an attempt to forgive the tension between us, I shook my head. "It was so stupid of me."

"Since we didn't receive a follow-up call, I assume you left the party after we did?"

A flare of anger burned in my stomach at the thought of Susan. "Yes."

"What else did Emma say?" Anne turned her attention back to winding the cloth bandage between my outstretched fingers.

"Not much, other than I'm not allowed back at that house."

Anne raised her eyebrows. "Excommunication from the Charles and Susan Arztin Estate?"

I snorted. "Hopefully it means I'll see less of Susan. Em already has a lot on her plate. Mediating arguments between her bitch of a mother and me shouldn't be one of them."

"Hopefully." Anne fastened the wrap and held her hand out. "She seems to be doing okay . . . Emma."

"Yeah." I offered my unwrapped hand. "She's stopped mentioning the evil ex. I don't think she's wasting any more tears on the guy, either."

"Honestly, Alex," Anne said. "You make Mitch sound like a comic book villain."

"He was brainwashing people in his secret lair. He might as well have been." I tried to make my question sound like a casual inquiry. "Any news on the person we found in the river?"

"He was too young," she said. "Make a fist for me, please."

"How are they approaching the investigation?"

"Homicide. Here's the thing though . . ." She paused wrapping my hand and looked at me. "The whole situation feels off. At the crime scene, the ME commented he'd never seen a combination of lacerations and burns like on the kid's neck wound. When I asked Detective Grey about it later, he said he hadn't noticed any notes in the ME's report about burns." She frowned. "Grey is grumpy enough for a man twice his age, but he seemed extremely defensive."

"Like he'd forgotten that detail?" Had a wizard wiped it from Grey's memory? Was it Reginald? But he was an ally to the wolves. "It seems pretty important if it's so unique."

"No, as in, the medical examiner didn't include the note in the report. I think Detective Grey was embarrassed. He usually double-checks his sources and work."

"You could show him how it's done," I said.

Anne smiled. "I'd like to look at the case file to see what the crime scene photos and forensic autopsy include." She continued wrapping. "The last time I doubted an investigation was this past winter when I helped track down the two guys that attempted to kidnap you." She secured the cloth bandage and looked at me again. "One of those odd coincidences, I guess."

I was being processed by the *Anne Scan*, so I flexed my fingers and feigned an interest in how she'd wrapped my hands. It allowed me to avoid making eye contact. "What does Jakob think? You two talk about those kinds of things, right? You know, cop things."

She chuckled. "He wasn't interested, even though I shared how odd it felt to me. He's gunning for the rank of detective too, so that surprised me. Maybe he's overwhelmed getting up to speed at the department."

"Was there evidence at the river we overlooked?" I asked.

"Why are you taking such an interest? This isn't the first homicide case I've followed."

Dammit. Too far. I didn't have the healthy blush of a workout to disguise the reddening in my cheeks. "Can't I be interested in what my friends do? I mean, I was there when you found the body. I feel vested in puzzling out the case now." The last part was true.

"Uh-huh." She stood and tossed me the boxing gloves from her bag. "I call bullshit." She watched me while I put on the gloves. Realization dawned on her features. "Wait, did you know the kid?"

That would work. "Yes."

"I'm sorry, Alex."

Standing, I shrugged. "No, it's okay. I knew him through Hell's Bells, but we weren't close."

When I said the club's name, Anne frowned. "Why didn't you mention that when we found him?"

My mind flailed for an excuse. "Shock?"

"So, those people knew the kid? We could have had someone over there questioning them by now."

"*Those people* are named Trish and Nate," I said. "They're good people, Anne."

She snorted. "Good people don't get their friends arrested for breaking and entering. Did you forget your sleepover at the station this past winter?" She shook her head. "Those two are criminals. I wish you'd stop spending time with them."

My eyes narrowed. "You don't know them. They look out for me."

"They think they're above the law! Each has collected a list of infractions longer than my arm." She scowled. "You sound like Emma when she dated Mitch: complete and utter denial."

Holy hell, that was a low blow. I clenched my teeth to hold back any smart-ass retort. Anne didn't trust Trish and Nate, and

I was afraid I was losing her trust as well. I exhaled the frustration from my voice. "Maybe you should push Detective Grey more on why those report details were withheld."

Anne sensed I was backing down and checked her tone as well. "Already planned on it." She bumped the fronts of her gloves together. "Let's get started."

I VOLUNTEERED TO drive to the appointment Trish had scheduled for Nate and me. We were supposed to meet an informant who claimed to know a witness to Isaac's murder. The information seemed important enough for Trish to attend herself, but she insisted Nate and I go.

When I pulled up to Hell's Bells, Trish's car was already gone from the parking lot. Nate was still groggy when he got into my car wearing clothes that, judging by the smell, he slept in the night before.

We drove several minutes in silence before I asked, "Everything okay from last night? I almost came over when I read 'emergency.'"

Nate sat slouched in the passenger seat, his hand draped out the window. His other hand shielded his eyes despite his sunglasses. "About the time you messaged, we were dealing with the worst wolf versus wizard shitstorm to date."

"Oh no." I thought of Ben's upcoming performance there.

"A whole group got tossed out on their asses, and they didn't go quietly. One of those fucking wizards blew apart every bottle behind the bar." Nate frowned. "Not only did we lose money from the liquor, but we were forced to close early to clean up the mess."

"Is everyone okay, though?"

"Yeah. Trish got a call from the kid's parents," he said. "She's meeting up with them to get reimbursed for the damage."

"I wondered why she wasn't going to this herself. Who are we meeting?"

"The guy's name is Fillip. He's a vampire Trish works with when she's digging for hard-to-find information."

"Excuse me, what?" The car hit the rumble strip.

Nate's hand gripped the dash. "Need me to drive?"

"A vampire . . ." I corrected course and received a not-so-helpful horn blare from the driver behind us. "Like, *I vant to suck your blood* vampire?"

"Don't say that. It's rude." Nate gave the driver the finger as he passed us and slumped back in the seat again. "Never met a vampire before?"

I shook my head.

"I guess that makes sense. They aren't that social outside their flocks," he said. "I thought Emma runs a shelter."

"Yeah," I said, "but what does Another Chance have to do with meeting vampires?"

"They often shack up in communities overlooked or forgotten about by Commoners. It helps to keep the vamps safe." He pointed at a side street. "Turn here."

I turned down a street that took us toward the river. "Why would a vampire help the lupine?"

"Vampires are information brokers. He's going to make a hefty profit from what he knows about Isaac's murder." Nate pointed to the side of the tree-lined street. "Pull over and park here."

I parked and cut the engine. "Why do business with them? Aren't vampires parasites?"

Nate looked over at me. "Who told you that? I thought you hadn't met one."

"I assumed they were bad guys," I said. "You know, creepy monsters hiding in the shadows."

"Like werewolves?" he said. "I'm sure some aren't outstanding citizens, but most of them take care of their people. The guy we're seeing protects his flock from a lot of awful things. He doesn't kill his people when he feeds from them. I wouldn't define that as being a monster."

Nate got out of the car, and I followed him down into the tree line. Everything smelled of damp soil and stagnant water. A man-sized metal pipe jutted out from beneath the road and ran to the edge of the river. The ground was still soft due to seasonal flooding. As we drew closer to the pipe, the ripe scent of sewage filled the air. We pulled our shirt collars up over our noses to help mitigate the awful stink.

"Be careful of what you say around him." Nate's voice was muffled by the collar of his shirt. "Vamps can be crafty. You don't live as long as Fillip does by being an idiot."

"Wait a minute." Realization crept up on me. "You'll be doing the talking, right?"

"Doing the talking isn't my strength," he said. "I'm here to make sure you don't get yourself killed."

Trish had set me up. She expected me to lead the conversation with the informant. "This doesn't seem like a good idea," I said. "I'm in no way prepared for this."

"Trish seems to think you are."

I looked back toward the river. An old man waited near the side of the pipe. He hadn't been there moments before. A flimsy knit cap partially covered his balding head, and he wore a long-sleeved, heavily patched pea coat. His frame looked frail beneath the fabric, and a host of liver spots covered his wrinkled face and skeletal hands. When I got closer, his ruby-colored eyes settled on me with a glint of sharp intelligence.

I released the collar of my shirt, not wanting to possibly offend him. "Hello, Fillip." Despite Nate's words earlier on the grayness of vampiric morals, I kept what I believed to be a safe distance from the stooped man. Nate remained a step behind my left shoulder.

Fillip's gaze slid from Nate to me. His voice was as thin as his figure, sounding dried and cracked. "And you are?"

"Alex Steward and Nate Osterberg. Patricia Drake sent us."

"Ah, Alexandria Steward." His smile exposed rat-like teeth. "I'd wondered when Patricia would allow us to meet. You are close to

Miss Emma Arztin, correct? And a companion to the tethered wizard, Benjamin Sharpe?"

My body tensed, and my pulse skipped. How much had Trish told this guy about me? And why would she do that? "They've never mentioned you," I said.

"Have they had reason to do so?"

I could tell this guy was going to try my patience. Trish apparently thought I could handle the task though. "You know someone who claims to have witnessed Isaac's murder?"

"Yes. The werewolf was killed beneath an overpass, and his body was carried from the scene. The killer's description was shared through my network. This is what was returned." The vampire held out a blank envelope to me.

I approached close enough to take the envelope from his outstretched hand. Stepping back, I ran my finger under the envelope flap. Inside was a folded piece of letterhead from Another Way Ministries, Emma's workplace. Printed on the page was a low-quality photo of the man I'd shared an uncomfortably intimate moment with in Susan Arztin's hallway. Goosebumps broke out along my arms. "Are you sure this is him?"

Fillip nodded once. "The witness to the werewolf's death confirmed the man in the photo is the killer."

"Thank you." My hands shook as I studied the photo. "Where can we find him?"

"I apologize, but we do not know yet," he said. "This man has been challenging to track. I expect to have the information soon. Should we notify you instead of Patricia?"

"Yes." The beast behind my ribcage paced. She recognized the man in the photo. He'd killed a fellow wolf and threatened us.

Nate cleared his throat. I glanced back at him. His nose was still covered by his shirt, but his brows were drawn together. I could picture his frown.

"I'll call you two as soon as I get the info." I turned to Fillip before Nate could object. "Can I give you my number?"

"I do not have a phone, but we know where to find you when the information is available." Fillip's red eyes stared unblinking at me. "Do you know the man in the photo?"

I frowned and stuffed the folded paper back in the envelope. "I don't know him, but he threatened me at a fundraiser for Stone."

"The mayoral candidate, Joseph Stone?" asked Fillip.

"Yes," I said. "This guy knew my family. He said he'd been looking for me and that we'll meet again later."

If the Committee found out about my past, I could be tethered. I needed to silence the Hunter, Stone, and anyone else that knew before they reported me.

"Is there any way you can find out more about the guy?" I asked Fillip. "Who is he? How does he know me? *What* does he know about me?"

Nate cleared his throat again. I gave him an irritated glance.

"Of course. This is all information I can gather for you." Fillip slowly smiled. "Are you asking this of me?"

"Yes," I said. "Thank you."

Fillip bowed his head. "I look forward to growing our business relationship, Alexandria."

After catching and turning in Isaac's killer, I hoped not to work with the vampire again. It was uncomfortable having my back to him while Nate and I walked to the road. When I got into the car, I tapped Nate on the chest with the edge of the envelope. He took it from me and opened it while I started the car.

"Well, doesn't he look friendly? Big bastard, too." Nate studied the grainy photo. "There's something familiar about him . . . I don't like it."

"Trish said Hunters can mess with our shifting," I said. "They lure out our inner wolves."

Nate frowned and looked at me. "Is that what he did to you?"

"Yeah." I pulled away from the shoulder started driving. "He was taking orders from Joe Stone, the new Commoner rep on the Committee."

"I can let Trish know," Nate said.

"No need. I'm meeting her and Aiden after I drop you off," I said. "Hopefully Fillip can find where this guy is hiding and why he knows me."

Nate pushed his sunglasses up. "Okay, makes sense you'd ask about that, but did you notice Fillip didn't list a price?"

I gave him a sideways glance. "What do you mean?"

Nate tapped the paper with the back of his fingers. "Fillip found us this photo and will pass along the guy's location. Trish and I are paying a chunk of change for that. Fillip gets you info on how this big fella knows you. What did Fillip want in return?"

"Um." Sensing I'd made a mistake, my face warmed.

"Exactly. Vampires don't hand over info for free," he said.

"How was I supposed to know that's how it worked?" I said. "I've never dealt with a vampire! Weren't you supposed to be there to, I don't know, mentor me or something?"

"No, I was there to keep you alive."

"Fantastic." I scowled. "So, how do I fix this?"

"Calm down," Nate said. "You owe him something. At some point he'll decide what that is, ask for it, and you'll give it to him."

I disliked owing people favors. It was like a weight hanging around my neck. "What if I don't want to give him what he asks?"

Nate shrugged again. "It sounds like Fillip is interested in a long-term relationship with you. There's a chance he'll negotiate your first deal so you get comfortable working with him. You got lucky. Don't expect the same luxury with other vampires."

"I'd appreciate a bit more warning from Trish before she throws me into these situations," I said.

"You made it through, didn't you?"

I called him a few choice names.

"Trust in Trish. She knows what she's doing." Nate flipped his sunglasses back down on the bridge of his nose and grinned. "Owes a vamp a boon right out of the gate; that's our Alex."

"Shut up," I growled.

BY THE TIME I dropped Nate back off at Hell's Bells, the summer heat was rolling off the pavement in waves. It made the horizon in St. Anthony's square into a mirage. I spotted Aiden alone in the shadow of one of the trees. He was seated on a bench, his ankle resting on his knee as he watched some sparrows hop around the walkway. They launched into flight as I approached.

"Thanks for agreeing to talk on such short notice," I said as a greeting.

He squinted up at me, either due to the heat or the brightness of the square. "Of course."

"Trish isn't here yet?" I asked the obvious, feeling obligated to make small talk with him.

He shook his head and checked his watch. "But you're early."

I sat on the other end of the bench to wait with him. "Has Jakob or Detective Grey sent any info to you after visiting the morgue?"

"Not yet." Aiden dabbed at his brow with a handkerchief. "I hope to hear from them soon."

It wasn't long before Trish strode toward us, a bright splash of color from across the square. Aiden stood. Her yellow, halter-style dress displayed her beautifully tattooed sleeves. She slipped off her cat-eyed sunglasses and gave Aiden a curt nod.

"Patricia, please, have a seat." Aiden offered the space where he'd been sitting.

She sat on the bench beside me and crossed one leg over the other. "Alex, you had something you needed to discuss with us?"

I took a breath. "Susan Arztin hosted a fundraiser last night for Joe Stone's mayoral campaign. I caught Stone holding a private meeting with some guys who are on the Committee."

"The majority of the members are also active in other areas of the community," Aiden said. "Were they discussing Committee matters?"

"I'd think so since they discussed reinstating hunting in Hopewell," I said.

Trish's eyes widened.

Aiden frowned. "That's a strong accusation. Are you sure?"

"He was promising to 'roll back the ban.' Earlier I'd asked him why he wanted to be mayor. He told me how awful Hopewell has become and mentioned how the Noble Sons were wronged. The way Stone was talking to these other Committee guys, he believes by clearing out supernatural citizens, the city will be restored to this weird utopia."

Aiden's brow wrinkled.

"Even the mention of reinstating hunting will cause friction," Trish said to Aiden. "I won't tolerate Stone bullying the wolves. We're already near a breaking point because of Isaac's death."

Aiden nodded. "I understand. I'll request Mr. Stone see me by this evening and provide an explanation. I'm sure this is a misunderstanding."

"Stone also had some huge guy with him I hadn't seen before." I took Fillip's envelope from my pocket and handed it to Trish. "At one point Stone ordered him to destroy my phone because I'd recorded part of Stone's meeting. The guy snapped it in half *with his bare hands*, no questions asked."

Trish studied the sheet of paper and passed it to Aiden. Her jawline tightened and her gaze snapped back on me. She wasn't pleased. I set my jaw as well, returning her stare. I didn't appreciate being set up on a blind date with a vampire.

Aiden interrupted our unspoken exchange. "Where did you get this?"

"Does it matter?" I growled. "This guy assaulted me on Stone's command because I didn't want to hand over my phone!"

"His name is David Williams." Aiden refolded the sheet of paper. "He requested a meeting to announce his arrival."

Trish tensed beside me. "That information should have been shared at the Committee meeting two days ago. Why did you keep it from us?"

"He only contacted and met with me this morning. I am waiting on details of his lodging and length of his stay." Aiden afforded me an irritated glance. "I planned to present the information when it was complete so as not to waste anyone's time."

"But why would he have to let you know he's here?" I asked.

"It's part of my role as Committee Chair. Since his family's heritage is one of hunting, he didn't want confusion about the reason for his visit."

My stomach lurched. There was no doubt left. The guy *was* a Hunter.

Aiden looked at Trish. "He'd heard of the unrest among our lupine citizens and didn't want his presence to agitate it."

"I doubt this man has the lupine's best interest in mind," Trish said. "He should be sent away. Hunters have no business in our home."

"There is no rule stating people should be denied entry into Hopewell based on who, or what, they are," Aiden said. "Mr. Williams is here because he was hired as extra security for Mr. Stone's campaign."

"That's bullshit," I said. "I told Stone I'd let you know what he was peddling at his secret meeting. I bet you wouldn't have even heard from this David guy otherwise."

"Everyone is innocent until proven guilty, Miss Steward," Aiden said.

"Except we have a dead wolf and silver as the murder weapon," I said. "And now this Hunter shows up in Stone's company, the politician who's promising he'll have hunting reinstated to get rid of all the scary monsters allowed in Hopewell."

"Miss Steward." Aiden looked down at me. "Like I said, I will request that Mr. Stone meet with me by tonight. Of course, knowing this, you'll keep your distance from Mr. Williams."

I gritted my teeth.

"We'll give you a day," Trish said. "If David Williams isn't gone, *I'll* ask him to leave."

"Erring on the side of caution might be for the best," he said.

"Exactly." Trish stood and put on her sunglasses. "One day."

"Of course." He looked between the two of us as I stood as well. "Rest assured, it will be resolved."

Trish and I left together across the square. I waited until we had put some distance between ourselves and Aiden before I asked, "Do you think he'll actually meet with Stone?"

"He'll attempt to," she said. We stopped beside her car. Trish watched Aiden climb the cathedral stairs. "I'm not as confident Stone won't weasel out of the request."

"Thanks for coming down here at the last minute," I said.

Trish looked back at me. "Information from Fillip is extremely valuable and often expensive. You should have asked me before sharing it with Aiden."

"All I said is that the guy was in Stone's company at the fundraiser. If Aiden hadn't seen the photo, he probably wouldn't have told us about Williams." Somehow I kept the irritation from my reply. "And if we're on the subject of asking permission, you should've asked me if I wanted to risk meeting a vampire."

Trish's brows lifted above her sunglasses. "Nate was there with you, and Fillip is an honorable businessman. You weren't in danger."

A growl slipped into my voice. "That should be my decision to make, not yours."

There was a strong exhale through Trish's nose. She lifted her chin and pressed her lips together.

"I want to help you," I said, "but please give me a bit of warning next time."

"We don't always have the benefit of time. You need to think on your feet." She tucked the envelope into her purse. "But I understand your frustration. I'm sorry. Thank you for your good work."

Warmth spread in my chest. "You're welcome."

"Are you still able to meet Nate and me later?" Trish asked.

"Yes."

"We're outside this evening. I'll send the address." The corner of her mouth curled upward. "We'll practice thinking on your feet."

My chat with Trish and Aiden complete, my mind shifted to the next item for me to tackle. I was expected to meet up with Ben and his sister, Joan. Confirmation of the Hunter had me worried I wouldn't be able to focus on the visit. But I owed Ben for accompanying me to the campaign fundraiser, and I wanted to make a better impression with Joan. With all the stressful shit going on with Isaac's murder and now the Hunter as the prime suspect, I didn't need my guy's sister telling him I'm not good enough for him.

Plus, Ben promised ice cream. I couldn't say no to that.

11

WE LEFT THE frigid ice cream parlor and stepped back into the hot afternoon. Joan, Ben, and I crossed a narrow one-way street to a small park. The park designer fashioned it as a communal place for residents and visitors to enjoy every season of the year. We strolled past mounds of soft grass and small ornamental trees surrounding a paved area full of tables and chairs. In winter, the open space was converted into an ice rink. Tucked among the greenery were raised cement benches encircling shallow pools of water. Cool mist rose from the water's surface. Kids laughed and ran through the mist, watched from afar by socializing parents.

We chose one of the benches to perch on while we savored our dessert. I licked the peanut butter and chocolate ice cream from where it dripped down the side of my hand. Ben smiled and gave me a chilled kiss tasting of mint before handing me a napkin.

I grinned at him. "Thanks." His bright eyes gave me that fluttering feeling in my stomach. My connection with Ben was evolving and strengthening, which excited and terrified me at the same time. This ritualistic torture of exposing your insides to your partner's family seemed to be an unfortunate part of the process.

Joan sat on the other side of Ben, peering around him at me. "Alex, tell me about yourself," she said. "My brother doesn't share anything with us."

Ben made a face and signed to her. His gestures were too fast for me to pick out any words.

"Ha!" Joan said. "Just because we live out of town, Benjamin, doesn't mean you couldn't write."

I'd grown up an only child, so their sibling dynamics were entertaining. "I'm not sure there's much to say. What do you want to know?"

Her brother forgotten, Joan focused her full attention on me. She gave me a friendly smile, again making me marvel at the similarities between her and Ben. "Are you from Hopewell?"

I shook my head. "No. I moved here almost three years ago from out of state."

"How do you keep yourself busy?" she asked.

"Um . . ." I glanced at Ben, but he was preoccupied wrangling his melting ice cream. "I'm between jobs right now. Ben has gotten me into reading graphic novels. I like listening to music, going to shows, and spending time with my friends. I run."

"Run?" Joan arched her brow. "For fun?"

Ben grinned and I laughed. "Yes, for fun. It's good exercise, but it also helps me relieve stress and sort my thoughts."

"How'd you find this guy?" Joan gave her brother a playful bump in the arm.

I rescued him from getting his ass kicked by a rogue wizard and werewolf after him for damaging his tether? "We met through a mutual friend at a show he was playing."

"Of course," Joan said. "That's usually where I found him if Mom and Dad had lost track of him again. He'd either be at a concert or making an ungodly racket in the basement with his guitar."

I grinned and looked at Ben. "You play guitar? How come I didn't know this?" With him being involved in EDM, it never crossed my mind he'd learned any instruments. I'd only seen him messing around on his beat-up laptop, arranging music.

Ben shrugged and Joan laughed. "See what I mean?" She jabbed her ice cream spoon at him. "He doesn't share anything."

"Where's your guitar?" I asked. "I haven't noticed one at the apartment."

Ben's gaze jumped from me to Joan. She waited expectantly. He signed to her and turned his attention back to his ice cream.

Joan's smile flickered. "He pawned it."

"Oh." There was an awkward silence between them. I flipped the questioning to avoid more interrogation or anything that might make Ben uncomfortable. "What about you, Joan? Tell me about yourself."

She took another spoonful of ice cream. "I grew up here, of course, but have lived in Chicago for about ten years. The regional Delegation is seated down there."

"Is that who Reginald worked with several months ago? He was talking with some Chicago group to identify the guys who attacked Ben."

"Yes. A Delegation is the next tier up from local Committees. Some colleagues and I are trying to get rules revised at that level. Our hope is that the changes will filter down to the local level. It takes up a lot of my time, so I don't do much else." She motioned with the spoon at Ben again. "He'd be down there with me if it weren't for the damn tether."

Ben frowned and signed to his sister.

"No, I will not let it go," Joan said. "There will never be a time I'm not pissed about it. If this Committee weren't so skewed, you wouldn't be stuck in this hellhole."

My ice cream gone, I wiped the remaining mess from my hands with my napkin. "It's frustrating the Committee here is weighted to one side when it comes to membership. There are only three people like us out of about a dozen."

"The wizards and lupine have a seat, but why only one each? And where is everyone else? They're scared to even show their faces for fear of being persecuted by the Commoners' puritanical bullshit." Joan's eyes grew intense. "What do you think about tethering, Alex?"

I hesitated, glanced at Ben, then answered truthfully. "I think it's awful. It's inhumane."

Joan nodded. "Exactly. It's archaic, and for such a life-changing punishment, has no standardized system. That allows Committees like this one to dole out whatever severity of punishment they feel like at the time of sentencing." Her eyes lit up, similar to Ben's whenever he set a new album on the record player. "It's going to change. We've been working since last year to outlaw tethering."

I raised my eyebrows. "How're you managing that?"

"We're hoping local pressure from the Committees' supernatural citizens will support the request made at the Delegation. In fact, we have a protest scheduled in Hopewell for this evening, over at Union Street Church where the Committee meets."

Protest? "Wouldn't wizards and wolves marching around holding signs about tethering alert the Commoners?"

Joan shook her head. "I'll use a spell to veil the protest. It's similar to what's used to hide the Village Pub from the Commoners. They'll walk by while we blend in as some protest about dumping waste into the river or whatever their minds supply."

"If no one is going to notice the protest, why would the Committee even care?"

Joan held up a finger. "No one is going to notice . . . yet." My eyes widened and she grinned. "Yeah. We're done being ignored. If the Committee refuses to sit down with us and discuss banning tethering, we'll threaten to drop the veil. It would be chaos for them. The very last thing they want is to lose control, and maintaining secrecy is a key part of that."

"That seems risky." I frowned and glanced at Ben.

"Don't worry," she said. "I told him I didn't want him anywhere near the church, but you're welcome to join us. Tonight should be a peaceful gathering."

Ben scoffed and signed abruptly to Joan.

"I think she can make the decision for herself if it's worth her time." Joan looked at me. "What do you think?"

I chewed at my thumbnail and glanced at Ben again. Tethering was a monstrous practice, and I lived in constant fear of it as I struggled to get my inner wolf under control. But I wasn't sure if threatening the Committee with exposure was the best way to get it changed. "Does everyone attending the protest know the risk?"

"Of course," she said. "Hopefully the Committee will talk before we have to take any drastic actions. But no risk, no reward."

Her passion was contagious but the protest made me uneasy. Joan was organizing a movement that could put participants at risk of being tethered. But the wizards, unlike any werewolves involved, would live to see the other side of that punishment.

"Thanks for the invite, but I have other commitments tonight," I said. "Good luck, though." Should I alert Trish to the protest? Or did she already know? She had to know. She knew everything going on with the wolves.

Ben smiled and signed to Joan again.

She laughed and flipped him off. "You can be such an ass."

I smiled, stood, and held up my wad of dirty napkins. "I need to find a trash can. I'll be right back."

I left the siblings and started toward a garbage can across the seating area. The jingling of a small bell caught my attention. As I scanned the tables and chairs for the sound's source, the scent of lemon drops reached my nose. It brought to mind images of my grandfather and the covered glass dish of hard candies kept beside his recliner. My parents had moved the candy dish and recliner from our family's living room shortly after he passed.

The bell jingled again, and I looked down to see a vaguely familiar white cat. There was a gold bell on its collar, and it carried some sort of food scrap in its mouth. The fluffy animal wove around my legs before it padded off between the tables and chairs. It stopped to look back at me and meowed, the sound muffled by whatever it carried.

I glanced around to see if I could spot the owner. A couple seated at the table the cat stood beside either didn't hear it or were ignoring it. The cat meowed again. Was it *calling me*? When I looked over at Ben and Joan, the two were still in conversation.

Curious and feeling all sorts of foolish, I followed the cat's winding path through the seating area. It periodically stopped as if making sure I wasn't lost.

The cat repeated the odd behavior across the small park until it reached an older man seated on the amphitheater-like steps. It bumped its head against the man's outstretched hand, then sat beside him and began to eat the scavenged food. After seeing the man, I realized why the cat looked familiar. The pair had been on Opal Street bridge the morning Anne and I had found Isaac. Did they live in the area?

I glanced back across the park again at Ben and Joan. They were still lost in conversation. Taking advantage of a moment to myself, I approached the seated man. The scent of the lemon drops strengthened. He smiled off into the distance, his wrinkled hand absently petting the animal beside him. The cat crouched over its meal, watching me with rounded eyes, one green and one blue. Its fluffy tail swished back and forth over the pavement.

"Excuse me, sir. Hello," I said.

The man emerged from his daydreaming to regard me. "Hello, young lady." He shielded his eyes from the sun reflecting off the buildings. One of his eyes was blue, and the other green. I blinked and he asked, "Is there something we can do for you?"

"This may sound strange, but I think I've seen you during morning runs," I said. "You're usually on the Opal Street bridge."

He smiled. "Yes, that may have been us. We go to the bridge often. We like to watch the ducks." The cat stood from its crouched position and drifted behind the man. It rubbed along the back of his worn, button-down shirt. Purring, the cat peeked up at me with its bi-colored eyes.

"Have you noticed anything suspicious there this past week? Maybe people you're not used to seeing?"

"Suspicious?" asked the man. The cat sat down and the bell on its collar jingled. The man smiled again. "Why do you wish to know? Are you a police officer? A detective?"

"No." It was a weird question to ask a complete stranger. "I'm sorry." I dropped my gaze to my shoes. "I've been searching for a missing friend. The police know he's missing, but I'm anxious to find out what happened. He was—is—about twenty. He's my height with brown hair and eyes." I turned my forearm to expose the inside of it to the man. "He has a large cross tattoo here."

The cat's tail swished as it looked up at me. The man gave its head a gentle stroke. He tilted his own head to the side. "Yes. We may have seen this friend of yours."

I tried to keep him talking. "Was anyone else with him?"

The man shook his head. "We can't quite seem to remember. We're an old one, trying to get by on so little, and making sure there is enough for us to eat." He looked up at me expectantly.

It took me a moment to realize what he was waiting for. I got out my wallet. The cat padded to me and rubbed against my legs, its body thrumming with purrs. The scent of lemon drops was almost overpowering.

The man watched me count out several bills. I never carried a lot of cash and wasn't in the habit of bribing strangers, so I hoped it would be enough. He accepted the money with a smile and a nod.

"We appreciate your generosity." The man filed the money in a broken bifold. "A Wordweaver visited the Veiled One as he lay in rest."

"Wordweaver?" I asked.

"She did not approach until the man made of dark light left the water's edge." The old man studied me. "Why do you ask after the Veiled One if you know he is no longer here?"

I began to feel uneasy. A light trill sounded near my feet. The cat was seated there, staring up at me as if awaiting my answer. I backed away. Startled by my movement, the animal scampered to the seated man. It jumped onto his shoulder to watch me.

"We saw you that morning when we were watching the ducks. You were with one of the Commonfolk. She does not know you are a Veiled One," the man said.

The hair at the nape of my neck rose.

The man reached up to give the cat a scratch behind the ears. "Did we frighten you with what we said?"

I looked between the two. "I'm sorry. I don't understand how you know about—"

"You don't find the mystery entertaining?" the man asked. From its perch on the man's shoulder, the cat rubbed against his head. The rumbling purrs vibrated loud in my ears. Too loud.

I frowned. "No. A young man is dead. That isn't entertaining. What more can you tell me about the people that were with him?"

He frowned as well. At first I thought I'd offended him. Then he got a distant look in his eyes and mumbled, "An old one like us? Our sight is poor, and our memory is dusty—" He stopped speaking when I got out my wallet again. I handed over my last bit of money. The man's frown vanished as he pocketed the new bills.

"The Wordweaver was hooded and wore your friend's mark in metal," he said.

"And the man of dark light?" I asked.

"He was large. He wraps himself in hide and carries silver to cut the life from the Veiled Ones. There was no hair on his head, but much from his chin. We were frightened of him and hid so he would not find us." The man and cat both looked up at me with unblinking eyes.

I felt light-headed and nauseated from the unsettling information and the constant sweet aroma swirling around the man and his cat. "I'm sorry—" I lurched to the nearby trash can to brace myself over its pungent opening. The cat brushed against my ankles, and another wave of nausea hit me. Spots hovered at my vision's edge.

"Alex, are you feeling okay?" It was Joan. "What are you doing over here?"

"I think I ate my ice cream too fast," I lied. "I don't feel good."

"She looks like she's going to pass out," Joan said.

I recognized Ben's touch as he took a hold of me.

"Go away!" Joan swatted at the cat, causing the creature to flatten its ears and hiss. "Find someone else to play with."

The cat growled. I turned in Ben's arms and watched the animal from around his shoulder. It slunk away toward the old man but stopped every few feet to turn and hiss vehemently at Joan. The man sat silent again, a pleasant smile on his face, staring into the distance.

Ben guided me away from the pair. He scanned my face and signed to me. I knew this one. "Are you okay?"

I nodded, my hand on my stomach. The nausea faded the farther I was separated from the man and his cat. "That guy saw Isaac and the person who killed him at the river," I said.

Ben helped me to sit on a bench. He pulled out the small notepad he always carried in his back pocket. He scribbled a word and turned the paper toward me. *Description?*

"Yeah. It sounded like the big guy who was with Stone," I said. "The description is too similar to be a coincidence. The guy must've killed Isaac and dumped him. The old man said another person was at the river, too. He talked about a 'Wordweaver.' Do you know what that is?"

Ben nodded and sat down beside me. He wrote on the paper again. *Slang for wizard.*

Crossing my arms over my knees, I leaned forward to close my eyes and rest my forehead on my arms. The nausea had passed, but the spots hadn't cleared.

There were footsteps. Joan's voice asked. "Doesn't she know to stay clear of the fae?"

Ben's body shifted.

"You're kidding me." Joan crouched beside the bench and placed a hand on my back. "Haven't you ever met fae kind before?"

"No." I'd of course *heard* of them. Vampires and now this. Apparently it was my season to meet the extended family.

"Did they steal anything important from you?" she asked.

"No. I gave them some money."

Her hand rubbed over my back, a gesture of comfort. "The remaining fae are extremely old and clever. They have potent glamour magic and a wicked streak of mischief. It could've happened to anyone."

I sat up, my vision finally clearing.

Joan smiled at me. "Feeling better?"

I barely heard what she said. My attention rested on the gold, ornate cross hanging from the thin chain around her neck. It was almost an exact duplicate of Isaac's Shield.

12

MY FINGERS ENTWINED with Ben's, I remained silent as the three of us walked back to the apartment. I had questions for Joan about Isaac but didn't want her bolting when I asked why she was there the night of his murder. Having Ben with us further complicated the situation. Since he had to run to the Sound Refuge after we returned, I decided to pin her down then. After saying goodbye to us, Ben left for the concert venue to rent equipment for the upcoming memorial show at Hell's Bells.

Joan smiled. "Ben says you're a busy person, so thank you for spending time with us."

"You're welcome," I said. "Full disclosure: I'll do almost anything for ice cream."

She laughed. "Understood."

"Can you stick around a bit longer to talk?" I asked.

"Sure." Her smile wavered. "Did I say something offensive?"

"No, you didn't." Not today anyway. We sat down in the chairs on the landing. "I noticed your necklace. It's pretty."

"Oh, thank you." Her fingers closed around the cross. "I've had it since I was a little girl. We receive one at St. Anthony's for our First Communion. My family went to church there when we still lived here."

"It reminds me of someone I knew. He wore the same cross as his Shield." I fixed Joan with a critical stare. "His name was Isaac Laska. Maybe you knew him, too?"

All airs of pleasantries vanished. Her smile gone, Joan returned my stare. "Please don't waste time with implications. If you have something to say to me, say it."

"Were you there when Isaac was murdered?"

Lips pressed together, she paused. Her gaze was unflinching "I was late to meet with Isaac that night. We were . . . reconnecting. When I arrived, another man was there. Isaac was already dead."

Reconnecting? Were they friends or more? Did Julia know about their meeting? "But you were at the river," I said.

"Yes." She frowned. "I followed the killer to the river where he dumped Isaac's body. I should've continued following the man to identify him, but I was too upset over Isaac. So, I went down to the riverside instead."

"What did the killer look like?"

"I don't see as well as you in the dark, and I didn't want to be noticed by that man," she said. "Whoever he was, he was large and he'd overpowered a werewolf."

"Why wouldn't you use your veil spell to get closer?"

"I was upset. I'd lost a friend." Her cheeks colored. "I couldn't concentrate on casting."

"I talked with Aiden Clark and Trish Drake earlier today," I said. "Aiden said the guy descends from a line of Hunters."

"Father Aiden knows the man?" she asked.

"Aiden said the guy was hired as Joe Stone's campaign muscle and, because of his hunting lineage, made Aiden aware he was staying in Hopewell."

Joan shook her head. "That isn't going to sit well with the lupine when they find out."

"No shit." I frowned. "Why haven't you spoken to Trish about Isaac?" I touched my hand to my chest. "Or to me, for that matter? You must know through Reginald that the Committee is investigating Isaac's murder."

Joan frowned as well. "I suspect other Committee members, not only Joe Stone, played a part in Isaac's death. Patricia is too close to the Committee. I don't want them finding out through her that I'm looking for the killer."

"Trish wouldn't expose you to them," I said. "She's given Aiden twenty-four hours to meet with Stone and send the Hunter packing. Otherwise, she'll be asking the Hunter to leave."

"I don't understand why you waste time with the Committee." Joan looked me up and down. "Don't you care what they did to my brother?"

"Of course I do," I growled. "But Trish believes we can change the Committee from within." I had doubts about the approach, but I didn't let Joan know that. It seemed for every step of progress Trish made with the Committee, she'd been sent back two.

Joan gave a sharp laugh. "Do you know how long Granddad has been working on accomplishing that? And he's a wizard! The Commoners here are too scared of us. They see us as a threat to their way of life."

She sounded like Nate. "But we were able to unseat William Jansen for his support of the Noble Sons hate group," I said. "That wouldn't have happened without Trish's Committee ties."

"Agreed. But the remaining Commoner representatives nominated Joe Stone to take Jansen's place." She smirked. "Do you know who's dumping truckloads of money into Stone's campaign?"

"I know Susan Arztin held a fundraiser for him."

"Yes, Susan Arztin, the leading donor at Robertson Street Church, home of Reverend William Jansen. I believe you know her daughter."

I immediately felt defensive. "Leave Em out of this. She isn't anything like her mother."

"My point is that working within the Hopewell Committee is like beating your head against a wall. People like Susan Arztin have too many resources. You aren't going to make any lasting change." The pity in Joan's eyes irritated me. "We have to make so much noise here it'll startle the Committee and be heard all the way down at the Delegation."

"Trish and I are focusing on Isaac right now," I said. "If you have information to add about his killer, you should share it. If you think the Committee is responsible for Isaac's death, I agree that should be explored, but right now we don't have the luxury of time. The Hunter should be detained and charged soon before he kills someone else."

"Are you working outside the Committee on the investigation?"

"I'm working with Trish for the benefit of the wolves."

She lowered her voice, and the spark I noticed from before returned to her eyes. "The two of us could handle this." Joan gestured between us. "You and me . . . no Committee rules and procedures to slow us down. We wouldn't need to report to anyone. We'll turn the killer over in half the time."

I chewed at my thumbnail and studied Joan. The offer was tempting. I'd already experienced the frustratingly slow movement of the Committee, even on urgent matters like this. The faster Isaac's killer was detained, the sooner the wolves would be safe.

"Someone is working on locating where he's staying," I said. "They'll tell me when they find him."

"How long will that take?"

"Hopefully I'll know soon," I said. "I could message you when I go to meet the informant."

"Yes. Please do so." She extended her hand to me.

I glanced down at her hand, still unsure. Instead of accepting the handshake, I handed my phone to her. "I'll need your number."

She smiled and took the phone from me. A pang of guilt twitched in my chest as I watched Joan type in her information. Trish and Nate had made every effort to include me in their pack. They'd shared so much of themselves with me. Now I was entertaining the idea of joining forces with a wizard and going after the Hunter without them.

And why was Joan *really* interested in finding the Hunter? Was it because he'd taken a friend of hers? Was it her dislike of the Committee and what they did to Ben?

I reasoned that the choices I made about the investigation were to benefit the wolf community. But a part of me wanted to prove to myself that I deserved Trish's and Nate's confidence . . . and to show Joan I was more than the primal beast trapped inside me.

SINCE OUR CONFRONTATION with the Hunter at Stone's event, it was a challenge to get from one location to another without Ben wanting to know who was accompanying me. When I got ready to meet Trish and Nate that evening, he offered to give me a ride. We suited up in our helmets and left on the motorcycle.

Trish texted me the name of a large county park on the west side of the river about ten minutes outside of the city. I peeked around Ben's shoulder as he drove, my enhanced vision allowing me to see despite the quickly fading light. The warm air felt pleasant blowing against my face, and a whole slew of scents raced past us as the distance between houses grew larger.

Eventually we reached the park's closed gate. The padlock hung from the gate's latch, already open. Ben slowed the motorcycle, guided it around the gate's edge, and back onto the paved drive.

Farther into the park, Trish and Nate reclined atop the hood of Nate's old sedan. Both sat up as Ben pulled the motorcycle beside the car and cut the engine. The rumbling of its motor was replaced by a symphony of frogs from the surrounding wetland and prairie. The odors of exhaust and restaurants were replaced by wildflowers and damp soil.

Ben held the bike steady as I used his shoulders to brace myself and get off without falling on my face. With my friends present, there had been a fifty-fifty chance of it happening.

I lowered my voice to speak to Ben. "Thanks for the ride. If you want to wait at your place, I'll call when we're finished. Nate and I can get rough. I don't want you caught in the crossfire."

Ben smiled and shook his head.

Nate gave a low whistle and slid off the car's hood. "Where were you keeping the bike, wizard?" He drew closer to examine the motorcycle.

I answered. "The owner of Rear Window Records lets him store it in the shop during the winter." After my two failed attempts, Ben helped me find the helmet strap. I took off the helmet and stowed my earplugs in my back pocket.

Nate nodded as he admired the bike. "Trish, love, I think we need one of these."

Trish smiled. "I don't think we do."

Ben set our helmets on the motorcycle's seat and joined Trish on the front edge of the car hood to wait. Hopefully he would stay put and not feel the need to intervene.

I looked above us at the open expanse of sky. "The light pollution isn't as bad here. I actually see stars." Traces of clouds drifted through the inky sky. A patch opened between them, and the moon was unveiled. A long swath of pale light fell across us and the park's large prairie.

I turned my face up to the light, lowering my eyelids and enjoying the feeling of it washing over me. Despite pop culture lore, a full moon doesn't cause werewolves to shift against their will into uncontrollable, snarling monsters. It acted more as a shot of adrenaline or amplification of our gifts.

The moonlight sent a wonderful, tingling sensation racing across my skin. The creature inside me uncurled from her resting place and stretched. My body filled with warmth, and my pulse strengthened. A swat on my arm disrupted me from my basking.

Nate's eyes glowed a warm copper, and he flashed his toothy grin. "So, let's see what you can do where we have some space." He backed away, and I followed him into the tall grasses and flowers of the field.

Nate halted his retreat, causing me to stop as well. I felt foolish and self-conscious with an audience. "I'm not sure I can do this. It feels weird having people watch me," I said.

Nate didn't reply. The goofy grin faded, and his glowing eyes locked onto me. His body steadily lowered, and he crept forward. Apparently, my comfort level was not an important factor.

"Alex, you won't always be able to choose the location and bystanders," Trish called.

I turned. "I know, but—"

I realized my mistake too late.

The plants barely whispered their movement before Nate's mass struck me and I went down. He was off me just as quick. Already a safe distance away, he chuckled.

I rolled to my side and gasped for air. Grimacing, I climbed back to my feet. "How in the hell are you moving so fast? That guy at the club did the same thing." I kept him in my line of sight as he circled me.

"I've seen you jump. What gives you so much lift?" he asked. He feigned a lunge forward, and I stepped back. A growl sprung up into my throat, and the hair immediately stood at attention on the nape of my neck. Okay, so maybe control was a *bit* more slippery in the moonlight. I tightened my focus, and my wolf twisted painfully.

Just like shifting, when I tried any feat of strength or endurance, I directed the primal force inside me to fuel the act. Nate feigned another move forward, and I growled again, trying to keep an eye on him while figuring myself out. I gradually loosened my hold on the energy inside me. Cartilage snapped and popped. My fingers elongated, and I flexed my claws. Sweat beaded on my forehead.

He faked twice more before he leapt at me. At least he didn't take me by surprise. His claws sank into my shoulders, and we crashed to the ground yet again.

I winced at the pain sent through my shoulders and back. My teeth clenched in effort, even as they shifted shape. Unlike before, I stopped Nate's retreat by hooking my claws into the flesh of his biceps. I pitched my weight and rolled over on top of him. I grinned, pleased with myself for pinning him.

My victory was short-lived as he launched me forward over his head. He twisted his body, leapt forward, and pinned me down onto my stomach. "C'mon, quit screwing around," he growled. "This Hunter isn't going to wait for you to be ready."

"I'm trying!" I wanted to learn, not to be humiliated.

"No, you're not! You're supposed to be fighting me, not her." Nate cuffed me on the back of the head and leapt to his feet. "Get up." He was out of reach when I stood again.

I trembled with frustration. My inner wolf strained to be let loose and defend me. If I eased my control further, I wasn't sure I could maintain it. I gave a worried glance at Trish and Ben waiting on the sedan's hood. I didn't want Ben getting injured. It would kill me if he regarded me as something to fear.

When I looked at Nate, he'd noticed. A slow, menacing grin curled the corners of his mouth. My stomach dropped, and my heart lurched.

Nate tore off toward the car in a burst of speed.

I let go.

My limbs flooded with strength. I raced to intercept him. Ben hopped down and scurried back from the hood. I collided with Nate. We crashed into the car's side. The vehicle rocked and groaned on its worn shocks.

Nate snarled, flashing sharp teeth. He slashed at my face.

I blocked and channeled all my frustration into a single, well-aimed punch. Nate's collarbone crunched. His sharp yelp diffused my anger. My inner wolf flinched back. "Shit! Nate, are you okay?"

Nate staggered away from me, swearing like a sailor and clasping his collarbone.

There was light applause. "Well done." Trish smiled from her side of the car hood. "Could you feel the difference?"

"I sure as hell could," Nate growled.

I grinned at them, elated. For that brief moment, she and I moved in sync within our shared body. "It's so slight." My chest rose and fell from the exertion. "It felt incredible."

Trish nodded. "It's a fine balance. Don't muzzle her. Give yourself permission to feel that anger. It doesn't have to dictate your actions, but let it be your fuel."

Ben walked back to stand by Trish, the car's body separating him from me. My grin faltered when he offered me an unsure smile. Having two snarling werewolves dash at him with inhuman speed was probably unnerving. And he hadn't seen this side of me often. How had I appeared to him? Like a monster?

Nate stretched his neck from side to side and popped his knuckles. "Ready to try again?"

BY THE TIME we were finished, I was tired and ready for a shower. Trish and Nate had already left when I climbed on the bike behind Ben. I clasped my hands together at the front of his waist and rested the side of my helmet against his back. We glided along the road back toward the heart of the city and the apartment.

A shrill siren rose above the sound of the motorcycle. Ben slowed the bike and stopped along the shoulder as a firetruck screamed past us. I watched it cross the bridge ahead of us and turn toward downtown. Sirens were a common occurrence in cities, but I frowned when three police cars from a neighboring town to the west zoomed past us, following the firetruck.

Across the river, several patches of black smoke rose above the skyline. A fire and extra law enforcement called in? What was happening? I tapped Ben's shoulder and leaned forward to shout near his ear. "Can you follow those police cars?"

He turned his upper body to look back at me. His frown clearly communicated his opinion of my request.

"There's smoke over there!" Didn't he see it? I pointed toward the dark plumes.

I felt his sigh. He shook his head, glanced back briefly for traffic, and merged onto the road again. We turned toward downtown and passed Rear Window Records and his apartment. The only event I knew of planned for tonight was Joan's protest. Did something go wrong? I grew more anxious the closer we got to the middle of downtown.

Ben pulled the bike over again as another group of police cars, this time from the east, zipped past us. The traffic grew congested along the city's main street running east and west. We slowed and came to a stop. Ben lowered his shoes to the pavement to brace the bike upright as we waited.

A dense group of emergency lights flashed beyond the snarl of traffic. Curious drivers leaned out their car windows to see the cause of the wait. I couldn't stand sitting still. I got off the motorcycle, and Ben caught my arm. He frowned and shook his head.

"New plan," I shouted above the honking horns and sirens. "I'm going on foot." I was able to get the helmet off and pushed it toward him. When he released my arm to accept the helmet, I gave him a brief kiss and stepped back out of his reach. "I want to get a closer look. I'll meet you back at the apartment." Before he could object, I turned and jogged toward the chaos and Union Street Church.

13

THE SCENE UNFOLDING ahead of me was one I didn't expect in a sleepy city like Hopewell. The traffic was at a standstill because of police barricades erected several blocks from the church. I immediately thought of Anne. Was she caught up in this?

As I drew closer, collisions of noise, scent, and movement assaulted me from all directions. The smell of burning garbage and scorched metal stung my nose. Everything was loud despite my earplugs. Confused, I pressed back against a wall to regain my bearings. Between whoops and shrieks of sirens were shouts and screams.

Red and blue lights from squad cars danced on the buildings' walls around Union Street Church. The stench of burning metal was an abandoned cruiser, ablaze and blocking the street. Crowds of people were thicker here with the scent of fear heavy in the air. I wove among them, detecting some to be wolves. It wasn't only their scent. I noticed their eyes.

I broke out into a cold sweat. Rule number one: Don't reveal yourself to the Commoners. Why would they be so careless? What the *hell* was going on? My need to find Anne doubled.

Officers in riot gear had created a protective line across the church's front entrance. With all the ambient noise, I couldn't decipher the shouts being hurled between swarming citizens and clustered law enforcement. What had happened to the plans of a peaceful protest?

The screeching sound of twisting metal came from beside me. A large garbage can was lobbed past as a projectile. I ducked away as the shop window behind me shattered. The person who threw the garbage can pushed past. Another werewolf.

The window's destruction was like a spark.

The rioters erupted. Bodies surged toward the neighboring businesses and the church. I tried to dash across the street, hoping Anne wasn't part of the police line. With angry werewolves around, I didn't want her opposite a riot shield from one.

An object flew into the crowd, struck the pavement, and rolled as it spewed smoke. People scattered. I started to cough and my vision blurred.

Tear gas.

I nearly tripped over a young woman who fell during the crowd's hasty retreat. She heaved and coughed on her hands and knees. I seized her under the arm and hauled her to her feet. She'd be trampled otherwise. We made it across the street, but I almost wiped out as we stumbled up over the curb onto the sidewalk.

Unfortunately, our escape from the tear gas brought us within reach of the living barricade in front of the church. The odors of fear and anger were so thick, I could have waded through them. My tear-filled eyes made it difficult to see the officers. One shouted at us. "Step back!"

A second canister deployed. We were pressed closer toward the officer by another wave of bodies evading the gas. The woman's arm slipped from my hold. I was separated from her. Completely disoriented, I pawed frantically at my eyes to clear my vision. The officer I nearly fell into jabbed his metal baton into my gut.

I doubled over. Anger rose sharply inside me. Suppressing frustrated growls, I pushed away from the line of officers. With one hand over my head to protect it, I retreated up the sidewalk and scanned the blurred faces for Anne.

Another baton struck the back of my thigh, and another my shoulder bone. I was trapped between the officers and the rioters.

Clenching my teeth, I struggled to control the beast twisting inside my chest. She was done being attacked. It was time to terminate the threat.

The next baton that swung at me I caught. Once again I smelled another werewolf. I glared up from the baton to see Jakob. Thin rings of gold shone in his brown eyes.

"What are you doing here?" he shouted.

I released the baton. "Trying to find Anne!" There was a bang and a flash of light. We were nearly knocked off balance as a wave of people crashed into us. I cursed, my blurred vision now riddled with spots.

Jakob seized my arm and pulled me through the narrow space between his body and the next officer. He replanted his feet. His wide stance made him essentially a wall. "She's inside!" His gaze fixed back on the rioters. "Now leave before you get arrested!"

Not before I spoke to Anne. I needed to know she was okay. I turned and surveyed the church facade for the first time since arriving. There were scorch marks on the stone, and only shards of glass remained in the window frames. Sparkling fragments of shattered glass lay strewn along the sidewalk. They crunched under my shoes as I rushed into the entrance hall.

Voices echoed off the stone walls of the enclosed space, adding to the confusion of activity in the hall. A handful of paramedics tended to a small group of people either sitting or standing along the walls. Anne stood near one of the doors to the sanctuary, speaking on her phone. The hair around her face was damp with sweat, and dried blood was crusted around her nostrils.

I waited until she ended the call before I approached her. When she saw me, her eyes widened. "What are you doing here, Alex?" She shook her head. "And they've brought out the tear gas. Come with me." Limping, Anne ushered me over to one of the paramedics. She handed me a bottle of water. "Here, for your eyes."

"Thanks." I attempted to flush the irritant from my eyes. I blinked rapidly as the stinging momentarily increased.

"You weren't part of this, were you?" She'd already filed me with the offending party. That's how low her confidence in me had fallen. It hurt.

"No," I said. "Ben and I were out for a ride. I saw the smoke."

"Are you fucking kidding me?" Anne looked around the large hallway with a scowl. "Ben is here, too? We don't need any more people down here!"

"No. I left him in traffic with the bike. There's a huge traffic backup before the barricades, so I told him I'd see him at the apartment." I glanced back over my shoulder at the maelstrom beyond the front doors. "What the hell happened?"

Anne shook her head. "Jakob and I were sent over because of complaints by neighbors in the loft condos across the street. There was a protest being held here. The size of the crowd and the noise they were making was growing. No one was doing anything illegal."

I looked quickly back at her. "Are the protestors the same people outside now?"

"I don't know. It seemed like a standard peaceful protest. As it got dark, there was a disagreement between Jakob and one of the protestors. He asked everyone to go home. It quickly escalated." She took off her hat to push the hair sticking to her forehead away from her face. "I think a lot of the protestors were caught off guard. I helped extract a lot of them from the crowd so they could either leave or shelter here. The angrier ones are outside. I'm stuck in here babysitting since I twisted my knee."

Did Joan's veil spell not work? "Do you know why they're here?" I asked.

Her green eyes fixed on me. They turned glassy. "It seemed like a standard peaceful protest." Her eyes refocused. "Did the water help?"

I studied Anne and nodded. Was her odd reaction my imagination? I hesitated before I asked again, "Anne, do you know why the protestors are here?"

The same dream-like look clouded her eyes. "It seemed like a standard peaceful protest," she repeated. "Be sure to shower and throw your clothes in the wash when you get back to Ben's place."

"Sure." Something wasn't right. "Is there anything I can do to help?"

"You can leave. The fewer bystanders we have to manage, the better." She gave an annoyed glance around. "I wish *I* could help."

I didn't. I was glad she was pacing around inside rather than in the middle of the mess outside. Yes, I knew her job was inherently dangerous, but it didn't usually involve hostiles with sharp teeth and claws.

My phone buzzed. I'd missed three messages from Ben. He was probably worried. I looked back up at Anne. "I'll be thinking of you. Please be careful."

I tried to hug her, but she held up her hand. "Your clothes." She smiled, her eyes tired. "Go take a shower. I'll be fine." She pointed to the opposite end of the hall. "There's a side entrance you can leave through."

"Right." I reluctantly left her behind.

I slipped out of the church and skirted the crowds to get back to Ben's apartment. It wouldn't take long, so I didn't waste time messaging him.

It wasn't normal behavior for wolves to be so openly aggressive among Commoners, especially their police force. I thought of Stone's private meeting. What had he said? *Convincing won't be necessary when the other members witness the damage the werewolves are capable of.*

Had Stone known about the protest? Or had he banked on anger boiling over in the werewolf community?

I called Trish and Nate but only reached voicemail. I sent a quick message instead. *Trouble downtown at Committee meeting spot involving wolves and the police.* They probably knew what was happening, but I didn't want to leave it up to chance. I'd try to call again later.

I'D BEEN SORE on our ride back from the park, but my body really ached as I crossed the parking lot to the apartment. A hot shower was my first objective. My pace slowed when I scented an unfamiliar smell. Someone sat on one of the two small chairs we kept on the landing. When I ascended the stairs, she looked up from typing on her phone.

"Hello?" She greeted me in an unsure voice.

"Who are you?" Many wolves' and wizards' residences had been simultaneously raided the past winter. Since then, I preferred Ben's doorstep clear of strangers.

"I'm a friend of Joan's." She extended her hand, but I was distracted by the sound of a raised voice from inside the apartment.

Frowning, I opened the door and walked straight into an ongoing argument. My nose picked up traces of smoke, blood, and another wolf. Joan stood at the kitchenette sink, cleaning a wound on a young woman's upper arm.

"What do you want me to do?" Joan scowled across the apartment. "Take them to Granddad's?" She dropped a bloodied kitchen towel on the counter and snatched up some clean bandaging. "Great idea! 'Hey Granddad, we were actively promoting an overhaul of the governing body you serve, and we got a bit banged up. Mind if we crash here for a bit?'"

Ben was a storm of angry facial expressions and gestures as he argued with his sister. When he saw me, he hurried across the apartment. He did not look pleased.

I stopped him as Anne had me. "They had tear gas, and I don't want any of it getting on you. I need a shower and fresh clothes."

"Get in line," Joan said. She secured the bandage and tossed the extra medical tape aside.

The bathroom door opened, and a man around Joan's age emerged drying his hair with a towel. "Next."

The additional werewolf. I didn't recognized him.

There was a slight quiver of his nostrils. He looked warily from me to Joan. "Who's this?"

I snorted, growing more irritated by the moment. "Who the hell are all these people, Joan? And why are they here?"

Joan's next scowl was aimed at me. "I'm sorry, is this now your apartment, too?"

Her words caused a flare of anger in my gut, not because of the assumption this couldn't be my place as well, but because she'd brought random people to Ben's home. Why would she endanger him for the sake of one of her protests?

I failed to hold back a snarl. The unknown werewolf immediately growled low at me and slunk up beside Joan.

The hair rose on the nape of my neck. I shouted at Joan. "Why are you here instead of down there cleaning up the shit you started?"

"What am I supposed to do, Alex?" Joan wiggled her fingers at me. "Hocus Pocus it better? It doesn't work that way! I can't wipe away all the damage the Committee has done with a wave of my magic wand."

Ben's hand settled on my upper arm.

I turned on him, snarling. "What?"

His eyebrows angled downward, and he stepped back. Frowning, he signaled between him and me before he stabbed his finger toward the door. He placed his hand flat over the center of his chest before moving it in a clockwise circular motion. *Please.*

I turned on my heel, stormed from the apartment, and paced at the bottom of the stairs. Ben closed the door behind us and followed me.

"What does she think she's doing? Does she realize what kind of trouble she and anyone else she was with could get into?" The Committee forbade supernatural beings to reveal our gifts to Commoners. I was pretty sure that included using our gifts to trash the city. "And to bring that to your home!"

Ben frowned up at the landing and back at me. He signed a quick abrupt response.

I threw up my hands. "I don't know what you're saying!"

He motioned for me to follow him alongside the building and farther away from the woman seated outside the apartment. Despite my effort to pull my arm out of his reach, he caught my elbow. I bared my teeth at him, growling, but he coached me closer. His voice was an angry whisper. "Where the hell have you been? I messaged you three times!"

"I know," I said. "I was trying to find Anne, and then I was on my way back."

"You can't run off into whatever that was and not expect me to be scared out of my fucking mind! Did you not think of that?" He shook his head. "Joan showed up at the apartment, all banged up, and told me what was happening down there. I didn't know where you were or if you were hurt or if you needed help—"

The beast inside me balked. Why should I have to check in? I didn't need his permission. But that wasn't what this was about. I searched Ben's face and could see the worry behind the anger. From between clenched teeth, I managed, "I'm sorry."

"Next time, at least let me know you're okay," he said. "Please."

He understood there would be a next time. Ben wasn't the kind of guy who needed to control his partner, but he constantly worried about my safety. This was a compromise I'd have to make if I wanted to stay with him. I dropped my gaze and nodded. "Yeah, all right."

Ben exhaled. His body relaxed a bit. "Thank you." He released my elbow. "About Joan . . . she's been organizing protests like this for years. She misjudged the amount of pent-up frustration over the Committee's use of tethering. I guess the police were called on the protesters, and everything quickly got out of hand. There were a lot more lupine than she expected."

My gaze snapped up to meet his. "The lupine, huh? They were the cause of the problems."

"No, I meant—"

"A bunch of wolves decided to go apeshit in the middle of downtown because 'why the hell not?'"

"What I mean is . . ." He fumbled for words. "They can be more unpredictable."

I flinched. "Unpredictable? Ben, most wolves die after being tethered! They're either executed for another offense or end it themselves because they can't handle the tether's feedback. Many kids don't believe they'll make it to middle age." Why was it so hard for the wizards to grasp? I motioned toward downtown. "We aren't going to risk our lives to screw around and bust some windows!"

He glanced back at the apartment. "Alex, please—"

"Isaac was loved by a lot of people," I said. "He was *murdered*. It shouldn't be such a struggle to get the Committee's help! But what's one less wolf to them, anyway, right?"

"I'm sorry," Ben said. "It was a poor choice of words."

"What's 'unpredictable' about getting angry when the only paths allowed to you set you up to fail?"

Ben knew the challenges of living with a tether, but he was still a wizard. And a wizard's tether didn't destroy their mind. He held his hand out to me. "I'm sorry about Isaac, and I'm sorry you're all hurting."

The constant stress and anxiety among the werewolves had affected me more than I realized. With a low growl, I stepped back, overwhelmed by conflicting thoughts and doubts. Why didn't the wizards care about what was happening? Were they going to blame the wolves for the riot just as Stone predicted?

"Maybe I should have been at the protest with Joan," I said. "Maybe she's right. The only way for change to happen is through threats to the Committee." If I was going to be cast as an uncontrollable monster either way, why not make it count?

Ben lowered his hand. "I'm glad you didn't go with her."

The beast inside my chest halted her pacing and watched him through my eyes. I wrapped my arms around myself. "I'm not staying here tonight. Will you go with me to Em's place?" I looked past him toward the apartment. "Joan can do what she needs to do here, and neither of us will be caught up in it."

"I'm staying," Ben said.

I looked back at him and my chest tightened. "What? Why?"

He avoided my gaze. "She's my sister. She screwed up, but maybe there's some way I can help."

Someone he cared about was in trouble, and he wanted to help. To have my own reasoning thrown back at me made me want to scream. "I understand, but I'm not happy about it."

His smile was weak. "Believe me, I know the feeling."

Joan, on the other hand, wasn't on board. Ben and I returned to the apartment so I could grab a change of clothes before leaving for Emma's house. Joan spoke to me, completely bypassing her brother though he stood right beside us. "Can you take him with you?"

Ben readied to launch into another tirade of expressions and hand gestures. Joan snapped at him. "Don't be an idiot about this. You're tethered. I know I messed up coming here. I'm sorry. We'll be gone by morning. You can help me by going with her."

When Ben left in a huff to retrieve the helmets, Joan offered me her hand. "I'm sorry I behaved so poorly earlier. I know you're looking out for him, and I appreciate it. Tonight has been hell. I miscalculated the tension between the lupine and the Committee."

Her apology wasn't going to change the fact that fallout from the riot would be worse for the wolves than the wizards. Was that even considered when she planned the protest? I looked at her outstretched hand and back at her. For Ben's sake, I shook her hand. "I'm glad you and your friends are okay."

Her handshake was firm, and I shivered from a draw on the energy around us. With her eyes looking into mine, Joan's voice spoke inside my head. *We need to find the Hunter as soon as possible. We'll talk tomorrow.*

Startled, I yanked my hand away. My heart hammered in my chest and sweat beaded on my forehead. The beast inside me leapt toward the surface. I narrowed my eyes, and my lips pulled back from fangs. "Don't *ever* do that to me again."

It was not okay for anyone to step uninvited into my mind.

Joan swallowed. "I'm sorry." The sharp scent of her fear tainted the air. The other werewolf stood, eyeing me.

I thought of Anne's odd behavior at the church. "Did you mess around in Anne Reid's head tonight, too? She's a Hopewell police officer. Red hair."

Joan frowned. "She saw things she shouldn't have. I only removed what endangered her and us."

"What makes you think that's okay?" No one should have their mind unknowingly or unwillingly altered.

"If I didn't, the Committee would have ordered Granddad to do it," she said. "I was careful, I promise."

Ben rejoined Joan and me, helmets in hand. He looked between us, no doubt noticing something had raised my hackles. He passed me the helmets so he could sign a question. "Are you okay?"

Joan answered. "We're fine."

Were we? I didn't know about her, but I struggled to reign in the fangs.

"Just a small disagreement." She hugged Ben. "I love you, little brother. I'll let you know when we're gone."

I handed Ben his helmet, and we left the apartment for the motorcycle parked in the lot.

14

I called twice before Emma answered the phone. Her voice was thick with sleep. "Hello?"

"Hey Em, could I stay at your place tonight?" I asked.

Bed covers rustled over the phone line. "Alex, it's one in the morning. Where are you?"

I glanced at Ben and then looked back at her house. "Outside your front door."

Her exhaled breath blew across the phone receiver. "Hold on." The phone clicked, and the front door lock buzzed as it was temporarily overridden. I pushed open the ornately carved wooden door, and Ben followed me inside.

Compared to others in the neighborhood, Emma's house was modest. However, she lived in a wealthier area than us. Her overbearing parents had insisted on buying her a house for a college graduation gift. The compromise the three had reached lay in the details. The two-story home had five bedrooms instead of seven, a two-stall garage instead of four, and a maid that visited once a week instead of a full-time maid and cook.

Ben and I entered the high-ceilinged living room. I'd been there many times before, but it was his first visit. He took in the designer furniture and draperies. I murmured to him. "Wait until you feel the bedsheets."

I caught the scent of vanilla, followed shortly by the sound of Emma's footsteps. She called ahead, "What on earth are you doing coming over at this time? Did you get into another fight?" She entered the room, bleary-eyed, in a light robe over her thin-strapped, satin sheath of a nightgown. Her blonde and pink hair fell in soft waves past her round face.

Emma stopped, surprised to see another person. She pulled her robe around herself, clasping its front closed with her hand. "Oh, hi Ben! Welcome back. I'm sorry I didn't get a chance to chat with you at the party before Alex had you thrown out."

I cringed. Ben averted his eyes and raised his hand in greeting.

She looked between us. "Is everything okay?"

"There's some trouble downtown. We wanted a quiet place to sleep."

Her eyes widened and her fingers tightened on her robe. "What's happening? No one has called from work."

"It doesn't involve Another Chance in any way." I filled Emma in on what I knew as she led us upstairs to one of the spare bedroom suites.

"That's awful," she said. "I hope Anne is safe."

"I hope so, too. She seemed to be when I tracked her down. It's hard not to message her and check in," I said. "I'm sure the last thing she needs right now is me bothering her."

"Did you contact Trish and Nate yet?"

Shit. With the surprise of finding Joan at the apartment, I'd forgotten to call again. "I couldn't get them on the phone, but I sent a message. Not much goes on with the wolves without their knowing. I'll try calling again later today. Right now I want a shower and sleep."

"See you later this morning then. Sleep well."

Emma left down the hall. I immediately began shedding clothes on my way to the bedroom's private bathroom. A soak in the bathtub sounded amazing, but I didn't trust myself not to fall asleep. When I emerged from the steam-filled room, wrapped in a huge fuzzy towel, Ben was on the bed among the dozens of decorative pillows.

He'd kicked off his shoes, rested his back against the headboard, and sat with his knees drawn to his chest while listening to music on his headphones. His brow was creased, and he seemed miles away in thought. With his dark hair and clothing, he looked ridiculously out of place on the stark white bedding, like a scrawny stray cat dumped into the lap of luxury.

I dropped onto my stomach atop the deeply cushioned mattress and grinned as, startled out of his thoughts, Ben looked quickly over at me. His gaze softened, his brow smoothed, and he returned a smile. He pulled off his headphones.

"I'm surprised you haven't passed out by simply coming into contact with this bed," I said. "We should ask Em if we could vacation here sometime for a long weekend."

He reached over and pushed up the bottom edge of my towel. His smile faded. "Is this from tonight?" He'd noticed the bright new bruise on the back of my thigh.

"The police," I said. "I'll be okay. It'll be gone in a few days."

Ben took my hand in his and ran his thumb over the back of my fingers.

"You seemed pretty deep in thought. Are you worried about Joan?" I asked.

"Yeah," he said. "I hope whatever happened tonight gets sorted, and she isn't blamed for the damage. She got everyone together but didn't intend for it to turn violent."

My immediate thought was that Joan had nothing to worry about. She may have organized the protest, but the wolves would be accused of starting the riot.

Instead of voicing my thoughts aloud, I encouraged Ben to keep talking. "You two seem close."

"Yeah, I guess we are. When we were growing up anyway." He shrugged. "She doesn't have much time to visit anymore. Not like after she first moved. She has more important things to do, I guess."

"Has she always been so . . ." I selected my words carefully, not wanting to offend him. ". . . politically active?"

"Yeah." He smiled and looked up at me. "Some of my earliest memories of Joan are her arguing with our parents. She constantly questioned the rules. As we got older, she wanted explanations for the Committee guidelines." His shoulders lifted again. "A lot of the rules didn't make sense; they still don't. Joan spoke up when everyone else was too scared. And she didn't only talk about problems but also tried to solve them."

I arched an eyebrow. "Who're you and what've you done with Ben?"

He smiled. "What do you mean?"

"Since I met you, you've wanted no part of other people's problems," I said. "I'm surprised you admire Joan's efforts."

"Staying out of other people's business is how I've made it this far with a tether. But Joan—" He shook his head. "She's willing to make these sacrifices, except the loss isn't always her own." His smile flickered and was gone again. "At one point, a new Commoner rep whipped up fear among the other Committee representatives. They declared a curfew for the wizards and lupine. We all thought it was bullshit, so Joan organized a protest."

"Did you go to it?"

"I had a habit of finding trouble back then. Joan was in charge of keeping track of me, so yeah, I was with her." Ben paused and shifted uncomfortably. "There were over fifty of us gathered outside Union Street Church. Some officers rolled up in their cruiser. They demanded to see our permit. When Joan handed it over, the officers bitched at us for blocking the sidewalk and street. A friend of Joan's didn't take that well. Words were exchanged, tempers escalated, and then the batons came out."

The hair on my arms rose as I recalled the confusion and violence I'd experienced between the Hopewell police and the protestors. The past and present sounded so similar.

Ben frowned as he recalled the memory. "Joan threw herself in front of her friend who was being beaten. The officer was already bringing down his baton. My only thought was to stop the guy from splitting open my sister's skull." He swallowed. "The spell was cast before I realized what I'd done. The officer was pinned to a brick wall with his rib cage crushed. He died within minutes."

Music drifted from the headphones resting on the back of his neck as we sat together in silence. I didn't know what to say to comfort him. Everything I thought of seemed wrong. What a terrifying experience for anyone, let alone a sixteen-year-old. More confident with touch, I sat up, slid closer, and wrapped my arms around him. He leaned into my embrace.

I'd never pushed Ben to tell me why he'd been tethered. I'd poked and prodded before, but never pushed. Frustration and anger simmered in me for a frightened young man, barely an adult, who'd acted rashly to protect a loved one. How many of his possible futures had been taken from him as a consequence?

"They didn't consider you were protecting your sister?"

"It didn't matter. The officer was a Commoner and my magic killed him," Ben said. "They tried and convicted me within the week. The Commoner reps also wanted me to serve time in their prison system, but Reginald fought against it. They struck a deal by adding more years to my tether instead."

"Are you glad you chose the extra years over going to prison?"

"I didn't choose anything. I was a kid. Reginald made the choice for me." He was quiet a moment before he added, "I'm not sure what I would've chosen."

"Two years left." I hugged him. "Then you'll be free of it."

"Yeah, two years." He shifted to slip his arm around me.

We lay back on the bed and fell asleep listening to the faint music from his headphones.

I AWOKE TO the delicious aroma of coffee. The sun was up and filtered through the bedroom's curtains. Birdsong drifted in from the backyard, along with the suburban chorus of barking dogs and lawnmowers. Despite the comfortable accommodations, I hadn't slept well. Images of the previous night's violence invaded my dreams. I stretched my body long and it lit up with aches and pains. When I turned over, the space beside me was vacant. I wondered if Ben hadn't slept well either.

After getting dressed, I descended the stairs and followed the sound of Emma's voice to the back patio and pool. She and Ben were seated at a table. A spread of pastries and fruit was set out, along with coffee and juice. My stomach growled in longing. I was starving.

Emma laughed as she conversed with Ben. She was fluent in sign language, the study of which was responsible for their friendship. I stepped outside to join them, and they turned in their seats. Emma's smile brightened. "Good morning! Join us and grab some breakfast."

"Good morning." I bent to kiss Ben on the cheek before I sat at the open place setting between them. "Em, this looks amazing. Thank you for taking us in at a moment's notice." I filled a plate to near overflowing. Ben poured me some coffee.

"You're welcome. Ben was telling me about the tour. It sounds like so much crazy fun. I told him next time to put my name down as a roadie." The EDM artist he had toured with, Derezzed, was one of Emma's favorites.

"I'm not sure you could pull off the scruffy roadie look," I said.

Ben chuckled and shook his head.

Looking at Ben, I asked, "Did your sister check in yet?" I took a hefty bite of croissant.

He nodded and pushed his phone over to me. I read the message from Joan.

We're gone. Left your key downstairs with the store clerk like you asked. Thanks again.

I only made it halfway through my cup of coffee before my phone rang. It was Trish. She rarely called, preferring to text. I set my croissant aside and excused myself to answer the call.

Trish's tone was terse. "Alex, we need you at Union Street Church. Aiden called an impromptu Committee meeting to discuss last night."

My stomach dropped. I didn't know the whole story yet and didn't want to inadvertently get Joan into trouble. "Can you fill me in afterwards? I just woke up." I cringed. I might as well have told her I couldn't come because I was washing my hair.

"This isn't a request," she said. "A Committee member reported seeing you at the riot. You're being summoned."

15

MY STOMACH WAS a mess of nerves, so I couldn't even cram down a few more bites of food. The ride downtown to the church didn't take long. The empty window frames were already secured with sheets of plywood. I got off the bike, not looking forward to whatever awaited me inside.

"I'll see you tonight," I said over the rumbling motorcycle. He had a full workday before the show. I secured the extra helmet to the bike and gave Ben a quick kiss before heading inside.

Raised voices echoed into the main hall outside the sanctuary. I slunk into the enormous room. Trish and Stone were on their feet.

Stone pointed a finger across the table at Trish. "Either your people can't be trusted to handle themselves, or you aren't doing your job!"

"You believe the lupine were responsible for what occurred in your poorly managed city last night?" Trish snarled. "We will not be the scapegoats for your inadequacies."

Ever serving the role of mediator, Aiden spoke. "Enough! Both of you. Carelessly throwing blame around benefits no one."

I frowned. Stone would benefit if he could pin the riots on the werewolves. A reversal of the hunting ban was within reach.

Trish turned on Aiden, her golden eyes ablaze. She pointed past Stone to someone standing behind him. "This is absolutely unacceptable and a blatant disregard of agreements this Committee has forged between the people of Hopewell!"

I stopped at the front pew and my blood chilled. A large man stood stationed behind Stone. Aiden said his name was David Williams, but I could only think of him as the Hunter. His eyes trained on Trish, he watched her every move with a cool calculation that made my skin crawl.

"I'm glad you could be bothered to join us, Miss Steward." Aiden's voice broke into my thoughts.

All eyes at the table turned on me. I wanted more than ever to be back on Emma's patio. "I got here as fast as I could."

Aiden gestured to the seat open beside Trish. Had she requested I be seated with them? As I climbed the stairs, the Hunter's predatory gaze shifted to me. The same uneasiness as before came over me, and my inner wolf bristled. With my pulse thudding in my ears, I slumped down into the chair and stared at the table's surface.

Reginald spoke. "I agree with Ms. Drake. I can't imagine how this wouldn't be viewed by the lupine citizens as a threat."

"Of course you agree with her," Stone said. "You magicians have nothing to worry about. You can abracadabra yourselves and be safe." His thumb jabbed back at his chest, and his voice rose again. "We're the ones who end up being dog food when they decide the rules don't apply to them!"

Trish snarled, and before I could stop it, a low growl rumbled in my chest. I glared across the table at Stone. This guy needed to go.

"Mr. Stone!" Aiden reprimanded sharply. "Show some respect for your fellow Committee members." He looked between Trish and Stone. "And as Committee Chair, I'll ask both of you a final time: please take your seats."

Trish and Stone begrudgingly sat back down.

Reginald's voice was edged. "Mr. Stone, let me remind you that every member of the lupine community is also a citizen of Hopewell. As a commissioner, you are charged with serving your citizens, not frightening them into submission."

"If they aren't breaking the law and destroying private property, they have nothing to worry about!" Stone said.

"It wasn't only the wolves," I said.

Everyone at the table looked at me again.

"Are we really going to listen to more excuses?" Stone smirked and held out his hand to me. "How can we trust anything she says? She was caught trying to sabotage my campaign fundraiser, hosted by a big donor who happens to be a wizard!"

Trish growled, and my face flushed. The fundraiser? Why was he talking about me misbehaving at a wizard's house if he had info about my past? Did Stone not know? Then how did the Hunter?

"Tell them, Reggie," Stone said.

Reginald grimaced and cleared his throat. "Charles Arztin informed me Miss Alex was dismissed from the event because she was *suspected* of foul play."

"Mr. Stone and Mr. Sharpe, if either of you would like to file a formal complaint concerning Miss Steward's behavior, you can do so after this meeting," Aiden said. "We are currently discussing the events of last night's riot."

"Sure thing, Father," Stone said.

"Apologies," Reginald added.

Aiden nodded at me. "Please relay your account of last night's events, Miss Steward, and why you were there."

"I was making sure a friend of mine was safe," I said. "There was so much chaos and confusion. It was hard to tell what was happening, but there weren't only wolves rioting. There were Commoners and wizards, too." I looked at Jakob, seated beside Stone. "Ask him."

"Officer DeBoer already gave his account," Aiden said.

I frowned at Jakob, but he avoided my gaze. He must have been the one to report me. Who else could have? That asshole. Wasn't he supposed to be *our* representative? "It was organized by a wizard!" I blurted.

There was shocked silence. Everyone stared at me as if I'd grown a second head. The guilt hit me like a slug in the stomach, but I'd made my choice.

Reginald's eyes were saucers in his pale face. "Excuse me?"

"The riot started as a protest organized by a wizard," I said. "Why is all the blame being heaped on the lupine?"

"Miss Steward, take care what you say next," Reginald said. "Your reckless accusations and irresponsible behavior will hold severe consequences for others."

Reckless and irresponsible? I narrowed my eyes at Reginald.

"Mr. Sharpe," Trish said, her voice low, "let me advise you to take care how you address one of my people. She is not giving her valuable time to be berated in front of this Committee."

Reginald frowned and leaned back from Trish.

Stone held up his hands. "Listen, people, I hate to be the new guy who upends everything, but until your people are under control," he pointed at Trish and Reginald in turn, "my guy stays." Arms crossed, he rocked back in his chair.

"That is not for you alone to decide," Reginald said.

Aiden nodded. "You are new to this organization, Mr. Stone, so I encourage everyone," he scanned around the table, "to be patient. The Committee's mission is to ensure a peaceful meshing of all citizens, not to irritate differences. Hunting has been outlawed for decades. It targets supernatural citizens for being different, not for being a threat. No peace has ever resulted from the practice, and frankly," Aiden turned his gaze on the Hunter, "it's barbaric."

I blinked. Aiden always toed the line between the Commoner and supernatural reps. Not only was it necessary because he was the Committee Chair, but it seemed ingrained in his nature. This was as close to him taking sides as I'd witnessed.

"So if I keep my guy around, I get kicked out of the club?" Stone looked around the table. His hostile gaze stopped on me, and anger roiled in my stomach. The hair on the nape of my neck rose, and my inner wolf drew forward.

"No." Even Aiden's patience was being tested. "If you are certain that installing a Hunter is necessary, we will put your proposal of lifting the ban to a vote."

"Aiden, you can't be serious!" said Trish. "It will destroy years of progress."

The Hunter's presence loomed large and threatening across the table. He stared into me like we were the only people in the enormous room. My pulse quickened, and it didn't go unnoticed by the beast inside me. Sweat broke out on my forehead. Beneath the table, I flexed my hands as my claws emerged.

Reginald spoke to Aiden. "I also ask for this vote to be reconsidered. No good will come of allowing hunting."

Aiden's expression was grim as he looked around the table. "As I told Mr. Stone, this isn't a choice for one person to make. I'd like each of you to consider what your decision could mean for *all* of our citizens."

My attention darted from the Hunter to Stone. The corners of Stone's mouth twitched into a smile. He was winning, and he knew it. Men like him always seemed to be winning. It was infuriating. He made a grave mistake when he winked at me.

I jumped up onto my seat and launched myself across the table at Stone, claws outstretched. Exclamations of surprise sounded around the table. Chairs tipped and crashed to the ground. Stone's smugness morphed into fear.

That's right, jackass. I'll open you up and show everyone how ugly you are inside.

The Hunter yanked Stone's tipped chair away. The commissioner's body lurched and fell backward. Instead of Stone being at the end of my leap, it was the broad body of the Hunter.

Energy whistled past my ears and collapsed around me. My body seized its descent midair, as if I'd been frozen in a photograph. I couldn't move my limbs, but my chest rose and fell in short pants. My Shield burned as if it had caught fire. Only one person here could wield magic. "Let go, Reginald!" I snarled.

Stone stumbled to his feet while pointing at me. "See! Do you see?" His frantic gaze darted around the table. "How can we trust them not to harm us? They're barely human!"

A low murmur of conversation began. The acidic scent of fear wafted off the Committee members. Aiden stood, causing the room to go silent. "Mr. Sharpe, please show Miss Steward to her seat."

My body floated back toward Trish. The spell ceased, energy dissipated, and I was dropped. Control of my body was returned to me, ensuring I landed on my feet instead of my ass. Trish closed and tightened her fingers over my clawed hand. I glared past her at Reginald. He returned a look of utter disapproval.

"Ms. Drake, please remind your guest of her manners, or she will no longer be allowed to sit at this table." Aiden's voice grew tight. "Mr. Stone, another outburst and you will be suspended."

"Unbelievable," Stone muttered.

"The vote is tomorrow evening," Aiden said. "Adjourned."

A rumble of conversation overtook the silence. Trish's grip on my hand grew painful. She seethed, her golden eyes locked on the Hunter as Stone spoke to the larger man. Jakob stood beside the two, occasionally glancing over at us.

"Trish." I shrunk beneath the weight of her gaze. There was no excuse for my behavior. I'd let Stone manipulate me. "I'm sorry."

She released me. Her tone was neutral. "We'll deal with him."

Did she mean Stone or the Hunter? Movement drew my attention back to the three men. Stone and Jakob walked around the table. The Hunter followed behind them, dwarfing them with his ominous presence. As they descended the stairs behind us, I called. "Jakob, hold on."

"I'll only be a few minutes, Mr. Stone," Jakob said. He waited at the base of the stairs while Stone and the Hunter left the sanctuary.

I joined him. "What did you tell everyone?"

"I was asked to tell them what I witnessed last night. That's what I told them."

"Did you defend us, or do you think it's okay for a Hunter to be here?" I wrestled with keeping my voice at a reasonable volume in the cavernous room.

Jakob's jaw tightened. "I don't like the idea of a Hunter being in Hopewell, but you saw last night how we were struggling to keep everyone safe."

"I did," I said. "I have bruises to show how I was kept safe."

"We were being overwhelmed," he said. "Mr. Stone wants us to have the resources we need to keep order. A Hunter's presence will deter another riot." His brows drew together, and he glanced up at the table. "Why are you on my case after pulling a stunt like that here, of all places? How does that help us?"

I frowned. He was right. My actions hadn't done much for instilling confidence in the wolves. The thought I'd botched the vote for us didn't improve the raging frustration in my gut.

"Jakob, did you ask Stone where he found this guy? Did you forget we have a dead wolf with silver as the murder weapon?"

His confidence wavered. "That's not my department."

"Are you kidding?" I gave a short laugh. "You were asked to check on Isaac's body!"

Jakob hesitated. "I was removed from the task after we got back to the station. Mr. Stone said he would take care of it himself."

"What! Did you ask why?" My voice rose. "You're supposed to be looking out for us!"

"I was following orders," he said.

"Alex." Trish's eyes still glimmered a soft gold. "Let Officer DeBoer return to his day."

I growled, struggling between my respect for Trish and my irritation with Jakob.

"Thank you, Ms. Drake," Jakob said. "I apologize if anything I said makes your work more difficult."

Trish didn't respond. Her gaze rested on Jakob, but her expression was devoid of emotion. He stepped back with his hat held to his chest, gave a brief nod, and exited down the aisle.

With all other Committee members gone, Aiden approached Trish and Reginald. He rested his hand on the back of the chair I'd been sitting in. "Patricia," Aiden spoke in a soft tone. "I'm so sorry."

Trish narrowed her eyes.

"I wish there was more I could do," he said.

Her voice was a low growl. "Go to hell, Aiden."

Aiden's jawline tightened. He withdrew his hand. Reginald quickly stood. "Ah . . . Ms. Drake, would you be interested in a bit of brunch?"

"With a man who'd so easily abandon his ally?" Trish descended the stairs.

Reginald's face flushed and he followed her. "Patricia, I'm sorry. The accusation caught me by surprise. Naturally I would default to defending the wizards."

Trish's reply was a question to me. "Can you join us?"

For a tongue lashing over my attempted disemboweling of a Committee member? It didn't sound like a good time, but I nodded.

Aiden stood alone beside the empty table in the enormous sanctuary as we left.

THE THREE OF us walked out into the sunshine. I was surprised to see Detective Grey waiting, his rumpled suit jacket over his arm. He'd already loosened his tie and rolled up his sleeves. He gave our group a nod. "Could I interest you all in some coffee?"

"We were on our way to share a meal," Reginald said. "Would you like to accompany us?"

"I don't have time to eat, but I'm good for a coffee or two."

Our party chose outdoor seating beneath large umbrellas at a small diner. The delicious aromas of toast, eggs, and bacon caused my stomach to rumble. Everyone but Detective Grey ordered food, and the waitress brought us coffee while we waited. Grey placed Trish between him and me, no doubt because of my earlier behavior.

"I wanted to apologize for the mix up with the ME's report in Isaac's case," Detective Grey began. "It was sloppy work, and I find it embarrassing. Once in a while, my department is pulled into a case involving one of your people. Investigation and secrecy aren't good bedfellows, so there's always a chance things will go off the rails. I'm not making excuses, but letting you know that I can get pushback. Right now, I'm getting pushback."

Reginald refolded his napkin in his lap. "While we appreciate the sentiment, Sam, I want to remind you it is frowned upon to discuss Committee matters at length outside of official meetings."

"I've been with the group for a while, Sharpe. I know the rules," Grey said. "I choose to view them more as guidelines, especially when I see something rotten festering."

It seemed Joan wasn't the only one suspecting foul play within the Committee in regards to Isaac's death. "Jakob said he was told not to check on Isaac's body with you," I said.

Grey nodded. "Upper management at the station pulled us from that task. The kid and I were surprised to find out it was at Stone's request."

"Why didn't you tell us?" Reginald asked.

"Because instead I went to my desk and called up the coroner. I ordered additional reports, including a heavy metals and poison panel."

"For the silver," Trish said.

"Yes." Grey nodded. "I figured if I was blocked from visiting the body, chances are it wouldn't be staying around the morgue much longer. He'd be released to his family and a mortuary. Getting him back into the lab after that would require a hell of a lot of paperwork." He frowned at his coffee. "Those reports I ordered take days, even weeks, to come in. I wouldn't have anything new to share on the case, so there was no need to draw the Committee's or Stone's attention to it."

He was keeping the panels from Stone and the Committee because he sensed foul play. I was beginning to understand why Anne admired the guy.

"Stone doesn't know about the extra reports you requested?" Trish asked.

Grey shook his head before he flagged a waitress for more coffee. "That way the reports will make it to my desk instead of mysteriously disappearing in the bureaucratic shuffle."

I waited for the waitress to refill our coffee mugs and leave. "We don't have weeks. Can't you put a rush on the lab reports?"

Mild irritation crossed his features. "Listen kid, this is actual police work. We're not living in the movies or on TV. Things take time." He sipped his coffee. "There's a certain level of confidentiality required for Committee cases. Otherwise, I'd like nothing more than to bring your friend, Officer Reid, on board to help with this."

He didn't want to expose Anne to the knowledge of the supernatural. I'd never given thought to how Commoners-in-the-know like Grey managed life with one foot in each world. I'm sure the lifestyle carried its own set of challenges.

"Is there anything else we should know?" Trish asked.

"No, that's all I've got. Short and sweet." Grey checked his wristwatch for the time. "I'm due over at the station for a briefing on last night." He stood, took a worn bifold from his pocket, and counted out some wrinkled bills.

Reginald nodded and touched the brim of his hat. "Thank you, Sam."

"Yes. Thank you," Trish said.

Grey nodded and placed the bills under the coffee mug. "I'll be in touch when and if anything comes back from the lab." He collected his suit jacket from the back of his chair and started down the sidewalk.

I watched Grey cross the street and walk in the direction of the police station. The rumpled man was a Committee fixture, but I didn't know much about him. "Do you two trust him?"

"Detective Grey?" Reginald looked surprised by the question. "Of course. He's always been an honorable man."

Trish looked from Grey's retreating figure to me. Her taut jawline and critical gaze provided her answer. She was undecided.

Grey seemed to be open and honest, but I know Trish had been let down by the Committee before.

Anne, on the other hand, adored Grey and his unrelenting dedication to his work. I hoped she was right about him. The metals and poisons panels would be evidence Isaac was killed with silver. He was targeted because he was a werewolf. Stone's gang warfare bullshit would be thrown out.

The killer knew Isaac was a wolf, was aware of the effects of silver, and had the strength to overpower a werewolf. The list of suspects would be short, and Stone's Hunter would be at the top. I hoped the results arrived soon before the Hunter could take another life, possibly mine.

16

THE STRESS OF the past few days had me looking forward to the concert at Hell's Bells. Since first being invited to the club by Trish and Nate, I'd returned many times for rock and punk shows. I was curious to see how EDM would feel in the space.

People already lined up, waiting for the venue to open. I waved to the doorman as I entered. He was a large but quiet wolf everyone knew not to argue with. Trish was busy with a final check of the newly stocked bar, so I headed for the stairs to the right of the front door.

I was halfway down the stairs when music started for several beats before cutting again. A handful of flickering fluorescent lights illuminated the basement. I crossed the stained and sticky cement floor toward the low stage where Ben stood. He was focused on a laptop beside a board covered in buttons and lights.

The walls were decorated with old show posters, band stickers, and chewing gum. Graffiti was spray-painted across the brick wall behind the stage. Large speakers were stacked at the stage's corners. The ceiling was left open with exposed beams and pipes. Some large industrial fans had been added to help manage the summer heat when the space filled with people.

I stepped up onto the stage and walked to Ben's side. He looked up from his laptop, smiled, and signed, "Hello."

"There are people waiting outside. Did you invite your sister?" I asked.

He shook his head and made an adjustment to the board.

"Oh." Weren't they supposed to be close? "Why not?"

Ben looked up at me again and shrugged.

"How're you feeling in general about tonight?"

He placed the fingertips of his right hand against his lips and then lowered them into the open palm of his left. "Good."

"Hey!" Nate called from the other end of the room behind a makeshift sound booth. "Go back upstairs. I need him to focus."

I replied to his command like a lady. Flipping him the bird, I disregarded it. "You're not nervous, are you?" I asked Ben. I was anxious enough for both of us, despite Trish's reassurance of Ben's safety.

He grinned and shook his head.

"I didn't think so."

Ben loved music. Though the majority of his free time was spent alone, or more recently with me, he thrived most when sharing music. Discovering it, splicing it, rearranging it, and presenting it as a new piece to an audience helped fill the hole left in him by tethering.

He looked past me and his grin widened. Footsteps caused me to turn and see Nate before he lifted me off my feet and slung me over his shoulder. I laughed and pummeled his back with my fists. "Okay! Put me down. I'll go."

"Sure you will," he growled. He carried me up the stairs. "Those doors are going to open any minute, and your wizard is still dicking around with the sound. He doesn't need any distractions."

We reached the lounge, and he let me down. I yanked at my clothes to get everything back in order. "I'm worried about him being here, Nate," I said. "Look what happened with Em."

"I'll be with him all night. I won't let anyone hurt him," Nate said. "Tonight's important to a lot of people who knew Isaac. We're going to celebrate him and hopefully bring in enough money so his family can give him the sendoff they want. Ben gets that and wants to help."

"You said his name." I smiled, already feeling better. It was the first time Nate used Ben's name.

Nate turned, muttered to himself, and headed back down the stairs.

THE FRONT DOORS opened, and Hell's Bells was swamped with people. There were familiar faces, but also new ones as Isaac's worlds collided in the wake of his passing. A dedicated area in the lounge was arranged for his father, mother, and younger sister to receive condolences. Isaac had made an impression upon a lot of people during his short life.

Trish said Isaac had got the werewolf gene from his father. They weren't sure if it would skip his sister. It was like a bad game of genetic Russian roulette. Most kids knew by fourteen if their lives would be turned upside down. It brought a whole new meaning to puberty. My family thought I'd escaped it like my father, but to everyone's surprise, I was a late bloomer.

After admitting the people attending in honor of Isaac, Trish left the doors open to fill the building to capacity. People packed the downstairs venue and a staff member was posted to regulate traffic. Emma arrived before the doorman started to turn people away. She was in her element dancing beside me, unaware of the other patrons drawn to her like moths to a flame.

The first set ended, and the beat spun down to be replaced by house music. I glanced at Emma to let her know I was going to talk to Ben. She was preoccupied with bewitching another concertgoer. I wove through the sweaty bodies toward the stage, but the crowd grew so dense it was impossible to get close.

Ben stood beside the stage with Nate and attempted to communicate with the people waiting to talk to him. He repeatedly nodded and signed, "Thank you," while trying to juggle his small notepad. I didn't care for the way people leaned in close to him to read his notes in the dim light. A club patron ambushed him with a hug, and an uncomfortable prickle of jealousy soured my stomach. When he closed his arms around her to return the hug, I decided it was best I went upstairs to rehydrate.

I sat down at the bar and asked for some water. A barstool's width to my left, a young teen sat by herself. She stared at her untouched soda. Her eyelids were red and swollen, so I assumed she was here for Isaac.

"How're you holding up?" I asked her, and then internally cringed. *Ugh.* I was awful at social skills.

Her tone was flat. "My brother is dead. How do you think I'm holding up?"

Perfect. I'd asked "how's it going" to Isaac's little sister. "I'm sorry, that was a stupid question. I didn't mean . . ." I fumbled with my apology.

My floundering prompted something resembling a smile from her. "No, it's okay. I'm not doing well, if it wasn't obvious. I miss him." She added, "I'm Hanna, by the way."

"Alex," I said.

"Your name is familiar. Are you the person who found Isaac?" When I nodded, she continued, "Mom said the Committee doesn't want to investigate my brother's death. They want to blame it on a gang. Is that true?"

"Who told your mom that?" I thought that wasn't public knowledge.

"I overheard the werewolf cop talking to Mom and Dad about it. He wanted to know if Isaac had been running with a gang again," she said.

"Some people would prefer that," I said, "but Trish is pushing them to do their job." I wasn't sure how much Trish shared with Isaac's family about her plans to find the murderer if the Committee stalled.

Hanna opened her mouth, but then closed it and glanced around the lounge. She frowned and shifted her weight.

"What is it?" I asked. "Do you know something about what happened to Isaac?"

She looked back over her shoulder in the direction of her parents. Hanna lowered her voice when she spoke again. "Before my brother was . . . found, he became part of this new group. He was in a lot of groups, but this one wanted to change the rules for people like you, dad, and him."

"Werewolves?" I clarified.

She nodded. "Werewolves, wizards, all the people with gifts."

It sounded like the goals of Joan's group. Was Isaac her local contact?

"There are chapters all over in different cities," Hanna said. "Isaac didn't tell Mom and Dad because the changes would wreck the Committee. He didn't want them worried about him getting tethered. I didn't know about it until I overheard Isaac and Julia arguing. She thought it would put Isaac in danger."

"That was his girlfriend, right?"

Hanna nodded. "Julia Visser."

"Did he mention the group's name or any other members?" I asked.

"No. He was mad I'd found out. He didn't tell me anything else because I might 'say something to the wrong person.'" She looked back at her drink. "I should've told Mom and Dad. They could've stopped him, and he'd still be around to yell at me for it."

I shook my head. "There's no way to know that."

If the Committee had heard about the goals of Joan's group, her suspicion of the Committee's involvement in Isaac's death sounded more plausible. "Did Isaac ever meet up with anyone from this group?"

She nodded. "He must have. That was another thing he and Julia argued about. She accused Isaac of sneaking around on her because he was never where he said he'd be. I know he wouldn't do that because he was crazy about her." She rolled her eyes. "She's okay, but not *that* great."

The meeting planned between Joan and Isaac the night he died must have been about Joan's group's plans to tank the Committee. They weren't simply "reconnecting" as Joan had said.

Hanna paused. "Do you think a wizard murdered him?"

I blinked. "What? Why do you ask that?" A wizard wouldn't risk getting so close to a werewolf when they could attack from a distance.

She shrugged. "Dad says wizards never care about what happens to werewolves. Maybe a wizard thought no one would bother finding out who killed Isaac."

"I'm not sure, but I don't think so," I said. "It sounds like your dad isn't a fan of wizards." It reminded me of all the times Nate had grumbled about them.

"He doesn't trust them and thinks they're all snobs." Hanna frowned. "I think that's why he didn't like Julia. She never wanted to come over to our house."

"Julia is a wizard?"

"Yes."

The night we were introduced, I'd noticed Julia wasn't another wolf and assumed she was a Commoner Isaac was invested in. "Is she here?"

"No. She's probably across town with her rich friends." Hanna stood and gave her parents another glance. "I need to get back to Mom and Dad. They keep looking over at us. Thanks for caring about what happened to Isaac." She picked up her soda and left to rejoin her family.

My mind buzzing, I finished my water and went downstairs to find Emma. I caught her eye, and she excused herself from the company of yet another club patron. She beamed at me. "Ben is great tonight! How's he feeling?"

"It was too crowded, so I couldn't get to him. I went upstairs for some water instead."

"Oh. Well, it looks like he's having fun." She laughed. "I'd be so nervous up there."

"Yeah, me too." I bit at my lip, reluctant to kill her buzz. "Hey Em, do you know a Visser family?"

"That's an odd change of subject," she said. "Why are you asking about the Vissers?"

"So you know them?"

Emma nodded. "I dated a few of them in school. It's one of the larger wizarding families in Hopewell. My mother has always been jealous of the oodles of children they have running around."

"Remember Isaac's friend Julia? Her last name is Visser."

Her eyebrows rose. "I wouldn't expect a Visser to be at a lupine hangout. Maybe the younger generation isn't as concerned with the status quo."

"Isaac and Julia were dating when he was killed," I said.

"Did you say Julia killed Isaac?" a voice asked at my elbow. I turned. Two young women stood beside us, staring at me.

Emma frowned. "No. She didn't say that."

"You believe that?" One woman's hand settled on her hip. "Is it because she's a wizard?"

My eyes widened. "What? No. I—"

"Why are you werewolves always so suspicious of us?" her friend asked. "Just because most wizards have great jobs and nice things, doesn't mean we're villains."

You werewolves?

"Suspicious?" Roger pushed his way forward from behind us, two of his friends in tow. "Why waste time on you?" He scoffed. "We barely ever think of you people. You're here in *our* space."

One of the wizards rolled her eyes and spoke to her friend as well as anyone else listening. "My father told me the werewolves started the riot last night and were destroying everything."

"What?" I said. "Wolves weren't the only people causing trouble." And what was this bullshit about them starting the riot? Was Stone trying to alter the facts by spreading lies?

Emma addressed the two wizards. "Spreading rumors isn't going to help Isaac *or* Julia."

One of the women let loose a sparkling laugh. "We're here for the music, not some Romeo and Juliet sob story."

Growls started rumbling within Roger's group, and my own inner wolf took notice. She pressed forward, and I broke out into a sweat from withholding a snarl.

"Hey," I shot Roger and his friends a warning look. There could be Commoners here, so none of us could afford being caught displaying our gifts.

One of the women lifted her chin and smirked. "Maybe pay closer attention to your own kind if you're looking for Isaac's killer." She strode between Emma and me and continued to the stairs.

Her friend followed, muttering, "Fucking mongrels."

Roger lunged, and I barely caught the back of his shirt. He spun and twisted out of my grasp. "What the hell, Alex?" He yanked on his shirt to straighten it. "What are you doing?"

"Don't be stupid," I stepped toward him so I could lower my voice. "Trish and Nate don't need this tonight. It's about Isaac and his family, not tangling with some diva wizards."

Roger glowered at me, shook his head, and pushed away through the crowd with his friends. I hated the sense that I'd wronged them somehow.

"You okay?" Emma said.

"No," I glanced at the stairs. "I'm not."

THE LAST OF the remaining club patrons exited in the early morning hours. I checked the time while I waited on one of the lounge's sofas. I was exhausted, but I'd promised to meet Anne later this morning for a run. I'd also be able to make sure she was okay after the riot. There'd be no sleeping in today.

Trish took a seat across from me, slipped off her heels, and pulled her legs up to tuck them beneath her. She rested her arm along the back of the couch and looked over her shoulder toward the stairs. The sound of Nate's laughter caused her to smile.

Ben and Nate emerged from the doorway of the downstairs venue. There was an unsteady sway to Ben's step, and Nate guided him over to us. The scent of alcohol surrounded the two. Ben settled next to me, reeking of several types of perfumes. With a sweep of his arm, Nate gave me a low bow. "Your wizard, mademoiselle. As promised, not a scratch on him."

Ben collapsed to lay his head in my lap, leaving his long legs to hang over the end of the sofa. I raised an eyebrow at Nate. "Except I'll have to carry him up the stairs to the apartment."

Nate dropped into the space beside Trish and waved aside my complaint. "Details. What's important is that he's alive and in one piece."

I brushed some hair away from Ben's glassy eyes and smiled down at him. "The music sounded great tonight. Did you have a good time?"

Ben's grin was lopsided and he nodded. With each blink, he struggled to keep his eyes open.

Trish stretched her legs out across Nate's lap. She wiggled her eyebrows and toes at him. He smiled and began to rub her feet.

"How much did we bring in?" he asked.

"Quite a bit," Trish said. "Isaac's family was grateful. I'll transfer the money to them later today."

"I talked to his sister, Hanna," I said. "Did either of you meet Julia Visser, Isaac's girlfriend?"

Trish nodded and Nate answered, "He introduced her the first time he brought her to a show. The Vissers are awful, but she seemed okay. I didn't see her often after that."

"I don't think she felt comfortable here," Trish said. "As you saw with Emma, there are still some wolves who struggle sharing this space with wizards."

"I thought Isaac having a close relationship with a wizard was interesting," I said. "Since there's so much goddamn tension between our communities, maybe someone who wanted to exploit that gave Isaac's name to the Hunter."

"Someone who knew Isaac and Julia," Nate said. He gave a low whistle and shook his head. "Friend or family member?"

I nodded. "Hanna mentioned Isaac's dad didn't care for Julia. I wonder if Julia's family felt the same about Isaac."

"Reginald may know," Trish said. "The Vissers are a large family and very outspoken about how the balance of power should be maintained in Hopewell."

"But if you ask Reginald, he isn't going to let you nose around that family without being there himself," Nate said.

"I thought I could ask Julia about it," I said. "I met her briefly with Isaac. I'm not sure how to find her though."

Trish drummed her fingernails on the back of the couch. "I'll ask Isaac's family for her phone number and address when I see them later."

"Hanna might know Julia's contact info before his parents do."

Trish nodded. "I'll send it to you when I get it."

"Thanks." I hesitated before I echoed Hanna's earlier question. "Is it possible a wizard had Isaac killed?"

"Of course," Nate said. "The Visser family is lousy with wizards."

Trish shook her head. "I don't think so. My suspicions lie with Stone. From what you heard at Stone's campaign fundraiser, I believe Isaac was hand-selected as a target. His death was more visible and upsetting to a larger number of people."

"Which was one of the factors that led to a riot," I said. "Do you think the Committee members will consider that when they vote on the Hunter?"

"I wouldn't hold my breath," Trish said. "Stone is directing their attention to the property damage caused by out-of-control lupine, not on Isaac's murder."

I growled. "I hope Stone doesn't win his run for mayor."

"With Susan Arztin's bottomless pockets, he has a good chance," Nate said.

"But tonight was encouraging," Trish said. "A lot of different people showed up to remember Isaac and enjoy music together. They were reminded of what we share rather than dwelling on our differences." She looked over at Ben. "We'd love to have you back again."

When he didn't answer, I looked down. He was fast asleep.

I carried Ben to the car. He slept as I drove, leaving me alone with my thoughts. Even though Trish felt good about the evening, Roger's, Emma's, and my interaction with the two wizards bothered me. If the two wizards were told the wolves were solely responsible for the riot, the lie was well on its way to being spread. Would it get back to Reginald? Would he be pressured into voting for the Hunter to be posted in Hopewell?

I shuddered. The Hunter knew oddly specific details about me and Stone didn't. I worried a yes vote would remove the last barrier keeping me from the Hunter's reach.

17

WHEN RUNNING SOLO, I preferred to stay close to downtown in the company of the city's heartbeat. I felt safer surrounded by the tall buildings, loud traffic, and bustling people. But Anne suggested we try a trail system paved for cyclists, joggers, and people wanting to escape the congested grid of concrete and noise. I understood the concept of escaping into nature, and had once cherished it myself, but I hadn't been able to reclaim it yet.

"How's your knee doing?" We were stretching before our run, and I'd noticed the winces Anne attempted to conceal.

Anne shook her head. "I almost asked if we could hit the heavy bags instead of this, but decided the fresh air may wake me up. I'm still exhausted."

"We could do that," I said. "Wouldn't it be better on your knee?"

"My knee is fine." Her answer was sharp, which she noticed. She sighed. "Sorry. It's a sore spot, pardon the pun, between my supervisor and me. He's trying to shackle me to a desk."

"Did you find out what happened? What caused the riot?"

"I'm sorry, Alex. I can't share that with you right now," she said. Anne hesitated, her brow wrinkling. "I'm also concerned my memory is so foggy. I hope it's the lack of sleep."

Our stretching complete, we began our run. The wide trail was edged by woods running along the river, not unlike where Nate and I had met Fillip. The shade afforded by the tree canopy allowed a reprieve from the seasonal heat.

"How're things with you?" Anne asked.

I glanced over at her, instantly on guard. "What do you mean?"

"In general," she said. "Some time has passed since those guys burnt up your apartment and tried to kidnap you. This is a basic mental health check-in."

"Oh." I shrugged. These conversations with her were becoming increasingly difficult to navigate the more involved I became in the wolf community. "I'm okay, I guess."

"Really? Because you seemed stressed at our boxing meetups," she said.

"I still feel a bit silly at those heavy bags, trying to look competent in front of people that know what they're doing. You know how I am with an audience. Must have been nerves."

Anne was silent for a few strides before she said, "Yeah, no, I don't think that's what was bothering you."

I didn't like where the conversation was going, so I deflected. "Hey, Jakob mentioned he sparred with you before. How many more boxing drills do I have before I can do that?"

"Alex, are you okay?" she asked.

Our pace slowed and we stopped. "I'd rather not talk about it," I said.

She frowned. "Are you getting caught up in something you shouldn't? Is it with the people from that club?"

"No." Nothing I couldn't eventually sort out, anyway. "Where is this coming from?"

"Are you looking into that young man's murder?"

I couldn't think of how to not outright lie to her, so I stared and didn't answer.

Anne's frown deepened. "Why?"

"You've said that something strange is going on with that case."

"If you're withholding information, stop," she said. "Tell the police."

"Now you're telling me to trust the police? Which is it going to be?" I asked.

"Then tell *me* what you know! This isn't television. You're not a detective, Alex. Let the police handle this. It's our job," she said. "I don't want to arrive to a scene and find your body next."

I hated keeping this part of my life from Anne, but the rules couldn't be ignored. "We're here to run together. Spending time with you makes me feel better. Running makes me feel better. Can we do that?"

Anne shook her head, turned from me, and started to jog again. I followed, drawing up to and falling into stride beside her. Our footfalls pounded out that repetitive rhythm I found so centering. One foot fell in front of the other. It was something predictable I could control.

My mind and body were on the verge of fully committing to the exercise when my sensitive hearing picked up the runner behind us. He moved at a faster pace and steadily drew nearer. A surge of panic caused my heart to race and my palms to dampen.

It's okay. I held tight to the thought. *You're safe.*

Eventually, Anne heard the additional runner. She glanced back before she looked ahead and refocused on our run. It wasn't curiosity; it was reflex. It was so deeply ingrained in women, we did it without thinking. In that brief action, she'd located the person moving into her space, assessed his intentions, decided he wasn't a threat, factored in her environment in case she was wrong, and moved on with her day.

Despite Anne's comfort with the approaching jogger, I couldn't shake my uneasiness. I forced myself to concentrate on the path ahead of us instead of looking back. I wanted to push through the difficult moment.

The footfalls grew louder. Closer. The familiar stirring began in my chest. The creature inside me was receiving my mental telegram: *danger.* The breeze shifted and a strong dose of the stranger's sweat and deodorant reached me. I clenched my jaw, and my whole body broke into a cold sweat.

It's okay. You're safe.

I focused on keeping my breathing even. Inhale. *It's okay.* Exhale. *You're safe.* Inhale. *It's okay.* Exhale. *You're safe.*

He was only a few paces away from us. My skin crawled as I imagined how his gaze wandered uninvited over my body. He planned to seize and drag me deep into the woods. He'd silence me so no one could hear my cries for help.

He was right behind my left shoulder. I clenched my fists and my nails began to lengthen. They bit into my palms.

"Alex, watch out!"

The other jogger's body collided with mine. The noise that was torn from me wasn't human. I spun and slashed at the jogger while leaping back. My claws caught him in the chest with a dull ripping of fabric. His face was a mixture of startled surprise and horror.

He saw me.

Then something large, coming from the opposite direction, struck me in the hip. With a crash, I was on the ground tangled with another body and a bicycle.

"What the hell was that!" The stink of fear rolled off the male jogger.

"Please sir, calm down. Are you injured?" It was Anne's voice. She'd shifted into her *dealing-with-hysterical-citizens* tone.

"Did you see her eyes?" He demanded. "You must have seen—" He paused. "Look at my shirt! She tore my shirt!"

"Sir, please. I'm an officer with the City of Hopewell. Are you injured?" Anne asked.

"Look at my shirt! Does she have a knife? That crazy bitch has a knife!"

"Sir, she does not have a knife," Anne said.

Groaning, the cyclist pushed her bicycle off of us and untangled herself from me. "Are you okay?"

I closed my eyes and wished to be anywhere but there.

It didn't work.

"Yeah, I'm fine." I pushed myself up into a seated position and kept my gaze lowered to hide my eyes. My fingers were curled into fists against the pavement. "Sorry, I didn't see you." My hands, bracing my body upright, appeared unremarkable.

"We're so sorry," Anne said. She extended a hand and helped the cyclist to her feet.

"It happens. It's not my first crash," she said.

"I thought I could get around her before you passed," the jogger said to the cyclist. "I didn't think she'd jump in front of you. Everyone saw that, right? Did you hear her? Are you sure she doesn't have a weapon?"

"I assure you, sir, she does not have a weapon." Anne crouched beside me. My stomach clenched as I smelled the faintest traces of fear, this time from her. She reached out to touch my shoulder but drew her hand back at the last second. "Are you okay?"

She didn't want to touch me. Was it because she was scared? Of me? "I'm fine." Embarrassment made my tone sharp. I stood and walked to the path's edge to brush off my clothing.

"Everyone okay then?" Anne asked the group of us.

"Yes," the cyclist said. "Are you sure your friend is okay?"

"Yes, thank you for asking," Anne said. "We'll be all right."

I heard the clicking of the bicycle gears, and the woman slowly coasted past me going the opposite direction. The bike picked up speed, and she continued on her ride.

"This was an expensive shirt," the jogger said.

"I'm sorry about your shirt, sir," Anne said. "If you give me your address, I can send money for a replacement."

"There's no need for that." He paused. "She's lucky I wasn't injured."

"Yes, sir, we're lucky no one was hurt," Anne said.

Anne's acknowledgement seemed to appease the man. Without another word, he continued in the direction we had been running.

My body crashed from the adrenaline rush. I wasn't sure if that was why I started shaking, or the fact I almost sliced up a random Commoner out for a run.

Anne approached me. The odor of her fear strengthened.

"You're bleeding." Her tone was cautious. She didn't know what to expect from me.

Hell, *I* didn't know what to expect from my own goddamn body.

I inhaled slowly through my nose and tried to stop my trembling. The road rash on my knee and one of my forearms stung. "He startled me."

"You must've been in the zone not to have noticed the cyclist." Anne paused. "How did you do that to his shirt?"

No, no, no. Shit! My thoughts raced. "I must have caught it somehow and it ripped when I jumped away."

"It wasn't that type of tear. It was sliced apart, like with a knife," she said. "Except, there were three tears, and you don't carry a knife. Or do you?"

"No." My thudding heartbeat was beginning to overpower her words.

"What happened to your hands? Did you try to catch yourself?"

I opened my clenched fingers. My claws were gone, but they had carved perfect bloody crescents into my palms. I quickly closed my hands again. "I must have." Another bright drop fell from my fist to the pavement, joining the smattering of blood there.

Frowning, Anne stepped forward, clasped my wrist, and jerked it toward her. "Open your hand, Alex."

My chest tightened. "No."

"Now. Open it."

"No! Let go of me!" I yanked my hand away. The movement's strength almost pulled Anne off balance. I'd barely kept the growl from my voice.

Her eyes widened briefly. A more potent wave of fear curled off her. She took a step back and cleared her throat. "I have a first aid kit in my car. You shouldn't run after taking such a hard fall. Did you hit your head?"

"No, it doesn't feel like it." I couldn't bring myself to look at her. Not only was I ashamed of my reaction, but I also suspected she'd seen something she shouldn't.

We walked through deafening silence back to her car. Even though the scrapes would be gone tomorrow, I let her bandage me up. She was applying some ointment to my forearm when she said, "You know you can talk to me, right? If something is wrong, or you're not feeling like yourself. I'm here for you."

I bit my bottom lip and nodded, willing myself not to cry.

Emma knew about my assault, the trigger that awoke the dormant gene in my body. But, like the fact I was a werewolf, I'd kept it hidden from Anne. The two were closely linked, and Anne excelled at following links.

"You're more of a private person. I get that. But there are other options if you're uncomfortable talking to me. All of us at the department have access to a network of mental health professionals," she said. "I can pass along some contact information."

I imagined myself stretched out on a sofa, dropping my very specific issues on a shrink. *I've tried several pet shampoos, but I can't find a single one to work with this mop of hair!* I shook my head. "Thank you for the offer, but I'll pass for now."

"Something doesn't feel right. I'm worried about you, Alex."

The struggle to control this being inside of me weighed heavy on my mind and heart. Anne was offering to listen, to help, but I couldn't tell her anything.

"I'll be fine," I assured her for what felt like the hundredth time. Maybe with enough repetition, I'd believe it myself.

THE DRIVE BACK to the apartment allowed me time to settle my nerves. I showered, redressed the oozing road rash, and joined Ben on the landing outside.

He noticed the new bandage. "Rough morning with Anne?"

"I was hit by a bike," I said. "First a table and now this."

Ben's eyebrows rose above his sunglasses and he smiled. "Are you going to be okay?"

He got points for not laughing.

"Not really," I said. "I'm not sure how much longer I can keep my secret from Anne. She's too damn perceptive."

"I'm sorry," he said.

"Me too." A small stack of graphic novels, each spine tagged with a library sticker, sat beside him on the landing. "How're you feeling? After the late night, I thought you'd still be asleep."

"I wasn't doing well when I woke up, but the fresh air on the walk to the library helped," he said. "Head still hurts."

"I have some pills in the medicine cabinet that can help with that. Want me to grab a few?" I asked.

"No thanks."

As a werewolf, my body burned through the effects of alcohol faster than a Commoner's. Even so, monitoring my intake was something I kept in mind. Getting too tipsy could quickly get dangerous for any woman, but I also had to ensure I wouldn't disembowel anyone who tried to take advantage of me.

I sat down beside Ben. "Aren't you worried if you have too many drinks you'll blow your cover? Start talking to people?" It would land him in a hell of a lot of trouble with the Committee if they found out.

His cheeks flushed and his chin dipped. "Yeah, I know. Nate kept handing me full cups." He rubbed at the back of his neck and shrugged. "I mean, it's not his fault. I could have said 'no,' but I let my guard down."

"This isn't a reprimand. I'm glad you had a good time," I said. "It was something I wondered while you emptied your stomach in the parking lot."

His whole face reddened. "I don't remember that. I'm sorry."

"It's okay, just don't make a habit of it." I motioned to the books at his feet. "What did you bring home from the library?"

Thankful for the change in subject, he handed me the first book. "While I picked up a few holds, I grabbed these thinking you might want to give them a try."

I was deep into the first *Sandman* when I noticed a man crossing the parking lot. He was dressed in worn jeans, a faded t-shirt, and a sweaty Lions ball cap. His beard was a wild tangle of brown and gray hair with eyebrows to match. I stood as he reached the stairs. He paused at the first step, his hand on the railing, to squint up at me. "Good morning, Miss. Are you Alexandria Steward?"

Ben looked up from his book at the sound of the man's voice.

I scented the air, only picking up sweat and cigarette smoke from the guy. "Who's asking?"

"My name is John," he said. "I have some information for her."

Grinning, Ben stood. He gave the man a wave.

"Ben!" John laughed, and a smile brightened his face.

I looked at Ben and lowered my voice. "You know this guy?"

Ben nodded and motioned John up to join us.

John made it to the top of the stairs, out of breath, and leaned against the railing. There was a handkerchief and envelope tucked into his pocket, and a pack of cigarettes rolled into his shirt sleeve.

He shook Ben's hand. "How are you, son?" Squinting, he mouthed each word as Ben signed. John slowly and clumsily signed a reply. "Two jobs? Give me one?" His throaty chuckle broke into coughing.

Ben smiled and signed again, motioning to me. I recognized the letters of my name.

"It's nice to meet you, Alex," John said.

"It's nice to meet you as well." I glanced between the two. "How do you know each other?" Ben didn't have many close friends, none that he'd introduced me to anyway.

"We met at Another Chance," John said. "How long has it been? At least twelve years."

Ben shifted his weight from one foot to another and signed a response.

"Sorry, Alex." John retrieved the crumpled envelope from his back pocket. "I'm sure you're wanting this instead of listening to some old man ramble." He handed it to me.

"Thanks." I opened the blank envelope.

Ben asked another question.

"Taking it day by day," John said. "Had a place with several other guys, but they kicked me out when I lost my job. My lungs were bothering me again, and I didn't make my shift. Then I couldn't make rent. You know how it goes."

I withdrew a slip of paper from the envelope. Handwritten in elegant script was today's date and a time in the late afternoon.

John turned his head and coughed. "Those stairs took it out of me."

Ben signed again, and John shook his head. "Thank you, but I'll leave you two kids to your morning. It was good to see you again." John nodded to me. "And it was nice to meet you, Alex." He turned and carefully descended the stairs.

John crossed the parking lot before Ben looked over at the envelope. "What's that?"

"I'm not sure if I should say." I returned the paper to the envelope and stowed it in my back pocket. "It might upset you."

"I don't want you to feel like you can't share something with me because of how I'll react," he said.

"Trish has a contact she works with when digging for information. I asked him to look into something for me." I patted my back pocket. "This is the day and time I need to meet him."

"Is it Fillip?"

I blinked. "How did you know?"

Ben settled back into his chair and picked up his book. "John is part of Fillip's flock."

And how did he know that? "Why haven't I met John before if you know him so well?"

He shrugged, not looking up. "I haven't had a chance to introduce you."

Joan was right. Ben never volunteered information about himself. Extracting it from him was like pulling on a brittle thread. Only bits and pieces broke off at a time.

"Ben."

He looked over the top of the book at me.

"Another Chance is down the street. I could have met John by now."

"I'm not a client there anymore, so we don't see each other often. He invited me in when I was first tethered. My parents had moved." Ben looked back at his book and turned the page.

I'd forgotten Ben relied on Another Chance at one point in his life. That's how he'd met Emma. She'd been a student volunteer there. But I hadn't known his family left him to fend for himself. "Your sister didn't take care of you?"

"I was an adult, and she was in Chicago."

"Don't you have an older brother?"

"I'm too much of a hassle for him." Ben looked up and frowned. "Why are we talking about me when you've set up a meeting with Fillip? You won't be alone with him, will you?"

"No." I excluded the detail that it would be his sister with me. Joan had pissed me off barging into my head, but she knew Isaac and wanted to bring in his killer as fast as I did. Her stealth skills would give me an advantage sneaking up on the Hunter.

"Good." Ben looked back down at his book. I wanted to reassure him everything would be okay, but I couldn't guarantee that.

I sat down and texted Joan a time to meet me at the apartment. While doing so, a message popped up from Trish. It was a street address. I checked the time. My visit with Julia would have to wait until after Joan and I met with Fillip.

BEN WAS AT work when Joan arrived. We were silent while I drove to the same riverside location where Nate and I previously met Fillip. Joan followed me from the edge of the woods down to the large drainage pipe. Fillip waited, wearing the same knit cap and large coat as before.

"Hello, Fillip," Joan said. Like me, she kept her distance from the stooped figure. "I suspected Alex's contact would be you."

Did everyone know this guy except me?

"Joanna Sharpe." His ruby eyes glinted. "Tell me . . . How goes the revolution? I've not heard of any progress."

"It's ongoing."

Fillip looked disappointed Joan refused to react to his needling. "Were you able to find the man in the photo?" I asked.

"Of course, though it was a challenge," he said. "I hope you are equal to the task of killing him."

"We can't promise that," Joan said.

I frowned and glanced at her. I'd brought her along as a courtesy.

"Then why was time wasted with this request?" Fillip asked me. "Will the lupine yield to the wishes of a wizard?"

"He'll stand trial with the Committee for his crime," Joan said.

Fillip scoffed. "This man is a Hunter. He will play through the charade of a trial, be pardoned, and be released back onto our streets. You are as spineless as your grandfather, girl." He spat on the ground.

"If he isn't charged here, he will be in Chicago with the Delegation," she said.

"No final decisions have been made on what will happen to him," I said. "Where can we find him?"

Eyes narrowed at Joan, Fillip handed me a slip of paper with the same elegant handwriting as the note delivered by John. It was an address. "He is staying in an abandoned service garage south of the city. He leaves each evening at dusk and returns a few hours before sunrise." Fillip's gaze slid from Joan to me. "My people say he watches a den every night as if awaiting an order."

My eyes widened, and his thin lips curved upward.

"Hell's Bells?"

He nodded. "Alexandria, you must see the need to rid us of him. Permanently. Joanna is a wizard." Fillip made a face like the word left a foul aftertaste. "She cannot understand the fear a

Hunter strikes into our hearts. Wizards have never had their skin or teeth taken as trophies."

His canine teeth were missing.

It was a detail Detective Grey reported to the Committee. Isaac's canine teeth were removed. Did the Hunter take the young man's life and keep his teeth? Anger seared my insides, and a low growl rumbled in my chest.

Joan watched me cautiously. The faint odor of fear curled off her body. "Don't let him sway you, Alex. The Hunter should stand trial and be convicted."

I snarled, and my attention swung to Joan. Fillip had spoken truth to the darker side of the creature nested inside me. Of course the wizards could afford to trust the Committee to bring the Hunter to trial. The Hunter wouldn't be tracking down the wizards if he was released. Maybe letting him live to face trial wasn't the best choice.

"Yes!" Fillip gave a thin laugh. "You've seen how the wizards are favored while the lupine struggle under the Committee's thumb, haven't you? What have the wizards done to address this? Nothing. It should be the lupine's right to deal with the Hunter as they wish."

"Thank you, Fillip," Joan interrupted. She attempted to end the conversation by turning away and walking back toward the car.

I looked back, and Fillip held my gaze with his red eyes. His rasp of a voice was quiet. "And you, young one, are of special interest to this Hunter. He carries your name with him."

I froze. "You found out how he knows me."

He nodded once.

"Tell me."

Joan called from the side of the road. "Let's go, Alex."

"This Hunter believes his only master is St. Hubert. He finds and vanquishes monsters who have avoided punishment for their crimes," Fillip said. "He has been searching for Alexandria Steward, the werewolf who nearly took a man's life and escaped."

I swallowed, pulse hammering. "Stone didn't tell him. The Hunter already knew about me."

"He arrived in Hopewell with a contract to kill you."

My stomach roiled and the world seemed to tip. I covered my mouth and took a stumbling step. The beast inside me bristled and twisted against my hold.

Run.

Three years since the thought had crossed my mind.

"Patricia will help," Fillip said. "Kill him."

Mindless beasts killed people.

Run.

He would follow me.

"Alex!" Joan stood at the tree line.

Nauseated, I asked. "Is he alone?"

"No one else is staying with him," Fillip said. "He is a sole man."

"Thank you."

The vampire gave a slight bow of his head. "A pleasure, Alexandria. I wish you luck."

I staggered away toward the car, and my steps grew more sure. My mind raced with the new information. I needed to alert Trish and Nate to the Hunter prowling around Hell's Bells. When I did, I'd have to decide whether or not to share his location.

The Hunter was strong, but he'd taken me by surprise when we first met. Now I knew what to expect. With the help of Joan's magic, I could get the jump on him. And then . . .

Joan waited for me beside the car. "Be careful around Fil—" She frowned. "You look like shit. What did that undead bastard do to you?"

I scowled across the car roof at her. "What he said was true. What do *you* have to worry about if the Hunter's trial is fumbled?" I got into the car and started the engine.

The passenger side door opened and Joan sat down. "I know I've bitched about how awful the Committee is, and I meant every word. Currently, it's our only option for sending the guy through a legal trial. If they won't do it, we'll move up the chain to the Delegation. I don't want to wait for the Committee to arrest the Hunter, but I'm not willing to kill him."

"Can you please shut your door?" I asked.

"You don't seem like someone who's comfortable taking lives."

"You just met me. How could you know what I'm capable of?" I shot her a glare and growled. "Shut the door."

Joan pulled the door shut. "Are you going to share the Hunter's address with Patricia?"

"She's been waiting for the information," I said. "Even if I don't tell her, she'll ask." She trusted me, and keeping information from her felt like a betrayal of that trust.

"Can I see it?" Joan held out her hand.

I passed her the slip of paper.

She copied the address into her phone and brought the location up on a map. "It looks like a ten-minute drive south on the highway from Benjamin's apartment." She handed back the paper. "We should go tonight. We'll slip in after he's left and collect any evidence. If we find enough, we nail him when he gets home."

I shook my head. "I need some time to think this through."

"There's no reason to wait. Every night that pass—"

"Give me some time!"

Joan's jawline twitched, and she turned her gaze out the passenger window. Our car ride back to the apartment was as silent as before. After a brief goodbye with Joan, I sat in the car and rewrote a text several times to Trish and Nate. Finally I hit the send button.

Found out Hunter is watching Hell's Bells every night after dark. Be careful.

I HAD ANOTHER reason to postpone making a house call on a Hunter. I still hadn't talked to Isaac's girlfriend, Julia. The address Trish sent belonged to a renovated historic home that'd been divided into six condos. I rang the doorbell and waited. Not getting an answer, I knocked on the door. The window was cracked, and when the breeze shifted the curtains, I glimpsed a figure darkening the front hallway.

I pressed the edge of my hand to the window to shield the sun's glare and get a better look. "Hello? I'm looking for Julia Visser. Is she home?"

The female voice was toneless. "What do you want?"

"I have some questions about Isaac Laska," I said.

There was a pause. "Isaac is dead."

"Julia, is that you? I'm sorry to bother you, but we're looking into his death."

"I already told the detective what I know."

"I knew Isaac through Hell's Bells." I hoped the comment would communicate what I intended, that I wasn't here on behalf of the police. I heard movement in the hall and a deadbolt being flipped. The door opened a crack, revealing only a sliver of the tall young woman inside.

"Oh, it's you," she said. "You're the bitch who barked at him when he asked if you were okay."

I cringed. "Yeah, that was me."

"They're saying a Hunter killed him. Is that true?"

"Can I please come inside so we can talk in private?"

She eyed me a moment before the door was pushed shut again. I sighed, waited a minute or two, and was about to give up when there was more movement inside. A chain jangled, another lock flipped, and the door opened.

Julia Visser stood in the doorway, her hair gathered away from her face into a ponytail. She waited for me to enter the condo and closed the door behind me.

"Thank you," I said. "I'm Alex, a friend of Patricia Drake's."

"Was it a Hunter?" Her eyes were swollen and red.

"We believe so," I said, "but we're still trying to determine exactly what happened. I hoped you could help."

"Now that you suspect I know something you need, you people are going to contact me?" Her arms crossed over her chest. I couldn't tell if it was a gesture of defiance or of self-comfort. "No one thought to tell me he'd been killed?"

I frowned. "No one contacted you?"

"I found out when I went to that trashy club looking for him," she said.

"I'm sorry. I didn't know that."

She wiped a stray tear from her cheek.

"We want anyone involved in Isaac's death to be held accountable," I said. "Isaac's sister told me you didn't get along that well with his family."

Julia scowled. "That little creep was always trying to follow us. We never had any privacy at his house."

"What did your family think of him?"

She shrugged. "I don't know. Who cares. They can't tell me who I can and can't date."

"They didn't have a problem with you seeing Isaac?" I asked.

Julia tilted her head and narrowed her eyes. "Are you accusing my family of having my boyfriend murdered?"

I took a slow inhale and exhale. "Hanna said you and Isaac argued over an organization he'd joined?"

"Isaac had bought into this ridiculous idea that he would lead a group of people to implode the Committee and build something different in its place," she said. "I told him he was being unrealistic. The Committee has been around forever. That's how things work for us, and we have to accept it if we want to live in Hopewell."

"Except it works differently for the wizards than the wolves," I said.

"That's what Isaac said all the time." Her brows gathered. "Sure, it isn't *perfect* for everyone, but it's not that bad either."

Julia seemed clueless about why Isaac had strong feelings about the Committee, but I felt bad for her anyway. She'd lost someone she loved.

"Did the group Isaac was part of have a name?" I asked.

She shook her head and sniffled. "I don't think so. But he was supposed to meet someone from the larger organization the night he was killed." Her voice hitched and she began to cry. "I told him to stop associating with that group. He could get into trouble, even be tethered, and I didn't want that to happen."

It all lined up with what Hanna had told me. Isaac was Joan's contact for the Hopewell chapter of her activist group. "Julia, did you tell anyone how worried you were about Isaac and why? Maybe another friend?"

"No, I only—" She paused. Her crumpled features smoothed, and her gaze became distant. Comprehension flashed in her bloodshot eyes.

"Julia?" I reached out to touch her arm.

She balked. Her gaze jerked back into focus, and a sudden wave of fear rolled off her. She briskly wiped away tears as if it would hide her distress. "No." She shook her head. "I didn't tell anyone anything."

I frowned. *Bullshit.* "I won't—"

"I said *no!*" she snapped. "I'm done answering questions." She yanked open the front door. "Go away and stop bothering me."

"Who did you tell about Isaac? Please, all I need is a name and I'll go." I gasped as streams of energy were torn from the air. The hair on my arms and the nape of my neck stood on end.

"Leave me alone!" Julia's anger was punctuated by a smoldering fit of violet flames escaping her clenched fist. It reminded me of the rogue wizard I'd dealt with the past winter. If it was the same as his, Julia's area of magic focused on attacks and destruction.

I raised my hands and backed away. "I'm sorry. I'll go." My Shield offered protection against most magical attacks, but pissing her off wouldn't get me any answers. I turned and passed through the doorway. The door almost clipped my heel as it slammed shut.

If I was going to find who she'd told about Isaac, Julia wasn't going to be the one to tell me.

18

BEN WAS WITH me when Joan messaged later. It was dark and we were sitting outside, enjoying the pleasant summer evening. I settled beside him at the edge of the landing and handed him the chilled beer I'd brought from inside.

While he opened the bottles, I leaned over and kissed his jawline. My eyelids lowered and I inhaled deeply to smell the day's sun on his skin. It caused the creature curled inside me to stir and stretch.

Our noses almost touched when he turned toward me. He smiled, handed back a bottle, and studied my features. "You have the most stunning eyes."

My cheeks warmed. I'd always been clumsy at receiving compliments. "They're actually a bit embarrassing."

"Why? Because you're supposed to hide them?"

"Not really." I bit at my lip, admiring his blue eyes and how his mop of dark hair tangled in his eyelashes. "It makes what I'm thinking about you pretty obvious. No intrigue there."

Ben chuckled, and my stomach did that little flip it did around him. My phone buzzed from where it lay between us on the landing. The screen lit up and we both glanced down. Joan's name stood in stark relief on the bright screen. We looked up at each other at the same time.

"My sister is texting you?" he asked.

I looked into his eyes, frozen in indecision. Swallowing, I answered. "Yes. She is."

He waited for me to elaborate.

I didn't.

"Did everything go okay earlier for you two?" he asked.

My mind raced through the paths our conversation could take. It didn't look good. "Joan and I plan to break into the abandoned building where the Hunter is staying to look for incriminating evidence linking him to Isaac's death."

Ben's eyebrows drew together as he listened. Silence hung heavy between us after I finished. He opened his mouth to say something but closed it again and looked away. He stood and went into the apartment.

I watched him go before I snatched up the phone and read the message from Joan.

He just left. Can you meet me in 15?

Joan had decided I'd had enough time to think over my next steps, and the time to visit the Hunter's hideout was tonight. Not telling me ahead of time forced me to make a split-second decision. Was I serious about helping her or not?

I need at least 25. I sent the message, pocketed the phone, and went inside the apartment. Ben glanced at me before continuing to browse through his wall of records.

"We found out the Hunter is watching Hell's Bells," I said.

"What!" He turned to me. "What did Trish and Nate say?"

"I told them the Hunter was lurking around the club, so they know to watch for him, but I didn't share the guy's address." I chewed at my thumbnail. "Joan and I are worried he's going to kill someone else before the Committee bothers to collect enough evidence for his arrest. But Joan also doesn't want to work with Trish because of Trish's Committee ties. I don't know what to do."

"Tell Joan no. Tell Trish and Nate where to find the Hunter," Ben said. "Then stay clear until he's hauled in and charged."

I frowned and began to pace. "You know I can't *not* help. This is my community the Hunter is threatening. The next body that turns up isn't going to be a wizard's."

It might be my own.

"I don't know what you want me to say, Alex," Ben said. "If it were my choice, you wouldn't put yourself in danger, but it's not."

No, it wasn't. It was mine, and I owed Trish and Nate. I'd tell them where to find the Hunter, and we could face him together.

"What about Joan?" I stopped beside him. "Would she try to take out the Hunter alone?"

"Why are you asking? Did she text to say she was there?"

I called her even as I nodded. It rang straight into voicemail. "She has her phone off."

Ben cursed.

"I'll stop by the address before going to Hell's Bells," I crossed to the kitchenette counter for my car keys. "I'll convince Joan to come with me. Maybe after meeting and talking to Trish, Joan will feel more comfortable working with her."

"She won't listen to you." Ben retrieved his own keys. "We can go together. She'll leave to make sure I'm not caught there."

I bit back my immediate refusal. He grabbed our helmets and was out the door.

My stomach was in knots. I held tight to his waist and we sped along the highway. What if we ran into the Hunter? Ben would be defenseless. What if the Committee found out he was meddling in the investigation by helping Joan and me? They'd extend his tethering if not worse.

After exiting the highway, we drove past a park and down the poorly lit street where the building was located. The area included empty storefronts, broken sidewalks, and an occasional home that'd resisted being bought up when the block flipped from residential to commercial.

We found Joan's rental car parked on the shoulder. Ben pulled up beside it and cut the bike's engine. I checked over the car. Joan's scent lingered, but the vehicle was empty.

"The building should be up ahead. I'll go get her. Wait here." I offered him a smile. "You're my getaway driver."

He didn't smile back. "Let her know I'm here."

I crept down another block, following Joan's scent. Other than a barking dog and shouts from one of the houses, I didn't notice anyone else. When I approached the one-story building, the few windows near the front were dark. It appeared to be a deserted garage or some type of commercial vehicle storage. Two large garage doors faced the street. At the gravel drive, Joan's scent disappeared. She'd taken the extra caution of cloaking it again.

The metal side door was cracked open. I slipped into the building, and my eyes adjusted to the absence of light. The first room was small, like a lobby. Undisturbed layers of grime and odors of wood decay spoke to the building's age. Chunks of water-damaged drop ceiling lay scattered on the chipped tile floor. Across from me was another doorway, the door having long gone missing.

I detected the stink of oil and gasoline before I stepped through the second doorway into a much larger room. To my left, across the space and through yet another doorway, a soft glow of light emanated. I crept along the wall toward the light. Halfway there, a small spark flashed near the toe of my shoe. It burned in a bright line across the width of the room, like some sort of magical trip wire, and then vanished. The soft light in the back room extinguished.

I waited, motionless and straining to hear anything. A soundless shadow swept into the doorway ahead of me, paused, and then Joan's voice whispered. "Alex?" A soft, marble-sized point of light appeared, hovering over her shoulder. "I wasn't sure you'd come."

"I'm only here to get you. I don't think we should do this alone," I said. "Come with me to see Trish and Nate. We could use their help."

"I'm already here, and arguing the point is a waste of time." She returned to the smaller room, the sound of her movements still cloaked.

I stepped through the doorway. The room was long and about a third the size of the previous. "You can talk to Trish about not mentioning your name to the Committee."

She arched her eyebrow and ran her hand along the surface of the wall. "You were with Benjamin when I messaged, weren't you?"

"Yes."

"I'd thought so," she said. "That's why I went ahead without you. My little brother has a tendency to be overprotective." She tapped on the wall with her knuckles. "I'm surprised you've stuck around this long."

The knots in my stomach clenched, and a surge of frustration filled me. "Ben came with me. We don't want you to be here alone."

Joan quickly looked back at me. "What?" She cursed. Her movements became rushed. "And you were bitching at *me* for putting him in danger?" She pulled some moldy boxes away from the wall. "There has to be something here. There's no reason Fillip would lie to us."

My phone buzzed. Joan threw an annoyed glance my way. It was a text from Ben.

He's here. Passed me. Black truck.

The words vibrated on the screen. Instant fear paralyzed me.

"What is it?" Joan asked.

"The Hunter is here." I looked back toward the larger room.

Gravel crunched in the driveway. Headlights swung along the larger room's walls.

"Shit! He's not supposed to be back yet." She frantically looked around. "Give me your hand."

"What?" Eyes wide, I turned to her.

She held out her hand for mine. When I extended it toward her, she seized my wrist and began to murmur. The telltale rush of energy swirled from the room toward her. She opened her eyes to look at me, still speaking the strange language I'd heard every wizard use to cast magic.

The effect of the spell rushed up my arm beneath my skin. I tried to pull my hand from her grasp but was unable to move. Her body grew semi-transparent from head to toe, as if a bucket of water had been poured over her.

She released my hand, her voice quiet. "I can't see in the dark, so I need your help finding the front room. I can take care of myself from there. We'll slip out together."

I held up my hand and spread my fingers. The same semi-transparent effect allowed me to look straight through my hand at Joan. "Are you able to see me?"

"Yes, of course I can. But we're invisible to him." She swatted at the bobbing point of light at her shoulder and it dispersed.

The faint creak of the front door caught my attention. Another pang of anxiety coursed through me. Joan nudged my side and pointed in the same direction I'd heard the door. Her hand was light at my elbow as I moved us from the back room to the larger one. There was no other noise. Did the Hunter suspect something?

I retraced my steps along the wall of the larger room. Still no sign of the Hunter. A swath of light shone through the empty doorway from the front room into the larger one. At the edge of the doorway, I peeked into the front room. The door leading outside stood wide open. An exterior light illuminated the space.

I froze again. My breath came in short bursts. I covered my nose to muffle the sound and tried to get my nerves under control.

Joan crept around me to look into the front room. She glanced back, gave my arm a squeeze, and then let go. She passed through the doorway into the front room.

My stomach spasmed. Despite Joan's cloaking spell, I felt exposed. As soon as I crossed into the front room, I smelled bleach. I began to tremble. My gaze darted about in a frantic search for the Hunter.

The room appeared empty.

Joan was already several feet ahead of me. She inched toward the building's entrance door. I followed, and the bleach scent grew stronger. Joan stepped slowly and lightly, not unlike a cat, through the doorway. She paused for a moment and then looked back. She motioned me along. Shaking, I continued forward.

I was at the entrance door when I saw him.

Crouched in the shadow of a large truck, the Hunter focused on the ground outside the door. The loose gravel and sand displaced under Joan's weight as she soundlessly passed him. He watched her footprints appear out of thin air. The Hunter realigned his grip on a crowbar. When Joan looked back to check my progress, he sprang from his hiding place. He swung the crowbar around at the height of her waist.

"No!" With an inhuman burst of speed, I rushed through the doorway and grabbed his arm. The trajectory of his strike was thrown, and the bar swung up to graze Joan's shoulder blade instead. She cried out in surprise.

When the improvised weapon made contact, the veil of invisibility melted away. I wrestled with the Hunter and realized the spell's effect was spoiled for me too. He glared over his captured arm at me. His eyes filled with recognition.

I tried to snap his wrist, a simple task with a Commoner, but he only winced and dropped the crowbar. After a minute more of struggling to take him down, I leapt back out of his reach. He'd pinned me like a bug to Susan's hallway wall, but I thought I'd at least put him on his heels in a fair fight.

The Hunter straightened and rubbed his wrist. I continued to back away toward Joan as I watched the man. He kept an eye on us while he calmly retrieved wound rope from the bed of his truck.

"Go and tell Ben we have to leave," I said to Joan. "He's waiting at your car."

"I can help you," she said.

"He's too strong for the two of us."

She nodded, turned away, and ran down the remainder of the drive to the street. The Hunter's gaze flitted to the fleeing woman and back. Every step he took toward me was intentional. I was his sole focus.

The hair rose on the nape of my neck. A growl rose from deep within my chest.

He whistled a soft low tune as he unwound a length of the rope. He spoke like one would to a nervous animal. "Shh . . . Calmly now. No more running. No more hiding."

At the end of the drive, I stopped. I didn't want to lead him down the street to Ben. Though my whole body trembled, my words left me as a snarl. "Stay the hell away from me."

"Shh . . . Be still." He continued his advance. "You're barely a person, Alexandria. The blight, it rots your humanity and leaves only a beast." His dark eyes glinted.

I flexed my clawed hands, and the urge to retreat faded. It was being overtaken by anger at his brazen disregard of my request. "Stop!" I bared my pointed teeth. "Don't come closer!"

He smiled, and his steady gait didn't falter. "I see it . . . The deadly creature that tried to kill the young man. It's just behind your eyes. Let me free you from it."

Fillip was right. The Hunter planned to kill me.

My body tensed. I lowered my frame and shifted my weight toward the front of my feet.

The Hunter took another step.

I lunged at his throat.

For someone with so much mass, his movements were swift and graceful. I barely clipped the side of his neck as he ducked past me. He turned and struck a solid hit to the middle of my back. My momentum and the force behind his punch threw me off my feet.

I landed in a forward slide. Gravel lodged into the heels of my hands. Growling, I spun on my knees. I found my feet in a cloud of dust to face him. The Hunter had put himself between me and my getaway ride.

He followed me step by step up the drive and began to whistle again. The sound of it made me want to scream. He was playing with me, like a cat with a mouse. It pissed me off. Ben's motorcycle raced down the road. The Hunter heard it as well. He asked in his low voice, "Aren't you tired of running, lupa?"

I lunged again, repeatedly slashing at his neck and face. He raised his forearms to block me. My claws shredded the fabric of his sleeves but were hindered by thick bands of leather he wore beneath. Despite the leather bracers protecting him, my attack forced him to back away. Ben waited on the motorcycle at the end of the drive. Seeing my chance, I made a run for it.

A rope snapped tight around my upper body. My retreat was halted. I turned, seized the rope, and wrenched it toward me.

The Hunter's feet slid in the gravel, but he kept his body anchored at the other end of the rope. I struggled to free myself from the binding. Every time I slackened the tension to escape, he yanked the rope one length toward him to pull it tight again.

A set of headlights rushed toward us. Joan drove directly at the Hunter.

He held on longer than I would have before he dropped the rope. He dodged the car and a spray of gravel.

The rope fell slack, and I slipped free. I raced toward the motorcycle, jumped on, and in my haste, almost fell off the other side. My hands barely clutched Ben before the bike took off. Joan's car was behind us. An arm hooked around Ben, I looked back.

The Hunter was a large, dark figure standing motionless in the drive, watching our retreat.

We were several blocks away before Joan's car passed us and pulled over. Ben followed suit, the headlight of the motorcycle shining through the back window of her car. He handed my helmet back to me.

Joan jogged up beside us and shouted over the rumble of the motorcycle. "We need to talk. Where do you want to meet up?"

My hands shook as I put on the helmet. "Hell's Bells."

She looked disappointed but nodded. She gave Ben a brief pat on the shoulder before she hurried back to her car. Joan pulled onto the road and drove quickly in the direction of the highway.

Ben's upper body twisted to check that I was ready. His eyes widened. His face brightened to a ghostly white from oncoming headlights. I jerked around. The large truck bore down on us. Ben accelerated, and the front of the bike hitched as it tore from the shoulder back onto the pavement. There was a crash behind us as the front corner of the Hunter's truck destroyed the mailbox we'd been idling beside.

We raced toward a park situated on the corner of the block. Ben steered the motorcycle toward and across it to gain a lead on the truck. The Hunter was restricted to the street, but he accelerated around the corner in a way that brought a messy end to several parked cars' side mirrors.

The motorcycle skipped off the sidewalk back onto the road, and we flew toward the highway on-ramp. The motorcycle's engine screamed as it accelerated up to speed for the faster traffic. The Hunter was delayed as his truck caught the corner of a sedan. The smaller car was spun out of the way, and he turned onto the ramp after us.

My hold around Ben's waist tightened, and I kept my head behind his body. The wind roared in my ears, and my shirt billowed out behind me like a sail. Ben sliced dangerously between vehicles and crossed three lanes to put traffic between us and the Hunter. The truck still accelerated after us.

A large spotlight on top of the truck's roof turned on. The bright light blasted into the rearview mirrors of other drivers. The flow of traffic decelerated and clustered. The highway was filled with the sound of blaring horns. The Hunter whipped his truck into the far-left lane and quickly gained ground.

"He's going to cause accidents," I shouted into the wind near Ben's ear. "We have to lead him back off the highway."

Ben nodded and eyed the upcoming exit. With a brief glance back at the Hunter's truck, he waited until the last moment to shoot off the exit ramp. We climbed the ramp fast as the motorcycle whined back down in speed. The traffic light at the top of the ramp shone yellow. The motorcycle didn't decrease in speed.

Ben planned to blow through the light.

At the last second, a panhandler stepped off the curb. Ben's body jerked and the motorcycle's brakes locked up. The bike slipped sideways on loose stones, and the bottom half slid out from beneath us.

I wrapped my arms around Ben, hoping to shield his body with my own. A swift surge of energy collapsed around us, and my body went numb. When we hit the pavement, we were traveling fast enough to slide across the intersection. The concrete should have torn up our clothes and any exposed skin. Instead, we skated across the street surface like it was polished ice, completely unharmed.

The bike hit the curb ahead of us and bounced back off it to spin toward the left of the intersection. Ben and I struck the curb and lay in a heap. An enormous amount of energy buzzed around us. My eyes watered, and my teeth and fingernails vibrated with it.

The blur of a large dark truck crested the ramp. It didn't slow.

The Hunter planned to crush us.

Ben pushed himself up onto his hands and knees and looked into the oncoming headlights. He raised his open palm toward the truck's grill and spoke a single word.

Crackling light exploded outward from our figures into a large, webbed sphere. The front of the Hunter's vehicle struck the sphere and crumpled in on itself. Ben twisted his wrist and the sphere rotated, pitching the truck up into the air.

The back of the vehicle eclipsed the front as it passed over us. The truck fell back to the pavement onto its roof with a tremendous crunching of metal and shattering of glass. It slid and rocked to a stop in front of the on-ramp. The shield-like sphere collapsed out of existence with the zapping sound of discharged electricity.

Eyes wide, I looked at Ben.

He lowered his hand to grasp his throat, and the reek of singed flesh filled my nostrils. The cross shape of his tether burned bright from between his fingers. He leaned forward on his knees and coughed. A spew of blood dripped from between his lips.

The metallic scent hit my nose so hard I could taste it.

Shaking, I stumbled to my feet. "Can you stand?" We had to leave before the accident was reported.

He nodded, his features distorted by pain. I held out a hand to help him up. His balance wavered, and he turned away to spit up more blood.

My heart hammering against my ribcage, I hurried to the motorcycle lying on its side in the street. I'd asked Ben before to teach me how to drive it. I was sure these were great circumstances for my first lesson.

The motorcycle was in one piece, though horribly scratched. I pulled it upright and got onto the bike. I attempted to start it as I'd seen Ben do by kicking down on the pedal. The bike lurched forward, but the engine didn't start. Ben tapped on my left leg and pointed to a lever on my left side. I pressed down the pedal, tried the kick starter again, and the bike rumbled to life.

When I attempted to idle ahead, the bike leapt with a jerk and stalled. I growled and tried to start the bike twice before succeeding. Ben closed his bloodied hand around mine to press a lever at the bike's handlebar and nodded. I shifted and the bike crept forward.

Ben sat behind me and gave me a light pat on my shoulder. Thankfully I got the shifting correct and we continued to move in an upright position. Progress.

Something sharp struck the back of my shoulder. I screamed as an explosion of pain shot down my arm and across my collarbone. The tip of an arrow protruded through the front of my shoulder. I looked back and my eyes widened.

Bloodied and bruised, the Hunter walked toward us from the wreck of the truck. He was reloading a crossbow.

I fumbled with the motorcycle, and it threatened to stall again. Finally, it accelerated. I shifted gears, and it began to pick up speed.

The throbbing pain in my shoulder made it difficult to concentrate. I tried to decide where to flee. I had no idea what was happening with Ben's tether, but the amount of blood scared me. Trish stitched and bandaged beat-up wolves, but this seemed like an injury for an expert healer. I abandoned the plan of going to Hell's Bells and drove toward Emma's house instead.

19

THE TRIP SEEMED to take forever. Emma must have heard the engine because she came to the front door after we pulled up into the drive and idled there. She rushed outside and did her best to help Ben get off the bike. I let the bike stall out and climbed off.

"Did you get into an accident?" Wide-eyed, Emma took in the state of the motorcycle and the front of Ben's shirt, bright with fresh blood.

"No, it was the Hunter."

"The Hunter? Your shoulder! Is that an arrow?"

"Also the Hunter." I stowed the bike in a garage stall. My shoulder flared with pain when I reached up to take off my helmet.

Emma followed me into the garage. She tried to keep Ben upright, but struggled, being a full head shorter than him. "Why was a Hunter after you?"

I set my helmet aside and removed Ben's for him. "We snuck into the place where he's staying. He has strong feelings about trespassers." I took over for Emma and guided Ben into the house.

She hurried ahead to the bathroom for towels as I helped Ben settle at the dining room table. He slumped forward and rested his forehead on his crossed arms. I sent a message and Emma's address to Joan.

Ben and I were injured. We're at the address for medical care.

Emma rushed back into the dining room with an armful of towels. "How bad is your injury?"

I looked it over. The sight of the bolt protruding through the front of my shoulder made me queasy. "The tip looks like it's silver, but it passed through. I can wait until after you help Ben. He's vomited a lot of blood. I think his throat was injured."

She pulled a chair to him, sat down, and touched his shoulder. "Ben?"

At the sound of Emma's voice, he lifted his head. His gaze was distant as if he were looking through her. It frightened me even more.

"Can I see your throat?" She reached toward the area of his tether. He frowned, shook his head, and tried to lean away.

I crouched down on the other side of his chair. "Please, let her help. I don't understand what's happening, and it scares me. I don't know what else to do for you."

He struggled to focus on my features before he reluctantly sat up straighter in the chair. Emma gently blotted away the blood from where it had run down the front of his chin and his throat. He grimaced as the damp cloth came in contact with the skin around the mark of his tether. It looked freshly burnt into his skin, but there was no trace of the strange light I'd seen.

A repeated loud pounding on the front door marked Joan's arrival. I stood back up and hurried to let her into the house. She pushed past me, looking for Ben. "What happened? Did he follow us?" Joan asked. I smelled the fear trailing after her.

"He was chasing us and tried to hit us with his truck when we got off the highway." I followed her toward the lights of the dining room. A tingling sensation brushed across my arms, and I knew Emma's magic was at work.

"Is he going to be okay?" Joan demanded. Her expression was a mixture of anger and worry. She stopped beside Emma's chair and noticed the raw area of Ben's throat. Joan paled, and the scent of her fear thickened. Tears welled in her eyes.

"I'm still trying to see the nature and extent of the injury." Emma was calm, despite Joan hovering near her shoulder. Her delicate fingertips were placed lightly at the tether, her eyelids partially lowered. Her voice murmured, trance-like, "It seems internal for the most part."

A verse of gently spoken and indistinguishable words left Emma. A soft glow spread across Ben's throat like a light beneath the skin. I held my breath and searched Ben's features for some sign her efforts were making a difference.

Emma's finely shaped brows drew together, and she frowned. Her eyelids snapped open, and she yanked her hand back from Ben's throat. A bright arc of light, crackling like electricity, snapped at her fingers. "Ow! What the hell?" She sat back, startled, and held her hand. The foul scent of singed fingernails filled the room. "I think the tether blocked me."

"You can't help him?" I asked.

"I stopped the bleeding, but something is barring me from completely healing him. The interior of his throat suffered some sort of burn or trauma," she said. "The Hunter did this?" She leaned forward and looked closely at Ben's tether, as if the answer were written there.

I swallowed, unsure how to respond. I had sworn to Ben I'd keep his secret, even from Emma. "I'm not sure what happened, Em." It was a partial truth. Even though he'd found a way to weaken the tether, I'd never seen Ben use magic. He still didn't have full access to it. The wards on his apartment were of Reginald's creation.

Emma turned her attention to her next patient: me. "I'm going to make sure a room is ready for you two." Her nose wrinkled as she pointed at the crossbow bolt. "Then we'll get rid of that thing." She stood, offered the still-lurking Joan a friendly smile, and left the room.

As soon as Emma was out of earshot, Joan leaned forward and placed her hands on the table beside Ben. The volume of her voice was kept low, but her eyes were alight with anger. "You goddamn idiot. What have you done?" A tear escaped down her cheek.

"He protected us from getting killed," I growled.

She glowered at me. "I'd like to talk to my brother without you here."

I watched her, suspicious of her intent. Why couldn't I be in the room? Would she do to her own brother what she did to Anne? Mess with his mind? "No."

Ben opened his mouth, but his face contorted. Eyes watering, he withdrew his notepad and pencil. He scribbled two words.

She knows.

We both looked at Ben in surprise.

Joan's face flushed. "Why would you do something so asinine, Benjamin?"

He laid his head back down on his arms.

She fumed and threw a gesture in my direction. "You just met this person! How do you know she's trustworthy? Of all the stupid things you've done in your life, this—"

"It was a mistake. He didn't mean for me to know." And I thought I was the only one who knew he'd cheated his tether. Suspicion nagged at the back of my mind. "Joan, those two guys who attacked Ben this past winter . . . Were you the one who told them what he'd done to his tether?"

She turned on me, her eyes widening. Her mouth moved, but no words came out. "Why was he out there with us? He's tethered! The Committee burned a bullseye on him, and you brought him along to break into a Hunter's hideout! What were you thinking?" Her tears flowed freely, her face distorted. "How are you not dead yet?"

I swallowed back the lump in my throat and looked at Ben's hunched figure. He was barely conscious. Emma cautiously reentered the room. There was no way she couldn't have heard the shouting. Joan turned away to hide her outrage and wipe away her tears.

Emma spoke in a quiet voice. "The bed is ready if you want to take him to your room, Alex."

I looked at Joan's back. My voice wavered only a bit. "Any other words before he gets some rest?"

Joan turned to Ben and wrapped her arms tightly around his slumped form. She whispered, "I'll fix this. Please be careful until then." She kissed the top of his head. "Sleep well, little brother." She straightened and offered her hand to Emma. "Thank you for stabilizing him."

Emma daintily accepted the strong handshake and smiled. "You're welcome. I'm happy to help."

Joan strode from the room. The front door opened and closed. It felt as if all the wind had been knocked out of me.

Emma invited me to take the chair she'd sat in earlier. "Since she's gone, let me help with your shoulder first. Then you both can rest." There was the sound of snapping wood as Emma cut the shaft behind my shoulder. I winced as the action jostled the wound.

"I should have followed my gut and told him no," I said, "but I don't like when he tries to stop me from doing what I want to do."

"Ben is a grown man capable of making his own choices," Emma said. "He knows all the rules of being tethered. And it sounded like Joan spoke more out of fear for her brother than believing you're to blame." There was another wiggle of the crossbow bolt. I clenched my teeth against the sharp pain. "Alex, I don't think I'm strong enough to pull the shaft out. Can you do that?"

Hearing the suggestion made me feel light-headed. I took the thin pair of gloves and towel she handed me. I looked away from the wound and yanked the bolt the remainder of the way through my shoulder. There was a sickening tug from within the muscles of my shoulder, a wave of nausea, and a burning pain afterward that caused my eyes to tear up. I firmly pressed the towel to the front of my shoulder to staunch the bleeding long enough for Emma to literally work her magic.

"Breathe," Emma coached before she swiftly wove another healing spell.

A comforting warmth, like the soothing feeling of a hot bath on sore muscles, seeped outward from where Emma's hand covered the wound. The pain throughout my shoulder, arm, and back dulled. It took longer to heal than Ben's injury, but when I removed the towel, a fresh swath of new skin covered the front of my shoulder.

I rolled my shoulder forward and backward to test it. The only uncomfortable sensation was a tightness in the muscle. "Thank you for helping us. Again."

"You're welcome. Again." Emma wiped her bloodied hands on a towel.

I stood and roused Ben. He made it to his feet, and I put my shoulder under his arm to support him.

Emma collapsed in the chair I'd vacated. She surveyed the mess of her dining room and sighed. "Let me know if you need anything."

I guided Ben to the same room we'd stayed in before and helped him sit down on the bed. I crouched in the dark to take off his shoes. My voice was hushed. "Even if she suspects something is up with your tether, I don't think Em will tell anyone." I looked up at him. "And I want to talk more about what happened tonight . . . what you did to defend us."

Ben slouched at the bed's edge. He frowned and placed his hand at the front of his throat. He spelled out a word in sign. "Burns."

"It doesn't have to be right now."

He let me help him out of his clothes. The scent of his blood was still strong even as it dried on the fabric. I tossed our shirts in the bathtub and closed the bathroom door to dampen the odor. Ben's eyes were already closed when I crawled into the bed. I curled up close beside him and focused on the steady beat of his heart to help calm my thoughts.

Our encounter with the Hunter had scared the shit out of me. The guy was eerily focused and extremely strong. He was too much for Joan and me to take on alone. We needed help. We also needed to know more about Hunters. How were they so powerful?

Joan may not want anything to do with me now since I'd endangered Ben. But like Emma said, he knew the risks. It didn't help the dread and guilt I felt. Would the Hunter tell the Committee about Ben? He'd be punished for slipping his tether.

I reached my arm across Ben, pressed my nose to his skin, and inhaled his scent. His breathing gradually fell into the regular rhythm of sleep. It wasn't long after that I slipped off to sleep, too.

THE NEXT MORNING I awoke to several missed calls and a message from Nate asking if I was okay. Joan had made it to Hell's Bells last night and was waiting there when she received my text that Ben and I were at Emma's. I sent Nate a message assuring him I was safe and would be by the club later that night. Our encounter with the Hunter had finalized my decision to include Trish and Nate.

I quietly dressed so Ben could sleep longer. Two folded shirts waited on the floor outside the bedroom. After swapping out my ruined shirt for the clean one, I set the shirt for Ben on his shoes.

Fragrances of comfort, vanilla and coffee, led me down the hall to the kitchen. Emma stood at the coffee maker dressed in an aquamarine sundress, pouring a cup of coffee. Her hair was drawn back into a messy ponytail that somehow appeared stylish. She smiled. "Oh good, you found the clothes. You should really keep some here in case you need them."

I sat on a barstool at the kitchen island. "Ideally I won't."

She placed the steaming mug of coffee in front of me. The woman was a saint.

"I love you, Em." I took the delicious first sip.

"I love you, too." She sat beside me and picked up a cup of tea. "How's Ben feeling?"

"He hasn't stirred since he passed out, so I'm letting him sleep," I said. "Do you think there'll be permanent damage from his injury?"

"It's possible any remaining damage could be healed once the tether is removed." She watched me take another sip, biting at her bottom lip.

"What is it?" I asked.

"Did Ben break his tether?"

I choked on my coffee and started coughing. Was it that obvious to another wizard? Thumping on my chest, my eyes watered as I cleared my throat. "I told you already, I'm not sure what happened."

"Because the injury was internal," Emma said. "I thought about it more while I cleaned up last night. You never told me *how* he was attacked. You at least know that, right?"

My gaze dropped to the wisps of steam rising from my mug. "We appreciate your help, but I can't discuss this with you . . . at least not right now."

"I understand." She frowned at her tea. "I was up until 3:00 a.m. scrubbing your blood out of my carpet so the maid won't ask questions, but heaven forbid I ask the details of why. You roll up to my door and expect me to help, no questions asked."

"Em."

"And I swear he was talking in the video from my parent's house. There was no audio, but his lips moved."

Why hadn't I thought of that? I suddenly felt sick. "Does your mom suspect anything?"

Emma's eyes widened. "So he did it? He broke his tether?"

"Emma! Your mom."

She shook her head. "No. My mother doesn't even know Ben. She was too focused on kicking you out of her party." She sat back in her chair, staring at her tea. "Why would he do that? That's so dangerous."

"I know." My stomach clenched. "It's why you can't say anything to anyone. Promise me."

She nodded.

"Em?"

Her eyes flashed. "Of course I won't say anything. I promise."

"Please let me tell him . . . that you know."

"Okay." She took a sip of tea. "Can you at least tell me more about finding the Hunter?"

I hesitated. Emma had reminded me Ben was able to make his own decisions. Maybe it was time I trusted her to do the same instead of not telling her things to keep her safe.

Our conversation progressed in fits and starts at first, but then smoothed out. I told her about the investigation of Isaac's death, the Hunter, and my growing concern that Anne would discover the secret I was obligated to keep from her.

"Anne called yesterday to ask about you," Emma said. "She's concerned you're in trouble and hiding things from her."

Shit. "What did you say?"

"That you're a private person. She didn't sound convinced."

"Was it because of our run?" I asked.

Emma nodded.

I put my elbows on the counter and leaned my face into my hands. "It was awful, Em. I should have stepped aside and waited for the other jogger to pass, but I thought I could push through it. I practically wolfed out, right there, in front of Anne and two strangers." I lowered my hands and shook my head. "I don't know what to do."

"Maybe you ghost her until the situation with the Hunter and Isaac has blown over," she said. "I'll still be here for her."

"Maybe." Talking to Emma about Anne eased some of my stress. "Thanks."

Ben joined us about an hour later. His features were pallid, but he seemed more alert. His throat was still tender when he woke, so he wasn't interested in eating. I took my breakfast to go so he could rest in his own bed and not feel obligated to answer Emma's questions. Plus, she had an awful poker face and constantly stole curious glances at his tether. I was afraid he'd notice.

When we arrived back at the apartment, he assessed the motorcycle's damage. He shook his head and ran his hands through his hair. His two jobs covered bare necessities and his music addiction, not pricey cosmetic work for a beat-up motorcycle.

I placed my hand at the small of his back. "Why don't you text Rear Window and ask for the day off?"

He frowned and gestured at the bike.

"One day won't make much of a difference. You can save up, and I'll help pay for the repairs," I said. "Right now, you could use the extra rest."

The battered motorcycle brought back memories of last night. I gave an involuntary shiver. Fighting the Hunter had been a rude reminder of how little I knew about them. I thought of the daggers kept in St. Anthony's and called to request a meeting with Aiden. Mrs. Murphy let me know how fortunate I was that he had an available time slot that afternoon. I had waited until the last minute after all.

I showered and mentally prepared myself for my meeting. The motorcycle had put Ben in a foul mood, so he stretched out on the sofa for some disgruntled napping. I debated if this was the best time to share that Emma had discovered his secret.

Footsteps sounded on the stairs. A familiar scent reached me through the open front door. My stomach turned and I gave Ben's shoulder a few taps. "You have company."

Bleary-eyed, Ben blinked up at me a few times before he sat up. He raised an eyebrow, clearly not expecting anyone.

Reginald appeared outside the doorway. The wizard was dressed as sharply as ever in a dusty blue suit. Dropping in on each other unannounced must run in the family. Ben's eyes turned stormy, and he greeted his grandfather with an immediate frown.

Reginald waited and cleared his throat to ensure his presence was known. "Salutations!" The greeting was good-natured and punctuated by a tip of his hat.

Ben stood, crossed the apartment in several long strides, and closed the apartment door. He returned to the sofa and laid back down. Like I'd mentioned, Ben's relationship with Reginald was complicated. He strove to have as little to do with his grandfather as possible.

I swallowed, unsure what to do. "Should we see what he wants? It might be about the investigation."

Ben's only reply was a heated glance. He turned onto his side, which placed his back to the door. Well, that wasn't a no. I opened the door and offered Reginald an uneasy smile. "I'm sorry."

"Thank you, Miss Alex." He grimaced. "May I come in?"

I stepped aside. Reginald took off his hat and entered the apartment. His brief scan around seemed to distress him. He straightened and cleared his throat once again. His tone was firm. "Benjamin, I've respected your wishes by keeping my distance, as difficult as that has been for me. However, your recent actions forced my hand." Reginald frowned when he wasn't acknowledged. "Please, sit up and give me your attention."

Ben gave his grandfather the finger instead.

Reginald's face flushed red, and his bushy eyebrows drew together. I dropped my gaze and debated stepping out of the apartment to give them privacy. The idea was abandoned when a whisper of energy gathered from around us. I stepped in front of Ben, narrowed my eyes at Reginald, and growled.

Reginald glanced between Ben and me. Was a tangle with a werewolf worth the effort to discipline his grandson? The energy he'd collected was harmlessly released. Reginald sighed and wilted into a chair at the table. "Peace, Miss Alex."

He spoke to Ben's back. "I find myself in a difficult position. When I created your tether, I made the selfish choice of including a safeguard. It would allow me to sense any violation of your sentence before word reached the Committee. I justified the action by assuring myself it would never be needed."

The uneasy feeling in my stomach grew. I backed closer to Ben until my calves touched the front edge of the sofa.

Reginald ran a hand over his face. "Benjamin, I know you've overpowered your tether."

The words were like a sucker punch. I looked back at Ben in panic. He'd sat up and regarded Reginald with wide eyes. The acidic smell of Ben's fear flooded the room and caused my chest to tighten.

"The Hunter was trying to kill us!" I said. "We'd be dead if Ben hadn't stopped him."

Reginald looked startled. "Why would the Hunter have reason to attack the two of you?"

Because I thought spying on a Hunter with your grandchildren would be a great night out? Nothing I thought of wouldn't also drag Joan into this. Instead of answering, I said, "If you don't believe me, I can show you." Reginald could glimpse people's recent memories. He'd done it once before with me. "Ben shouldn't be punished for saving us."

Ben's thin frame trembled, and his breath came in quick, short bursts through his nose.

Reginald looked from me to his grandson, unsure. "The Committee has never been faced with this specific situation before. I would, of course, be required to repair any damage to the tether."

"No." Ben signed the word and shook his head. "Please. No."

"Don't be ridiculous, Benjamin. You broke the law." Reginald frowned. "I cannot allow you to complete a criminal sentence with a broken tether."

"No. No. No. Please. No." Ben's hands seemed caught in a loop, and he repeatedly shook his head.

"Imagine the optics if a family member of mine received special treatment. I hope your years served thus far will work to your advantage, and your sentence won't be lengthened by too much."

The color disappeared from Ben's face.

Witnessing him this frightened was like a knife twisted in my gut. "What if we run into the Hunter again?" I asked.

"No more arguing! Need I remind the two of you how serious the repercussions are for this?" He scowled at me. "When we first met, I'd asked you to consider what consequences your actions hold for him." He drove his fingertip down onto the tabletop. "*This* is exactly what I was speaking of."

That knife jerked in my gut again. Reginald was as scared for Ben as I was. But there was something condescending in his tone I didn't like. Growling and baring my teeth, I lowered myself to sit close enough to Ben that our arms touched.

He sat dazed at the edge of the sofa. His hands latched behind his neck, elbows on his knees. He stared down at the floor between his feet.

Reginald's next words to Ben were orders. "You are to remain in this apartment until I have this sorted. You can go to your job at the shop below, but do not leave this building," he said. "Do you understand?"

Ben gave a nod but didn't look up from the floor.

Reginald turned his stormy gaze to me. "Do you?"

Grasping tightly to my control, I nodded.

"I'm hopeful the matter of Isaac's murder will remain the Committee's priority, for Patricia's sake and now ours. We will revisit this infraction afterward." Reginald stood and looked down skeptically at his grandson. "Benjamin, you've worked hard for many years to reach this point. Your sister and I miss you and are eager for you to rejoin us in the study of our craft. Don't lose focus by being short-sighted." Reginald replaced his hat and left the apartment.

We sat together, listening to Reginald's steps depart down the stairs. Ben's body shook in spasms beside me. I'd never seen him this scared, and I didn't know what to do to help. I twisted my hands in my lap. "Do you want me to stay here with you? I can reschedule my appointment with Aiden."

He shook his head.

"Do you want to talk about what happened?" I tentatively reached out to touch my fingertips to his arm.

Ben turned toward me, scowling, and curtly signed. "No." He stood and left the couch for the mattress.

It stung, and my immediate thought was to follow him. I wanted to lay beside him and be there when he was ready to talk. I wanted to understand what had happened last night. And I wanted him to know I cared for him and he wouldn't have to face whatever lay ahead alone.

But I wanted information on the Hunter more.

I hovered near the front door, momentarily paralyzed by indecision. Ben lay curled on the bed so he faced away from me. I wondered if he was thinking what I was thinking, that the Committee wouldn't listen to *why* he'd cast magic. They'd be focused on the fact he disobeyed them. It could be the excuse they needed to make an example of him . . . to have him executed.

A sudden flood of anger coursed through me. This Hunter was not only threatening the wolf community, my family away from home, but now he'd endangered Ben. I was not okay with that. Neither was the creature inside me. The mix of fear and anger agitated her, and she pushed a low rumbling growl from within me.

"I'll be back as soon as I can." I hurried from the apartment, locking the door behind me.

20

I ENTERED ST. ANTHONY'S unsure of how the last-minute meeting would pan out. It was always a toss up, guessing how successful my conversations with Aiden would be. I knocked on the door before entering the administrative offices. Mrs. Murphy, positioned dutifully at her post, looked up from her computer. Her smile was thin. "Can I help you?"

"Yes." I kept my hands tucked in my pockets this time. "I called this morning and scheduled an appointment with Father Aiden."

"One moment, please." She looked back to her computer, and the mouse clicked a few times. "Alex Steward?"

"Yes." The appointment confirmed, I started toward the edge of the counter. "Can I go in?"

"No." Mrs. Murphy shot me a disapproving look. "Please have a seat. I'll let Father know you're here."

I looked around the little area where I stood. There were no chairs or any place to sit down.

Mrs. Murphy spoke into the phone, "Father, your next appointment is here." She nodded, smiled, and hung up the receiver. "He's ready for you."

"So, I can go in then?" I asked, hesitating.

She frowned, like the question was absurd. "Yes, of course. Step around the corner."

When I opened the door to Aiden's office, the fragrances of soap, incense, and leatherbound books wafted out. Aiden, seated at his desk, waved me in without looking up from his work. I shut the door and sat down in one of the leather chairs. It was more comfortable than I remembered. But the last time I sat in the chair, Aiden interrogated Ben and me about why we'd broken into the cathedral's basement.

The room was as I remembered, more of a study or library than an office. Two of the walls were lined with built-in bookshelves. The shelves sagged beneath the weight of books of every size and color. Ben would love to have a room like this. We both would. I'd more than once tripped or knocked over piles of books he'd left around the apartment.

Aiden put down his pen and looked across the desk at me. "How can I help you, Miss Steward?"

"I need more information about Hunters," I said. "Since you're a keeper of their weapons, I thought you might know how they get their superpowers."

"Superpowers?" The priest set aside his reading glasses. It was a sign he was preparing for one of our classic arguments, which confirmed my suspicion he had more knowledge to share. "Why do you want information about them?" he asked.

"We need to know how to protect ourselves."

Aiden steepled his fingers. "The Committee has yet to vote on the Hunter's installment. That vote will take place today."

I gave a derisive snort. "Even if you voted no, Stone has the majority of the other members scared of us. We'll be outvoted."

"If I gave you the information you're seeking, would you use it for defense only?"

I clenched my jaw. It would be faster if he gave me what I came for instead of first running me through his list of pointless questions. I remained silent and refused to break my stare.

Appearing weary, Aiden was for once the first to look away. He stood and walked around the desk to sit in the chair beside me. "I apologize for the stress this is causing you, Patricia, and the rest of the lupine."

His apology wasn't going to protect us. I frowned. "Do you have information to share with me or not?"

"What exactly do you want to know about Hunters?" he asked.

"They're Commoners, aren't they?"

"Yes, they are."

"When the Hunter looks at me, he sees my wolf. I can feel it. But it's different from when a wizard prepares a spell." I held my breath, willing him to speak.

"They do not access power like wizards," he paused. "Hunters carry with them a token, or object, of their faith. Unlike wizards who draw on the raw energy surrounding them, a Hunter will tap into an object to gain abilities beyond those of a Commoner."

"Where do they keep the object?" I asked.

"They will always have it on their person," Aiden said.

"Like those daggers?"

"No," he said. "The daggers are a tool and can be easily taken away."

I tried to recall what the man was wearing. Did he have any jewelry? A charm pinned to his clothing? The thought of the Hunter caused me to shift uncomfortably in my seat.

"Miss Steward," Aiden interrupted my thoughts. "If you've decided to do something rash, I ask you to please wait until after the Committee holds the vote today."

Was he giving my plan to go after the Hunter his blessing? "I've found two witnesses identifying the Hunter as the person who murdered Isaac."

Aiden frowned. "You said the information will be used by the lupine to protect themselves from a Hunter. Why are you investigating Isaac's death? That is being handled by Officer DeBoer and Detective Grey."

"At the last Committee meeting, Jakob told me he was pulled from his visit to the morgue. He never went to see Isaac's body. And someone messed with the ME's report. Details of the burns on Isaac's body were excluded. Remember Detective Grey's confusion at the meeting?" I tapped on the chair arm. "It's Stone's Hunter. He killed Isaac."

"You believe the man Mr. Stone wants to put into place to protect the city is the same man who killed Isaac?" he asked.

"I don't know where you've been, but the wolves have been living in a state of heightened anxiety for the past six months. Those riots didn't materialize out of nothing. It wasn't a group of thugs getting together to break things." I leaned forward in my chair. "I wouldn't put it past some Committee members to order Isaac's death, knowing it would spark the riots. Then they could justify the Hunter's placement in the city."

Aiden listened as I explained my current working theory. An ever so slight smile appeared on his lips. He stood and walked to the bookshelf behind me to scan the titles. "You remind me of Patricia when I first met her," he said.

I turned in my seat to watch him. "Thank you."

"She was a constant thorn in the Committee Chair's side as well," he said.

I smiled. I'd take that one as a compliment, too. "How long have you known each other?"

He pulled down a book and continued to run his fingers along the spines. "Many years now," he said, "before my position as Committee Chair bound my hands to neutrality."

Had they been friends? Trish always defended Aiden when Nate ranted about the priest, but otherwise she never talked about him.

Aiden selected a second book from the shelf and returned to the desk, placing both books on its surface. With a hand on the top of the stack, he looked at me. "You were correct. As a keeper of the Hunters' artifacts, it is important I understand the history behind them. The Hunters are an ancient order with beliefs deeply rooted in old traditions. Since our last Committee meeting, I've been reviewing some texts to refresh my knowledge of their ways."

"So you don't trust him, either," I said.

He didn't answer. Instead, he added, "Lending said texts to anyone could be viewed as favoritism and jeopardize my position as Chair." Aiden emptied a canvas tote on his desk, folded the bag, and set it atop the books. "Unfortunately I will have to cut our meeting short, Miss Steward. I've promised Mrs. Murphy I would take her to lunch. We have the very important matter of discussing why her grandson should sing the solo in the youth concert despite the choral director's objections."

I grinned.

Aiden returned a fleeting smile. "I've been counseling many grieving parishioners over the loss of Isaac. I'll let Mrs. Murphy know I've given you permission to stay in the office to collect yourself. Please lock the door when you leave."

"Thanks, Aiden."

He nodded, gave the books a final decisive tap of his fingertips, and exited the office. I picked up the first book and flipped through the pages. It was dense with text and illustrations. Sections had been flagged with scraps of paper. I needed information about the Hunter fast, before he attacked or killed anyone else. That meant I also needed help getting through the books.

I put them in the canvas tote and cracked open the door to check if Aiden and Mrs. Murphy had left. With the office dark and empty, I flipped the lock and left down the main hall and back out into the bright afternoon.

I RETURNED TO the apartment to find it dark and quiet. Ben was asleep on the mattress. After getting a tall glass of ice water, I set up camp on the floor in front of the couch. I could get started on sifting through the books and ask for Ben's help when he woke up.

I pulled the books out of the tote and set them on the floor in front of me. Both had patterns embossed on the covers and smelled of leather. The swirling medallion-like design on the smaller of the two matched the symbol on the pedestal, box, and daggers at St. Anthony's. I opened the cover carefully, the scent of dust and old parchment filling my nostrils. The illuminated letters of the title page read *Ordo Sanctus Hubert*.

I flipped through the book slowly, admiring the beautifully adorned pages. Various creatures were tangled and trapped within ornate borders, reminding me of a book of fairytales. I lingered on a page with a gruesome wolf man, his jaws agape as he prepared to devour a flailing infant. *Lupus*, read the illuminated subtitle of the page. I ran my finger down the text and frowned. I'd been so taken with the illustrations, I hadn't noticed the entirety of the book was written in what looked like Latin.

The second book was in English and seemed to be a historical recount of Hunters. I was so engrossed in the book, I didn't notice Ben was awake until he stood from the mattress.

I closed the book and looked up as he walked past me toward the kitchenette. "Hey, how's your throat? Did the sleep help?"

His shoulders lifted briefly.

"Aiden grew a backbone and gave me some info about Hunters," I said.

Ben returned with a glass of water and his phone. He lowered himself to sit beside me and stifled a yawn that ended in a grimace.

I motioned to the books. "Apparently somewhere in these pages is the info I need to keep everyone safe. I was going to ask for your help to read through all of it. You know, divide and conquer."

He typed on his phone, and the device read it aloud via text-to-speech. *Info you, Trish, and Nate need to keep everyone safe.*

"Yes, that's what I meant."

I showed the history book to him. "So, Hunters belonged to this type of royal order, like a knighthood. Each knight had a squire studying under him, so if the knight was killed or died, the squire would have all the information, training, and weapons to take his place. It reminds me of what Emma told me about wizards and apprentices."

Ben nodded as he typed. *Wizard specializing in the type of magic we want to study will teach us the language for spellcasting and some basics. Then we study on our own.*

"Did you apprentice under Reginald?"

Ben frowned. I took it as a "yes." He held out his hand for the larger book.

I passed it over. "The cover has the same symbol as the creepy dagger box in St. Anthony's."

Ben nodded as he opened the cover and read the title page. He balanced the book on his legs and typed into his phone. *The Order of St. Hubert. Aiden mentioned him when we looked for the daggers.*

"You can read that one?" I asked.

He skimmed through a few pages. *Yes. It's just Latin.*

"I'm going to see Trish and Nate, but that won't be until later tonight. What do you think about a study session?" I asked. When he didn't look up from the book, I stood. "Do you want to try to eat something? I can make you some soup."

He shrugged and leaned back against the couch, already reading the book again. I walked to the kitchenette to make us lunch. The text-to-speech app read, *Doesn't look good. They have heightened abilities similar to yours.*

"The purpose of this session is not for you to tell me how awful this guy is and that I should hide," I said. "Our goal is to find out how to survive him when we're ready to bring him in to the Committee for killing Isaac."

Increased strength, speed, and stamina. A Hunter fuels an ability from something called Saint Hubert's Key.

"That must be what Aiden was talking about." I glanced over at Ben. "He said they carry around an object symbolizing their faith that gives them supernatural abilities."

Was the Hunter wearing anything, like a charm?

"No, but to be honest, I'm not sure I would have noticed. The guy made my skin crawl, so I looked at him as little as possible. When we were face-to-face, I was more focused on leaving." I returned with the lukewarm soup for Ben and a sandwich for myself. I set the bowl beside him.

Ben skimmed the text and flipped ahead a few pages. He rubbed at the front of his throat before taking a tentative sip of water.

"Try your food," I said.

He continued to read, the book open in his lap, and ate a half bowl of soup. Diving into the book improved his mood. I was thankful we had something other than the earlier meeting with Reginald to focus on tonight.

"Can you think of anyone old enough in Hopewell to have dealt with Hunters while they were still around?" I asked.

He thought a moment before typing his reply. *Vampires live pretty long. Most fae are ancient.*

"What about Cat Man?" I asked. "He's fae, right?"

Fae can be difficult if you need info. They never feel obligated to tell the truth. Ben glanced over with a small smile before he typed. *Can you afford another meeting with Cat Man?*

I threw up my hands. "I've never met or asked about these beings before. Why does everyone expect me to know about them?"

Bring them a gift. Fae love gifts and flattery. Might want to bring someone along so you're not lured away. He smiled again. *Leave your wallet here.*

I grinned and gave him a mock slug in the side of the shoulder.

HOLDING MY HELMET, I waited for Emma outside the apartment. I'd asked her to be my plus one for a visit downtown to look for Cat Man. She'd been delighted by the fae since childhood, so she agreed. I think she also was excited to be included in my efforts to find information about the Hunter.

A mechanical buzzing noise announced Emma's arrival. She pulled up to the stairs on a pearlescent Vespa with airbrushed fuchsia and violet flames. She waved at me, flashing her brilliant smile. Her nail polish, helmet, and heart-shaped goggles matched the violet on the scooter's body.

"What do you think?" she asked.

"It's . . . perfectly you." I grinned and put on my helmet before getting on the scooter.

She pulled away and we drove farther into downtown. Her silk scarf, shimmery and echoing the Vespa's flame pattern, fluttered back into my face.

We parked the scooter, bought tea and coffee, and found a table where Joan, Ben, and I had visited for ice cream. I told Emma about my first encounter with Cat Man and how woefully unprepared I'd been. She giggled at the fae's antics instead of properly feeling sorry for me.

"I once lost a bag of marbles to one," she said. "I was playing in my parents' back garden, and the fae had taken the form of an adorable, pudgy squirrel. I still remember how loud my mother shrieked when she found me with them."

"Did she know what they were?" I asked.

"No." Emma rolled her eyes. "She thought it was an actual squirrel. She rushed me to the ER to make sure I hadn't contracted rabies."

"That sounds like Susan."

The light jingling of a small bell caused me to scan the crowd. I caught sight of the fluffy tail and pantaloons of the white cat as it padded across the seating area. A small child, maybe two or three years old, followed the cat through the crowd of tables and chairs. Several feet back, an attentive father shadowed the child. I looked ahead to where the cat was going. The old man snoozed beneath a tree. "Right there," I said, pointing.

Emma looked over her shoulder, and then turned back to me, her eyes sparkling. "Well, are we going to talk to them?"

We made our way to the old man and his pet. As we drew nearer, the scent of lemon drops reached my nose. The father towered like a gentle giant beside the child, clasping one of her tiny hands. She shook her other hand and squealed with delight as the cat purred and wove around her stubby legs. The father passed the little girl a dollar bill. She toddled over to the old man and dropped the money into the hat he held out.

"We thank you, sweet little one," he said.

The father waited as his daughter stroked the cat's head. "Gentle . . . Be gentle." He lifted the child up into his arms. The two waved goodbye to the man and cat before walking away. Emma and I approached.

"Hi again," I greeted the man.

Upon seeing me, the cat slunk quickly away behind the man's seated figure. The man's brow wrinkled. "Do you bring the loud, angry Wordweaver with you?"

I chuckled as I thought of Joan. "No. She's not with me today. I'm sorry she was rude to you. I brought a different friend."

Emma was already crouched several feet from the old man, talking to the cat hiding behind him. "Aren't you gorgeous?" She held her hand out, open palm up, and wiggled her fingers. "Come see me, sweetheart."

The old man tilted his head and smiled. "We already like this one better." The cat came out and bumped its head against Emma's hand.

"Look how fluffy they are, Alex!" Her excitement reminded me of the child's. She withdrew a can of tuna from her purse.

The man's eyes brightened and his smile grew. "How gracious!"

"Can we sit with you?" I asked the man.

"Yes, yes!" he said. The cat meowed and head-butted Emma as she peeled back the can's metal lid. It almost jumped up into her lap before she set the open can down on the pavement.

"What is your name?" Emma asked the cat as she stroked lightly along their back. The cat rumbled as it gobbled the tuna.

"Pangur," the old man said.

"Hello Pangur. My name is Emma. This is my friend, Alex." She settled on the step beside the cat, and I took a seat next to the man.

It felt odd to speak to the cat and have the man answer. I followed Emma's lead anyway. "Pangur, I found a photo of the man you described, the man of dark light. Can I ask you more about him?"

The cat stopped eating to look at me. The old man looked at me as well. "We are frightened of him."

"We're frightened of him, too. I want to learn more about him so I can protect all of us," I said.

"When Alex realized she would have to find someone very wise and knowledgeable, she immediately thought of you," Emma said.

The cat stood and their tail snaked back and forth. They gave Emma's shin a brush with their head before resuming their rhythmic purrs and tuna feast. The man asked, "What is it you wish to know?"

"I've read these men gain strength from an object or a key. When you saw the man that night, did you see a key on his person?" I asked.

The old man lightly scratched at the side of his head, as if excavating for the memory. "We did not see an item like you describe," he said.

"You said the man was made of dark light. What did you mean by that?" I asked. "Did his eyes glow?"

"Wordweaver Emma's eyes glow, but the man's eyes do not glow." He grew solemn. "The man's eyes are dark like the light at his hand."

Was the Hunter wearing some sort of bracelet? Maybe the fae creature couldn't see any jewelry because it was underneath those leather bracers. Or the bracers were covering a type of magic-infused tattoo like my Shield.

Emma's laughter brought my attention to her and the cat. The creature was stretched out on their back, bending their body this way and that. They swatted at some keychain charms Emma shook in the air above them.

"Thanks for speaking with me, Pangur," I said. "Can we visit again sometime?"

The cat rolled to its feet and strode over to me. My nose was saturated with the sweet scent of lemon drops. I started to feel light-headed. "We would very much like that, as we would very much like more gifts of canned fish," the man said. The cat trilled and pushed their head against the side of my leg.

I reached out and brushed their soft head with the back of my fingers. A tingling sensation ran up my forearm, like the kind of shiver I got when I drank one too many cups of coffee.

Without a word of farewell, the man reclined back again under the tree. He placed his hat over his eyes. The cat hopped up onto his chest, turned a few circles, and settled down to join him for a late afternoon nap. Emma picked up the empty tuna can. We walked from the area, pitching our to-go cups and the can into a bin on our way back to Emma's scooter.

"How cute! And what a lovely molasses scent," she said. "My grandmother used to bake the best molasses cookies. What did they smell like to you?"

"Lemon drops." I smiled. "My grandpa kept a dish of them next to his chair."

"Did you understand the answers they gave you?" Emma's cheeks turned rosy. "I lost track of the conversation. In my defense, they were extremely precious."

"Yeah, I think so. I'm going to talk to Ben. He's more of a research nerd than me, so he can help piece everything together."

"You two should open a PI business," Emma teased. She spread her hand across the span of an imaginary marque. "Steward & Sharpe: Private Investigators."

I snorted. "Don't you need a sweeping trench coat and a stubbled, square jawline for that?"

"We could go shopping! Think of the cute trench coat we could pick out for you. Maybe a red one. And of course you'll need a hat."

Grinning, I shook my head.

21

EMMA DROPPED ME off at the party store a block or two away from the apartment. I wanted to pick up a frozen pizza and beer for dinner. Well, the pizza for me, but Ben should be able to enjoy a cold beer. On my way to the register, I passed a small display of office supplies. A single design of lined notebooks, the cover of which had a photograph of a puppy and the words *Don't Forget to Be Awesome* in hologram foil, sat on the shelf. I grabbed two.

My plan was to spend a quiet evening researching with Ben before heading over to Hell's Bells. He loved to deep dive into research, especially on topics of religion, science, or the arcane. Hopefully doing so would continue to ease his anxiety brought on by Reginald's visit.

I bounded up the stairs to the apartment. The familiar sound of music and Ben's scent made me smile. I walked into the apartment, teasing, "If it gets too hot tonight, I suggest we strip—" I stopped. A new table and four chairs, appearing misplaced in the shabby apartment, were situated in the kitchenette area. Ben sulked on the sofa. "What's this?" I asked.

There were footsteps in the parking lot, and I turned toward the open door when they started up the stairs. "Is someone here?"

Joan walked through the doorway. She offered a cautious smile. "Hi. Sorry to drop in unannounced again."

I frowned. She was cloaking her scent again. I motioned at the new furniture. "Is this from you?"

"Sort of. It's from Granddad. I felt terrible about breaking the table, so he offered to replace it. I threw the old set out into the dumpster."

"Ah." I carried the shopping bag to the counter. Ben's behavior made sense now. "We saw your grandfather earlier," I said. "It wasn't a pleasant visit."

Joan followed me. "Benjamin mentioned that somewhere between telling me how I acted like an utter bitch to you and suggesting where Granddad could put the table and all four chairs." When I didn't reply, she continued, "I'm sorry about my behavior last night."

"Don't worry about it."

"I'm concerned about what's going to happen to him," she said.

"So am I." My reply was quick and sharp.

She took a step back and nodded. "Of course." She glanced at Ben before she asked me, "Did you get any information from Father Aiden?"

Ben must have told her about my visit. "He said the Hunters have tweaked abilities, but it's because of an object they carry." I avoided looking at her by turning on the oven for the pizza. I wasn't sure if I wanted to tell her about the books. The last time I'd shared information with her, she'd rushed ahead without me. "Do you want to ask Reginald if he knows anything about Hunters?"

"I'm not sure that's a good idea," Joan said. "Granddad is even a higher risk than Trish. He still believes in the Committee. If he finds out we're going after the Hunter, he'll try to stop us. But he does have an extensive library. I can go spelunking for information."

I turned, crossed my arms, and leaned back against the counter. "I've decided to work with Trish on finding evidence to charge the Hunter for Isaac's death. He's too strong for you and me to take on alone."

Joan's jawline twitched. "I was afraid you'd say that."

"I'm going to Hell's Bells tonight to share the info we've gathered so far. We could use your help."

"I'll give it some thought while I explore Granddad's library." She surprised me with a brief hug. My body went rigid, not knowing how to respond. "Please enjoy the table once or twice before he sells it." She left the apartment.

I looked over at Ben. "You needed a table. It's a nice table."

He stood, scribbled on his notepad, and walked over to shove it at me with a frown. *It's bullshit. Instead of not choking me with a tether, he bought a table. Fuck him.*

"Okay." Managing Ben and Reginald's relationship was way above my paygrade. I looked up from the notepad. "How's your throat?" As he wrote his reply, I grabbed two already sweaty beer bottles and threw the rest in the refrigerator. I swapped one of the bottles for the notepad.

Doesn't sting as bad. Cold drinks feel good.

"Do you want to talk about earlier today?" I asked. "Or even last night?" I did. His unexpected use of magic and now the fallout for doing so affected both of us.

"I want to shut down this Hunter." He winced. The scratchy words were less audible than his usual whispered voice. Scowling, he blinked back tears from his watering eyes.

He was angry. That worried me less than the fear-filled funk he'd been in earlier. I decided not to press him on the matter. "I think I found out where the Hunter might be wearing his key," I said.

Ben's brow smoothed. The two words he signed were ones I knew. *Cat Man?*

I smiled. "Yes. Their name is Pangur. Emma charmed them, like she does. They talked about the Hunter having 'dark light,' and that the light's origin was his hand. Do you think the key could be a tattoo? Something arcane like our Shields?"

He held his palms upward, the beer bottle's neck caught between his fingers, and sea-sawed his hands. *Maybe.*

The oven beeped. I set aside my beer and put the pizza in. I remembered the notebooks and grinned. "Wait until you see the amazing research tools I got for us."

He watched me with part suspicion and part curiosity as I unveiled the notebooks from the shopping bag. Beaming, I presented one to him. Ben raised his eyebrows, obviously left speechless by the amazing gift.

"Don't worry." I displayed my own notebook. "Mine matches."

He chuckled and shook his head.

Three hours later I had fallen asleep on the floor with my head resting on my open notebook. Ben woke me by nudging my leg with his foot. I awoke with a start, quickly and unsteadily sat up, and tried to locate my pen.

Want to compare notes? The robotic voice caused me to look over at Ben. He'd switched to his glasses, and held his phone. He tried to hide his amusement by flipping back through his notebook.

"Yeah! Sure, great idea." I blinked and rubbed at my eyes. "You first."

He typed into his phone. *Book is a Hunter 101 guide for guys in The Order of St. Hubert. In book are Tenants, abilities called Blessings, battle techniques, and prayers. Whole section on what they call Accursed.*

"People like me?"

Ben nodded and typed. *Anyone who "assumes the visage of a person, but is consumed with blight" is who they feel called to hunt.*

"Except wizards."

He shook his head. *Male wizards. Females are considered witches and the Accursed.*

"Wait. That was amended..." I scanned my notes, "...in 1815. Witchcraft was redefined as the type of magic the wizard practiced, not the absence of a penis." I looked up at Ben. "I also read about how the keys were created. There is a finite set of keys passed to the squires with all the knowledge of how to live life as a Hunter. The keys were originally made and imbued with magic by a wizard."

Ben shook his head again. *Wizards and lupine are allies. Doesn't make sense. Wizard wouldn't give Commoner power to harm werewolves.*

"Maybe at that time it was more than the Commoners who were scared of gifted beings like Pangur and me," I said. "There's a whole section in the book talking about how a splinter of wizards migrated into the priesthood."

He frowned. *Never read anything like that in my studies.*

I shrugged and motioned to the book. "This one was in English, so I didn't misread it. I'm telling you what's in the text."

He nodded, but the frown didn't wane.

"Did you find out anything more about how the keys work?" I asked.

Ben nodded and scooted forward from near the couch to sit next to me. He pointed to his notes. *St. Huberts Key (magical charm): used for physical feats or enhancements of perception. Identifies the Accursed since many appear to be human.*

"That must have been what I felt when he looked at me," I said.

Ben's brow wrinkled in the way it does when he worries about me. He wrote on the notes I'd been reading. *Sure Trish and Nate can't handle this on their own?*

"The Committee is holding the vote tonight on whether or not to let the Hunter loose in the city. We're sure it's going to pass," I said. "Trish and Nate need all the help they can get to bring him and the evidence tying him to Isaac's death to the Committee as soon as possible."

He used his thumb to rub ink from my cheek. "Be careful."

"I will." I leaned into his touch. "Speaking of being careful, can we please talk about last night and what that means for you?"

He lowered his hand and frowned.

"How long have you been able to use magic again?" I asked. "That's what it was, right? It felt like it."

He pushed his glasses up on his head, closed his eyes, and pinched the bridge of his nose.

"All that blood scared me," I said. "I didn't know how to help you. I felt completely lost." Helplessness was a feeling I despised with every fiber of my being.

Ben's eyes opened. He twirled his pencil between his fingers. "Please."

He blew out an exhale and turned the page in his notepad. *Picked up study of magic again halfway through tethering sentence. No casting until slipped tether several years ago. Small spells.* He frowned, the tip of the pencil pausing above the page before he wrote, *Balance of satisfying need to use magic and not getting caught. Never tried anything as large as spell last night. Surprised it worked.* His fingers lifted to his throat and he croaked. "Somewhat."

"What are we going to do about Reginald finding out?"

Ben scowled and shrugged.

Was now a good time to tell him Emma knew about him getting around the tether? He was already scared and angry about his grandfather. Would it make things worse?

Footsteps on the stairs caused me to look at the front door in alarm. That stupid fan. The musky scent of a werewolf was blown into the apartment. I silently stood and walked to the door. A resounding knock hit the door moments before I opened it.

Jakob, dressed in uniform, stood on the landing. He seemed unsurprised and not at all happy to see me. "Good evening, Miss Steward."

The greeting's formal nature made me uneasy. I looked past him. His cruiser was in the lot. "Is Anne here with you?"

"No. I'm here on Committee business," he said.

"Did you come from the meeting?"

"Is Mr. Sharpe home? If so, I'd like to speak to him, please." Jakob's request was another formality. I'm sure he smelled Ben.

At the mention of his name, I heard Ben move in the apartment. I narrowed my eyes at Jakob. "Why?"

"I'm taking him into custody on behalf of the Committee."

Jakob's words landed like a slug to the gut. Committee business? Taken into custody? My palms dampened. He was here to take Ben away to be punished for using magic. A low growl rumbled in my chest, and I bared my teeth. "Go away, Jakob."

"He broke the law, Alex," Jakob said.

"Do you know why?" I asked. When Jakob remained silent, I muttered, "Trish was right. You don't give a shit about us. You're just Stone's lap dog, aren't you?"

Jakob's expression darkened. "This will be the last time I ask. May I speak to Mr. Sharpe?"

I heard Ben behind me and felt his touch at my elbow. I looked back at him, and my stomach plummeted. Fear was draped around him like a thick blanket, souring the comforting scent I associated with him. He occasionally shook as he greeted Jakob in sign.

"Benjamin Sharpe, on behalf of the Committee of Hopewell, I have with me an order for your arrest in relation to violating guideline 7b. I ask that you come with me. If you resist, I have permission to use whatever force necessary."

"Reginald said Ben can stay here until Isaac's killer is in custody." I glared at Jakob. "Have you looked into the Hunter yet, Officer DeBoer? That's the guy posing an actual threat."

"Reginald Sharpe's signature was required for this arrest," Jakob said. "He knows I'm here."

My eyes widened. What happened that Reginald signed off on what could be his grandson's death warrant?

Ben's expression didn't hold the same naked surprise as mine. His eyes dark, he scowled at Jakob. The energy pull around us was so abrupt it caused me to gasp.

Jakob felt it too. His muscles tensed, and he stepped back to brace himself.

Shaking my head, I grabbed Ben's trembling wrist. I placed my body between the two men. My mind raced, trying to think of a way out of the situation without anyone getting hurt. "What about your brother, Jakob?"

Jakob's eyes briefly widened and then narrowed.

"You know firsthand how much damage tethering can do to a person and the people around them. Ben didn't do anything wrong. He was protecting us from the Hunter."

Jakob's hands tightened into fists at his side. "Don't lecture me on what I know and don't know about my family." His gaze shifted to Ben. "Even wizards have to face the consequences of breaking the Committee's laws."

So much for talking.

I glared at him. "You'll have to come back with help because I won't let you take him."

Jakob realized it wasn't an empty promise, but the guy had patience. He didn't haul me aside so he could seize Ben. Instead, he met my gaze and growled, "Get out of the way."

I didn't have his patience.

My initial shock over Reginald's actions was replaced by anger. I stepped toward Jakob, but he simply took another step back. He refused to be the first to throw a punch. I pushed my luck and stepped out of the apartment toward him. He retreated again. Soon I had moved him all the way back down the stairs. My bare feet came into contact with the parking lot's warm pavement, and he finally halted his retreat beside the cruiser.

Jakob glanced up at the apartment door before he spoke to me. "You're not thinking this through, Alex. They'd love to use this as a reason to tether you."

His suggestion I wasn't fully aware of the situation inflamed my anger. "I'm not thinking this through? He did nothing wrong! You're willingly taking a man to people who would execute him because he saved our lives!" The creature inside me struggled against my hold. My hands shifted shape, and I flexed my claws.

"What are you doing?" Jakob's gaze darted around the parking lot. "Get control of yourself. Someone is going to see you."

A car pulled into the parking lot, and I recognized it as Joan's rental. Ben must have messaged her before he came to the door. Was he trying to run?

Jakob and I flinched in unison as a sudden rush of energy surged around us. All windows on the cruiser blew out in an explosion of tinkling glass. I raised my arm to shield my face from the small shards. They bit into my exposed skin, and my whole body lit up with pain. I lowered my arm and looked back toward the apartment. Ben dashed from the bottom of the stairs across the parking lot to Joan's car.

I jerked my gaze to Jakob. He grimaced, and his uniform was peppered with blood stains, but he'd seen Ben as well. Jakob moved to follow, and I lunged at him. I grappled with him and sunk my claws deep into the flesh of his arms to anchor my weight to him.

Jakob's eyes were bright with anger as we struggled. "Alex, get out of the way!" he snarled. The sound of a rapidly accelerating engine marked Joan and Ben's rushed exit from the parking lot. With squealing tires, the rental car sped away down the street.

"Dammit!" Jakob twisted his upper body and pulled me off balance. A hollow, metallic thud sounded as my hip and shoulder struck the side of the cruiser. I released him, panting. Jakob stepped back, his face flushed and his uniform sleeves torn and bloodied. He surveyed the wrecked cruiser and turned a furious glare on me. "Nice work. You've handed them an excuse to give the Hunter his first case."

Joan, Ben, and I would be cast as villains. Now we'd be placed in the crosshairs of the man who murdered Isaac. We were running out of time.

22

I ATTEMPTED TO shower the glass from my body and hair before I drove to Hell's Bells. The bleeding from the tiny cuts stopped, but I had to bandage my forearm. There wasn't anything at the apartment to extract the larger pieces of glass.

Nate met me outside the club. His nostrils flared at the scent of my blood. "Christ, Alex. Did the Hunter track you down?"

"No, it was Jakob. He showed up at the apartment to arrest Ben for the Committee."

Nate's gaze hardened at the mention of Jakob's name. "Arrest? For what?"

I swallowed. If Jakob knew, that meant Trish did as well. "Ben cheated his tether. He used magic last night to stop the Hunter from killing us."

Nate's eyes widened and he gave a low whistle. "Holy. Shit. I did not think the wizard had it in him to try something like that."

"He escaped with Joan," I said.

"Where are they now?" We walked into the club and toward the bar. Trish was perched on a barstool, talking on her phone.

"Hopefully somewhere safe." Heads turned as I passed, the odor of my blood drawing attention.

"Let's talk in the back," Nate said. He caught Trish's attention and pointed toward the hallway. She nodded and held up her index finger to let us know she would join us soon. Nate led me to their apartment.

"Did the Committee hold the vote?" I followed him down the hallway. "Jakob wouldn't tell me."

"Yeah. It went as expected," he said.

"What does that mean for us?" I sat down at their small table as he rifled through cupboards in the kitchen.

He brought a bottle of whiskey and a tumbler over to the table and sat down with me. Whiskey was Nate's go-to for painful injuries. "We're not exactly sure. Trish is working on that." He filled my glass. Since our bodies burned through the effects of alcohol so fast, more than a few shots were required to dull pain. "Where did the three of you find the Hunter last night?"

"South on the highway. He's holed up in an abandoned garage." I accepted the tumbler he passed to me. "We thought he'd gone out for the night, but he returned sooner than expected."

Trish entered the apartment, her shoulders tense and her brow wrinkled. "The Hunter?"

Nate looked across the table at her. "Alex said he's down the highway a bit."

She nodded. "We'll be visiting him." She stopped beside me, saw my bandaged arm, and held out her hand. "Let me have a look."

I unwrapped the bloodied fabric bandage. She studied my arm and left for the bathroom to return seconds later with a small med kit. Trish sat down beside me and searched through the kit's contents. She retrieved a set of intimidating tweezers. I surrendered my forearm and reached for the whiskey Nate had poured.

"Fillip found the Hunter?" She set to work extracting the glass. I flushed with shame. "Yes."

"What did you find when you searched the place?" A chunk of glass, sticky with blood, dropped from the tweezers to the tabletop.

"We didn't find much besides a deserted building, but it angered the Hunter enough that he tried to kill Ben and me. There must be something we overlooked."

"The wizard who showed up here last night," Nate said. "What's your read on her?"

"Her name is Joan Sharpe," I said. "Isaac was her local guy in building a group to oppose the Committee's tethering practices. She wants the Hunter held responsible for Isaac's death, too." I winced and another shard of glass dropped to the table. "She and I were going to search the building alone, but I changed my mind. I thought we should come here first and share the address with you two. When I tried to contact her and let her know, she'd already gone inside alone. I couldn't leave her there by herself."

"Joan is reckless," Trish said. She set the tweezers aside and retrieved a thread and needle from her kit. "Reggie believes she will someday surpass his own skill. Right now, she's headstrong and possesses a fraction of his patience." She looked to Nate. "Could you grab the vodka, love?"

"You've just described Alex," Nate said. I wasn't sure whether to be flattered or offended. He sorted through the cupboards again and returned with a large, unmarked bottle of clear liquor.

Trish frowned at him. "Alex is different. She's a wolf. We can rely on her loyalty."

I hissed at the sting of the vodka, emptied my glass of whiskey, and looked away from my arm as Trish swiftly set to work with her needle and thread.

"You're disregarding a powerful wizard who'd stick her neck out for the wolves?" Nate asked. "Yet you're willing to collaborate with that old fool she's related to? I can count on one hand how many times he's risked his seat for us."

"Even though we have the same end goal, it doesn't guarantee Joan will listen to us when needed. That makes her a liability." Trish tied off the thread and asked me, "Why would she risk revealing her strong opposition to Hopewell's Committee just to see the Hunter brought to trial? The impact of his presence will be minimal, if that, for the wizards."

I shifted in my seat and glanced between the two. "She was supposed to meet up with Isaac on the night he was murdered. When she arrived, the Hunter was there and Isaac was dead."

Nate looked at Trish. "Isaac did have friends everywhere, even some wizards."

Trish still watched me. I dropped my gaze to the table. "I went over to the cathedral today, and Aiden gave me some books on Hunters. Ben and I were researching them when Jakob showed up."

"The priest agreed to help you with the Hunter?" Nate asked.

I nodded.

He sat back and scratched behind his ear. "Huh."

Unlike Nate, Trish wasn't surprised. "What did you find out?"

I explained to them what Ben and I read regarding the Blessings and Saint Hubert's Key. "Pangur mentioned something about the Hunter's hand. We think that's where the Hunter is wearing his key. I think if we remove the key, he won't have the advantage of these Blessings."

"Who's Pangur?" Nate asked.

"A cat," I said.

He tilted his head. "What the hell is happening right now?"

I clarified. "One of the fae."

Nate raised his eyebrows. "Now we're fucking around with the fae-kind?"

"I agree with Alex," Trish said. "If what she read is correct, seizing this key from him should be our first priority. Then he won't be an immediate threat to anyone while we wait for Detective Grey's lab results." She frowned. "Since the medical examiner's report excluded the burn details on Isaac's body, we'll need Grey's tests to show evidence of the silver. If we can find possible murder weapons where the Hunter is hiding, it'd be even better."

"I found a lead on who passed Isaac's name to Stone's Hunter," I said. "I spoke with Julia Visser yesterday. She'd been worried for Isaac because he was working with a group planning to replace the Committee. I think she told someone close to her who she shouldn't have."

Trish nodded. "So we take a closer look at the Vissers and Julia's friends. Let's start with the immediate family."

An enormous boom sounded outside. The club's foundation shook and the dishes inside the apartment's cupboards rattled. Nate was out of his seat and through the door of the apartment in a shot. Trish was quick to follow. I ran after them down the hall to the building's entrance.

Thick clouds of black smoke billowed up into the night sky from the flaming wreck of a car. A chaotic wave of scent, sound, and movement hit my senses. People yelled and dove behind vehicles to take cover.

A large, unmarked van blocked the parking lot entrance. Striding up toward the building was the Hunter. Calm and unhurried, he walked through the lot armed with some type of rifle. He wore additional leather guards over his clothing, like bits of armor.

I ducked out of the doorway and rushed to crouch with Trish behind her car. Not ten feet away, Nate was backed up against the long length of his sedan. He yelled over to Trish through the noise, "Tell the people downstairs. They might not have heard anything over the music."

Trish shook her head. "We stop him, right here. Now!"

"Alex can help me out here," he yelled.

Me? Sweat broke out on my forehead and upper lip. *What the fu—*

"No!" Anger thickened Trish's voice. "We need to kill him before he gets inside."

Kill him. My body began to tremble.

Nate looked around the edge of the car, checked the Hunter's advance, and scurried across to huddle beside us. He gripped Trish's arm. "Patricia, one of us has to go in there and get everyone out the exit through our place. Then call for help. You're their leader. They'll listen to you. Alex and I will slow him down. Then you can come back to us."

Rage quickly overtook any fear in her. She visibly struggled against it, furious to be forced from our sides. Trish leaned forward and gave Nate a kiss. "I love you, Nathan."

"I love you, too." He grinned. "We'll see you soon."

Trish peeked over the edge of the car's hood and made a hurried retreat back into the club.

Nate watched her go. He took a deep breath and looked at me. "Are you ready for this?"

"You can't be serious." My voice shook. "What in the hell are we going to do, Nate? The guy has a rifle!" I'd taken a bullet or two before, but not from a man aiming to end my life.

"Yeah, I know. That will have to go." He took another glance over the hood and was driven back by a gunshot. "He's not going to wait for us to get our shit in order, so we need to move. Let's try to find that key thing you were talking about. I'll head over to his other side if you can take this one." Nate took off across to his car again and then to the next.

My pulse pounded in my ears. Was he really going to rely on *me* to back him up? He'd witnessed my control issues firsthand. What if the police rolled in and I'd gone all-out Hollywood Wolfman?

But, if I wasn't where I should be when Nate attacked, he'd attempt to delay the Hunter on his own. The people here meant too much to him. Despite Nate's mastery of his abilities, I knew the Hunter could take down a single werewolf.

After the initial confusion of the Hunter's arrival, anyone who was outside had taken cover behind the parked cars. What if the Hunter decided to flush people out and start shooting?

There was so much adrenaline coursing through me, I clenched my teeth to prevent them from chattering. This community meant a lot to me, too. My inner wolf paced. She pushed a snarl past my lips. Loss of control was a risk I'd take to keep the other wolves safe.

The makeshift shield of cars kept me hidden as I crept in the opposite direction. I paused to check on the Hunter's location before I sprinted between the vehicles. He was already halfway through the parking lot.

Across the lot, Nate crouched with his copper eyes trained on the Hunter. The sight of Nate readying his attack caused a type of calm focus to settle over me. I allowed more freedom to my inner wolf. My fingers grew longer, and my knuckles larger, as my claws emerged. Scents and sounds became magnified.

Beneath the distraction of the burning car, gravel crunched on pavement from the Hunter's steps. His breath entered and left his body as evenly paced bursts of air.

The Hunter took one step beyond the waiting werewolf, and Nate tore out of hiding with barely a sound. A moment after Nate moved, I rushed the Hunter from the opposite side.

The Hunter sensed Nate but didn't spin fast enough to aim the rifle at the oncoming werewolf. Instead, he braced the gun's length horizontally across his body at arm's length. Nate's chest collided with the gun. He swiped a clawed hand at the Hunter's face, but the distance was too great.

I crashed into the Hunter's other side and raked my claws across the area of his kidneys and waist. My talons carved gashes out of a thick, wide leather belt he wore. The Hunter scowled and released one end of the rifle to seize ahold of my bicep. His grip tightened like a vise, and I yelped. Pain, and then numbness, shot down my arm.

Nate tried to wrestle the rifle away, but it was secured to the Hunter's body by a strap. Instead, Nate seized the gun's barrel and bent it into a sharp angle.

The Hunter released me and stepped back. He yanked the gun from Nate's grasp and drove the bent barrel beneath Nate's ribcage. The Hunter swung the buttstock across to hit the side of Nate's face. Nate stumbled back with a shake of his head.

"Nathan." The Hunter detached and tossed the firearm aside. "I'm not surprised you're at the center of this cesspool."

"Sorry, handsome . . . Do we know each other?" Nate lowered his body into a crouch. "I'm not remembering your name."

I hovered near the edge of the Hunter's field of vision. It forced him to divide his attention between Nate and me. From where I stood, I couldn't see any markings or jewelry. Most of the skin around his hands, wrists, and forearms was covered by leather bracers.

"You were always slow, weren't you?" The Hunter grinned. "Even before the blight took hold. A waste of skin, bone, and blood. A complete fuck-up."

Nate's lip pulled back from his pointed teeth. He crept forward.

Another werewolf emerged from hiding near the Hunter's back. It was Roger, the young wolf who'd introduced himself to Emma. He slunk toward the Hunter.

I lunged again.

The Hunter used the bracer across his wide forearm to protect himself from my claws. I shredded at it, desperately trying to tear it from his arm.

Faster and smaller, Roger slipped up from behind. He slashed the back of the Hunter's legs. The Hunter lurched forward out of Roger's reach. Nate landed a solid punch to the Hunter's temple.

The Hunter staggered to the side. He attempted to separate himself from the three of us.

Seeing him pull back, off-balance, my inner wolf strained against my control. She wanted to stop the prey's retreat. Clenching my teeth to maintain focus, I launched myself at him. We both crashed onto the pavement. Roger instantly fell upon him with repeated swipes at the Hunter's head and throat with his claws.

The Hunter yelled in rage as he struggled to block Roger's onslaught of attacks. He grasped something from near his belt. I recognized the archaic dagger with ornate engravings. It looked identical to the silver blades kept at St. Anthony's.

I grabbed his wrist before he could run a blade into Roger. Just as quickly, the Hunter risked a strike to his face to grab another dagger with his opposite hand.

I cried out. "Roger!"

Nate seized the Hunter's other wrist. His eyes widened as the Hunter began to overpower him with brute force. "Roger, get out of the way!"

The young werewolf hopped up and away from us. Growling, he paced and waited.

Nate met my gaze. I found my footing and retreated. Nate hopped up, but fell backward.

The Hunter drove the dagger to the ground where Nate had been crouched. The strike's force caused the soft metal to bend against the pavement. The Hunter twisted his body, seized Nate's ankle, and hauled the werewolf toward him.

I dashed over to the ruined rifle and snatched it off the ground.

Sliding on his back, Nate growled. "You're coming on a bit strong." He smashed his combat boot into the Hunter's face.

The Hunter didn't let go. Grinning through bright blood from his nose, he made it onto his knees. "Let me jog your memory, brother." He dropped his weight on Nate's thigh and wrenched upward on Nate's ankle.

An awful crunch came from Nate's knee. He howled.

The Hunter clutched the handle of the dagger and raised it over his head.

I loosened my hold on the beast inside me. My upper body flooded with strength as she leapt forward. I swung the rifle like a bat. It smashed into the Hunter's hand. The dagger spun out of his grasp and clattered to the pavement.

The Hunter ducked my next swing aimed at his head. He looked back at me, his dark eyes full of hate.

Screaming sirens of approaching emergency vehicles were a welcome sound. No amount of fabricated reports could erase him from the scene, especially if he stayed any longer and engaged the police. There were too many witnesses.

The Hunter cursed and rolled up onto his feet, bleeding from his nose and several gashes across his face. He grabbed the dagger from the ground. Not removing his gaze from us, he retreated several paces. He turned and bolted toward his van.

As soon as the Hunter's back was to us, Roger sprinted after him. My heart seized. "Stop!" I ran after Roger.

As if he expected the werewolf, the Hunter turned on Roger and caught hold of him. With a broad arm across Roger's chest and shoulders, the Hunter restrained the snarling, younger man. He lifted the dagger beneath Roger's chin.

I pulled up short, panting and wide-eyed. Nate limped up beside me, his face contorted.

All my senses vibrated. The mixed odors of the Hunter's blood and Roger's, Nate's, and my fear caused my inner wolf to throw herself against my ribcage. We couldn't let this man kill another wolf.

My nose caught the scent of another werewolf, and then another. Roger's friends were slinking up behind us. Multiple pairs of glowing eyes fixed on the Hunter.

The intensity of the sirens signaled the police and rescue vehicles were seconds away. The Hunter's calculating gaze moved slowly over our group. I growled, the creature inside me responding to the unspoken challenge.

In one swift movement, the Hunter pulled the silver blade across Roger's throat.

Nate let loose a strangled, guttural cry.

The Hunter released Roger.

Roger's eyes widened. His forehead wrinkled as if he found something confusing. His trembling fingers rose to his throat, and his knees buckled.

We couldn't seem to move fast enough.

I caught Roger before his body collapsed to the pavement. I lowered him clumsily to the ground. "Help!" One hand pressed tight over Roger's throat, I supported the back of his neck with my other. "No, no, no . . . Shit!"

The sound of the van's engine caused my attention to snap up to the end of the drive. The van pulled out onto the road and swerved around an oncoming ambulance. With a screech of tires, it accelerated and sped away.

I looked at Roger's friends. "Go! Get Trish!"

A few young wolves took off toward the club. The others huddled a step away.

The stink of skin seared by silver fueled blinding anger. Every muscle in my body screamed to run down the Hunter . . . to slice him to pieces. My wolf wanted to put an end to him.

Kill him.

Soon, I promised her.

23

SEVERAL SQUAD CARS and a fire truck arrived within minutes after the ambulance. The smoking wreck of the car was extinguished. I waited outside the nervous fringe of people by the ambulance, yielding the space to Roger's friends.

Trish stood with Nate, her chin lifted and her eyes dry as she watched the medics work. They'd given Nate a temporary leg brace. He held tightly to Trish's hand and pressed as near to her as possible as if the proximity provided strength. Dazed, he stared at the ground.

A medic hurried to Trish and spoke with her. Trish turned to look at the cluster of people and waved over one of Roger's friends. The young man, his eyes bloodshot from tears, hopped up into the back of the ambulance. The medic shut up the back of the bus before retreating to the driver's seat. The ambulance pulled out into the street and drove away.

As soon as the ambulance left, I scanned the lot. Anne and Jakob were two of the officers to arrive at the scene. Jakob had heard the emergency call come in and insisted on taking it. Additional officers moved through the parking lot to question the club goers. No one was allowed to leave before they had given a witness statement.

I found Jakob writing in a small notepad as a young couple spoke to him. He thanked and dismissed them.

My anger caused me to blurt out words that were different from what I'd intended. "What the hell are you still doing here? While you're playing twenty questions, the Hunter could be moving."

"I'm doing my job." Jakob scowled at his notepad as he finished writing. "Do you know where he went, because I don't."

"Yes."

Jakob looked up with a frown.

"He messed up," I said. "Not only did he publicly attempt to murder someone, he attacked Roger the same way he killed Isaac. We can use that as additional evidence now."

Jakob glanced across the parking lot. "Do Trish and Nate plan on going after him?"

"Yes, but Nate is hurt and the guy is strong." I narrowed my eyes. "You haul people in for the Committee, right? I don't see why you're even debating this."

"I have Anne with me," he said. "I can't tell her to take the night off, not after this."

"I'm not going to wait, so I hope you figure it out and we see you there." A familiar scent tickled my nostrils. My stomach lurched.

"See him where?" Anne stood behind me. She tucked her own notepad away and looked at Jakob. "Where are we going, DeBoer? Do you have a lead?"

"Miss Steward believes she knows where we can find the suspect," Jakob said.

Anne crossed her arms and gave me a flat look. "Imagine that."

I frowned. "Anne, please, trust me and sit this one out?"

"Absolutely not," she said. "I'm not sure why you think you're more qualified than I am to handle this. It's my job, Alex." She jabbed a finger at me. "In fact, *you* need to stay here. Don't interfere with our work." Her finger swung toward their cruiser. "Otherwise, I will throw your ass in the back of that squad car."

My heart sank. The last thing I was going to do was wait here while they went to confront the Hunter alone.

Anne spoke to Jakob. "Let's go and pick this guy up."

"Alex, the address?" Jakob reopened his notepad.

I glanced at Anne. She waited, arms crossed again, glowering. I gave Jakob the details.

He flipped the notepad closed and they walked to their car. The police cruiser pulled out of the lot as I chewed at my thumbnail. Trish walked over with Nate limping beside her.

Nate glared over his shoulder at the departing car. "Where are they going?"

"They're on their way to arrest the Hunter," I said.

Nate winced and looked at Trish. "Do we let them try? Or do you want to call Jakob off and we can grab the Hunter?"

Trish eyed Nate's leg. "You'll only be going to the hospital, love."

"I gave Jakob and Anne the wrong address," I said.

Nate grinned, but I doubted my split-second decision. We could have used Jakob's help, but who knew if we could trust him. Plus, I didn't want Anne there.

"We have a matching attack. We have the ruined dagger," Trish said. "Alex and I will pay the Hunter a visit."

"Will we be able to handle him on our own?" I said. "He took on three of us at once."

"Yes," Trish said. "I'll get my keys and we can leave." She strode off toward the club.

"The Hunter was looking rough, and now you'll have Trish beside you." Nate shifted his weight and grimaced. "I didn't see anything on his hands that could be a key, did you?"

I shook my head. "He acted like he knew you."

"Yeah. It's my stepdad's and mom's son." Nate swallowed and looked away. "He was only a kid the last time I saw him."

"Your stepbrother is a Hun—"

"He's not my brother." Nate turned a copper gaze back on me. "He's a demented jackass with a chip on his shoulder."

Trish walked back up to us. She jingled her car keys. "Time for us to leave, Alex."

"Kick him in the teeth for me and Roger," Nate said. "And for Isaac."

I GRABBED THE seat's edge as Trish sped past a changing traffic light and turned sharply onto the ramp for the highway. "Are you worried the Committee will be pissed you're bringing in their Hunter?"

"No." Her jawline was tight and her eyes glowed a warm gold. She smoothly shifted through the gears, and the little coupe raced up to speed.

"Will Roger be okay?"

"We don't know." She spared me a glance. "Address?"

I gave Trish the address of the building Joan, Ben, and I visited the night before. We neared the exit. Smoke hung like an ominous cloud against the light pollution of the sky. My heart sank and Trish cursed.

The coupe paused at the top of the ramp, and a firetruck raced past the intersection. We followed the firetruck toward the Hunter's hideout. Trish pulled the car over a few buildings away and turned off the headlights and engine.

The flames engulfed the majority of the deserted building, causing it to shine like a beacon in the dark. I jumped out of the car and jogged toward it. The fire's scorched scent and blazing heat forced me to stop at the end of the drive. Firefighters shouted to each other above the crackling flames as they attempted to contain the blaze. The Hunter's van was nowhere in sight.

I blinked against the bright light and heat. A boiling rage filled me. I should've immediately left Hell's Bells to follow the Hunter. I gave him too much time. Footsteps approached and a low growl sounded beside me. Trish stared into the fire, her eyes alight.

"What the *hell* is Jakob doing?" I shouted. "He could've left to go after the Hunter instead of wasting time! Is there no part of him that wants to help us?" I motioned toward the wrecked building. "How will we find the Hunter now? He could be anywhere!"

Trish turned away. Her tone was calm despite her glowing eyes. "I'll report the attack on the club and Roger to Aiden. He can set into motion what is needed for the Committee to detain the Hunter." She looked at me as we walked back to the car. "Fillip is our best bet to find where the Hunter is hiding. One of his flock would have been posted here." Trish glanced around. "May still be, in fact. While I speak with Aiden, will you locate where Fillip is tonight?"

I nodded.

"Anything Fillip charges for the information should be put on my personal tab," she said.

"Do we have time?" I asked. "I had to wait for Fillip to send someone. It'll give the Hunter even more time to disappear."

Flashing lights approached, and Jakob's cruiser pulled over in front of Trish's car. I'd fed him the false address, so I should've waited in the car and let Trish do the talking. Instead, I thought of Ben scared and in hiding, Nate badly injured, Roger possibly dead, and the Hunter having slipped through our fingers. Jakob had multiple chances to help but stubbornly clung to his rules and procedures. I strode toward the driver's side door of the police car where Jakob was getting out of the vehicle.

"Alex." Trish said my name as a command.

I ignored her.

I let loose a vicious snarl and drilled Jakob square in the jaw. He fell back against the body of the car, eyes wide. He almost didn't block my next strike in time.

"Alex!" Anne rushed around the car. She hauled me aside by the back of my shirt. "Have you lost your mind?"

Panting, I stepped back. The realization Anne was here as well materialized in my consciousness. How could I possibly have forgotten that? The dread that hit me next was so intense it made me nauseated.

Anne shouted my next thought aloud. "What the hell is wrong with you?"

I couldn't look her in the eye. I cast a frantic glance at Trish.

"Officer Reid, we are all under an extreme amount of stress tonight," Trish said.

Anne pointed at her. "You. Be quiet. Do not talk to me right now." She spoke to me, eyes flashing. "Giving false information to an investigating officer is a misdemeanor! Did you know that? Or did you just not care?"

I shook my head. "I'm sorry. I wanted—"

Anne held up her hand to silence me, then jabbed her finger toward the crackling building. "This fire came up on the dispatch, and do you know what my first thought was? That's where we'll find Alex."

My gaze dropped. "Anne—"

"I've tried to understand what is going on with you. Multiple times now, I offered to help. I'm done." Her tone changed, shifting to a formality she'd never used with me. "Place your hands behind your head."

I did as she asked, and without a word, Jakob handcuffed me. He escorted me to the back of the cruiser.

"We'll be in contact about tonight's attack on your business, Ms. Drake," Anne said. "You have my card if you come across any other information. If you see the suspect, contact us immediately. Do not engage him."

"Thank you, Officer Reid," Trish said.

Anne returned to the police car. She settled into the passenger seat, closed her eyes, and inhaled deeply through her nose. She exhaled, opened her eyes, and asked Jakob. "You okay?"

"Yes. I didn't expect it." He glanced up into the rearview mirror at me and frowned. He made a U-turn and drove back toward the highway.

I twisted my body to see Trish's shrinking form through the back windshield of the cruiser. She was speaking on her phone.

THE BRIEF CAR ride to downtown passed in a haze. My mind was a whirlwind of anxiety and anger. Anne didn't speak to me. With each interaction I had with her, intentional or not, more cracks formed in our friendship.

We neared the police station, and Anne spoke to Jakob. Her voice was quiet and tired. "Can you get this one on your own?"

Jakob nodded. "Not a problem." He pulled the cruiser to the side of the street, and Anne exited. Her door slammed, and she walked to the station's front entrance. She didn't look back. Jakob pulled away from the sidewalk and continued down the street.

I frowned. "Where are we going?"

Jakob didn't answer. He drove around the block to a narrow street that ran behind the station. Another cruiser was ahead of us and pulled into the building via some sort of loading bay. An industrial-grade door lowered behind the car, sealing it inside. Once we were in there, my chances to get out of this mess were slim to none. Jakob put the police car in park, took off his hat, and tossed it aside onto the passenger seat.

I leaned forward. "You know this is a waste of time. We need to find the Hunter."

His eyes remained stony and focused on the door. My idiotic mistake mocked me as a bright welt on his clean-shaven jawline. Talking my way out of here wasn't going to work, and there was only so much time before that huge door opened again. I glanced around the backseat, finding absolutely nothing helpful. The only thing at my disposal was me.

I sat back and reached down inside myself, summoning the beast waiting there. She readily emerged, my anger and frustration having already agitated her. Strength flooded through my core and limbs. I focused on my arms, gradually pulling my wrists apart. The bracelets of the cuffs bit into my skin, but a link in the chain between the handcuffs slowly bent and snapped.

I glanced up at Jakob. He was still looking out the front window. I spun my body, reclined onto the seat, and pulled my legs up. Clasping the edge of the seat for leverage, I drove my heels into the car door near the lock. Pain shot up my legs. The door bent and the force of the blow made the car rock.

Jakob turned in his seat, scowling. He lunged for his own door handle.

I clenched my teeth, pulled up my legs, and struck the door a second time. The door flew open, bounced against its hinge, and almost swung shut again. I stuck my shoe in the way to stop it.

The next few seconds were a race between Jakob and me to see who could get out of the car first. I'd made it to my feet, but he caught me by the arm.

"Stop it," he growled. "You're not making anything easier on yourself."

I twisted in his hold, trying to free myself. "Why aren't you helping us? You're going to get more of us killed!"

A familiar scent reached me, and I looked down the sidewalk. Jakob noticed it as well, glanced past me, and swore beneath his breath. He wrestled my arms behind my back, his hands like a clamp at my wrists.

"DeBoer!" Nate called. He limped toward us, wearing the temporary leg brace, and cast aside a spent cigarette. "What a surprise we should run into each other tonight."

Jakob muttered near my ear. "Please don't put me in this position. I need to take you into booking. Send him away."

Nate stopped several feet from us and flashed Jakob a large grin. "It's been years. How've you been?" He scanned the officer from head to toe. "You fill out that uniform nicely."

"I'm going to have to ask you to back out of the way, sir." Jakob attempted to steer me toward the large door, but Nate stepped in our path.

"I know you're dutifully playing your part in this charade," Nate said, "but Alex has important things to attend to tonight." He nodded toward the building. "We could all go in there, run her through the whole tedious process, and have me bitch nonstop while I wait with bail." Nate shrugged. "Or you could release her and not waste everyone's time."

"Are you going to pay my rent when they fire me for not being able to follow standard protocol?" Jakob glared at Nate. "She made her choice when she assaulted me in front of my partner."

I swallowed and felt a stab of guilt.

Nate scanned Jakob's face. "Everyone makes mistakes." He shrugged again. "For example, you could mistakenly not see a stranger approaching while you are moving a person from your car to the building. Said stranger could overpower you, and your detainee slips away."

"There are cameras and you have an injury," Jakob said. "Someone will be out here any minute. Now get out of my way or you can join her."

Nate cocked his head. "Wouldn't someone have already been out here by now?"

I glanced toward the building, but the large door remained lowered. No one emerged from the regular-sized metal door in the wall beside it. Trish's contacts must run deeper into Hopewell's police department than I'd thought.

Doubt flickered in Jakob's eyes. "I don't take bribes."

"Are you sure?" Nate leaned forward and lowered his voice. "This bail money is burning a hole in my pocket, and I'm certain it's more than that Commoner politician is paying you to kiss his ass."

Jakob's face reddened, and he tried to shove me forward past Nate and toward the building. Nate's grin vanished, and he seized Jakob by the front of his uniform. Even with his leg in a brace, he still managed to be a pest. Jakob was forced to release me to maintain his balance and free himself.

I scurried back from the scuffling men. Nate had found himself in this situation multiple times before, but I hesitated anyway. The Commoner police officers he habitually tangled with weren't as strong as him.

Once I was out of reach, Nate released Jakob and raised his hands in a gesture of innocence. Jakob promptly had Nate's chest pressed against the cruiser, and swiftly handcuffed him. Nate yelped but gave me a nod.

I nodded and ran.

I HURRIED SOUTH of the police station toward Ben's apartment. Anne would be even more pissed that I'd slipped away, but they had the mess at Hell's Bells to deal with tonight. There was a chance she'd prioritize that over tracking me down. However, she knew I was staying with Ben. I wanted to grab Aiden's books and our notes before Anne could send an officer to the apartment.

The parking lot behind Rear Window was empty. The street-lights caused the broken glass littering the pavement to sparkle. It crunched under my shoes and reminded me of my earlier encounter with Jakob. I pushed myself forward, up the stairs, and into the apartment. Dissonance passed over me as the familiar scents I'd begun to associate with contentment hung in the dark and vacant space.

I flipped on the lights, chasing the shadows back into their corners. The apartment was as I'd left it. It didn't look like Ben had been back. He should be safe with Joan, but unease nagged at the edges of my mind. Why hadn't they contacted me yet?

I growled and refocused my wandering thoughts. My first priority was the Hunter.

Aiden's books lay on the floor with our notebooks. I grabbed the canvas bag and started to collect the items. My hand paused over the book Ben had been reading. It had been left open to an illustration of a human, male body. We'd been talking about the keys Hunters use to enhance their abilities. I thought the Hunter might have a bracelet or tattoo, but Nate and I didn't see either when he attacked us at Hell's Bells.

I set the bag aside and turned the book toward me. An icon of a key appeared at different points of the body: the head, chest, groin, feet, and hands. Aiden had said the key wouldn't be some artifact like the dagger because a weapon could be easily taken. I couldn't think of any charm to wear on the head we wouldn't have seen, and the Hunter definitely didn't have a tattoo on his scalp. Plus, Pangur had mentioned the Hunter's hand, and how the man was filled with dark light. I looked at the icon placed over the illustration's hand.

Filled.

My stomach turned as the pieces fell into place. The key must be *inside* the Hunter's body. "That complicates things," I muttered.

My phone buzzed in my pocket. I tried to get to it so quickly I dropped it. Pulse racing, I scooped it up and read the screen. It wasn't Ben or Joan. It was Emma.

What happened?! Anne called and said you evaded arrest?! She wants me to contact her if you reach out! WTF Alex?!?!?!

Anne was fast. It was time to leave.

I dismissed Emma's message and hurried to pack the last book and Ben's notes. Emma wouldn't turn me in, but if Anne was contacting her, there was a chance someone would be assigned to watch Emma's home. I stood and looked around the apartment to make sure I had everything I might need.

When my gaze fell on the empty bed, a part of me entertained the thought of crawling into it. I could toss aside the bag weighing down my shoulder, curl up on the mattress laced with Ben's and my scents, and close my eyes to let sleep take me. There'd be a brief reprieve from the running, fighting, and the stress of having my efforts seemingly make everything worse. I wondered how long it would take for someone to come collect me. How long before the Hunter found me.

I forced myself from the apartment, locked up, and rushed down the stairs. I hurried along the sidewalk toward Another Chance Ministries. Trish asked me to find Fillip, and after what

Nate had told me about vampires, the shelter seemed to be my best chance at doing that as quickly as possible.

I ATTRACTED NUMEROUS stares as I walked along the corner of the block where the shelter was situated. Some were curious, others the usual leers, and almost all were suspicious. Many who were without a home and stayed close to downtown opted to be awake during dark and sleep during the day. It was safer. I scanned over the faces, looking for one in particular.

Growing impatient, I stopped and asked a man seated in a doorway. "I'm looking for John. He's about my height with brown hair and a beard. He was wearing a Lions ball cap and carried cigarettes rolled in his shirt sleeve."

The man blinked up at me with glassy eyes. He looked at my hands. "Who's asking for him?"

I realized I was carrying a canvas tote as if shopping after hours and still wearing the bracelet-like parts of the handcuffs. I didn't have time to deal with the cuffs.

"Alex," I said. "I'm a friend of Ben's." If both Fillip and John knew Ben, maybe this guy would too? I was banking on Ben's name being familiar in Another Chance's social circle.

"Ben Sharpe?" asked the man.

I nodded.

The man pointed across the street to a pocket-sized park. "John is over there."

"Thanks." I jogged across the street straight into a barrage of shouts and wolf whistles. I clenched my jaw, and the hair rose on the back of my neck. The stink of alcohol, cigarette smoke, urine, and unwashed bodies permeated the area. The park was full of lounging male figures. I remained along the edge of the park, not trusting myself to enter it. The first guy to grope me would end up with broken fingers. "John?"

My request was answered with more cat calls and several men who were not John insisting that they were. John pushed past one of the younger guys. He shouted with a bleary smile. "Whatever it was, I didn't do it!" His comment was punctuated by a round of laughter.

"John," I called. "I need to talk to you. It's urgent."

His eyes narrowed, and he tried to focus on me. "Alex? Is that you?" The man stumbled a bit, and then shuffled toward me. The scent of alcohol preceded him in a thick cloud. It overpowered the smoldering cigarette grasped lightly between his dirty fingers.

I waited until he was close enough that I could lower my voice. "I have to talk to Fillip."

He nodded. "I'll see what I can do."

"No," I said. "I need to see him right now."

He blinked at me. My words took a moment to process. He shook his head. "That's not how it works."

"How do I find him, John?" A growl slipped into my voice.

"I'm sorry." He shook his head again. "I don't make the rules."

A young man approached from behind John. "I'll take you to him," he said.

John's surprised reaction was delayed. He scowled, confused a moment, before he turned on the rail-thin, hollow-eyed man. "No. He'll punish you." John looked back at me. "He'll punish him."

The stranger shrugged. "I don't give a shit what the old man does. If you can pay me, I'll take you to him."

My stomach knotted in indecision. "I don't have much on me . . . Maybe a twenty."

The younger man scratched at the back of his neck and then frowned at his fingernails. "Yeah, whatever, that will do."

John seized my wrist and raised his voice as he repeated yet again. "He'll punish him!"

I recoiled and yanked my hand away from him. An immediate sense of guilt struck me. "I'm sorry. I don't know what else to do." I stepped back from John.

The younger man started down the sidewalk, obviously not concerned with waiting for me.

"I'm sorry," I offered John once more before I jogged to catch up with the other man.

The young man walked ahead of me, silent, as we wove through alleys and streets of downtown. We went West toward the riverfront and then south beside one of the main highways passing through the city. He stopped beneath the highway's towering concrete supports and looked back at me. "You can find him through there." He pointed toward a large pipe used to discharge rainwater runoff from the highway.

I frowned and pointed up at the traffic rumbling above us. "You're telling me he's sitting up there?"

"There's a door in there. It leads beneath the street." The young man held out his hand, palm turned up, and waited.

I dug out my wallet. "You're not coming in with me?"

"Hell no." He took the bill I handed him and stuffed it into his jeans pocket. The man turned away and continued down the edge of the street.

"Thanks," I said to his back. The pipe was taller than me, and the scents of oil and exhaust washed from the road hung in the air. I cautiously stepped inside. The sound of traffic reverberated in waves down the pipe, the volume causing me to wince. Before the bend upward in the pipe, I spotted a metal door with the letters *Maintenance Staff Only* spray-painted on its surface. When I tried the handle, it opened.

The door closed behind me and mercifully dampened the noise from the pipe. The low hallway stank of stagnant water, rust, and sewage. At the end of the poorly lit, short hall was a metal rung ladder that led below. I looked down the hole in the pavement and began to doubt my decision to let the younger guy leave before he brought me in person to Fillip.

When the soles of my shoes hit the pavement at the foot of the ladder, I covered my nose and suppressed a gag. The scent of sewage clung like a film. From down the larger tunnel, I heard song and laughter. I didn't have to walk far before finding an open archway in the stone of the tunnel wall. Beyond the opening, there was a larger room with a gathering of people.

A bulky man dressed in a faded t-shirt and stained jeans stepped into the doorway to prevent me from entering. He scowled down at me and brandished a short blade. "Keep moving."

I held up my hands to show him I didn't have ill intentions. "I'm here to see Fillip."

He frowned at the mention of the vampire's name. "I don't recognize you. Are you new?"

"I've done business with him before." I tried to look around the man's figure, feeling the familiar impatience building. I didn't have time for formalities. "Listen, just get him for me. It's important."

The shadow was suddenly beside me.

There was no smell or sound. I spun on it with a snarl and backed away, hackles raised. Fillip stood as still as stone in the tunnel with me.

"Who led you here?" His unblinking eyes glowed red in the murky lighting.

My gut clenched. I thought of the young man and what John said. "I don't know his name."

Fillip looked at the larger man. "Give us some privacy."

"Sure thing." He glared down at me, an unspoken warning, and stepped through the doorway into the larger room.

"I know this isn't how you like to do business, but this is an emergency," I said. "The Hunter attacked Hell's Bells and escaped."

"I am aware," he said.

Trish had guessed correctly. Fillip's network already alerted him that the Hunter moved locations. "We thought you would know where he went," I said.

"It's unusual for the lupine to be indebted to me. Patricia Drake is very careful, very frugal," he said. "Or will you pay the price for this, Alexandria?"

My mind ran through the missteps I'd made leading up to this point. "I will." I suppressed a shudder when Fillip's slow smile exposed his pointed, yellowed teeth.

"The Hunter did not yet move," he said.

I blinked. "The building he was hiding in went up in flames tonight. We saw it."

"The fire was used to deter those who wish to find him. This city is riddled with mazes of tunnels and forgotten shelters beneath its streets," Fillip said. "He simply burrowed deeper in place while he seeks a new location."

My pulse leapt. When we first visited the building, it looked as if it had been abandoned. The fire department would leave after an initial sweep through the structure's remains for any squatters caught in the blaze. Trish and I could still get back there tonight to search before any other investigation took place. "Thank you." I turned to leave.

Fillip spoke to my back. "How is Benjamin?"

My chest ached at the mention of Ben's name. I turned to see another one of Fillip's eerie smiles. "You know where he is?" I asked.

Fillip gave the slightest bow of his head. Of course he did.

"You won't tell Reginald, will you?"

"The price of this information for Reginald Sharpe is more than he would be willing to pay. But you, on the other hand, may find it worth the expense."

It was difficult, but I needed to trust Joan to keep Ben safe. "I'll keep that in mind."

"Wise choice," Fillip said. "Your debt is already . . . sizable." He rubbed his hands together, his papery skin rasping. "Should I have you fetch the fool who brought you here? Perhaps, instead, I will order you to cut him down where you find him."

"I don't kill people," I growled.

"But you have already done so." Fillip tilted his head. The dim light reflected back from his eyes. "Whoever led you here will not live beyond tonight."

A pang of guilt caused bile to rise in my throat. I swallowed and took a step back.

"But you are busy tonight, and I am not an unreasonable business partner." Fillip waved his hand, dismissing me. "Go. I will send for you when you are needed."

I hurried toward the ladder to the maintenance hallway. It took all my willpower not to look back over my shoulder. I reassured myself that I'd made the right choice. Fillip was the fastest path to finding the Hunter.

But now my debt to the vampire had grown even more. Would he send me like an attack dog after someone? And would I be able to handle the consequences when I refused?

24

I MESSAGED TRISH to let her know I'd found Fillip and had the Hunter's location. She left St. Anthony's and picked me up at the overpass. I tossed the book tote in the backseat of the coupe, buckled in, and floated an idea I'd had while waiting for her. "Should we ask Joan to meet us there? I'm not sure she's still in the city, but I could try contacting her."

Trish frowned. "I don't know what to expect from her, and this will already be difficult."

The Hunter had withstood three wolves. Trish and I going in alone made me nervous, even if the guy was injured. He was aware of Joan, and the stealth her magic granted her, but we'd still have a better chance of getting closer to him with her help.

And I could ask if Ben was safe.

"Yes, it will be difficult," I said, "so I think having magic will give us an advantage. I've seen a bit of what she can do. She's not the best fighter, but I think it's because she never needed to be. She can move around unnoticed, even by us."

Trish was silent, seeming to weigh the option.

"We could use the extra help getting as close as we can," I said. "I think the key is kept inside his body, in his hand."

She finally nodded. "Tell her we are already on our way."

I texted Joan and was surprised to receive a reply briefly afterward. I reread the message twice before I looked at Trish. "She's already there." Hopefully we could get in and find the Hunter before Anne and Jakob figured out what had happened. "Trish, what happens if we run into Jakob again?"

Her jawline stiffened. "I've told him to let us handle this." She glanced over at me. "If you look in the glove compartment, you'll find a shim for those handcuffs."

"Nate's?" I opened the glove compartment and found a two-inch long, flat metal pin.

"Yes. He tucks them away like a squirrel does nuts."

I actually laughed. With a wiggle of the shim down between the lock house and the teeth of the cuff, the remains of the handcuff fell open from my wrist. Nate loved picking locks and had taught me how to release the rather simple locking mechanism on handcuffs. I removed the second cuff and could hear his voice in my mind.

It's designed to keep only one person locked in, and not even for that long.

"Thanks for sending him after me," I said.

"He was more than willing to sabotage Jakob's evening."

Trish and I left the car a few blocks away, and as quickly and quietly as possible, we moved toward the building's burnt remains. The street was empty of firetrucks. Joan materialized from the shadows when she stepped out from her cloaking spell. Trish backstepped at the wizard's sudden appearance, and her nostrils flared. She searched for a scent I knew she wouldn't find.

"Thank you for contacting me." Joan extended her hand to Trish. "I apologize for not introducing myself the other night. I'm Joan Sharpe."

Trish clasped Joan's hand. "Patricia Drake."

"Is he okay?" I asked Joan. I had a lot of questions, but all I needed to know right now was that Ben was safe.

Joan avoided my gaze but nodded.

Trish studied me. "I'm relying on you to remain focused. Your mind won't be elsewhere, will it?"

My face warmed. "No."

Trish looked back to Joan. "Have you seen the Hunter?"

"Yes." Joan pointed ahead toward the building. "He's been loading bags into an SUV. There's a door in the back room I overlooked when I was here last night. It's built into the floor."

"How are we going to approach this?" I asked.

Trish looked between the two of us. "We need to separate the Hunter from this charmed key that gives him strength. Alex believes it is inside one of his hands."

Joan screwed up her face. "Are we going to cut it out?"

"Unless we find a way to remove the hand, yes," Trish said. "Alex and I should be the only ones to physically engage him. Don't get too close. If he attacks or restrains you, I will not let Alex endanger herself to protect you."

I bit my lip and looked from Trish to Joan, unsure how the command would be received.

Joan nodded. "Understood."

"Can you get us to him undetected?" Trish asked.

"Of course." Joan held out her hands for ours. Trish hesitated. When I took one of Joan's hands, she accepted the other. Joan gathered the energy needed to cast the cloaking spell. Trish gasped at the unexpected tingling sensation sent under our skin. She examined the effect on her body as I had the first time. Joan explained, "The illusion will remain intact until you attack him or he strikes you."

Trish nodded. "Lead on."

The three of us crept toward the abandoned building. The lingering odors of smoke and burnt building materials surrounded the charred remains. The roof of the largest room had collapsed in on itself, but the metal entrance door stood. The walls around it had been destroyed by the blaze. An SUV sat parked beside the partially intact back room. The Hunter must have ditched the van he used in the attack on Hell's Bells.

Trish and I waited behind the SUV while Joan continued ahead. She crouched in what had been the back room, and seconds later, waved us over. I reached down into myself and invited my inner wolf forward. All of my senses shifted to become more acute as Trish and I slunk toward the building.

Joan tapped her ear and pointed at the square door. I crouched beside her and strained to hear anything. I didn't hear any sounds, but my nose picked up a faint scent of bleach. I looked back at Joan and shook my head.

She slipped her hand beneath the latch and found it locked. Joan withdrew a small, delicate-looking toolset from her pocket. With a few quick, deft twitches of her fingers, the door was unlocked. We paused to check again for any sound on the other side of the door. I gave another shake of my head, and Joan lifted the door to reveal a metal ladder.

The pungent odor of bleach hit me as soon as the door cracked open. I lifted my hand to my nose. The smell burned through my nostrils to the back of my throat. I looked at Trish, eyes watering. She frowned. The Hunter had been wounded at Hell's Bells. We'd hoped to use the scent of his blood to find him. The strong chemical stench of the bleach would make it impossible. Joan noticed our reactions, and the first signs of doubt shadowed her features.

I wiped my eyes and descended the ladder into the cooler air of a dimly lit tunnel. The passageway was barely wide enough for one person to squeeze past another. Unlike the maintenance hall or even the sewers, the floor was uneven and no lighting had been installed. Instead, at random intervals, small battery-operated lights were jammed into the crevices of the roughly hewn walls.

Joan followed us. She lowered the door shut, and the faint light from outside vanished. I sensed Trish's presence behind me as we started down the tunnel. Groupings of small, dark splotches marred the stone floor. I couldn't pick the scent out of the haze of bleach, but I suspected it to be blood. We passed another tunnel leading away into the dark. I glanced back at Trish, but she pointed ahead to where the lighting was brighter.

As we snuck closer, faint noises of movement reached me. My chest tightened and my pulse quickened. We arrived at a low-ceilinged room, lit by a couple of electric lanterns and the same lights used in the hall. The lanterns, hung on hooks, cast shifting shadows across the walls. A folded cot and bulging backpack waited in the corner near the entrance.

I crouched, frozen, as the Hunter walked into view. He stood at a wooden crate that served as a makeshift table. A large duffle bag and a small ornately carved box sat on the floor next to it. He began to assemble some sort of weapon from parts strewn across the surface of the crate. The swiftness of his movements were the only indication he felt pressed for time.

There were slashes, stitched hastily together, across the side of the Hunter's face and scalp. His left eye was almost swollen shut. The beast inside me responded to the sight of the injured Hunter, causing my muscles to warm and my senses to sharpen further. I smiled to myself. Roger's attack had caused more damage than I'd thought.

Trish tapped my upper arm. Her fingers rested on her chest briefly before she pointed into the room to the right. I nodded, though her leaving my side did nothing for the dread I felt in the Hunter's presence.

The embodiment of liquid grace, Trish stood and stepped over my crouched figure. She slunk into the room to the right of the Hunter, her footfalls barely audible to my heightened sense of hearing. Her features shifted as she watched him. The pointed ends of her ears slid up through the dark curtain of her hair. Her fingers elongated and the curved shape of her claws formed.

I stood and followed through the doorway. Even though the Hunter couldn't see me, I kept low to the ground and watched for any sign he realized he wasn't alone. I crept close enough to see the red of the inflamed skin around his wounds. The adrenaline in my body surged. My body twitched and trembled as I held tight to my control, waiting for Trish's signal.

Her lips parted slightly to reveal her pointed canines. From her position near his left side, her gaze met mine. She nodded.

In a single, arced strike with her claws, Trish removed several layers of skin from the side of the Hunter's neck, including part of his ear.

His face contorted in surprise and pain. The force of the unexpected blow sent him tumbling over the bag at his feet.

I scurried back out of the way. A spray of blood spattered around me.

The Hunter's large bulk struck the floor.

My eyes wide, I raised a shaking hand to touch my damp face. My fingertips were bright with blood. A roaring noise filled my ears and the edges of my vision blurred.

I could taste it . . . the red that stained my skin.

My name is being called. It's my mother. She and my grandmother run from our house to meet me on the walkway. They try to pull me toward safety. The spring breeze chills my wet face and arms. My mother is sobbing. She repeats my name over and over again.

But it wasn't my mother's voice calling me.

"Alex!" Trish yelled.

The cloaking spell had dropped away from her. She perched atop the Hunter, her knee driven into his lower middle back. Her claws were sunk into the base of his skull to hold his head against the floor.

I scrambled forward to help.

Unfortunately, the Hunter was also recovering from the attack. He struggled against Trish. He failed to lift his head, but braced his hands against the floor and began to move his body.

I dove for the leather bracer covering the back of his right hand, wrist, and the majority of his forearm. The hand and fingers were swollen from where I'd clubbed him with his rifle. I fumbled with the ties.

He realized my intent and doubled his efforts to free himself.

Trish let go of his head to hold his upper arm stationary for me. Her body quivered, and a soft down of dark fur emerged from the twitching skin on her forearms.

The bracer's ties knotted. I wrenched the Hunter's right forearm up and behind his back and bit through the leather cording. The cord snapped, his arm jerked to his side, and I fell back onto my ass holding the chunk of leather.

The Hunter, bleeding profusely, pushed himself up despite Trish's weight on his back. His muscles strained. The key bulged grotesquely from beneath the skin on the back of his hand.

With a frustrated snarl at being overpowered, Trish slipped away before the Hunter could seize her. I retreated from his reach, too.

One hand pressed to his neck, he stood. He withdrew a dagger with his free hand. His eyes, rabid with hate, darted between us.

Trish paced outside the Hunter's reach. Not breaking eye contact with him, she growled and bared her teeth.

It enraged him further, this woman patiently waiting for her opening to strike. There was a slight sway in his stance. His stamina was faltering.

I craved to finish him.

With his fingers clenched around the hilt of the dagger, the Hunter succumbed to Trish's taunting. He rushed her. The strength and swiftness behind his attack was superhuman. It forced Trish to retreat deeper into the room.

It also gave me the opening she'd been waiting for.

Instead of controlling her like a weapon, I allowed my inner wolf to blend herself throughout our body. I ducked under the Hunter's swings and snatched a dagger from his belt. My fingers and palms sizzled. Tears sprung into my eyes. I stabbed the weapon deep into the muscle of the Hunter's thigh. He bellowed.

He turned from Trish and swatted me aside. The force of it pitched me back away from him. The Hunter lowered the dagger he held and clasped at the one in his leg. He caught Trish a moment before she descended upon him.

The Hunter grappled with her, and his attention shifted swiftly between the two of us. He held the snarling and snapping werewolf at arm's length and stepped back toward the entrance.

He planned to run.

The Hunter dropped the dagger he held, freeing his hand. With a grunt, he twisted Trish's arm down toward her body and drove her into the wooden crate. The contents of its surface clattered to the floor. The small box on the ground tipped to its side.

I tore a strip of fabric from my shirt, darted after the two, and scooped up the discarded dagger. The Hunter slammed Trish's forearm down onto the edge of the crate. There was the awful crunch of bone breaking.

Trish howled, the vocalization more feral with each passing breath. She rolled to the side and cradled her arm. The crate stood between her and the Hunter.

I blocked the room's entrance. It took extreme effort to prevent the dagger from shaking in my sweaty grasp.

The Hunter's gaze bore into me. It burned with a deep level of disgust and hatred. "You can end this, Alexandria. The beast nearly killed a man and escaped. Don't let it run free and endanger anyone else." His voice was steady, despite his injuries. "Bury the blade in your body. It will rid you of the blight."

"You're wrong," I said. My voice was *not* steady. "She's not some disease. She's a part of me. We're not a mindless monster for you to track down and kill."

He took another step toward me, and I jerked the dagger higher and bared my teeth.

"Then come forward, creature." His words weren't for me. They were for her. "With St. Hubert's blessing, I will cleanse you from this world."

My inner wolf flared like a fanned flame through bone and muscle. Our fear of the man skewed into hot anger. My ears and teeth warped and grew pointed as my body reshaped itself. But then we stopped. Waited. Because no Hunter was going to dictate to us where I ended and she began.

"Are you afraid?" He tilted his head. "Will you instead run away again like a small animal?"

It was always about size and fear with these types of guys. "Frightened? Me?" I said. "What type of coward tries to kill a kid?"

"I didn't put the creature out of its misery?" He smiled. The gashes in his face pulled against their stitches. "That will be corrected once I'm fin—"

Trish's solid punch knocked the Hunter back onto the wooden crate. She struggled to hold him, wincing from her injured arm. Muscles in her arms, shoulders, and back bulged and slid beneath her skin as she pushed the shifting of her body further to access more strength.

I dashed forward, pinned the Hunter's wrist, and drove the dagger down between the bones of his forearm into the crate.

He screamed.

Trish held his free arm with her body weight.

With my curved thumbnail, I sliced open the skin above his key. The stretched skin split away from the raised surface to expose metal beneath. From my angle, I briefly glimpsed an inverted cross before the wound became obscured by blood.

"Stop!" It was Anne's voice.

We froze.

My back was to the room's entrance, but I imagined Jakob was with Anne. The bleach and the Hunter's screams had masked their approach.

Trish dropped her gaze and turned her face away. The thin layer of dark hair on the back of her hands and forearms receded.

"Back away from him—now!" Anne's command quavered. Without seeing her face, I couldn't tell if it was anger or fear. Maybe both.

Trish looked at me, her eyes still rimmed in gold. Her gaze darted down to the Hunter's hand and back at me.

"Alex!" Anne said, "Let him go. Step away."

My mind raced. If I didn't get the key, we wouldn't be safe. But Anne . . .

The Hunter pulled free from Trish. He reached for the dagger in his forearm.

Heat flooded through my arms and across my back. My claws hooked and tore the metal from inside his hand. His screams rose above the sounds of the cracking cartilage and tearing sinew. I grasped the key with slippery fingers and spun away to face the room's entrance.

Anne was pale and shaking, her hand resting near her gun. "What the hell is—" Her expression morphed through a series of emotions. Disappointment, confusion, shock, and horror.

Each left one more fissure in my heart. I'd stopped a monster, but not without my friend believing I was one.

Trish raised her open hands and stepped back from the prone man. Wincing, she placed her hands at the back of her head. She glanced at the key and then met my gaze. I curled my bloodied fingers closed around the metal object and raised my hands as well.

The Hunter lay staked to the surface of the crate. With the key removed, all the fight left him. His breathing was uneven and his skin appeared damp and grayish.

Jakob stepped past Anne toward Trish and me, acting as if nothing was unusual. "Miss Steward, I'm going to need you to place your hands at the back of your head." I did as he asked, and handcuffs snapped securely around one of my wrists.

"What are you doing?" I asked Jakob. "Why would you bring her here?"

He guided my hands down behind my back and secured my other wrist with the handcuffs. He noticed my fingers closed around the key. "Miss Steward, please drop what you're holding."

I looked at Trish. Her nostrils flared, and her gaze was locked on Jakob.

"Alex, drop it!" Anne stepped into the room, her face red and brows drawn together.

I uncurled my fingers. A tingling sensation brushed over my skin. The metal cross fell toward the ground before it stopped and hovered in the air a half foot from the floor. It rotated and zipped through the room toward the entrance.

Anne ducked and turned as it flew past her.

The key struck an invisible surface, and Joan's cloaked figure melted into view. She tucked the key away, turned, and ran.

Anne looked back at Jakob, her eyes wide. She swallowed and ordered in a hoarse voice, "Stay here with them." She sprinted from the room back into the tunnel. Her voice echoed back to us. "Stop! Police!"

"Who was that?" Jakob said.

Before I could answer, Trish clasped her hand tight around Jakob's throat. "I told you to stand down," she snarled. "Why are you interfering?"

Jakob grasped at Trish's fingers. His eyes began to shift color as he choked. "Let us bring him in as a suspect of the shooting. The Committee can still try him afterward."

Trish's fury burned bright in her eyes. "Will you follow through on this as you did with the mishandled reports, Officer DeBoer?"

"He won't be able to slip out of the Commoner's court system."

"Bullshit," Trish said. "Their system is built to let men like him slip through."

"Anne will make sure of it." Jakob gasped.

"He's right, Trish. Anne is with him. She wouldn't let Jakob do anything other than get the Hunter to the hospital and place him under arrest," I said. "And we have the Hunter's key. He won't be able to overpower them."

Trish glanced toward the Hunter. He'd lost consciousness. She released Jakob and narrowed her eyes. "If you insist upon playing policeman with the Commoners, keep your partner on a tighter leash when it comes to matters concerning us."

Jakob, his face flushed, fixed his uniform collar and nodded.

"Are you going to let me out of these, or should I do it?" I asked and gave the handcuffs a shake.

He unlocked the cuffs. "What am I supposed to tell Anne?"

"That isn't our problem," Trish said.

I looked at the Hunter. "Should we take anything so it doesn't get lost on the way to evidence?" The two blades he'd had on his person were now inside his person. I'd learned the hard way not to pull a dagger from a wound unless you were prepared to deal with the consequences. The Hunter wouldn't be able to stand trial if he bled to death beforehand.

"No," Jakob said. "We want a clear tie between him and everything here. Don't pollute the crime scene any more than you have."

I turned on Jakob. "Shouldn't you be checking on your partner? Why isn't she back?" The questions were meant to get rid of him, but the fact neither Anne nor Joan had returned worried me.

Jakob glowered but walked toward the entrance. "Don't. Touch. Anything."

As soon as I no longer heard his footsteps, I asked Trish, "Should we take photos?"

"Photos can be altered." She held out a pair of leather gloves. "Put these on before you start looking. Less trouble later with your cop friend."

Would she be my friend after this?

"Thanks." I put on the gloves, crouched near the crate's base, and rummaged through the large duffle bag. Trish cradled her broken arm and stood at the room's entrance to watch the passageway. There were other weapons in the bag, but no sign of silver daggers.

I picked up the small ornate wooden box from beside the duffle bag. It was covered in a scrolling pattern identical to the one on the daggers' hilts. I futzed with the latch mechanism and opened the box to reveal a row of glass tubes nestled inside.

"What is it?" Trish said.

"I'm not sure yet." I lifted a vial out of the box, held it up to the light, and squinted. When I realized what I was holding, I almost dropped the tube. I tossed it back in the box, slammed the lid, and came dangerously close to losing whatever was in my stomach. "They're teeth. This is filled with people's teeth."

Trish's lip curled back, and her glowing gaze moved to the unconscious Hunter. Her chest rumbled with growling. I could imagine the dark thoughts being whispered at the edges of her mind. Fillip had teased them from my own subconscious.

"Should we take this with us or leave it for the police?" I stood, the box with its grisly trophies in-hand. "Trish."

She pulled her attention away from the Hunter and hugged her injured arm to her body. "Bring it with us for Detective Grey."

We needed to distance ourselves from the Hunter before the temptation became too strong. I nodded and headed to the doorway. "Let's go, then."

We rushed back through the tunnel and out into the blessedly bleach-free air of the warm evening. There was no sign of Anne, but Jakob was posted at the door.

"If you're going, get the hell out of here," he said. "An ambulance is on its way."

I turned in place, scanning the area. "Where's Anne?"

Jakob frowned. "Whoever is with you is stringing her along a block over."

Knowing Anne was being led around so we could escape made me feel awful. She was a good cop, and this might not reflect well on her or Jakob.

Trish and I jogged down the shoulder of the street back to her car. Joan was waiting for us, tucked behind the body of the vehicle.

"The cop is several buildings down, so we should clear out of here quickly," she said.

"Do you have the key?" I said.

Joan handed the blood-streaked, metal cross to Trish.

"I'll take this to Aiden and update him," Trish said. "Then I'll go to the hospital to ensure Jakob brings in the Hunter. We'll want to check on Roger, too."

"Should I come with you?" I said.

"No," she said. "Go somewhere other than Ben's apartment to rest and wait for my call. I'll clear any warrants for your arrest first."

"I can give Alex a ride to where she needs to go," Joan said.

"Will you be able to drive with your arm?" I asked Trish.

"Yes. Fortunately, it wasn't the arm I needed for that." Trish gingerly and briefly embraced me. "Thank you." She extended her good hand to Joan. "And thank you for your help."

Joan accepted the handshake. "You're welcome."

I set the small box I carried in Trish's coupe and jogged to Joan's car. Now would come a period of not-knowing, of hoping Trish and Aiden could present the evidence we'd collected in a way the Committee couldn't dismiss.

What weighed on me heaviest was Anne. How the *hell* was I going to explain what she'd witnessed? Was it even possible? I'd have to sit with the knowledge that, after tonight, my friendship with Anne may be over.

25

WHEN I DROPPED into the passenger seat of Joan's car, exhaustion hit me like a train. "Can you take me to Em's?" Even beyond Trish's request, I didn't want to be alone at Ben's apartment. I rolled the window down to let the night air into the car. Joan drove past the highway, the fastest route to Emma's. "Where are you going?" I asked, immediately suspicious.

She glanced over. "I thought you'd want a few minutes to decompress. We'll take the scenic route."

Satisfied with the answer, I settled back against my seat again. I messaged Emma to ask if any police cars were lurking around her house. My phone buzzed with her response.

Funny you ask. Sent one away hours ago. Haven't noticed others.

Good. I could catch my breath there. I tucked away my phone. "I know Trish already said it, but thank you for helping us."

"You're welcome. It'll be a good day when that man is sentenced," Joan said. "Trish seems to place a lot of trust in you."

"I trust her, too. She's been a mentor while I get control of . . ." I searched for the right words but settled for a gesture up and down the length of myself, ". . . this whole mess."

Joan smiled. "She's grooming you, isn't she? Ready to become a Committee stooge?"

I shrugged away her question. It wasn't any of her business and was the least of my worries at the moment. "Are you going to tell me where he is?"

Her smile dissipated.

"What's the plan, Joan? Won't it piss them off even more if he runs and they have to track him down?"

"I don't trust them like you do," she said.

"Quit pretending you know anything about me," I growled.

"I'm in conversation with the Committee about the incident."

"You weren't even there!"

Joan cranked the steering wheel to the right, and the car veered to the shoulder of the road. The seatbelt bit into my chest, and the tires slid on the gravel to a stop. She threw the shifter into park and turned to face me. "Benjamin is *my* brother! He means the world to me. I'm not putting blind faith in the Committee when it comes to determining if he lives or dies. They have to give me concrete assurance he won't be punished for defending the two of you from a psychopath on their payroll. Since you're so wrapped up in the Committee through Trish, *no*, I will *not* be telling you where my brother is staying."

"And what does Ben think?"

"Honestly?" She slammed her palm on the edge of the steering wheel. "He's being a tremendous pain in my ass. After convincing him to ditch his phone so we couldn't be tracked, I caught him trying to lift mine. I was hoping for a bit more understanding from you since you supposedly care about him." Joan gave a theatrical shrug. "But then, according to you, I know nothing about you. Maybe you don't care at all. He's simply someone you're fucking until you realize it's going to be hard work being with him. Then you'll disappear, just like the last asshole he gave his heart to." She glared at me across the span of the front seat. "So *you* tell *me*: 'what's the plan' with my brother?"

My mouth opened, but my eyes immediately blurred. Did she still see nothing more in me than a primal beast, incapable of caring for her brother? Maybe she was simply scared for Ben. I turned my face away, not wanting her to know how much her words stung. "Of course I care for him. Why else would I put up with you?"

"Don't villainize me for trying to keep my family safe, Alex."

I looked back at her. "Does Ben know you sold him out to the two guys that beat him bloody this past winter?"

Joan's face flushed. "They were idiots. I didn't think they'd be able to find him."

"Em had to heal him so he could even breathe right," I said.

"I was in a tight spot and trying to protect someone." Joan's eyes shimmered as she frowned. "She's important to me, too. I honestly didn't think Benjamin would be in danger."

I looked out the window.

"Are you going to tell him it was me?"

I shook my head. "I don't want to upset him."

"Thank you." Joan pulled the car back onto the road. "I'm working as fast as possible to get him out of my hair."

The remainder of the car ride was silent. I couldn't talk to him, but I knew Ben was hidden and, at least for now, safe. My chest ached even more as I realized I wasn't sure when I'd get to see him again.

EMMA'S FRONT DOOR opened and, upon seeing me, her hands flew to her mouth. She reached for my arm and pulled me inside. "What happened?"

"Trish, Joan, and I went after the Hunter," I said.

"Did you catch him? Where are Trish and Joan? Are they okay?" She grimaced at my clothing. "I want to hug you, but I don't know whose blood that is."

I gave her an exhausted smile. "We got him, Trish and Joan are okay, and most of it is his."

"I was so worried about you and Anne. She wouldn't tell me anything beyond what I shared with you," Emma said. "I've been waiting for you to call or show up for hours."

"I didn't have time to explain. Everything happened really fast."

"I'm sorry, Alex." Emma wrinkled her nose. "I'm not able to focus on this conversation because your clothes are incredibly disgusting. This is why you can't have nice things."

I grinned. "I'll clean up if you have a bathtub you can spare."

Emma granted me access to her private bathroom, which resembled a personal spa. She drew a hot bath while I discarded my sweaty, and now somewhat crusty, clothes into a trash bag. After declining candles, wine, and a cheese plate, I was left alone to sink down into the steamy, lavender-scented water. The bath salts were the one luxury I accepted. I exhaled slowly and deeply, wanting to expel any lingering stress from my body. If all went as it should, the Hunter wouldn't take a life ever again.

Trish's horrific first strike against the Hunter, which had left slasher-film-grade blood spray up the front of my shirt and face, looped in my mind's eye. It was the closest I'd come to glimpsing the wolf interwoven with my teacher and friend. Trish was always so focused and in control, I often forgot she was like me—a woman with a ferocious creature curled and waiting in her breast.

Did I appear like that when in a fight, or did I look entirely inhuman? I'd sensed harmony again when my inner wolf and I were battling the Hunter. The balance was so difficult. I closed my eyes and let my body slip fully down beneath the surface of the water to block out all sight, sound, and smell.

I reached for her, seeking my connection with the primal force inside me. She stirred and stretched within my chest. The Hunters called it blight. My grandmother referred to it as a gift. The now familiar surge of blood and warmth unfurled from my core throughout my body.

Almost eight years had passed since this creature let herself be known to me, but I'd only recently decided to stop running away and hold my arms open to her. We made some people around me uncomfortable. We frightened others. At times she scared me. But I was making progress in understanding and accepting this person I was becoming.

I sat up in the bath, a cascade of water running from me. I pushed my wet hair back from my eyes. The wolf inside me was more finely parsed throughout my being than when I first met her. She was beginning to meld with my tissue and fuse with my bones.

I set to work gently washing away the dirt, sweat, and blood from my skin. I tried to be intentional as I ran the sponge over my body, thanking her for giving me strength and protecting me yet again.

After my bath, I wrapped myself in a lightweight robe and joined Emma on the back patio. She already had a glass of wine poured for us, even though dawn would be within the hour. We sat together at the edge of the pool, draped our legs in the water, and enjoyed the singing tree frogs and the warm summer breeze.

I looked down at the distorted appearance of my feet beneath the water. "Em, I severely screwed up things with Anne."

"She was angry when she spoke to me. What happened between the two of you?"

"Her new partner Jakob is a werewolf," I said.

Emma almost choked on her wine. "What?"

"Jakob and Anne responded to the emergency call when the Hunter attacked Hell's Bells."

"What! Is everyone okay?"

"Roger, the pup—kid—you met at Hell's Bells, was almost killed," I said. "He's over at the hospital now."

"Oh no." She frowned.

"And then I punched Jakob, so Anne arrested me."

"Alex, you didn't!"

"Nate got me out of that, but Anne and Jakob found Trish and me at the Hunter's place. Anne saw me . . . As in, saw what I am."

Emma winced. "How did she react?"

"Like she'd seen a monster." I shook my head. "I'm not sure how to even talk to her about it."

"Anne's brain might be short-circuiting trying to make sense of everything." Emma said. "After three years of knowing you, she found out you're someone different from who she thought you were. It's difficult to keep Commoners as close friends."

"You don't seem to have an issue with it," I said.

She arched an eyebrow. "My gifts don't alter my features."

My shoulders sagged.

Emma rubbed my back. "I think you'll have to wait for her to come to you. And it'll probably take longer than you'd like because you have zero patience." She refilled our wine glasses. "Did you remember to let Ben know you're safe?" She set the bottle aside and looked at me. "Alex? What is it?"

My jaw clenched tight enough I felt my teeth would shatter. I was so tired. "Um. . . Yeah. He knows by now."

"What's wrong?"

"Reginald found out about Ben's compromised tether. Jakob was sent to arrest Ben for the Committee. Ben took off with Joan to hide until she negotiates his punishment." I cleared my throat. "I don't know where he is or when I'll get to see him again."

Emma put her arm around me, which resulted in more tears. I shook my head and wiped my eyes. "I'm sorry. I'm exhausted."

"You need to rest."

"Yeah. This will be the last glass of wine for me."

I LOWERED THE blinds of the spare room against the rising sun. Several hours of blissful nightmare-free sleep followed. My phone woke me when it buzzed from the bedside table. I squinted against the bright light of the screen to read a message from Trish.

Roger out of ICU. Grey visiting him later.

I breathed a sigh of relief. Was the Hunter recovering under the same roof? Trish's violent attack flashed again in my memory. I wondered if he would have lived if Jakob and Anne hadn't interrupted us. I sent a message back inquiring about the Hunter. Trish's reply quickly followed.

In ICU. Police guard. When stable will be transferred to Northwestern University hospital. No word on time or location of trial.

The gears were already in motion to hold the Hunter accountable for his actions. I wondered if Joan had anything to do with the Hunter being transferred to Chicago.

But what about Trish and me? Anne and Jakob had caught us at the scene, and then we ran. Had Trish already dealt with any reports or warrants? No one had come to Emma's or called her looking for me. Trish's answer was short and to the point.

It's been handled.

I dressed in some clothes Emma lent me, had a brief breakfast, and we drove to the hospital. We paused at a glass-walled waiting room. Among vending machine food wrappers and decks of cards were his friends. Most of the teenagers were asleep, draped across the waiting room chairs and curled up on the small sofas.

Emma and I walked the hospital corridor to the room number Trish had sent. I knocked on the door and heard Nate's voice invite us in.

Nate hobbled to his feet from where he'd been sitting in a chair by Roger's bedside. A full brace held his injured leg straight. Emma gave him a small smile in greeting. I hugged him.

"Thanks for your help at the police station," I said as we parted.

"I hadn't been down there to see them in a while." He grinned. "I think they missed me."

"Any updates on Roger?"

"He has a much better chance now than earlier," Nate said.

Bandaged and asleep in the hospital bed, Roger appeared much younger than when he'd confronted the Hunter. Emma stood beside the bed with her fingertips resting on Roger's forearm while she watched him sleep. "Where's his family?" she asked.

"Trish tracked his dad down. He was out of state on work, but by now should only be a few hours away." Nate scratched at his stubbled cheek. "I was going to stay until he got here."

"How is Trish's arm?" I asked.

"She's upstairs having it set."

"Has she been to see the Hunter?"

"No." His eyes darkened. "We're not on the guest list for that floor. You and Trish have been removed from the police department's radar, but not Stone's. You ladies broke his toy."

"How could Trish and I be cleared after being caught by the police?" I asked. "Did Jakob decide to help us for once?"

"It was the priest," Nate answered. "Don't look so surprised. Men of the cloth hold a lot of power around here. This is no different from him getting us out of charges for breaking into the Mind Center locations this past winter. Any complaints against you two are suspended until the trial is held for the Hunter."

I hadn't realized Aiden was responsible for protecting us from the White family's legal wrath after we'd caused havoc at the Mind Center. I'd thought it was the Committee. "I'll have to thank him."

"I'm not convinced he did it out of the kindness of his heart." Nate smirked. "Or for you."

To be honest, I wasn't sure I believed that either, and that made me uncomfortable. I was used to my inner wolf weighing in on the character of people I met. Aiden remained confusing to us.

"IT'S GOOD NEWS you're not a wanted criminal," Emma said.

We stepped onto the elevator to leave. I gave her a worried look and pressed the button for the ground floor. "Can you even begin to imagine the magnitude of pissed off Anne must be right now? She already dislikes Trish and Nate."

"Part of her might be relieved."

"Maybe." The whole situation made me feel ill.

The doors opened onto the lobby of the hospital. Standing among other people waiting to board the elevator was Detective

Grey. He frowned at a small notepad he scribbled in, as it had disappointed him.

I hadn't seen Grey since our brunch together after my humiliating behavior in the last Committee meeting. Emma exited the elevator, and I followed, trying to slip by Grey without being noticed. But he was cut from a similar cloth as Anne.

"Alex Steward, right?"

Hearing my name, Emma stopped and looked back at Grey. She smiled as she recognized the rumpled and unshaven man. I turned to find him pointing his pen at me. The doors slid shut on the elevator, leaving him behind in the lobby hallway with us.

"Oh. Hi." I conjured a smile. "Sorry, I didn't see you."

"Hello, Detective Grey." Emma held out her hand. She'd met him during the investigation into her evil ex and the Mind Center.

"Hello, Miss Arztin." His hand, fingertips stained with ink from his pen, enveloped Emma's. "Were you two visiting Roger?"

I didn't reply, having noticed Grey never asked a question for small talk's sake, but Emma nodded. "Yes. He's sleeping right now, though."

"Maybe he'll be awake by the time I make it up there."

"Did you get the reports back?" I asked. The heavy metals and poison lab reports would be more evidence against the Hunter.

He nodded. "It's confirmed that silver was in the Laska boy's system."

"And what about Stone?" I asked.

"What about him?"

"He employed the Hunter," I said. "And what about finding the person who gave Isaac's name to Stone? We think it's another Committee member. Julia Visser said—"

"Whoa, whoa, whoa." Grey held up his hands, palms toward me. "Slow down. You know the whole horse and cart thing, right? You're worried about the cart. Our focus is on the horse."

Irritation simmered inside me. "And in the meantime, the cart is going to be hidden away and forgotten."

Emma frowned. "So . . . is the cart Stone? Or something else?"

Grey glanced from Emma back to me. He suddenly looked very tired. "You're not going to be happy hearing this, Alex, but I'll tell you now: nothing is going to happen with Stone."

"What!"

"Shh, calm down." Emma placed her hand on my shoulder. "You're starting to shout."

I shrugged away, scowling at her. "Stone was the one to bring the Hunter to Hopewell."

"He hired the guy for 'security,' not hunting," Grey said.

My stomach felt on fire. "He hired the guy to kill Isaac."

"Alex." Emma's forehead creased. She glanced down the hall.

I closed my eyes and focused on my breathing. This was not the time to wolf out. My record had *just* been cleared. I managed through clenched teeth. "It's bullshit."

"You're right. It is," Grey said. "But the case against the Hunter is solid, and he'll be shipped out to Chicago as soon as possible. The Delegation will be in charge of the trial. He won't be returning to Hopewell to hurt anyone else."

"The Delegation? They're regional. Can they do that?" Emma looked from Grey to me. "I thought the Committee in Hopewell was going to run the trial for the Hunter."

"Someone pulled some strings, and now it's the Delegation," Grey said.

Joan. It had to have been Joan. She'd had doubts, even with our evidence, that the Committee would decide upon a guilty verdict in the Hunter's case.

"At least this time an outside influence worked in our favor," Grey said. "It doesn't usually play out that way around here."

Our favor? Maybe Reginald was right about Detective Grey. He had a moral code that made him an ally. Anne sure thought he was a good cop.

"How's Officer Reid?" I asked. He must have talked to her since she was one of the arresting officers for the Hunter.

"She's . . ." Grey scratched at his temple with the back of his pen, searching for the words. ". . . confused. Unsure. A bit pissed. She's a sharp cop, and things aren't adding up for her."

What would the Committee do with her? Would Reginald alter her memories? I started to feel sick again.

He looked at the descending numbers above the elevator door. "There's a lot to do, so I should head upstairs."

"Good luck, today." Emma waved, her smile bright.

Grey gave something like a grunt, nodded to us, and stepped onto the elevator.

Emma walked with me through the bustling lobby and out into the summer heat. "Do you want to spend the day poolside with me? It'll give you some time to rest and destress," she said. "We can bask in the sun, swim, and drink cocktails."

The warmth and brightness of the sun was pleasant after being in the hospital's frigid, sterile environment. The offer was tempting. "There's a strong possibility I'll be terrible company," I said.

"Are you okay?" she asked.

"No." I was feeling quite distant from okay.

She gave me a tight hug. "It's settled, then. You're coming back home with me."

Emma drove us back to her house, and it wasn't long before we were beside the pool on her sunny patio. She was right. The sun did make me feel better. Stretched out on a lounge chair, I enjoyed the toasty sensation of it seeping through my tired and aching muscles. The warmth of the sun also made me drowsy, and I was almost asleep when my phone buzzed. I reached under my chair where I'd set the phone down in the shade.

"You should turn that off for today," Emma said, basking in the chair beside me.

"I want to be available if Trish needs anything," I said. The message was only two lines of text, sent from Joan's phone.

It was the final lines of Elliott Smith's song, "Happiness." My heart leapt into my throat upon reading the familiar lyric. Then

I chuckled, imagining the shitstorm he'd have to face if his sister found out he'd taken her phone. I typed back. *It's okay you're gone . . . but it'd be nice to have you here.*

Ben's reply quickly followed. *I miss you, too.*

"Alex, seriously. You deserve rest. Shut off the phone," Emma said, standing. "And I deserve a daiquiri. Would you like one?"

I smiled and returned the phone beneath the lounge chair. "Sure, as long as I can find my drink somewhere in all the fruit."

Emma gave me an exasperated look and left to fix our drinks.

My phone buzzed yet again. I glanced at the patio slider, made sure Emma was still inside, and snatched up the phone. It was Nate. A photo of a lone beer bottle atop a bar counter was attached to our text thread.

Tomorrow night?

My mind flashed back to my last test. The disappointment and humiliation of losing control. The memory of fighting Nate agitated her. My inner wolf paced, a sharp and painful flare of heat behind my ribcage. I lowered my eyelids, exhaled, and reached for her.

I see you. I hear you.

I embraced her.

The stinging heat diffused into an intimate warmth. I smiled.

And this time, we're going to win.

Bonus Preview

Thank you for reading *Cage the Wolf*. If you enjoyed the book, please consider leaving a reader review.

For a bonus preview of the next book in the Alex Steward series, simply scan the QR code or visit the author's website at **stefaniegilmour.com**

Acknowledgements

THANK YOU TO my husband and first reader, Josh, for entertaining my endless what-ifs as Alex's story expanded from one to three novels. Your honest critiques are truly appreciated, if not always in the heat of the moment. I love you.

Logan Austin, Rebecca Cooper, and Diane Telgen, my writing continues to grow because of your expertise and dedication to the craft. Thank you for being such patient and caring mentors.

Many thanks to the rockstar *Cage the Wolf* beta readers: Logan Austin, Emily Bevilacqua, Kelly Bungee Rogers, Hailey Fournier, Jen Hefko, M.A. Hinkle, Kelly Knapke Leckrone, Hillary Robin, Olivia Smith, and James Tingley. You keep me on my toes and true to the characters.

Finally, to family, friends, and readers I have yet to meet, thank you for taking a chance on Alex's story. Your continued support makes this rollercoaster ride less lonely.

Stefanie Gilmour

STEFANIE IS A graphic designer who enjoys creepy and fantastical stories. Her short fiction has been published in *The Quiet Ones* literary magazine.

Plants, concerts, books, and writing are a few of her favorite things. She's a Midwest native and lives there with her patient husband and their tolerant cats.

stefaniegilmour.com
Facebook.com/AuthorStefanieGilmour
Instagram: @StefGilmour